Born in the same hos[illegible]heena Easton, **Lauren McCr**[illegible] been a music addict since buying her first record – 'I'm The Noodle Doodle Man' – at the age of five. After moving 'abroad' to England, Lauren read Law at Cambridge before ditching the power suits to pursue her dream of becoming an author. Lauren's first novel *Serve Cool* was published by Time Warner Paperbacks in 2001. Along with her professional surfer husband, Lauren divides her time between the UK, France, Ireland and Hawaii. She is now a full-time author and freelance magazine journalist, preferring to write longhand on beaches and in cafés to the sounds of her Walkman and the scent of black coffee. Lauren harbours no secret ambition to be a DJ but has sung in bands, and has also been known to sing karaoke on many occasions without the need for Dutch courage.

Angel on Air

LAUREN McCROSSAN

A *Time Warner* Paperback

First published in Great Britain as a paperback original in 2003
by Time Warner Paperbacks

*All characters in this publication are fictitious
and any resemblance to real persons, living or dead,
is purely coincidental.*

A CIP catalogue record for this book
is available from the British Library.

ISBN 0 7515 3152 9

Typeset in Berkeley by M Rules
Printed and bound in Great Britain by Clays Ltd, St Ives plc

Time Warner Paperbacks
An imprint of
Time Warner Books UK
Brettenham House
Lancaster Place
London WC2E 7EN

www.TimeWarnerBooks.co.uk

For
Darcey Hope and Molly Michaela –
who give life new meaning
xx

Acknowledgements

Firstly, I would really like to thank every person who sold, promoted, bought and read *Serve Cool*. I am especially grateful to those of you who came along to my book launch and signings, thereby ensuring that my nightmare of sitting alone at a dusty table signing one copy for my mum didn't come true. I hope you enjoy reading *Angel on Air* as much as I did writing it.

Many of the people I want to thank probably don't even realise how instrumental they were in helping me to write this book. Sometimes it just takes a word of encouragement or inspiration, a smile, a shoulder to cry on or a guiding hand when I am threatening to drop-kick my laptop out of the window to turn a writing day into a good one and to help create a finished product that I can be proud of. So, a very special thank you and a big hug go to:

Patricia 'jings' McCrossan and Hugh McCrossan, for all your faith, conversation, Scottish terminology, golfing references (dad) and for telling strangers at bus stops to buy my books (mum).

Anthony, Martin and Debbie McCrossan for all the advice and laughs and for being the best brothers and sister a girl could have. Your support is never-ending.

The whole McCrossan massive (and it is) – especially my super-cool Glasgow advisors Caroline, Kathleen, John and David, and the medical geniuses Laurence and Pam. (If I've got anything wrong in this book, I will let you lot take full responsibility!) Also my 'wee' Auntie Cath, Claire and Terry for everything, as well as my Gran, Sadie.

My great friend Michaela, for always being at the end of a phone line wherever I am and whenever I need you. You are one in a million.

Máire and Joe Fitzgerald for reading my chapters in the early stages. Thanks for your enthusiasm and comments, Máire, and sorry there aren't any zombies, Joe.

My legendary agent Jonathan Lloyd, who could inspire an inanimate object into action. Thank you for everything you do. Thanks also to Tara Wynne at Curtis Brown Australia.

The Time Warner team who work so hard to make all this possible, especially my editors Tara Lawrence and Joanne Coen, Tamsin Barrack, Barbara Boote, David Kent, Berni Stevens and everyone who makes Time Warner a great team to be part of.

Neale 'Buzz Pictures' Haynes for all the amazing publicity shots (despite the bikini) and Amanda Perkins for your encouragement, drive and money-making ideas.

Owain, Jesse, Peter and Annette Davies; Juliet Hardy; Naomi and Rob Escott; Ching Man Chan; Alf Alderson; Elaine and John Divers; Caroline Knights and Frances Wiseman; Richard and all the wonderful Fitzgeralds; Matt Britton at Tyrconnell Holiday Homes, Bundoran; Gareth,

Dylan, Huw and Gruffydd at Boomerang; Imogen Taylor and Anna Telfer (I can never thank you both enough); Valerie Older; JDPP Perrin; Daphne and Pete Navin; Joel Conroy and Michael Doyle; Robbie Hildreth; Agence Dufau, Hossegor; all at Quiksilver, especially Peyo Lizarazu and Phil Jarratt; Guy and Jock on the Indies Trader; Bevan at BIC; Kahuna; Extreme; Marian Keyes; Jill Mansell; Louise Rennison; Imogen Edwards-Jones; Steve England; Chris Power; Alex Williams; Alex Dick-Read; Roger Sharp; DJs Chris Moyles, Mark and Lard and The Bees; and all the people I realise I have forgotten when this goes to print.

Above all, I want to thank my own angel on earth, Gabriel, for so many things that I could write a book about them. Thank you for buying me a laptop with a 'B' that works, for laughing at all the right bits, for going surfing whenever I needed to concentrate, for always being by my side as well as in my heart, for believing in me more than I could ever believe in myself and for simply being the man that you are. Thank you for being my music. xxx

CHAPTER ONE

Sit Down

I still remember what Connor was wearing the day we first met, which is definitely a girl thing. Ask most women 'What was he wearing?' or 'What did he look like?' and you will get every last detail down to the length of his nails or the colour of his socks. Ask a man the same question and all you'll get is: 'Er, well, she was, like, blonde, about this tall and, well, how am I supposed to remember what she was wearing?' Men must make rubbish witnesses.

We met in an English Higher (the Scottish equivalent of the dreaded A Levels) class. Double English, to be precise, which became instantly pleasurable when I realised I had inadvertently plonked myself down next to one of the rare studs of St Bridget's Sixth Form. The school had just opened its virginal portals to boys for the first time, I suspect to take the pressure off the solitary male geography teacher who was the object of fifteen hundred girls' affections, so the atmosphere was one of furious flirting as pre-pubescent hormones bounced off the walls with not enough boys to go round. Competition was fierce, talons were sharpened, bras were stuffed with socks and, in just a week, the local chemist sold out of Sun-In, lip gloss and pregnancy tests (the three seemed to be linked at the time). I, however, was the new girl – my father Steve, or Stéphane as my French mother likes to call him, having decided that the first year of A Levels was the perfect time to uproot us from our home in Norwich to move north to Glasgow. Dad's so-called great ideas never are. Like marrying a beautiful French woman from the vineyards of Bordeaux and whisking her off to East Anglia where she will be miserably sour for the rest of her married life and insist on speaking English peppered with errors so as not to be mistaken for one of the natives. Like allowing your daughter to be called Angelique Knights – that's Knights as in 'of The Round Table', although my father has about as much chance of being heroic Lancelot as I have of beating Carol Vorderman in a mental arithmetic contest. Like choosing to work in a whisky factory when he is a raging alcoholic, but more about that later.

My mother, Delphine, had misread the date for the start of term so I was already a month late and something of a novelty. I had no idea that the empty seat next to Mr Stud Muffin was unofficially reserved for Ceri Divine (and she was), the ice-cool leader of the lower sixth. Ceri was so cool that she was approximately seven minutes late for every class, safe in the knowledge that no other girl would dare place their bum anywhere near the man she had been on/off with since they had played pass the Polo mint at the age of fourteen when he was the talent at the boys school down the road. I dared. Obviously I had no idea that I was daring at the time, but Connor failed to inform me of my misdemeanour.

There I was, firmly ensconced with my shiny new ring binder, my copy of *Madame Bovary* and my James pencil tin, which I adored. It had the band's flower logo in 3D relief on the lid and I used to run my fingers over the petals humming 'Sit Down', one of the greatest songs of all time, despite the fact that the live single only got to number two behind Chesney Hawkes' one and only hit 'The One And Only', which really aggravated my teenage angst. That song meant so much to me then and still does now, as does most music, given the fact that I am a DJ. Well, sit down I did and the look Ceri Divine gave me when she swanned in that door could have melted my electric blue mascara.

It was only when Connor stood up to write something on the blackboard that I took a good look at his clothes. I had been too scared to turn my head to have a gawp before that, partly for fear of an awkward eye contact moment and partly because I knew Ceri Divine's eyes were firmly fixed on the back of my head like a fighter jet locked in to fire a whopping great missile at its helpless target. He was wearing jeans, faded almost to white, which hung from a worn brown leather belt around his slim hips. The denim fell loosely around his pert bum, the right pocket hanging off as if he had been clawed by a desperate woman on the way to school. A single razor slit under his left bum cheek gave just a teasing glimpse of thigh and jet black boxer shorts – phew, not washed-out grey or, worse still, comedy cartoon characters. I tried not to ogle his rear end as he ambled towards the front of the class but it drew me in until my saliva glands could have produced enough supplies for a pack of rabid dogs. He wore red Converse boots, laced halfway to the top, and a matching red cotton T-shirt, emphasising the squareness of his broad shoulders. When he turned around, I gazed at him. He had one of those distinctive faces – the kind that sticks in your mind when you close your eyes. His skin was slightly tanned, despite the fact that he lived in Glasgow where summer tends to be the third Wednesday in August and maybe Thursday morning if you're lucky. The Celtic part was evident from the dusting of freckles across his nose and the vibrant blue of his eyes. Even then he had a shadow of jet-black stubble across his chin, toning perfectly with his shiny black hair. Some people say he looks a bit like Gary Lineker, only rougher and without the juggy ears and outstanding footballing ability (shame). Gary Lineker or not, I thought he was gorgeous, and when I averted my eyes from his face to the logo on his T-shirt I knew for sure – James written in bold white letters, along with the same yellow and white flower from the top of my pencil tin. It was surely a sign.

Thirteen years on, I still have that T-shirt folded up safely in my wardrobe. I've probably still got the pencil tin too, although I remember it suffering somewhat in its hedonistic days doubling as a marijuana receptacle. I also still have the man – Connor McLean, my first serious boyfriend, who asked me out thirteen years ago next week and hasn't left my side since. I now know every freckle on that nose, every mole and chicken pox scar. And I don't need a delicately placed hole in his jeans to look at his bum. I see it almost every morning when he ambles (still the best description of how Connor moves) out of bed to go to work as a TV cameraman for an up and coming production company. Connor still favours casual clothes – Levi twisted seams and a thin-knit jumper with some label or other, heavy boots, usually unpolished, which is one bone of contention between us given that I am a complete shoe fetishist. But on the whole I like his look, and besides, sartorial elegance and I are not exactly well acquainted either (at least, not above the ankles). Connor is still gorgeous and he's thoughtful and good to me, which is why buying him an anniversary present is turning into a shopping nightmare. It requires thought and taste and it has to be apt and romantic and . . . er, not too pricey because I just had to purchase that pair of pale pink leather and suede cowboy boots (for myself) and a brown tassely cowgirl style rucksack which Meg said matched my eyes. Oops.

What do you buy a man you've been with for thirteen years? I would ask my mother but she left my dad almost two years ago and buggered off back to France. Sadly, I don't know anyone else who has been with their partner as long as I have. A sign of the times, perhaps, or a sign that my friends are either complete commitment-loathing slappers or are so desperate to walk up the aisle that they may as well carry around a sandwich board advertising *Brides And Homes*. A very apt time to introduce Megan, who is unfortunately the latter type, and Ceri, very much the former. Yes, the same Ceri Divine who wanted to shove *Madame Bovary* where the sun don't shine when we first met is now one of my best friends. Along with loveable Megan McCaffrey, who was heavily influenced by Ceri at school and thus was persuaded to cut off a lock of my hair when I wasn't looking so that Ceri could practise black magic on the bitch who had stolen her boyfriend. The three of us are now an inseparable trio – we have weekly 'coven meetings', as Connor likes to call them, on Saturday nights – and we know everything about each other. Which is why I thought they would be the best help a girl could get in choosing a thirteen-year anniversary present, considering we have every shop in Glasgow city centre to choose from. Well, we have covered three of the main shopping arcades in the city and are down to the last department in John Lewis and we are still no closer to finding that perfect gift. My mission is not going well but it's not entirely my fault. My two best friends are, if I am honest, completely crap personal shoppers. Ceri wouldn't know what romance was if it hopped about in front of her banging a drum, and is much more interested in looking at her own reflection in every shop window, while Meg tries hard but thinks helium balloons with satin ribbons are a tasteful present for a modern man. I may as well give up right now.

'What do you have to buy him a sodding present for?' Ceri says loudly, which is not unusual. Ceri likes to be heard and has adopted a fake English accent that she believes makes her sound more posh than her natural Glaswegian. A plastic Sassenach, Megan calls her. Pouting her full, perfect lips at a display of umpteen gold mirrors, Ceri sighs, 'You've been together for, like, *ever*, surely some of this would do the trick?' She lifts up a bottle of £6.95 Old Spice and waves it disinterestedly at me.

'Hardly, Ceri,' I tut, peering at a phallic-shaped bottle of aftershave among the rows and rows of fragrances along the wall and gasping at the price ticket. 'We may have been together a long time but we're not quite that dull. I need something romantic.'

'Just For Men?' she smirks.

'That is not romantic, Ceri, and anyway, Connor doesn't have any grey hair.'

'But he will have, babe, so you'd be investing in his future appearance, thinking long-term the way you commitmenty people do. Now *that's* romance.'

'God, Ceri, I'm glad all the men you date expect nothing in return for the attention they shower on you. You have absolutely no idea about romance.'

'It's all bollocks if you ask me,' Ceri shrugs, sweeping her way towards the glittering make-up counters. 'I'm not into all this equality rubbish. Men should buy the presents, not women.'

'Well, Connor and I have a system and it works, Ceri, so I'll keep it that way if you don't mind.'

'Suit yourself, but remember it is your thirteenth anniversary.'

'So?' I frown, holding my breath as I pass the perfume counter, where clouds of fragrance are wafting around like napalm.

'Thirteen, Angel; not a very lucky number, is it? I wouldn't be so quick to celebrate if I were you.'

'Well, thank you, mate,' I reply, raising my eyes to the ceiling. 'I'll keep that cheery thought in mind.'

'Hey, Angel, how about this teddy bear then?' Meg hollers, bounding towards me, all red curls and freckles, and thrusting a pale blue ball of fur in my face. 'Look, he's holding a wee velvet heart and it says "Be Mine".'

'Be sick, more like,' Ceri snorts, clicking her fingers to attract the attention of the woman on the Chanel counter. 'That is totally gross.'

'I don't know if Connor's really a teddy bear kind of guy, Meg,' I smile charitably, giving the bear a friendly squeeze before placing him on the nearest shelf.

Megan's other offerings – a bracelet engraved with the words 'My Guy', an eternity sovereign ring, a photo frame adorned with glittery hearts and lips, an Elvis pen that plays 'Love Me Tender' while it writes – have also been strategically dumped around the shop. It's definitely time to call it a day before I run out of excuses and am forced to buy him the red satin boxer short and handkerchief set she spotted when we first came into John Lewis what feels like many aeons ago.

'Let's go grab some lunch,' I say, clapping my hands together to feign enthusiasm.

Meg, who never fails to be excited by anything to do with food, makes a bolt for the exit like a seagull swooping on a bag of chips.

'Hold on a sec, I just want to buy this lipstick – if that bloody woman can get her fat backside over here before the colour goes out of fashion,' says Ceri. 'She probably can't see me through all that mascara. Look at it, like ten years of soot on a chimney sweep's brush. Someone should give these women some guidance.'

I grin and lean back against the counter on my elbows, closing my eyes and trying to focus on Connor and what he would like for an anniversary gift.

'What did he give you last year?' Ceri asks as if reading my mind.

'Erm, underwear, I think. Yes, that red La Senza set and a St Tropez fake tan kit.'

'Oh God, how could I forget? Your fingers looked like cheesy Wotsits for about a week after that.'

'How was I to know you had to wash your hands afterwards? I mean, the whole point of the stuff is to put it on your skin. Washing it off again seems like a waste, especially at that price.'

Ceri shakes her long blonde hair and raises a perfectly plucked eyebrow. 'Oh dear, you're not really Cat Deeley are you, love? So, what about the year before?'

I bite my lip in thought. 'Um, I think it was underwear again. But a different kind, white and lacy.'

'Bit of a theme running through these gifts, isn't there, hon? Do you think your boyfriend is sexually frustrated, by any chance?'

'No!' I retort quickly.

'Just give him a blowjob,' Ceri smirks. 'I'm sure that would be a treat for him these days.'

'I'll have you know, Ceri Divine,' I huff, my face reddening, 'that I am a regular explorer in that department. In fact I gave Connor a blowjob on Thursday morning before he went to work and he said it was the best one he'd ever had. Apparently I get better every time.'

'Fascinating,' says a stern female voice behind me. 'That'll be twelve pounds for the lipstick.'

I turn to be greeted by a look of disdain from 'Judy, happy to help', as if I were a lump of chewed chewing gum on the sole of her Ecco sandal. Narrowing my eyes at Ceri, who is clutching her sides and making snorting sounds as if she is trying to suck a family of slugs through her nostrils, I scuttle off in search of Meg. This anniversary shopping is giving me a headache.

'I cannot eat here,' Ceri spits, stepping over a squashed chip in her turquoise Patrick Cox mule and screwing up her nose at the aroma of fried food.

'Och, away ye go, Ceri, it's fine,' Meg tuts, barging towards the shortest queue, her big green eyes growing even larger at the photos of giant burgers on the walls of the food hall.

'Yes, and I'm sure BK Flamers are on the Weight Watchers plan,' I add, recalling the booklet I paid four quid for and read only once over a chicken madras. 'They're only twenty points or something.'

'I don't care how many points they are, Angel, I am not a bloody Weight Watcher.'

'I'm no' surprised,' Meg giggles, 'you haven'y got any fucken' weight to watch.' Pulling her white cotton gypsy top over her rather large midriff, Meg adds, 'A whopper cheese meal, onion rings, full fat Coke and a portion of diddy donuts please. Oh, and a box of lettuce for my pal.'

'I'll be in Morgan,' Ceri announces, striding off towards the escalator with her ankle-length cream suede coat flapping behind her. 'Join me when you've finished gorging. If you can still move.'

'Away with the fairies, that one,' Meg laughs. 'Less fat than this flippin' plastic straw and no' making the most of it. What an eejit.'

I must explain about Ceri Divine. You see, she is not like most humans. In fact, if I had not seen it with my own eyes, I would never have believed that a grown woman could survive on a diet of vitamin supplements, coffee and rice cakes. While Meg and I indulge in cooked breakfasts or rounds of toast and Marmite, Ceri takes a combination of pills ranging from vitamin A to zinc, two cups of tar-like espresso and a glass of lemon-tinged hot water. Not a morsel of food passes Ceri's lips until midday and even then she eats like a vegan stick insect on a diet. Admittedly she has the body of Kylie

Minogue stretched out onto a five foot nine inch frame and a bum firmer than any chair she parks it on, but her habits are unhealthy and, I must say, intensely boring. I mean, why go out for dinner if you're only going to order a dressing-free salad? And why put jobs in the chocolate and savoury snacks industry at risk by not indulging in the occasional KitKat Chunky or tube of Pringles? She may turn every male eye as she glides down the street – with the exception of my Connor who describes her as thinner than a prawn cracker and not half as tasty, although I sometimes wonder if he just says that to make me feel better – but I enjoy food far too much to be like Ceri, as does Megan who is a girl after my own heart. Meg loves Ronald McDonald almost as much as she does Ewan McGregor and claims to have a potentially fatal allergy to exercise – largely because her boobs could quite possibly maim or kill if sent into a high velocity bounce. She is voluptuous and proud – a black mama trapped in a lily white ass, as she likes to say.

I am somewhere between the two, having neither the assets of Meg nor the angles of Ceri. I don't like to say 'average' but I am a comfortable size twelve, apart from one week every month when I become an uncomfortable size twelve. In my days of buckteeth and frizzy blonde hair I used to have a certain Continental gangliness, thanks to my mother who is more French than French fries and twice as thin. The frizz has gone, largely due to the John Frieda section in Boots, and the blonde has naturally turned more French mustard than Moet. I like my hair now. I have outgrown trying to keep it long and girly and have cropped it into a spiky, just got out of bed boyish style. I suppose it would be nice if my body decided to follow suit and become a bit more boyish but unfortunately my skinny limbs are now concealed by a layer of insulation. I'm not fat by any means but I do have curves, which are a necessity for surviving the cold Scottish winters. In fact, if it weren't for the plunging temperatures up here in Glasgow I would be Kate Moss, only shorter and not as stylish. Connor likes my curves; he thinks they're womanly. In his eyes they are second only to my nose – his favourite feature of mine – which is small and turns up at the end. I used to think it made me look like a half human half piglet but luckily I have grown into that too and it now fits comfortably with the rest of my face.

I have to admit, though, to not being one of those girls who is obsessed by how they look, which probably makes me distinctly unfashionable. I haven't even got an eating disorder – unless enjoying food is considered 'disorderly' these days. I have my moments, of course, but usually I am far too lazy to be a textbook beauty. Firstly because all the manicures, pedicures, facials and aerobic classes are a waste of good eating, drinking and being merry time, and secondly because I am a radio DJ. I have a fairly large audience and my listener figures are rising steadily, but they can't see me so it doesn't really matter whether I have a well-groomed celebrity image or not. Now if I were, say, Sara Cox on Radio 1, or Suzie McGuire – my equivalent at rival station Clyde One, who pulls in more listeners on her daily twelve till three slot than I have in eighteen months and has her face splashed around Underground stations and buses – then looks might be an issue, but I am several long-haul flights from their radio land. I am not famous. I once had my picture in the school magazine for scoring six points during my goal attack debut netball match but I haven't quite made the cover of *Maxim*. I was also asked to turn on the Christmas lights at my local pub in the West End but the specky Proclaimers twins and the Krankies would be way ahead of me on the list of celebs to invite to star-studded Scottish parties. I'm working on it though, and Energy FM is making a conscious effort to increase the popularity of its DJs. At the moment all I am asked to open is the can of worms ever present during the phone-ins that make up the majority of my lunchtime show, but one day I will reach the dizzy heights of opening school fêtes and barber shop concerts. At least I hope so.

'Act as if,' my mum always says. 'Act as if you are successful and one day you will be.'

'Chicken royale meal with a Diet Coke,' I say as the lofty thought drifts across my mind.

Well, even famous people have to eat.

'Why not get him a chess set?' Meg shouts over the noise of the children's crèche behind our table.

'He doesn't play, and if he started I would have to play too, which would mean learning what all the stupid pieces do and I really can't be arsed.'

'Aye, right, I see what you mean. How about one o' they micro scooters?'

'No, he'd be racing little kids down the street and end up killing himself.'

'Pogo stick?'

'Bit wanky.'

'Parachute jump?'

'He hates heights.'

'Ehm, a caving expedition?'

I sigh and slurp the icy remains of my Diet Coke. 'I don't know, Meg. How can it be so hard to find a present for someone I've been with for thirteen years?'

'Because you love him, hen,' Meg replies dreamily, resting her chin on her hand and the edge of her sleeve in a dollop of ketchup on the table, 'so you want it to be special. It's pure brilliant, so it is, you're such a dreamy wee couple.'

I smile widely like a love-struck teenager, which is the way I often feel when I'm with Connor. I think it comes from the fact that we've been together since I *was* a teenager, so being with him makes me feel almost suspended in time. Shame my body didn't catch on to that idea.

'Meg, do you think it's sad still going out with the same man after all this time?'

Meg leans across the wrinkled burger wrappers and holds my wrist. 'Don't be daft, Angel, you're so right for each other. Jings, if I could find a fella like that I'd cling on till my fucken' knuckles turned white.'

I don't doubt it. Meg is the sort of girl who used to design her wedding dress on the inside of her Geography folder. She is *desperate* to get married, which is clear to every man she dates within ten minutes of their first kiss. As soon as Meg gets a man's phone number she starts to hang about outside jewellery shops, gazing at the engagement rings until the staff begin to think she's casing the joint and call the police. She's a brilliant person – loving, soft and hilarious, with a huge laugh that necessitates throwing her head forward and opening her mouth so wide that passing toddlers are in danger of disappearing down her throat. In my opinion, those men just don't know what they're missing.

'Of course he's lucky to have you. If you hadn'y rescued

him from Ceri-the-man-snaffler his poor wee heart would have been broken into a kazillion pieces by now. You did him a favour, hen, no doubt about that.'

'I hope he thinks so too. I mean, she is rather gorgeous.'

'Gorgeous smorgeous. Her and Connor had nothing in common, believe me. She'd talk to him about nail varnish colours and fashion trends and he'd sit there with a glazed expression on his poor wee face. I mean, they didn'y even like the same music.'

'Well, that is something we definitely have in common,' I smile, thinking back to that first day.

'Oooh!' Meg shrieks, clapping her hands excitedly. 'I've got a fucken' brilliant idea for a pressie.'

'Tell me, tell me.'

Meg raises both hands and flaps them like a chicken trying to fly. 'James are on an arena tour, singing their greatest hits, and one of their gigs is at the Big Red Shed around the time of your birthday.'

'The Exhibition Centre? Wow, that'd be ace, Meg.'

'Exactly, and we've got some tickets in the shop and a wee goodie bag with a T-shirt and a CD and a poster and stuff. He'd fucken' love it.'

'Oh Meg,' I beam, leaning across the table to hug my excitable friend, 'you're great. That would be absolutely perfect. Can you grab me two tickets and a goodie bag and I'll give you the money? Actually,' I say after a pause, 'I'll write you a blank cheque.'

Meg may be the assistant manager of probably the largest music shop in Glasgow but she somehow manages to have the bank balance of an Outer Mongolian yak farmer. A very poor one.

'Aye, nae bother. I'll get them when I'm at work the morra.'

I scribble a cheque and hand it to Meg. See, all it takes is a bit of thought and this anniversary shopping is a piece of cake. I think I'll have to buy myself something else to celebrate our successful mission. God, Connor is going to *love* me on Thursday. Even more than he does already, I think vainly.

'Get ready to genuflect, here comes Her Highness,' Meg giggles, nodding her head towards the escalator where Ceri is battling her way through the hordes of angry shoppers fighting each other for that elusive empty table in the food hall.

'I don't want the blasted table!' we hear her shout at a family of five in various colours of shellsuit. 'Do I LOOK like the sort of person who would eat in a place that serves food on plastic trays?'

'All right, Ceri?' I snort as she reaches us, red-faced and flustered.

'No, I am not bloody well all right. It's like feeding time at the zoo in here. Honestly, I don't know how you two can eat this stuff.'

'Onion ring?' smirks Meg, raising the grease-stained paper bag towards Ceri's suede coat.

'I'd rather chew on a flip-flop. Now, are you done? I think there's something you would rather like to see.'

'Ooh, have you found a present for Connor?' I ask, jumping up and grabbing my faded denim jacket from the back of my chair. 'Only I think we've already—'

'Not exactly,' Ceri pouts, moving out of the way of two old women who dive for our chairs before they've even had a chance to cool down, 'but I have *seen* Connor.'

'Where?' I ask, shuffling along behind her with Meg and her diddy donuts in tow.

'Downstairs,' she replies, flapping an arm towards the escalator, 'in a jewellery shop. With a woman. Quite a good-looking woman, I might add. It's all really rather cosy. In fact, I'd say it was rather suspicious.'

Tact is not one of Ceri's greatest assets when it comes to delivering earth-shattering news. Thank God she doesn't work for the police force. I can just imagine it: 'Is that your son out there on the road, Mrs Smith, splattered all over the white line by that ten-tonne truck?'

'It can't be Connor,' I whine, anxiously biting my lip. 'He's at work. You must have got the wrong person.'

'Believe me, honey,' Ceri replies, spinning around to face me, 'I know what Connor looks like. I know him rather well, remember?'

How could I bloody forget when you remind me every five minutes?

Ceri steps elegantly on to the escalator. 'And it was him. With her. Now are you coming to have a look or not?'

'Don't worry, pal, it'll be fine,' Meg whispers reassuringly as we descend the escalator, my heart sinking even faster than the metal stairs.

'Of course it will,' I cough. 'It won't be him, and even if it is I'm sure there's a perfectly reasonable explanation.'

But somehow I wasn't so sure.

CHAPTER TWO

Trouble

It was him. And her, whoever the fuckety fuck *she* was. Her hair was enormous, not just big – like a shaggy dog that has got its fur wet and then stuck its head out of the window of a moving car to dry. Her clothes were garish and skin-tight, apart from two giant shoulder pads jutting like breeze blocks from her tiny jacket, the low-cut neckline of which revealed a pair of boobs bigger than Premiership footballs. Speaking of which, I felt as if I'd been hit in the stomach by one, kicked at a hundred miles an hour by David Beckham himself.

I was seething – largely because it looked as if Connor was doing the dirty on me but also partly because he'd chosen to do it with someone like her. I mean, if he's going to have an affair he could at least do it with someone decent a) to show that he's got taste and b) to show that they could have had anyone they'd wanted but had chosen Connor as their number one option. Shoulder pads, for God's sake, *shoulder pads*.

However, despite my feelings of near devastation, I didn't make a scene. I didn't shout, scream or stamp my feet, or confront her in true soap opera fashion by demanding to know what the hell she was doing with my fella and finishing with a spectacular slap to her face. No, I was dignified. I simply tailed them from the Buchanan Galleries shopping centre to Princes Square with Ceri and Meg following close behind. All right, it may not be your dictionary definition of dignity but I thought it was better than a catfight at the time. Although now I'm at home, alone with my thoughts, I'm not so convinced. I want to tear the little hussy's big hair out at the roots, not to mention what I'll do to Connor when he eventually comes clean. The thing is, I just cannot believe Connor would cheat on me. OK, I know all the sappy girlfriends on those bare-all TV shows are always the last to know and defend their man to the last breath while he's off shagging everything with two X chromosomes, but Connor really isn't like that. He's an honest man; he buys the *Big Issue* even if he's already got that edition and he feeds stray dogs. He doesn't even flirt – at least not when he's with me, which is most of the time. But maybe I'm kidding myself. Maybe Ceri is right and thirteen is unlucky. He might have thought of our impending anniversary and been overcome with a sudden feeling of intense boredom. To think I spent all day looking for a sodding thirteenth-anniversary present for the two-timing git. Oh God, maybe I am one of those sappy girlfriends after all.

'How's my Angel then?' says a very familiar voice from the front door of my flat. A soft Scottish voice I can usually listen to until my ears melt.

I turn my head from my rigid position on the sofa to see Connor stride into the room wearing his faithful brown suede jacket and a smile wider than an American freeway.

I know why you're smiling, I think sourly, *good, was she? Better at shopping than me?* But I sit, tight-lipped and silent, pretending to read a magazine.

He bends down to kiss me, the way he always does when he arrives, and I breathe in the familiar smell of Dune for Men.

'All right, baby?' he asks, running a hand through my spiky hair.

'Yes, fine,' I reply curtly.

'Hmm,' he coughs and makes his way to the lime green kitchenette attached to the bottom of my L-shaped lounge.

I raise my eyes from my magazine and watch as he lifts two Safeway shopping bags on to the worktop.

'I got that pasta sauce you like,' he calls to me while bending down to look for a beer in the fridge. 'You know, the one with the prawns and scallops and loads of chilli and garlic? So I suppose I'll have to eat it too if you want a snog later.'

'I doubt it,' I hiss as he laughs and pulls up the ringpull on the beer can.

'Sorry?'

'Nothing,' I grumble, turning the pages of my magazine as loudly as possible. Shiny paper can be annoyingly quiet sometimes.

I say nothing while Connor bangs cupboard doors, putting the shopping in all the right places. He is from that unusual breed of tidy man. In fact, he's often cleaning up my mess, being as I am from the rival tribe of messy-as-fuck woman.

'Glass of wine for the lady,' he smiles, walking towards me with a glass of freshly poured red in one hand and a bowl of olives in the other. 'It's the Chilean one we had the other night that you said tasted like Cherryade.'

Trying too hard. I nod, taking the glass without saying thank you. *Obviously has a guilt complex.* I take a sip, screw up my nose as if he has handed me a glass of methylated spirits and return to reading an article about what I have absolutely no idea.

Connor sits down on the edge of my low pine coffee table – I've spread myself out so much that there is no room on the sofa and the rest of my lounge suite consists of a squishy pink beanbag and a small pouffe that has seen better days and slopes to one side. He leans towards me, resting his arms on his long, slim thighs. I keep my eyes averted.

'All right, what's the matter, Angel?'

I sigh dramatically and pout my lips, which comes very unnaturally to me. 'What do you mean, what's the matter? Why should there be anything the matter?'

Apart from the fact that I saw you cavorting with some floozy in the centre of Glasgow for all and sundry to see, you WANKER.

'Because,' he replies calmly, 'you're acting like Kevin the Teenager, you've got a frown on your face like a tramline, you're pouting like your mother and you haven't dragged me into the bedroom to see the new shoes you bought today.'

'How do you know I bought new shoes?'

'Educated guess,' he grins. 'You always buy new shoes when you're looking for presents for someone else.'

'I wasn't looking for presents actually,' I huff. 'Don't be so bloody presumptuous.'

'Pardon me, Kevin,' he smirks, biting his bottom lip. 'So are you gonna tell me what the matter is or shall I get on with cooking us a feast?'

Now this is the problem with Connor; he just will not argue. While some men holler and throw tantrums and sulk for weeks, Connor does none of these things. He is calm and sensible and far too laid-back to take a hairy fit about something. It's not that he doesn't like to discuss any issues we may have, preferring to sweep them under the proverbial carpet the way my father did throughout his marriage until my mother finally had enough, rolled up the carpet and bolted for the Continent. No, Connor is very good at confronting issues by way of reasoned discussion. Our private life in that respect is like a series of exam questions: 'You have seriously pissed me off by getting bladdered and vomiting in the bed. Discuss' or 'Why do we have to go and see this stupid chick flick when Wesley Snipes is shooting people on the screen next door? Discuss'. I guess it's better than 'You are getting on my thrupenny bits, now fuck off out of my flat and don't come back. No discussion', but sometimes it can be very therapeutic to have a bit of a rant. Don't you agree?

'Shall I put some music on then?' he asks when I continue to stare dumbly at the pages of my magazine.

'If you like. Don't care.'

OK, that was a bit Kevin-ish but I have my reasons.

Connor walks around the sofa and pauses to stare at my extensive music collection, which stretches the entire length of one wall. Well, it saves on paintings and I do live my life to a backing track in my head.

'Will Coldplay do, baby?' he asks, pulling out the CD and

biting the tip of his tongue as he concentrates on selecting his favourite song.

I shrug. This silent moody stuff is actually really difficult. Maybe I should have gone for the rant right from the beginning, made it a bit more obvious and in-your-face-ish.

'"Trouble",' I sniff as I recognise the track he has chosen, 'that'll be right.'

While Connor potters around in the kitchen for the next fifteen minutes, washing my dirty dishes from the night before and preparing our dinner, I remain steadfastly silent. Silent, that is, apart from regular incredibly exaggerated sighs and the odd tut, just to let him know that I am in a mood and not just being quietly content. I am desperate for him to ask me again what the matter is. I thought the first couple of times were trial runs for the big question, just him giving me a chance to respond with one syllable answers and shoulder shrugs. The problem is he doesn't seem to be interested in asking me again. Irritatingly enough, he is leaving me to my own devices, giving me space while he cooks my dinner and refills my wine glass. What a git. And I can't just launch into one. I'm not very good at impulsive hissy fits; I need my anger to be dragged out of me with questions and pandering. Call me attention-seeking but . . . all right, yes, I am attention-seeking but I bloody well deserve to be when my boyfriend, whom I thought was lovely, honest, gorgeous and faithful, is putting it about in broad daylight and doesn't even have the decency to tell me.

I turn my face away as Connor finally comes back (all of twenty paces) from the kitchenette gingerly carrying a large wooden tray loaded with two steaming plates of pasta, a rather colourful salad, hot garlic bread and the rest of the bottle of red wine. He carefully bends down, places the tray on the coffee table, biting his tongue the way he does when he's concentrating hard, and then raises his long arms with a flourish.

'Spaghetti à la McLean,' he beams, 'with a wee bit of help from Mr Safeway. Now get stuck in, my Angel, before I eat all the garlic bread.'

He hands me a plate, which I try to snatch but end up placing carefully on my lap because it does smell bloody good.

'Anything else I can do for you?' he asks, sitting down next to me on the sofa.

'No.'

Apart from owning up to your dirty business and offering to castrate yourself with that bottle opener.

'Great,' he grins, making a popping sound with his lips, 'well, *bon appetite*.'

'It's *appetit*, actually; you don't pronounce the last "t",' I reply sullenly, wishing that he wasn't so nice and bubbly and enthusiastic and caring. It makes it all the more difficult to hate him.

'Sorry, *mademoiselle*, my French is truly *le crap*. I will have to, er, marry a half-French girl and take some lessons perhaps.'

'Not bloody likely,' I grumble as he gives me a playful nudge in the ribs.

Connor rubs his hands together before reaching for a slice of garlic bread. He takes a bite and chews it slowly. I can feel his eyes burning into the side of my face.

'I take it you didn't have a good day in town, Angel,' he says eventually. 'Was Ceri getting on your nerves? Dragging you into every shop where the prices are more like telephone numbers?'

I shrug as a lump moves into my throat. I don't say a word in case I start to cry.

'Were you looking for an anniversary pressie?'

I turn towards him and stare into his blue eyes. They look mischievous and I know why.

'Yes. Yes, I was, although why I bother I don't—'

'Ooh, so was I,' he interrupts excitedly.

'Were you? I thought you were working today, Connor,' I say sharply.

'Aye, I was, but I bunked off this afternoon and went into town.' He bites his bottom lip with a perfect white tooth and grins happily. 'It's supposed to be a secret but you know I'm rubbish at keeping secrets.'

Oh God, I think as my stomach somersaults nervously, here it comes.

'I thought I'd see you and your coven, actually, but you must have been in different places from your usual haunts,' he carries on, the smile still playing on his kissable lips. 'But it's probably just as well because I went into town with someone and we were looking for something very special.'

I hold my breath and sit frozen on the sofa while half of me wants to run screaming from the room before I hear what he has to say. I don my best angry, temper-tantrum expression and wait for *it*.

'At work I said I was going to buy you something but I wasn't quite sure and then Beth, well, she offered to come with me.'

'Beth?' I spit.

'Yeah, Beth. She's our new director's wife.'

Oh.

'Nice enough lady, very friendly. I suppose you girls would think she was a wee bit tarty perhaps but she's pretty . . .'

He does this when he's excited; Connor could waffle for Scotland.

'. . . not the smartest tool in the shed, you know, the wheel's there but the hamster's missing, that sort of girl. Anyway, she does have good taste though, so when she offered to come and help me choose your present I thought what a great idea.'

'Good taste, has she?' I smirk, an image of big hair and shoulder pads floating past my eyes. It is true, men are from Mars. And she was from the Land of Hairspray.

'It was weird though, wanderin' around Buchanan Street with another woman,' Connor carries on oblivious. 'It felt horrible, actually. I much prefer shopping with you. But we found it in the end and I hope you like it but I have *got* to try and keep this one under my hat because it'll be a lovely surprise. I can't wait to see your face.' He bends forward and kisses my cheek, which has fixed itself into an uncomfortably wide grin. 'Thirteen years, eh, baby, who'd have thought it? And you're still as beautiful as ever.'

I grab my emotional gearstick and quickly shift it into reverse, zooming out of the Moody cul-de-sac and into Easy Street. Didn't I tell you my boyfriend's the best? Huh, it's a good job I'm not one of those over-reacting types – I didn't doubt him for a second!

I love Sundays. It's the only day of the week when neither Connor nor I work and so we can spend the whole day just being us, a couple. We tend to be at my flat in Byres Road, which is a trendy, I suppose you would say up-and-coming, area in the West End. It is about fifteen minutes from the centre of Glasgow on The Clockwork Orange – our mini equivalent of the London Underground, nicknamed as such because of the orange colour of the tiny trains chugging monotonously around the circular track. Meg, Ceri, Connor and I all live in the same area within five minutes of each other and Gibson Street – otherwise known as Curry Alley due to its impressive selection of Indian restaurants. This does not impress Ceri, who will rarely even indulge in a poppadum, but the rest of us appreciate its culinary splendour.

My flat is my one true asset, give or take a hundred pairs of shoes and an original painting of a ballet dancer by Robert Heindel which my mum bought me for my sixteenth birthday in the hope I would become the next Margot Fonteyn rather than follow in the footsteps of the likes of Tony Blackburn and John Peel. It didn't work but I still have the delicately painted ballerina hanging in my hallway, clashing completely with the rest of my furnishings but covering an unsightly crack in the plaster.

Connor rents a place in an archetypal old redstone building just around the corner. You see, we may have been going out for umpteen years but we haven't quite taken our relationship to the next level by getting one of those very mature joint mortgages and officially moving in together. Connor is at my place most of the time – his toothbrush is firmly ensconced in the turtle-shaped toothbrush holder in my bathroom, he has a key and he keeps the cupboards stocked with food. But I am immensely proud of the fact that the flat is mine, bought with the help of a small inheritance from my French grandmother who passed away five years ago, much to my mum's delight because they couldn't stand the sight of each other – it was a competitive thing, with mother and daughter constantly striving to be thinner, younger-looking and more glamorous than each other. Fortunately Delphine doesn't have that problem with me, given that she will always be thinner and more glamorous than I am and has nurtured a self-confidence that would make Britney Spears look like a shrinking violet.

Although the building is still clean and new, the inside of my flat has, I have to admit, a thrown-together look about it, largely because it is. I am a hoarder, a collector of stuff – empty bottles, mugs, cinema tickets, carrier bags. You name it, I probably hoard it, and thus I will never achieve the minimalist interior design favoured by Ceri and people leading organised, uncluttered lives. My L-shaped lounge is painted deep red, which clashes drastically with the lime green kitchenette, but in my world clashing isn't a problem and it's bound to be considered fashionable eventually the way trends zoom in and out of favour. The walls and furniture are adorned with hundreds of photographs, spanning almost every year of my life. Black and white ones, passport ones with too many grinning faces squashed into a tiny booth, holiday snaps of Connor and I in places ranging from Thurso to the South of France and Lanzarote. Some of the pictures are in proper frames, some stuck to the fridge with colourful magnets and others arranged as collages in A3 clip frames. I love photographs almost as much as I love music, which is the other major collection vying for space in the lounge.

Connor says my flat is comfortable, which is his code for a complete tip but with a friendly vibe. It is the kind of place that invites you to come in, put your feet up on the furniture, eat crisps without worrying about crumbs and generally make yourself at home, which is exactly the look I was going for. I could not live in a perfect showhome, although I did for the majority of my junior years. I hyperventilate when I go into houses with white sofas and highly polished surfaces. I love my flat and I love it even more when Connor's there. Having a man about the place just makes it feel complete somehow.

Connor and I wake up around ten o'clock, have a kiss, a cuddle and – well, I'm sure you can use your own imagination as to the way things can progress when you're not knackered and craving sleep, you don't have to go to work and your boyfriend has morning horn – before snuggling under the duvet with a cup of coffee and Marmite-covered toast to watch *T4*. It seems the older I get the more I can relate to programmes aimed at the younger viewer. Give me *Breakfast With Frost* and the *News* or *Hollyoaks* and *Popworld* and I will go for the latter every time. I mean, I went into a state of mourning when Ant and Dec left *SMTV: Live* and I know I'm not the only one of my generation who felt like that. We want to be entertained rather than informed. We like to be children because it keeps away the horrible responsibilities of growing up in the big wide world. I'm sure when I'm eighty I'll be living on a diet of *Grange Hill* reruns and *The Rugrats* while important current affairs pass me by in an intellectual blur. In fact, my generation probably won't even produce a Prime Minister unless the candidates are asked to take part in a fly-on-the-wall TV show called

Westminster Idol and the election is decided by a phone-in vote hosted by, of course, Ant and Dec.

Anyway, having watched every cartoon, American teen comedy and interview with the likes of Atomic Kitten available, Connor and I feel inspired enough to begin our day proper so we head out to the café across the street for brunch and a read of the Sunday papers – yes, I *do* read the news parts, not just the fashion and horoscopes, I'm not completely stupid. Several cups of coffee and a bacon with black pudding roll later, we take a wander along Byres Road to indulge in one of our favourite pursuits: people-watching.

We see the usual Sunday morning bleary-eyed hangover cases clutching bottles of Irn-Bru – the true Scots hangover cure, or bender mender as Meg likes to call it. We give directions to lost American tourists looking for the Glasgow Botanic Gardens at the top of Byres Road and Connor politely responds to their excited cries of 'Oh, man, you're, like, really Scottish. Your accent is so cool, say something!' without replying, 'Shove your maps up your fat arses, you condescending Yanks.' We pass the man selling plastic lighters and scissors from a suitcase on the pavement and buy a copy of *The Big Issue* from a girl with three-foot-long dreadlocks dyed every colour of the rainbow.

'Tell me rara skirts aren't back in fashion,' Connor laughs when a group of teenage girls stride past in a mass of lacy frills and a clatter of stilettos.

'I think they must be,' I reply, nodding at an almost identical group of girls across the street.

'What is the world coming to? They're even wearing leg-warmers. I feel like I've stepped into an eighties timewarp.'

'You never left it, my darling,' I pout, pretending to eye up his clothes.

'You cheeky wee thing,' he gasps, poking me in the ribs, 'and that's coming from a woman who still holds a torch for Marti Pellow.'

'I do not!'

'Well, you bought his solo album the other day. I saw it cunningly concealed under "M".'

'I had to, I'm a DJ. It was a purely professional thing,' I blush, 'and anyway, I saw you drooling over Kim Wilde on that gardening show.'

Connor raises both palms and laughs. 'All right, you got me, but I was only interested in the sweet pea potting, honest.'

He links his arm through mine and we cross over the road to walk back towards my flat.

'Oh dear, I think we must be getting old, Angel. Next thing you know we'll be complaining that *Top Of The Pops* is just noise and ticking young scallywags off for skateboarding on the pavement. Before you know it we'll be married with eight kids, a dog and a pension plan.'

'I've already got a pension plan, Connor.'

'Have you? Bloody hell, you are Little Miss Sense and Sensibleness. A pension plan and a mortgage, I canny keep up.'

'Well, you'd better try,' I shout over my shoulder, letting go of his arm and running off down the street (I say running, but a waddling jog would be more like it), 'the *EastEnders* omnibus is on and last one home has to be Pat.'

We sloth out on the sofa in front of an hour and a half of the goings-on in Walford – which we have already seen during the week but which assists our game of assuming the roles of several characters each. Connor unwillingly becomes Pat and the ceaselessly weedy Ian Beale. I am all the foxy ones (my casting choices). At the sound of the *duh duh duh* cliffhanger, I slip out to the hallway and call Meg at work.

'Hi babe, how's the shop today?'

'Och, no' bad really. Full of trendy wee things in Limp Bizkit T-shirts hanging about playing on the free Playstations and flirting with the lassies. And some big balloon knocked over my pyramid of Tweenie videos that I'd spent all morning building up to about four feet, the stupit eejit.'

'Might have been a bit of a hazard for kids, though, a four-foot-high mountain of hard-edged Tweenie goodies.'

'Aye, I suppose, but it filled a couple of hours. It meant I didn'y have to do refunds and direct endless tourists to the bagpipe easy listening section. Anyways, how's things with my two favourite lovers?'

'Who, us?'

'Well I'm no' talkin' about Beauty and the fucken' Beast. Course I mean yous two. Did you get it all sorted then, about the girl and stuff?'

'Yes' – I clear my throat and talk quietly in case Connor is listening – 'it was just a misunderstanding. They were looking for a present for me. She's the wife of his boss.'

'Oh dear, and there you were doin' your bunnit that he was shagging about. Did you ask if she had a licence for that hairstyle?'

A snort erupts from the back of my throat. 'No. God, Meg, he even said she's got good taste.'

'Jeez-oh. I dread to think what your pressie will be like.'

'Exactly. Speaking of which, er, you know I told you to rip up that cheque?'

'And shove it up Connor's arse?'

'Er, yes. Well, I was wondering whether . . .'

'No,' Meg interrupts, 'I didn'y quite get the chance. I haven't seen his arse recently. In fact, I didn'y even tear the cheque up. I knew you'd be calling me back and asking me to buy the tickets so I put them aside just in case.'

Typical Meg, so trusting and optimistic – that's what I love about her.

Meg agrees to buy the present and give it to me on Monday when we meet up after work. Feeling pleased with myself for finding such an ace anniversary gift, I skip into the lounge, plonk myself on the sofa next to Connor and pull his arm protectively around me.

'What junk are you watching?' I laugh, nodding my head at the television.

'Ehm, it's a video from work,' he says before pausing and sucking air through his teeth. 'It's the *Dollywood or Bust* show my company made earlier this year. Do you remember?'

Before we go any further, let me just explain the concept behind *Dollywood or Bust*. It is a fly-on-the-wall documentary following the progress of five big-breasted Essex glamour models trying to find fame and fortune in Hollywood. Unfortunately, or should I say fortunately for the male viewers, they rarely get past the lying-on-the-casting-couch-legs-akimbo stage but it somehow attracts good ratings nonetheless. A fine example of sensationalist modern TV tat. You get my drift.

'*Dollywood or Bust*; isn't that the fly-on-the-wall documentary following the progress of five big-breasted Essex glamour models trying to find fame and fortune in Hollywood but rarely getting past . . .?' (You know the rest.)

'Aye, that's right.'

'God, how could I forget? What a complete load of drivel.' I reach for a Jaffa Cake and dip it in my hot chocolate, freshly made by my thoughtful boyfriend.

'Yes, well.' Connor makes a clicking noise with his tongue and looks at me oddly.

'Why are you looking at me strangely? Have I got chocolate on my face or just grown another head?'

'Actually,' he replies, smiling nervously, 'I've been meaning to talk to you about work. It was something that happened yesterday but I didn't want to tell you last night because you were a wee bit—'

'Tired,' I interrupt before he can say, 'Moody bitch from hell'.

'Aye.'

Connor clicks his tongue again. I smile and continue to dip my biscuit, watching in amusement as the chocolate topping slides off into my mug. God, I'm in such a good mood.

'Tell me then, Connor,' I say with a mouthful of melted orange goo. 'I'm listening.'

'Right.'

He turns to face me on the sofa, shifts his bum on the cushions and smooths his hair back from his face.

'Well, you are looking at the newly appointed, as of yesterday, head cameraman *stroke*' – he makes a slash sign with his hand – 'temporary producer of the channel's leading show *Dollywood or Bust*. Which means more money, much more responsibility and a great opportunity for me to show them what I can do.'

'Wow, Connor, that's brilliant. I mean, the show's a load of old tripe but that doesn't matter. Well done.' I put my mug down on the coffee table and move forward for a congratulatory hug.

'And there's something else,' he adds, stopping me mid-embrace.

'Oh, let me guess. You're getting a big new camera with a huge zoomy thing and a giant fluffy microphone and lots of exciting bits like that.'

'Er, probably.' He scratches his cheek. 'More importantly, Angel, the series will involve filming for six months in California' – (pronounced, rather cringingly, Californ-I-A) – 'for the whole crew. What do you think of that then?'

I frown and chew thoughtfully on the remains of my biscuit. 'Filming for six months in Californ-I . . . I mean, California?'

Connor nods quietly.

'*You* filming for six months in California?'

He nods again. I cough as a lump of sponge lodges itself in my throat.

'But six months in California, Connor,' I repeat. 'I mean, it'd be exciting and everything but I can't just jack in my career and bugger off to LA for that long. I'm really establishing myself at Energy FM and they're relying on me to bring in the younger audiences. I'd be daft to walk out of something like that and they'd never let me have six months off to go gallivanting – listeners are too fickle.'

'I know that, baby,' he grimaces, 'and I wouldn'y expect you to. Anyway, we'll be staying in really pricey top-notch hotels on expenses and they wouldn't cover you. It just wouldn't be financially viable for you to come.' A wary smile fixes itself on Connor's lips.

The penny, or should I say the nickel, finally drops.

Drawing my lower jaw up from the sofa I whisper, 'You want to go to California for six months *without me*?'

The smile freezes, giving him the appearance of a wide-mouthed frog. He nods his head and searches my face for clues as to how I'm taking this news. My heart beats rapidly and I feel a bead of sweat erupting on my top lip.

'And your brilliant role is cameraman *stroke* what exactly?'

'Stroke temporary producer.'

'Stroke Essex tarts with humungous jugs and tiny knickers,' I growl under my breath.

'Och, you don't have to worry about them, Angel,' he tuts, taking my hand and giving it a squeeze. 'Don't feel threatened now.'

'I don't,' I pout. *Or at least I didn't until you bloody well said that.*

I stare at Connor, at my boyfriend who has been by my side for so long, and try to imagine what it will be like without him. Of course it's not as if I can't survive by myself, don't go getting all feminist on me, I'm just used to having him around. I like it. I like him. I like sex, for God's sake. I don't want to be part of a long distance relationship, having crappy phone orgasms, however they happen, and hugging my pillow at night for comfort. I take a deep breath and close my eyes.

'So,' Connor says after a very long pause, 'what do you think? Are you pleased for me?'

'You want to go to California for six months,' I hiss, 'without *me*, to film five busty slappers getting their tits out for the camera, for *your* camera, and you expect me to be *pleased* for you?'

Bloody hell, how can men get it so very wrong?

CHAPTER THREE

Rainy Days And Mondays

'It's Monday, it's twelve o'clock, you're listening to Energy FM and now it's time for *Angel on Air* with our one and only heavenly host, Miss Angel Knights.'

Jesus, they really need a good jingle writer at this station. It's not exactly what you'd call catchy, is it?

'Hello there,' I say into the microphone when the Energy FM music fades into the background and my producer Dan gives me the signal. 'It may be Monday, it may be raining cats and dogs out there, but have no fear – we're here to cheer at Energy FM. So if you've got any good stories from your weekend that will bring a smile to our grey-day faces and that you'd like to share with the people of Glasgow, give us a call on the usual number. And as well as all the general banter and' – I sub-consciously clear my throat – '*fantastic* tunes we've got lined up for you over the next three hours, our special discussion topic today is long distance relationships. Are you in one and does it work for you? Have you been in one and discovered it was a total waste of time?

Would you rather have one than the sort of relationship you've got at the moment? Whatever your opinion on LDRs, let us know and maybe we can help some of you out there who are in a dilemma about your own love life. So, get calling and let me know what my listeners think about love divided by distance. Can it work?'

All right, it may be a little self-serving but we needed a topic for discussion today anyway. The advice is free and I'm curious to know what an LDR is really like, so what better way than through my very own hotline? Waiting for the flashing red lights to appear on the studio telephone, I glance at the playlist and press a few buttons on the deck to my right.

'Now just sit back, relax and chill out to the beautiful voice of Karen Carpenter with one of their greatest hits: "Rainy Days And Mondays".'

Well, if the shite weather and having to go back to work doesn't push them over the edge, that ought to do it. I look at Dan, grinning broadly on the other side of the soundproof glass dividing the studio, and shake my head.

'What's wrong with that?' he snorts through my headphones.

'You're a bastard,' I laugh back. 'Now find me some modern, happy tunes before I shrivel up and die and all my listeners commit suicide.'

'Sure, Angel Fish, no problem. We've got Showaddywaddy up next – that'll bring a smile to your face.'

'Save me, Radio One,' I groan and press the button for the first caller.

I know what you're thinking: phone-in discussion therapy is usually the bastion of late-night radio – the twilight hours being prime-time for all the loonies such shows hope to attract. Energy FM see themselves as pioneers. To give them credit, it seems to be working so far and, after all, so am I. I may moan at times and, to be honest, Energy is not quite up there with the likes of the BBC or Clyde Radio but it certainly has potential and my job is great. I realise that not many people get to wake up every day and look forward to going into work. I do my show Monday to Friday from twelve till three so it's not exactly hour-intensive. I'm lucky, I know, although I have my moments of doubt when I'm tired and grumpy and I glance at the playlist to be greeted by a list of artists even Terry Wogan would consider uncool.

It was actually Connor who pushed me to apply to Energy FM in the first place. He has always been amazingly supportive – my crutch, my rock, my Gossard Ultrabra – and it helps to have someone supporting your dreams. I had dabbled as a DJ at college but had actually spent more time concentrating on perfecting my enigmatic DJ image than on the intricacies of mixing the decks. I'd then bagged a slot at a local pub, before landing my first real job on hospital radio. That was a challenge, let me tell you. I actually had to speak to my listeners rather than mumble song titles to comatose teenagers and, God forbid, entertain them. Not an easy task but I, as a twenty-two-year-old novice, rose to the challenge. Most of the time. Admittedly, playing 'Spirit in the Sky' was an unfortunate oversight on my part but I soon learned to screen every song on the playlist for borderline lyrics. I guess that's the reason I know almost every lyric ever written, apart from the Estonian winner of the Eurovision Song Contest and the Milli Vanilli, er, 'classics' (credit me with some taste).

I stayed at hospital radio for, would you believe it, four years before moving on to evening slots in a few of the swanky new wine bars springing up all over the city. I was back to mixing decks instead of broadcasting. I was making money but spending even more trying to keep my music collection up to date – a necessity in this profession – so I supplemented my income by scrounging a day job at Meg's shop and a handy discount on sounds to boot. It was there that I saw the advert for the DJ job at Energy FM. I was immediately excited, Meg almost had a baby trying to push me to go for it and Connor's insistence made up my mind. So here I am. And, believe me, I don't intend to be playing the likes of Mel and Kim and Rick Astley and trying to pass them off as modern-day pop music for much longer. Energy FM wanted a young DJ to drag them into the twenty-first century and build a fresh fan base and that is exactly what I plan to do . . . if I can just get a meeting with the station controller, one day when he's not on the golf course.

The first caller today, as usual, is Gladys, a sixty-something from Motherwell. I think Gladys has our number programmed into the speed-dial on her telephone and she presses it as soon as we come on air, before I've even announced the topic of the day. You see, there is no danger that Gladys wouldn't have a relevant view on the daily discussion because Gladys, it seems, has an opinion on everything – from the colour of the new black to the rights of public transport users. She is, I imagine, a formidable woman. Rather like my mother, although with a touch more homeliness about her than Delphine, who would never stoop so low as to clean a toilet or operate a hoover. Gladys likes to get the ball rolling.

‘Angel?’ she wheezes into my earpiece.

‘Yes, Gladys, good to hear from you. How was your weekend?’

‘Och, you ken, no’ bad, Angel, no’ bad. My Leslie came through with her wee-uns, Jack and Jodie, my twin grandkiddies. Och, they’re wee belters so they are, Angel, proper wee darlings. Brought me a box o’ they chocolate Roses, thirty per cent extra free too, and a new teapot so I was made up, so I was. Anyhow, that’s why I’m calling yous.’

‘Right, and why would that be, Gladys?’

Gladys sighs heavily down the phoneline, ending with a rasping smoker’s cough despite the fact that she has insisted during many a phone-in that a cigarette hasn’t passed her lips since 1964.

‘Well, my Leslie, you ken how she’s’ – Gladys clears her throat and almost whispers the next word – ‘*divorced*?’

‘Yes, Gladys, I remember. She’s had a hard time, your Leslie.’

‘Aye, she has, which is why I dinny want to see her make the same mistake again. Big waste o’ space her last fella was, upped and fleed as soon as he got a whiff o’ the first dirty nappy, so he did. Good riddance, in my opinion, he had a face like a camel eatin’ sherbet and he was totally useless. Send him oot for a tin o’ tartan paint and he’d spend all day lookin’, the big eejit. Anyhow, she’s got this new man. Nice enough fella, handsome and polite and all, but he works in Manchester through the week. He’s away Sunday night till Friday and only sees my Leslie on the weekends. Now that’s one o’ they long distance relationships and I’m no’ sure it’s right. My friend Maggie,’ she carries on without taking a breath, ‘well, her daughter Sadie’s best pal Paula over in

Edinburgh had this bloke and he was all sweetness an' light, or so it seemed. He worked away, two weeks on two weeks off kind o' thing. And do you know, Angel, I bumped inta the big sod one day in Argyle Street wi' another woman. Turns oot he was married and livin' a double life, stringin' them both along like knickers on a washin'-line, so he was. Well, I was tempted to give him his heid in his hands to play with but, you know me, I won't interfere where I'm no' wanted.'

I smile silently and wait for Gladys to finish her monologue.

'But I told Maggie and Maggie told Sadie and Sadie told Paula and Paula, well, she threw a flakey, of course. Matey got the heave-ho from the both o' them and Paula found herself a proper man, at home. You see, that's how it should be, Angel. The man should be at home where the wife can keep an eye on him and cook his dinners and build a relationship that way. None o' this long distance modern rubbish. That's no' a relationship at all.'

That's our Gladys, feminist and proud.

'So you're worried that Leslie might find herself in a similar sort of situation with her new relationship, Gladys?'

'Aye, well, I don't have any proof of that, mind, but it's a risk fer a girl these days. I mean, men like to have their cake and eat their scone, don't they, hen?'

'Hmm, yes . . .'

'I mean, he'd be daft tae do anything like that because I'd have him dragged doon the polis office and arrested for being a danger to lassies but how do you know? When a fella's away doon in Manchester or wherever and you canny keep yer eye on him, how do you know what he's up tae, Angel?'

I make agreeable noises and bite my lip. 'Well, I guess you don't know for sure, Gladys,' I reply thoughtfully, 'so it comes down to trust.'

'Aye,' Gladys tisks, 'and where did that get poor wee Paula, eh? Trust is a very disposable thing these days. Anyways, I better be off-ski, I've got a meat pie in the oven, but I suppose that was my point, hen, aboot these long distance thingummybobs. How do you know?'

'You, like, don't know,' says the caller on line two, who introduces herself as 'Casey originally from California but now an adopted Scot' (or 'Scart' as she pronounces it in her Malibu accent).

Casey is a new caller, which should keep the station controller happy. My network of interactive listeners is growing.

'I had a long distance relationship with my man in the States when I first came here. I had to, like, come for work, I'm a lawyer, and we had six months apart, divided by the Atlantic Ocean.'

Damn, this is sounding far too similar for my liking. Casey better be the bearer of good news or I might just have to cut her off, new caller or not.

'Well, I loved him as much by the end as I ever had,' she carries on confidently, 'but his eyes wandered and I'm sorry to say that he, like, played the field and got together with one of my girlfriends. I mean, *Gad*, I couldn't believe it. She's blonde and she's got these enormous fake boobs and she's a lifeguard, for Gad's sake. Like Pammy Anderson or something. I'm a lawyer, my IQ is, like, top two percentile and I make *soooo* much money. What was he doing with her when he could have been with me?'

Following his dick, I think sourly.

'Living the dream,' Dan groans into my headphones as his rising testosterone level begins to steam up his soundproofed room.

'Some men, eh?' I huff, trying to feel some sympathy for Casey but instead oscillating between hating her for compounding my fears about Connor and his glamour model friends and . . . hating her for being a brainy lawyer who makes *soooo* much money. Jesus, what the hell does she have to complain about, the self-indulgent whinger?

'You poor thing, Casey,' I say as sympathetically as I can muster while Dan holds up his hands in the shape of a square and then a big L for 'Loser'. 'And how long ago was all this?'

'About, like, four months but it's fine now. I don't miss him at all. Of course, I'm sure he wants me back; he'll get sick of looking at her fake boobs eventually.'

Dan vigorously shakes his head.

'And besides,' Casey carries on, 'I'm in a new relationship.'

'Oh really? Well, that's great, Casey. So there is a happy ending?'

'Yeah, sure. I'm having a new relationship with the beautiful people of *Glass-cow* and your wonderful country. I wake up every day and thank God he sent me to this great country, and I just have to listen to the adorable accents and play my bagpipe CD to know that I've come home.'

All right love, it's not bleedin' *Oprah*. In the distance I hear several thousand Glaswegians being sick into their haggis sandwiches, or at least that's what they would be eating if Casey had her way.

'Well, thanks for sharing that with us, Casey,' I smile, glancing at Dan who is miming 'Cut' quite dramatically through the glass, 'and call us again sometime.'

'Sure, Angel, I'm a regular listener and I totally love your show. Every day you connect with the beautiful people of *Glass-cow* and you make them feel so warm—'

'That was Casey from California, everybody,' I cough, cutting off the phone-line before she alienates my whole audience. 'And now it's time for the lovely voice of Charlotte Church, going out to Nora in Paisley who's just had her cataracts operated on and needs a little bit of cheering up. Keep those calls coming and this is for you, Nora.'

'I wish I had one o' they flippin' lang distance relationships, Angel, so I do,' grumbles Eddy, a taxi driver from Govan, close to three hours later and still on the subject of the moment.

I have had a certain amount of insight into the LDR as a modern form of relationship and, admittedly, it hasn't all been bad news. I've heard from Fran and Julie who have been apart for two years and spend their time writing love letters to each other which say more than they could ever have said on the phone; then there was Caroline and Kelly who got married after an LDR spanning five years and ten thousand miles; not forgetting Hatty and Bruce who have been in an LDR for fifteen years and like nothing better than their time apart during the week – 'It gives you time to be yourself,' said Bruce, 'and we make up for it at the weekends if you ken what I mean.' Yes, thank you, Bruce, we get the drift. I am still confused though, and still dwelling on the thought that at the end of this week my boyfriend is going to America with . . . well, you know who with. This could be a five-day countdown on our relationship. This could be the end.

'My wife, Janet, willny leave us alone, hen,' continues Eddy. 'Nag, nag, nag, all flippin' day. In my ear tae mend this and do that and take her here there and every bloody where. I'm a taxi driver fer my job, hen, I dinny want to be a taxi driver when I come hame as well. That'd be like asking a footballer to kick balls aroond the park when he comes back from a game. Speakin' of which, that couple, Thick and Thin, you know, Posh and Becks, they have a long distance relationship a lot of the time, so it says in my wife's gossip rag, and it works well fer him, doesn't it? He gets a bit of peace tae go off and be captain of England and practise his free kicks and all that. Och, what I could have been if I didn'y have Herself bumpin' her gums in my earhole all the flippin' time, nag, nag, nag,'

'Will you get off that flippin' phone right noo?' shrieks a female voice before I have a chance to comment on Eddy's problem. It seems Janet and Eddy have a telephone extension.

'Hey, I'm havin' a private converbloodysation here, Jan. Away ye go.'

'I don't care if you're havin' words with Prince Bleedin' Charles! You've got jobs to do and I want a lift to town. I've got a bikini wax at four so shift yer fat backside doon here now!'

'Thanks for your call, Eddy,' I grin, suppressing a laugh as the phone goes dead, 'and thanks to everyone for all your comments today. As usual, we're going away with a lot to think about. We'll have another special topic tomorrow, but till then have a great rest of Monday afternoon, despite the rain, and join me, Angel Knights, at twelve o'clock tomorrow for another three hours of *Angel on Air*. Now here's Europe to play us out with that unforgettable rock song "The Final Countdown", so get out that air guitar and let yourself go.'

'"The Final Countdown"? Jeez-oh, Angel, that's a fucken' terrible song to inflict on your listeners,' Meg snorts.

'But don't you see? It's a sign.'

'Damn right it's a sign. A sign that you work for a second-rate radio station with incredibly poor taste in music,' Ceri pouts, delicately lifting her mug. 'Do they still think The Beatles are a fancy new boy band?'

'No,' I tut, 'they're not that bad.'

'They bloody well are if "The Final Countdown" is all they can come up with to climax the show,' Meg giggles, reaching for a chocolate brownie. 'Maybe I'll have a whipround at work, see if we can get yous some nice new records. How about Climie Fisher, hen; I hear they're the next big thing.'

Meg and Ceri laugh loudly, Meg throwing her mouth open to reveal a mass of semi-ingested chocolate goo. I bite my bottom lip and stare moodily into my cup. I've got too much on my mind to indulge in idle banter. This is serious.

We are in Starbucks on the corner of West Nile Street and Sauchiehall Street at the top of town, near to the centre of the media world where Ceri works as some sort of assistant to the assistant features editor of a weekly glossy magazine called *Star*. She is far from the top of the ladder but, of course, Ceri manages to carry herself as if she were the Editor-in-Chief, blags her way into every important party and freebie give-away and even gets a huge discount from one of the waiters in Starbucks, who would clearly lick week-old coffee from the soles of her shoes if it meant getting a date with Ceri Divine. Thanks to Ceri, we now all have steaming mugs of green tea with *two* tea bags and a selection of mini cakes, which will not even touch Ceri's manicured hands never mind her glossed lips, for a highly discounted price. Definitely worth the five-minute uphill walk from Meg's shop where I met them after my show.

'Can I no' have a cappuccino?' Meg groans, holding her nose as she sips from the large cream mug. 'You wouldn'y even give this stuff to famine victims. It's like water that's been briefly introduced to a few wee blades of grass.'

'It's good for you,' Ceri replies firmly. 'It's full of antioxidants which clear the free radicals from your body.'

'Eh? I just want a drink, Ceri hen, not a friggin' Ph.D. in coffee shop science.'

'It's cleansing,' Ceri continues primly, 'and heaven knows you need some help in that department.'

She turns her nose up in disgust as Meg shoves half a caramel shortcake into her mouth and starts to chew.

'Look, girls, I really mean it about that song,' I say with obvious frustration, squirming on my purple velvet chair. 'I was just thinking how this trip to the States could be the end for me and Connor and then that Yankee girl comes on and tells me her story about the blonde lifeguard and makes it even worse. And just as I'm fretting that he's going on Friday, I look down at the playlist and there it is: "The Final Countdown". It's a sign.'

'Friday!' Meg shrieks. 'You didn't say he was going on Friday. What *this* Friday? As in four days' away Friday? As in the day after your anniversary Friday?'

I nod sadly. Meg and Ceri exchange loaded glances.

'Wow,' says Meg, 'that's mental, hen. As of this Friday, your Connor'll be, like, fucken' miles away on the other side of the world and you'll be here on your own, like me. Only not like me cos I haven'y got a fella and you'll still have one only he'll be thousands of miles away doin' whatever.'

'Thanks, Meg,' I croak, 'that really cleared up a few things for me.'

'Any time, pal,' she smiles, happily returning to the delicacies on the cake plate.

'So what do you think, Ceri?' I ask, nervously chewing the inside of my cheek.

Ceri crosses her long legs and sweeps her hair back from her shoulders.

'What do I think?' she says slowly, pausing to run her tongue along her full lips which, quite frankly, I would lick all the time too if they were mine. 'What do I think about Connor going off to America for six months out of the blue like this?'

'Yes,' I reply impatiently.

Ceri smooths down the arms of her caramel cashmere jumper and shrugs.

'I think that Connor needs some space. Maybe by taking this job without even consulting you first' – she emphasises this last point – 'he's trying to show you that he needs to do some things on his own for a while, see the world, meet new people and all that jazz. I don't know – maybe he's bored and wants to break up with you.'

'Bloody hell, Ceri, what is this? A PR exercise for The Samaritans or something? You're not doing a very good job of cheering me up here.'

'We're just being honest, Angel,' Ceri replies with another flick of her hair. 'If we weren't honest then there wouldn't be any point in us being your best friends, would there? Unfortunately, our opinions are not always going to be what you want to hear.'

'Well I think you and Connor'll be absolutely fine,' Meg butts in, just in time to stop my heart shattering into a million little pieces. 'Yous two are a perfect couple. You've been together for ever and you still laugh and get all romantic.'

Meg's eyes glaze over dreamily. Ceri raises hers to the ceiling.

'It's only six months, hen,' Meg continues. 'What's that when you've been lovers for thirteen years?'

'Thanks, babe,' I smile, leaning forward and touching her arm.

'I told you,' says Ceri, shaking her head. 'Thirteen years, it's unlucky. First that girl at the shops and now this.'

She finishes the sentence with a raised eyebrow. I take a deep breath and stare morosely at the crumby remains of our cake selection, most of which has disappeared down Meg's throat.

'That woman was the wife of his boss, Ceri.'

'Or so *he* says.'

'And he hasn't said he wants to break up, it's just a job opportunity.' I try my best to sound convincing while my friends watch me, the pity visible in their eyes. 'I'm sure, as Meg says, it'll all be fine. It just means getting used to having a long distance relationship.'

'Huh, what's the point in one of those?' Ceri tuts. 'All the hassle of commitment and absolutely zero bodily satisfaction. A complete waste of time if you ask me.'

'Well, we'll see,' I reply shakily, looking down at my feet and rubbing an invisible mark from the front of my red glittery trainer.

'Right,' Meg beams, 'now are we gonna go find you some shoes for your big anniversary date this Thursday? I'm gaggin' for a quick shop.'

'I don't know if I'm really in the mood,' I sigh woefully as Meg jumps to her feet and pulls on her fluffy green jacket. 'I mean, it's not going to be much of an anniversary. I've bought him a present that he won't be here for' – my eyes move to the James tickets and goodie bag lying on the table in front of us which Meg brought with her from work – 'and he's buggering off to America for half a year the next morning. I wouldn't call that perfect.'

'Och, away ye go. It's what you make it, hen,' Meg replies, grabbing my arm and pulling me gently up from the chair, 'Connor can still wear the T-shirt and we can go to the gig in his honour if we get Ceri a ticket—'

'Er, don't bother,' Ceri interjects, 'I don't like grungy, sweaty places.'

'. . . and I have never,' Meg continues, 'known my pal Angel, the Footwear Fairy, to let an important occasion pass without treatin' herself to a new pair of shoes. Come on the noo, it'll make you feel better. Put a wee smile on that fizzer of yours.'

I smirk as Meg grabs the skin on my cheek and shakes it like a granny would do to her young grandchildren.

'*All right*, I guess we could have a quick shifty before the shops shut,' I say, grabbing my jacket with the sudden urgency of a girl in need of shoes, 'and I do really need a new pair of wedge heels.'

The good old retail therapy trick, it seldom fails.

'That's the way, babe,' says Ceri over her shoulder as she strides out behind Meg and I scuttle happily along behind. 'Get a whole new outfit, make yourself look like a million bucks. Then if he's going to dump you at least it'll make him have second thoughts about what he's throwing on the scrap heap.'

'Thanks, Ceri,' I mutter, my confidence crumbling before we've even reached the door. 'You know, you should really consider a career in counselling. Roll on Thursday, eh? I can't bloody wait.'

CHAPTER FOUR

Diamonds Are A Girl's Best Friend

We haven't even looked at the dessert menu yet and already he has popped the question. Proposed. Asked me to marry him. It is bad timing really. Firstly because that last slice of raspberry pavlova on the sweet trolley has been sending me subliminal messages for the last hour and it doesn't seem right to disappoint it. And secondly (which should probably be firstly in the general scheme of things) because I have spent the last three days getting used to the idea of being without Connor for six months or even, if Ceri's opinion was anything to go by, for ever. Now all of a sudden I am having to get used to the idea of being *with* him. For ever. Till death us do part – except for the next six months when five pairs of silicone boobs and the hedonistic paradise of California us do part. In sickness and in health, for better, for worse and all that malarkey. Well, that's if I say yes.

I narrow my eyes at the glitzy little silver box sitting proudly on the table with an even glitzier ring inside it. The ring is a rather large, very sparkling turquoise, emerald and diamond cluster. It wouldn't have been my first choice but, then again, he is a bloke and they do tend to think big is best on the jewellery front, don't they? Show a man a diamond solitaire from Aspreys or a fist-sized lump of cubic zirconia set among brothel-red rubies from the Argos catalogue and ask them to pick the most expensive and I can guarantee nine out of ten fellas would plump for the latter. Subtlety doesn't come into it. Men like show rings. Rings that shout: 'Get yer hands off, this is my woman and I went into a jewellery shop all by myself' – or in this case as we know with a woman with big hair and shoulder pads – 'and picked her this marcasite-encrusted monstrosity as a token of my love, which she will have to grin and bear for the rest of our married life. Aren't I the cleverest man there ever was?' Although this isn't marcasite, it is the real McCoy. I also have to admit that, despite its grandness, the significance of the gesture is very touching. You see, turquoise and emerald are our birthstones – mine being in December and Connor's in May – and I guess the diamonds are in there for good measure, being a girl's best friend and all that. Connor assured me the birthstone thing was his idea and I like to think that was the case because it is genuinely romantic for a modern man. Besides, Big Hair Beth's brain was probably so weighed down with the amount of styling products on her coiffured mane that it wouldn't have had a hope in hell of coming up with something that complicated.

I snap the lid of the box shut as the ring's invisible price tag tugs on my conscience. I'm sure it set him back a pretty penny, which is pressure in itself to say Yes. Oh God, he must have saved for ages to get it, given that Connor doesn't do credit cards. And it must have cost so much. Probably even more than a case of this hugely overpriced champagne that I am gulping down like Panda Pops to steady my nerves. Steady my nerves because he, Connor, the man who I thought was sodding off to the States to get rid of me, has just proposed and sent my mind into a vortex of confusion, but also because I am sitting alone in an incredibly posh restaurant. We are in The Ice Palace, a beautifully extravagant eatery in the centre of town, a regular haunt of the stinking rich, incredibly famous and anyone either with a talent for playing professional football or shagging professional footballers. The cream carpets are as thick as a fresh falling of Alpine snow, the walls painted in swirls of metallic white and gold. Sparkling chandeliers hang like precious icicles from the mural of a snow scene on the high ceiling and two open log fires roar ferociously on opposite walls. The waiters and waitresses drift elegantly around the room in pristine cream suits, which I would be terrified of wearing within ten feet of a tomato ragoût. The menu is gold-embossed and every dish presented like a work of art. Personally I would rather eat my dinner than frame it but I appreciate the poshness of it all. Although such over-pronounced swank makes me nervous. In places like this I always feel as though I should be offering to wash the dishes or clear the plates away to justify my presence, or that people are staring at me wondering how someone like me can afford a place like this. Well, they're certainly staring at me now, sitting alone at a table for two slap bang in the centre of the restaurant like a complete desperado.

I nervously gulp more champagne, screwing up my face as the bubbles erupt into my nostrils. I wish he would hurry up and get back from the toilet; all this time on my own to think is making things worse.

I tap my feet – partly from anxiety and partly because the ridiculously pointy toes of my new black wedges, as chosen by Meg and Ceri, are starting to cut off my circulation. I knew they didn't fit properly but they looked so inviting in the shop and time was running out and I needed cheering up, as you well know. Besides, shoes are not about comfort, they're about style and sexiness and fitting the moment, not necessarily the *foot*. My legs shaking, I turn the ring box over and over in my hand. This is crazy; I didn't expect this at all. Which is pretty darned obvious from my contribution to the present-buying frenzy, which is lying on the table amid a mass of torn wrapping paper. Two tickets to see James, which he can't even use because he'll be thousands of miles away, and a retro-style T-shirt in blue with a green and purple flower on the front, among other goodies. I thought it was perfect, befitting that very first time we met, but it looks rather pathetic compared to his choice of gift.

I put the silver box to one side, still having failed to pluck up the courage to remove the ring from its red velvet cushion, and press the glass of cold champagne to my right cheek. How did I not see this coming? Of course Connor had seemed excited about the present he had bought, and I remember that he mentioned marriage and children a couple of times over the weekend but people do that when they're going out together in that off-the-cuff, teasing kind of way. I didn't think he actually meant it. I didn't get a whiff of a proposal in the offing and sneakily practise my acceptance speech in front of the bathroom mirror. In fact, I didn't even suspect anything was up right until the moment he produced the jewel and said those words. You see, my mind was on other things at the time. We were talking about tomorrow.

About Connor flying away to LA with *those* girls for *that* long. The mood was perceptibly sombre.

'I just can't imagine being without you for six months, Connor,' I said, morosely sliding a piece of lobster meat around the plate with my fork as 'Don't It Make My Brown Eyes Blue' played wistfully in the background.

'Och, I know, it's gonna be really weird,' he replied quietly, 'but I'm sure it'll go by dead quick.'

I sighed and tried to push Crystal Gayle's soulful lyrics to the back of my mind.

'And you can always come for a holiday once I'm set up and know where I'm staying. You'd like that, wouldn't you? A trip to LA?'

'Yes,' I smiled. 'I'll remember and pack my silicone breasts.'

Connor laughed uneasily, both our minds clearly dwelling on his travelling companions for the next few months.

'Well, we'll sort that out, Angel, but you'll be busy over here.'

'Yeah, I'll be busy,' I shrugged. 'I've got work to do at Energy; they really need a bit of a kick up the arse when it comes to their playlists. That is definitely a mission of mine. Then there's Meg and Ceri; they won't let me get lonely. And my dad – I really should see him a bit more often but, as you know, he can be a bit of a nightmare.'

Connor nodded knowingly.

'So I'll have lots to do. I'm not just going to sit around in a darkened room pining for you but it'll still be odd. Long distance relationships are strange things, Connor.'

'How do you mean?'

'Well, there's the communication thing. It's not quite as easy to keep a strong bond when you're snatching minutes on expensive phone calls or e-mailing sweet nothings and worrying whether some pervy computer hack is reading your private thoughts. Then there's the going to events on your own thing, like parties, and having to say, "I've got a boyfriend but he works abroad" while people nod and wink and think that your boyfriend is imaginary and you're really a loser who can't pull. Plus there's the trust thing, which can cause major problems. You'll be hanging out with women and I'm bound to bump into the odd man here and there but what if you don't trust me or I don't trust you or I trust you and you know I'm trusting you so you abuse that trust but keep it all a secret? It's just difficult.'

Connor raised his eyebrows as I paused for breath and stabbed my lobster with my fork.

'Jeez,' he whistled, 'that does sound complicated. In fact, you lost me somewhere around pervy computer hack. And here I was just worrying about my heart missing you too much.'

I stared across the table at his strong, smooth hand as he reached out and placed it on top of mine. We fell silent; staring at the stark white tablecloth while the piano music played from the concealed speakers around the restaurant and Crystal Gayle sang the last few words of her song.

'I don't want to make your brown eyes blue, my Angel,' Connor croaked eventually. 'I love them just the way they are.'

I raised my eyes and met his in the candlelight. They glowed against the vibrant blue of his smart shirt. He looked so handsome, so – at the risk of sounding like a Jane Austen character – dashing.

'Perhaps you've been thinking about all this a wee bit too much,' Connor suggested, holding my hand even tighter.

'Maybe. We did have a phone-in about it on the show.'

'What? About us?'

'No, of course not, just about long distance love in general.'

'And?'

I sniffed and looked at the tablecloth again. 'Not great news on the whole. Plus Ceri and Meg have been throwing in their ten pence worth.'

'Let me guess. Meg was hopelessly lovely and optimistic and Ceri foresaw doom, gloom and a locked door at the end of the tunnel.'

'Precisely.'

He laughed and wrapped his hand around the stem of a delicate crystal champagne glass.

'Those two are like chalk and cheese. You're somewhere in between, baby. What's between chalk and cheese?'

'Dunno – something a little bit chalky and a little bit cheesy?'

'Well, whatever you are,' he smiled, 'you're the one for me. You have been for the last thirteen years and you still are.' Connor raised his champagne flute and winked mischievously. 'Thirteen years today, baby. Cheers.'

I clinked my glass against his and forced a smile. We paused to drink the champagne. The tension in the air was palpable.

'Things are going to change though, aren't they, Con?' I said, biting my bottom lip. 'Especially Sundays. What am I going to do on Sundays now? They can be so boring without having someone to lie in bed with and have brunch with. As for normal mornings, I don't even know how to make porridge the way you make it.'

Porridge. Yes, I know it seems ridiculously insignificant but suddenly, as time pressed on and his flight the next day drew closer, the small things in my head were growing to the size of the big things. As for the big things . . .

We never had porridge in our house, what with mum being French and therefore anti anything non-French. Breakfast was a basket of warm croissants and pain au chocolat, which I blame almost entirely for my hips as not only are they packed with fattening butter cunningly disguised as tasty flaky crumbs and thick chocolate cunningly disguised as . . . er, thick chocolate, but they only fill you up for approximately half an hour after you've eaten. This is fine if you are a tiny French woman who then progresses to a few morsels of baguette for lunch, a glass of red wine and several cups of espresso, but I would always find myself raiding the cake and pie section of the bakery before I even got to school and then gorging on the delicacies of the tuck shop at first break just to make up for my early morning starvation. Luckily Connor later introduced me to the importance of having a hearty breakfast to kick-start my day which clearly didn't shrink my hips but seemed to take them to a curvy plateau.

'Try Ready Brek, baby,' Connor smiled, wrinkling his nose. 'It's almost the same, just the non-Scottish idiot version.'

'S'pose,' I sniffed, a smile crossing my lips, 'but I bet it won't give me that warm orange glow without you.'

'Actually' – Connor cleared his throat and wiped a line of sweat from his top lip, which I briefly thought at the time was unusual for him as he doesn't sweat much – 'I've got something that might give you a warm glow.'

'Connor!' I shrieked, the champagne bubbles coursing around my head, 'we can't do that here, it's far too posh a restaurant.' I glanced quickly around me, dismissing the disdainful expressions of the couple at the table to my left. 'Unless you fancy skipping off to the bogs for a quick bit of—'

'I didn'y mean *that*, Angel,' Connor whispered, his cheeks visibly glowing. He turned towards his jacket which he had insisted on hanging on the back of his chair when we first sat down, almost wrestling with the maître d' who had tried to whisk it away to the cloakroom. Sticking the tip of his tongue out and biting it with his teeth, Connor scrabbled in every pocket of the jacket while I whispered, 'What are you looking for? We don't need a condom, do we?'

Finally he found what he was looking for, turned to face me and wiped yet another line of glistening sweat from his lip.

'I meant *this*,' he croaked, staring into my eyes and reaching for one of my hands while lifting the little silver box from underneath the table and holding it out unsteadily towards me with his other hand.

My eyes flicked to the item in his hand and grew wide with disbelief. I almost threw up.

Well, it seems that *he* did, because immediately after uttering the words, 'Angel, will you marry me?', rendering me completely speechless, he dropped the box on to the table, jumped up from his chair like a rabbit with its tail on fire and scarpered across the restaurant towards the men's toilets. That was almost half an hour ago and I haven't seen him since.

I reach for the champagne bottle which clatters against the silver bucket as I try to lift it. I smile apologetically at the couple to my left who appear to be far more interested in my predicament than in anything they have to say to each other. Hardly surprising, I think, squirming under their contemptuous stares – he looks like a stiff suit with a personality bypass and she hoovered up four courses as if she were snacking on a packet of peanuts. Mind you, she probably needs the extra strength to hold up all that diamond jewellery.

Diamonds; fuck, don't talk to me about diamonds. Sticking my nose in the air in the general direction of Mr and Mrs Filthy Rich (my vision is starting to blur somewhat), I pour the remains of the bottle into my glass. Lifting it gingerly, I hold my breath and then throw it back like a tequila slammer. It tastes almost too good to be alcoholic; the liquid is cold and expensively dry and I hardly feel the bubbles popping in my throat. Apparently a good champagne has larger bubbles than sparkling wine. Connor taught me that while trying to wean me off the three-quid Asti Spumanti that Meg and I favour whenever we're trying to mimic the habits of Ceri.

Thinking of Meg and Ceri, I have a flash of inspiration. In times of trauma and indecision all a girl has to do is call her best friends. Delving into my bag – it requires *delving*, as I have never mastered the art of the postage stamp sized clutch bag – I locate my mobile phone. I have to share this news with someone just to hear the reaction. Perhaps then I will know what to do.

Five answering machines and a chip shop in Uddingston (wrong number) later, I'm none the wiser. In this age of being constantly contactable, why is no one ever there on the end of the line when you really need to talk? I leave a rather rambling message on Meg's home phone and mobile before remembering that she's got a date tonight with the new Italian Saturday boy – at thirty-two probably the oldest Saturday boy in Glasgow but Meg was instrumental in his selection. It's ten-thirty now so my guess is she'll either be trying to drag him back to her flat and asking him to move in for good or discussing how many children he would like and setting a date to meet his family. I also leave a bit of drunken abuse on Ceri's jewel-encrusted designer mobile and hi-tech digital phone at home. Of course Ceri is rarely in any night of the week, having so many men to choose from. By now she'll either be shagging her latest conquest senseless or kicking him out the door having made him wine her, dine her and declare his undying love. I even call my mum in France for advice, knowing before I dial that she won't be there. Since splitting up with dad and moving back to Bordeaux, mum has got a better social life than me and probably a better sex life too. Yuck, I can't believe I even let that thought grace my mind. Just thinking it makes me want to rinse my brain in soapy water.

'Is everything all right, madam?' a waiter asks, appearing at my side with a freshly opened bottle of Moet.

'Yes, fine thanks,' I reply quietly, stifling a hiccup and smiling benignly.

'Well, just let me know if I can get you anything else,' he beams pleasantly, clearly vying for a whopping great tip on top of the extortionate bill.

I nod timidly and turn my attention back to the champagne while the snooty cow next door whispers something to her husband and tuts louder than I thought humanly possible. Where is Connor, for fuck's sake? Men don't get cystitis, do they? I'll kill him for this. The whole evening has got me so rattled I'm starting to feel like one of Gloria Estefan's maracas.

So what is all the fuss about, you may ask? What is the big deal about your boyfriend of thirteen years asking you to marry him? The big deal – apart from the fact that I didn't see it coming when I thought I knew Connor inside out, which is worrying in itself – is that I thought we were happy the way things were. We have fun and we enjoy each other without the complication of feeling that we're tied to one another for the rest of our lives, although I suppose in a way I imagined that we were. I guess that might sound selfish or immature and to some extent that might be the case, but there is the obvious fact that he is leaving in about twelve hours for six whole months and the thought of a long distance relationship is terrifying enough. If I'm honest, though, a large part of the problem stems from having witnessed mum and dad's divorce in the very recent past. It scared me.

I suppose I always knew that they weren't the perfect match. My father is, generally speaking, a very private, quiet person. This can change entirely when he's had a few. Dad becomes loud, child-like and basically a bit of a tosser. Mum could put up with that to a certain extent, ironically having grown up in a family of French wine-makers, but she never really got to grips with the more British habit of chucking alcohol down your neck at an alarming rate until you fall over. I have to say, Dad is not a six-pack of Special Brew/bottle of cheap vodka in a brown paper bag type of alcoholic; he's much more subtle in his approach. As far as

Steve Knights is concerned, he is purely a connoisseur of fine wines and spirits and counts consuming almost an entire New World wine section of the supermarket in a single weekend among his finest achievements. Dad also has a penchant for whisky – hence the whisky factory job being a very bad idea – and the finest dark rums of the Caribbean. He thinks his tastes are refined, that he's simply indulging in a pastime like cookery or badminton. To the rest of us he's just an alco with a modicum of taste. I, on the other hand, know my limits when it comes to alcohol and I haven't let Dad's illness stop me from having fun. In fact, I should watch myself; this champagne is surprisingly easy to drink.

Drunk or sober, Dad does not communicate well when it comes to the important things in life, which was largely the reason why his marriage to my mum did not work. Mum is hotheaded, confident and opinionated and loves to be the centre of attention. She speaks her mind and doesn't care who she upsets in the process. Sometimes her honesty is refreshing in a nation famous for beating around the bush, but often she is downright rude. Dad worshipped her but didn't know how to show it, which Mum took as a sign of disinterest. He did everything for her, apart from listening to her troubles or recognising the homesickness that was eating into her heart. So two years ago Mum put herself first and left. They divorced, Mum moved back to Bordeaux and they have only spoken once since.

Add to that the fact that my dad's parents hated the sight of each other and my mum's father had two mistresses whom he paraded around Bordeaux like trophies in front of my grandmother's eyes and I think I'm justified in feeling wary about the whole Mr and Mrs thing.

And that's another point. Mr and Mrs McLean. Eugh, that is officially old people's territory. Mr and Mrs Connor McLean sound like dull, suburban strangers who mow their lawn on a Saturday, go to B&Q on a Sunday and cook only according to the Gospel of Nigella Lawson. Not that there's anything wrong with gorgeous, wholesome Nigella per se. The point is how can I be expected to answer to Mrs McLean when I've been called Angel Knights for the last twenty-nine years? I suppose I could be modern and stick to my maiden name but then it's bound to get complicated when we have kids and they go to school and their mummy and daddy have different names and . . . Bloody hell, listen to me. I'm already becoming mumsy and he only proposed less than an hour ago. I quickly refill my glass and gulp some more ice-cold bubbles. I'm beginning to scare myself but, you see, that's how these things snowball. That's the big deal.

So therein lies my dilemma. Am I just not cut out for marriage or does everyone feel this jittery immediately after a surprise proposal? Do I wait and see how our LDR works out and then decide? Would saying no to him now make him go off to Californ-I-A in search of someone who will jump at the chance to be his wife? More to the point, has he only proposed to me to keep me waiting patiently at home while he swans off to discover the world in a having it and eating it scenario? Or does he simply love me and would have done this anyway even if he weren't planning on buggering off tomorrow? All these questions and here was I thinking the biggest decision I would have to make tonight would be whether to have a starter, a pudding or both.

I clutch the edges of the table and lean to the side for a better view of the toilet door which, for once in my life, I haven't been seated right next to so that the door bumps my chair and I get a great whiff of urine every time somebody goes in or out. I almost let out a loud cheer when the door opens and my Connor appears. He has a pained expression on his face and a rather dubious mark on the front of his trousers but he's here. He hasn't jumped out of the window, or if he did at least he came back. I watch as he walks towards me, six foot tall but looking more vulnerable than I have ever seen him look in our time together. Is this what proposing does to a man? Reduces him to a nervous wreck? I smile, knowing in my heart how much I love him. My heartbeat quickens as he approaches the table.

'What shall I say?' I whisper to myself, hiccupping twice between each word.

'Hi baby, sorry about that,' Connor whispers, his face as red as the discarded lobster shell on his plate.

I take a shaky sip of water, spilling half on the table and dropping the rest down my front. I rub my chest, sit up straight and try to appear sober. I am failing miserably but I keep up the façade, smiling warmly.

'Ehm, I had a wee bit of a problem in there,' he carries on, his face moving in and out of focus in front of me. 'Tell you about it later. So . . .'

This is it. This is the moment I have been psyching myself up for over the last hour.

'So what?' I slur, running my tongue along my furry teeth.

'So, have you, ehm . . .' Connor coughs, nervously taking his seat. 'Have you thought about what I asked you?'

'I have.' I pout my lips and lean forward in my chair, ready to deliver the news.

'And?'

'And,' I hiccup, leaning closer still, 'I think . . . Oh God . . . I think I'm going to puke.'

I squeeze my eyes shut, my head spins violently and I feel myself falling. Falling. In a heap. On to the posh shagpile carpet. I close my eyes and flinch as a hard object falls from the table and hits me on the side of the head – a glitzy little silver box with an even glitzier ring inside it.

CHAPTER FIVE

2 Become 1

I wake up when Connor brushes his hand down the side of my face. I try to open my eyes but they are stuck together, my eyelashes congealed with last night's three coats of mascara. I kick myself for being too drunk to think about taking my make-up off before I went to bed. At least, I would have kicked myself but my legs don't appear to be working.

'I brought you a coffee, Angel,' Connor whispers gently.

My head pounds with the sound of the cup being placed on the table next to the bed. Even the duvet seems to be incredibly noisy for something constructed almost entirely of feathers and super-soft cotton.

'Shit,' I groan, rubbing my eyes until I find daylight. I start to panic that I've gone blind before I realise that there is no daylight because it's dark. It is still the middle of the night.

'Connor,' I splutter, slowly regaining the use of my tongue, 'it's night-time. Go to sleep. Sssh.'

I pull the duvet towards me and begin to recoil into the foetal position but he yanks the duvet the opposite way.

'No, you can't go back to sleep. We have to talk.'

'Later, Con, I have to die now.'

'No!'

Even in my semi-comatose state I can sense the urgency in his voice. I make a huge effort to sit up. My head spins as I try to focus on something, anything.

'Look, Connor, I'm hungover and you're really starting to piss me off. What is so important that you have to wake me up in the middle of the night and . . .' – I stare at him in the dim lamplight – 'Connor, what are you wearing? Why have you got your coat on?'

He moves towards me and perches anxiously on the edge of the bed.

'I've got to go, remember?' He smiles weakly. 'America,' he prompts, placing his hand on my arm.

'Oh my God; now?' Reality hits me with the force of being smacked in the face with a Le Creuset frying pan.

'Aye, baby,' he sighs, gently rubbing the skin on my forearm. 'I've got a taxi waiting outside and I'm already a bit late. I've got to go.'

'No! Oh, Connor.'

I lurch forwards and grab him, pulling him towards me. His arms envelop my body and I breathe in the familiar smell of his skin. I feel scared. My boyfriend is going away for six months and we have about sixty seconds to say goodbye. I have been preparing for this all week but all of a sudden it feels too soon, like this moment has crept up on me and I haven't said everything I want or need to say. As it turns out, I haven't.

'There was just one thing I wanted you to tell me before I

go,' says Connor eventually, pulling away slightly from the hug and wiping a tear from my face.

'Yes? What is it? Anything.'

He squeezes his lips together tightly and his hands grip my arms at the elbows. His eyes search my face. I stare at them, blue and sparkling, unlike my own which are, I imagine, a very attractive shade of bloodshot. My head aches at the intensity of the moment.

'Last night,' he begins, jumping as a horn sounds from the street below. 'Shit, wait a minute, will you?'

I bite my cheek and stare desperately at the window, knowing that there is a taxi revving its engine, ready to whisk my man away.

'Last night,' he says again.

'Yes, look, I'm sorry about all that, Connor. You were gone for so long in that toilet—'

'I know, I'm sorry. I explained that if you remember,' he replies shyly.

Jesus, how could I forget? But more about that later.

'Yes, yes, but I was uncomfortable sitting there and I thought posh champagne didn't get you so drunk or give you a stinking hangover like this.'

'Perhaps you had a wee bit too much, Angel, but that's all in the past.'

The horn honks again, louder and more impatient. I hear the protestations of an angry neighbour.

'All I need to know before I leave is your answer, baby. I can't leave until you say whatever it is you are going to say.'

I run my tongue along my bottom lip and stare at him. Then the frying pan appears for a second shot at my head.

Jesus, the proposal! How could I forget the proposal?

'Oh,' I gasp, my voice clearly shaking, 'that. I, er, gosh—'

'I know it's bad timing right now with me running out the door but I need you to tell me face to face and this is my last chance.'

The taxi horn honks exasperatedly, the neighbour shrieks again and is joined by the raised voices of several others. Connor looks at me anxiously from his position on the edge of the bed. He looks like he's in the starting blocks ready to run the 100 metre sprint. This is all too much; my head can't take this pressure. I need time. I'm just trying to come to terms with the fact that Connor is jetting out of my life for six months. In a couple of minutes I will be in a long distance relationship and I've never had one of those before. What if I'm not very good at it?

Take your time, my head urges me, *you can't rush it. If he loves you he'll understand.*

Say yes. Look at his face, he'll be so disappointed, says my heart.

'Angel Knights,' says Connor, looking me straight in the eye, 'will you marry me?'

I will think about it, I practise, trying to say the words. *I will think about it.*

'Connor,' I say, coughing to clear the breezeblock that appears to be lodged in my throat. 'This is a big step, especially with you leaving and everything, but I will . . .'

'YES!' Connor shrieks, leaping off the bed and running around the room. 'OH MY GOD, YES!'

I stare in disbelief as he sprints to the window, throws it open and yells, 'SHE SAID YES! SHE BLOODY WELL SAID YES!' to the dark street outside.

'Who fucken' cares?' an anonymous voice replies.

'Pal, d'you want this fucken' taxi or no'?' shouts another.

Connor runs towards me, lifts me out of bed and spins me around, kissing my neck until every inch has been covered.

'I knew you'd say yes, my Angel,' he beams. 'I love you so much. I'll miss you but I'll call as soon as I get there and we can talk about this some more. Now I know you'll be here for me when I get back.'

We kiss and hug all the way to the door, hardly a word crossing my lips other than noises to roughly correspond with his excited shrieks. It is a whirlwind of embracing, tears, grabbing suitcases, running out the door, coming back for the passport, embracing and running out the door again. Finally I close it, trudge to the window and watch as his taxi disappears along Byres Road and into the darkness. I pull the window shut, rest my head against the glass and sigh: 'Oh fuck, what have I done?'

'Wake up, beautiful blushing bridey McBride. The wedding dress shop awaits you.'

I open my eyes with a start to find that I am upside down in bed and my mouth is as dry as if I have been sucking on a roll-on deodorant all night.

'Eh? What? Why?' I grunt, hoping that the first time I woke up was actually a dream and I just imagined accepting a marriage proposal seconds before Connor rushed out of the door and into a waiting taxi. It is then I notice that the face three inches from mine is not that of my boyfriend but of a very excited Meg. She looks like she is about to explode into a million pieces right there on my bedroom carpet.

'Why? Why?' Meg shrieks, yanking back the duvet. 'Because you're getting married, hen, and there's no time tae waste. We've gotta find a dress and then there's shoes an' veils an' flowers, ooh, an' bridesmaids. Please tell me I'm gonna be a bridesmaid, Angel. I know I'm bein' bold and you're no' supposed to ask to be one but I'd be pure dead brilliant, so I would. Don't put me in the same dress as Skinny Malinky Long Legs Ceri but. Anyhow' – she flaps her arms in my dumbfounded face – 'we can sort all that out. Come on, pal, get up. I'm too excited to wait!'

I stare at Meg from my upside-down position and suddenly feel the need to vomit.

'But I can't be getting married already,' I whine. 'I only said yes about five minutes ago.' I struggle to pull myself up into a sitting position and clasp my head. 'No, Meg, not today. Don't make me get married today. I can't. Look at the state of me and I'm not ready. Not ready in my head.'

Meg tilts her head to one side and looks at my tear-stained face before screwing up her nose and bursting into uproarious laughter. She clasps her belly and opens her mouth incredibly wide. I pout and wait until she's finished.

'Ah, you wee mad skull,' she chuckles. 'You're no' gettin' married today, hen. He only asked you yesterday and weddings take a bit more preparation than that. Ooh, jings, it's gonna be so exciting you being a bridey McBride.' Meg laughs loudly again and clatters out of the bedroom towards the kitchenette.

'Oh. But' – I fall out of bed and search around the floor for my favourite grey trackie bottoms – 'how did you know? Did Connor call you?'

'Nuh,' Meg shouts through from the adjacent room, 'you

called me, you stupit eejit. Last night. I thought you sounded out o' yer box on my answering machine when I got your message but I couldn'y tell if it was because you were letting me know that Connor had just proposed' – she shrieks the last word at a level only audible to dogs – 'or if you'd had a wee bit too much o' the bendy juice.'

'Bendy juice,' I confirm from the bedroom, clutching my squirming stomach. 'Very bubbly, expensive bendy juice.'

'Och, well, you're entitled to that, hen, so don't go feeling all guilty about it like you do. It's no' every day a girl gets proposed to. Unless . . .'

'. . . your name's Ceri Divine,' we say in unison.

'You didn'y actually tell me you'd said yes,' Meg carries on, clanking cups around noisily, 'but I knew you would.'

'Mmmm,' I mutter under my breath. I shake my head and ruffle my hair, looking in the mirror through narrowed eyes. I think it will have to be the 'just got out of bed' look today. I scoop some fudge putty on to my head and pull my hair up into erratically arranged spikes. I put on a white T-shirt (thankfully Connor folded some up in my bedroom drawers) and a faded pink sweatshirt. Pulling on a sock, I hop through to the lounge to see Meg wrinkling her piggy nose at the state of my mugs.

'Jeez-oh, Angel, you live like a friggin' trampy student,' she laughs, turning a chipped Smarties mug around to show me the furry mould sprouting from its insides. 'You're a girl after my own heart.'

'Did I leave the door open, Meg?' I yawn, peering under the red throw on my sofa for my left Nike trainer.

'Nuh.' Meg gives up trying to find a clean cup and pulls herself up on to the worktop. 'I used my key.'

Meg and Ceri both have keys to my flat. I live in hope that one day Ceri will use hers to let herself in, tidy it as spectacularly as her own and leave some designer clothes in the cupboards. Fat chance.

'So where's the man of the moment then?' she chirps, looking from side to side as if she is checking for traffic on a busy dual carriageway. 'Can I give him a wee hug?'

'No,' I shrug, plonking myself down on the sofa, 'he's gone.'

'Gone? Gone where?' Meg replies, shifting her feet in her baby-blue trainers.

'Gone. Gone to America,' I sniff, 'early this morning.' I open my arms wide and smile at my friend. 'You are now looking at a long distance relationship girlfriend. I am all on my own.'

Meg shuffles towards me, sits beside me on the sofa and pulls me into a giant hug. That is one thing that can definitely be said for Meg – her hugs are *large* and much more satisfying than a stiff, bony embrace from Ceri.

'You are no' alone,' she sighs into my ear. 'You've got me and Ceri and all your listeners on your show an' your dad an' . . .'

We laugh at the dad thing. My dad may be in the vicinity, as it were, but he's not much cop at stuff like this. He just doesn't have the emotional capacity.

'Well, you've definitely got me and Ceri, hen, so you'll get through it. Anyhow, you're no' a long distance girlfriend' – she winks mischievously – 'you're a *fiancée*. An' that deserves a fucken' celebration, so it does. Let's jump on the Clockwork Orange, grab some brekkie an' then you can tell me all about this marriage proposal. I wanna hear every detail, so we need plenty of time for a wee natter.'

'Sounds good,' I nod, clutching my aching forehead with a rather shaky hand, 'especially the breakfast part. I need lard and caffeine, fast.'

'So where did he ask you?' Meg gawps, allowing me a clear view of a mouthful of fried egg and sausage.

We are in a café at the bottom of Buchanan Street, which becomes more designer the further south you go. The café is decorated in a Charles Rennie Mackintosh style and is cosy and relaxed while possessing a certain amount of natural class. The menu is a perfect mix of posh sandwiches and scones and full cooked breakfasts with eggy bread. Meg and I, of course, plump for the latter – bread rolls spread thick with real butter, slabs of square sausage, fried eggs, tattie scones, bacon, tomato, mushrooms, eggy bread and coffee, with a glass of Irn-Bru on the side for good measure. I think about calling Ceri to see if she would be able to skip out of work to join us for a chinwag – which has been known to happen before – but I remember she has some important meeting this morning about spicing up the gossip pages of the magazine.

'He took me to The Ice Palace no less.'

'Jeez-oh,' Meg gasps, spitting morsels of sausage across the table. 'If any man took me to the friggin' Ice Palace I'd marry him on the spot and get up the duff before the dinner mints and coffee. An' here I was thinking I was getting a treat with y'on Franco taking me to bingo night.'

'How did that go, by the way?' I ask, realising that I have been so caught up in my own Mills & Boon saga that I haven't even asked Meg about her big date.

'Rubbish,' Meg shrugs, stirring her coffee with the handle

of her knife. 'He couldn'y bloody well remember his numbers in English, the stupit eejit. So I spent all night trying to help him out and ended up messing up my own card. Then he tried to snog the face off me but I said I wouldn'y do anything until I had a bit of commitment.'

'Oh.'

'I mean, he was fit enough, nice bum and dark mysterious eyes like yon Ricky Martin, but I had the feeling he was just out for a bit of a rumble in the sheets. Aye, so we parted without any exchange o' bodily fluids and I ended up at home on my own with a bag o' cheesy chips and a bottle of fizzy ginger. Not quite The Ice Palace and definitely no romance.'

'Oh well, just give him the sack. Save his job for someone worthwhile,' I grin.

'I canny do that, Angel, that'd be abusing my position for my own benefit.'

'You only gave him the job for your own benefit in the first place, Meg. He's hardly a great asset to the shop if he can't even speak English, is he?'

'Aye, true enough. Maybe I'll give him his marching orders tomorrow. But I've got the day off today,' she smirks, 'and I wanna know more about this magical moment of yours.'

Meg shakes out her red curls, clasps her hands together and leans forward excitedly. I grimace as the tight top covering her rather large boobs comes to rest in a dollop of ketchup on the edge of her plate.

'Och, it'll come off,' she smiles when I point out the bright red stain, giving it a quick rub with a paper napkin. 'Right, hen,' she carries on happily, 'tell me everything.'

I guess I should explain the story so far. It turns out I was right; marriage proposals do turn men into complete jibbering wrecks, even if they do it of their own accord. Despite his initial bravado, nerves got the better of Connor in the final furlong, as I vaguely remember him trying to explain in the taxi home while I hung my head out of the cab window and treated the pavement to my regurgitated prawn cocktail. Much of the detail is a bit of a blur, I must admit, but the gist of it is that immediately after popping the question Connor had to disappear to the toilet to relieve himself of the adrenalin coursing through his body. ('Lose his world out of his bum,' as Meg so delicately put it.) But in his haste to return to the table to catch my response, Connor's shaking hands managed to trap his manhood in the zip of his trousers. Eventually, having cried, tugged (pardon the expression) and tried every which way to free his delicate parts, Connor swallowed his pride and emerged from the cubicle to enlist the help of another gent in the Gents. It apparently took three strangers, gallons of cold water, a third of a dispenser of bright pink liquid soap and the best part of an hour to return my boyfriend to his former glory – hence the dodgy stain on the front of his trousers and the pained expression on his face. And hence the inebriated state of his girlfriend.

'So after they picked you up off the floor,' Meg snorts, 'what happened then?'

I chew slowly on a rind of bacon. 'He wouldn't let me give him my answer,' I shrug. 'He said he wanted me to be sober and remember the magic of the moment, something like that. So he asked me again before he left for the airport this morning.'

'I don't know about magic, hen, but you'll no' be forgetting that night in a hurry. What a hoot. He's got the runs and you're boking out o' the cab window. God knows what your wedding will be like. Ha, that'll be a great story fer yer kids.'

I clear my throat and raise my eyes to the stained glass lamp hanging from the ceiling above our table. 'Hmm, kids.' I smile anxiously. 'That's a scary thought, isn't it?'

'No' really, you'll be fantastic parents, so you will. Mr and Mrs McLean and their wee-uns, eh? Ooh, ooh' – Meg claps her hands and bounces on her chair – 'can I be a godmother?'

See what I mean about that snowballing effect?

A shiver runs down my spine from the black hole inside my body where fear and anxiousness live as Meg continues to wax lyrical about my imaginary future. I let out a long breath.

'So, Angel,' Meg grins, leaning across the shiny table top, 'when are we gonna start planning the big day?'

'What, the w . . . wedding?' I ask shakily.

'Aye, of course the wedding. I'm no' talkin' about the Scottish Cup Final, am I?'

I laugh nervously. 'Well, there's a lot of time for that. Connor's away for six months and we haven't discussed anything yet. I'll have to wait until he calls me. I don't know what hotel he's staying in or anything and his mobile won't work in California. Apparently it's got to be a tri-band one and they're really expensive.'

'All gibberish to me. Anyways, it's probably just as well you canny call him; your phone bill would be like Ceri's weekly clothes budget.'

'God forbid. D'you know she bought a coat the other day for nine hundred pounds? Where the hell did she get that from? She only works for a magazine.'

'Men,' Meg replies, wrinkling her nose. 'Men with too much money and nae sense who wanna buy her presents even though she treats them like shite.'

'Amazing,' I say, shaking my head. 'She is truly amazing.'

Meg raises her glass of bright orange fizzy liquid and signals for me to do the same. 'And you're amazing too, Angel. After all, you're the one getting married. Here's an Irn-Bru toast to you and Connor, the best couple I know.'

I clink my glass against hers and gulp the drink until the bubbles fizz at the back of my nostrils. I want to say something to Meg, to tell her that even though I said 'I will', I actually meant to follow that up with 'think about it' but Connor jumped the gun and I hadn't the heart to tell him when he was rushing out of my life for half a year. I really want to air my doubts about the whole becoming a wife thing but I can't seem to get the words out. Even though Meg knows everything about me and would surely understand, I feel funny about admitting it all. Not only would Meg give her right arm to be getting married and is already incredibly excited, it feels as if I'm being disloyal to Connor by questioning whether I want to marry him or not. Damn, this day is confusing.

I sigh and glance at the giant clock on the wall to my left. 'Oh shit!' I shout, jumping up and throwing my faded denim jacket around my shoulders, 'I've got to go; I'm on air in ten minutes. God, what was I thinking? My boss will kill me.'

I open my purse and throw a ten-pound note on to the table, knowing that Meg would have a secret heart attack if

I landed her with the bill. 'We'll have to do that shopping another day, Meg. I've got a meeting after work about the direction the station is taking,' I say, hurriedly taking one more gulp of tepid coffee.

'Ooh jings, good luck, pal.'

'Thanks.' I lean down to hug my friend. 'Come round tonight, yeah?'

'Aye, brilliant,' Meg smiles, 'and I'll ask Ceri to come an' all.'

'She'll be busy,' I reply, fishing under the table for my mini rucksack.

'Not for this she won't be. Wait till I tell her the news. Bridey McBride,' she winks.

'Er, yeah, right.'

I squeeze Meg's shoulder, thank the waitress, then dash out on to the street. Now I have to run. In public. With a hangover. What could be worse?

CHAPTER SIX

Can't Get You Out Of My Head

'Hello line three; what's your name and where do you come from?' I say, kicking myself when I realise I sound like Cilla Black on *Blind Date*. I really must work on my catchphrases.

We are in the closing moments of a heated debate about the colour of Cherie Blair's lipstick during a recent visit to Glasgow's Royal Infirmary, initiated by, of course, our Gladys from Motherwell. Am I at the hub of political and social burning issues or what?

'Now I'm no' saying the woman doesn'y suit red, Angel, but there's a time and a place, you know what I mean? I was there in the hospital anyhow because, as you know, I'm a volunteer visitor. And my friend Maggie's daughter, Sadie, well her friend Flora is in cosmetics in the big Jenners store over in Edinburgh and she came across for a wee nosey. Angel, she said it was like one o' they Chanel ones and apparently they cost more than a six-month pass on the Strathclyde buses. Och, honestly; you'd think the woman would have more sense, what with her bein' a smarty pants lawyer. Don't you think?'

To be honest, Gladys, I couldn't give a flying fuck about Cherie Blair's lipstick. My boyfriend is currently on his way to LA for six months and he asked me to marry him and I said I will without actually meaning that and now I've really gone and done it and I'm confused! I want to say this aloud but I don't yet have the established, unshockable fan base and audience pulling power of Chris Moyles to be that rude. Instead I make an interested grunt, dip a digestive in my tea and console myself with the fact that it is five to three and this will all be over by three o'clock.

'Cherie Blair's got a mouth like a slot in a video player,' says a familiar voice through my headphones on line four.

I cringe and cast my weary eyes at Dan, who is sniggering silently through the glass. Bloody Malcolm from Hamilton. The man of irrelevant opinions with barely a good word to say about anyone. Dan always likes to save his call for the moment when I am tired and desperate to play a song. A very long one.

'Hello Malcolm.' I groan quietly. 'Now let's just hope Tony isn't listening to our show on his Friday off or he might be rather offended.'

Fair enough, his description is not far off but I am paid to protect the reputation of Energy FM and not to piss off important people like the Prime Minister.

'Dinny worry yoursel' aboot that, Angel,' slurs Malcolm, who has clearly had a liquid lunch today. 'Tony will be tuned into one o' they good radio stations like Radio Four. He willn'y be botherin' hisself with this tripe.'

'Thanks very much,' I seethe, signalling to Dan to cut the phone line.

Dan waves back, a wide grin on his impish face.

'And is that all you'd like to share with us today, Malcolm, or was there something else?' I ask, sticking two fingers up at my producer.

Malcolm snorts and mumbles into the receiver, the alcoholic fumes on his breath almost audible in my headphones. Which reminds me, I really must phone my dad. The very moment I think it, I am saddened by the fact that my dad only instantly springs to mind when I have a drunk caller on the other end of the phone-line.

'Now is there a song you would like to request, Malcolm? We could try and fit it in for you on Monday's show,' I suggest, desperate to get him out of my head. 'One for a special lady in your life, perhaps?'

'HA!' he howls. 'A special bleedin' lady. There aren't any, are there? Ha. Ha. Away ye go and fu—'

'Oh dear, we appear to have lost Malcolm there,' I interrupt hastily, always impressed by the speed at which Dan can sense a Class A swearword coming and manage to cut off the caller before the first syllable. Very few slip through the net but when they do they usually require a lot of apologising on my part in response to the calls of complaint jamming the switchboard from my more elderly listeners.

'This is "You" by Ten Sharp,' I say into the microphone, trying not to laugh as Dan holds up a sign reading 'Thank Fuck For That!' against the window, 'going out to Baz, a local taxi driver, from his fiancée Shaz, with love.'

As the musical intro to the love song clicks in, I pull my headphones away from my ears and lean back in my faux leather chair to glance at the clock. Four minutes to three. Will Connor have landed by now? How long does it take to fly to LA? Long enough for the glamour models to introduce every male passenger to the mile high club between them? He's only been away for a few hours and already there are details of his life I don't know about. My stomach flutters nervously. I replace my headphones.

'A beautiful song there for Baz,' I say, forcing a smile, 'and we'll have more great songs on Monday's show' – *maybe even the odd one or two from this century if you're lucky* – 'as well as a fresh discussion topic for you to get your teeth into. So have a fantastic weekend, whatever you're doing, and join me again on Monday at midday for another three hours of *Angel on Air*.'

'Will you stop picking up that bloody telephone?' Meg tuts when I lift the receiver for the tenth time in five minutes just to check there is a dialling tone, 'It is working, Angel, but how's he gonna get through if you keep picking it up, ya big eejit?'

Meg is sprawled on my sofa, dressed in copious amounts of bright orange velvet which gives her the appearance of an elongated pumpkin. She is reading my *Smash Hits* – well, I have to read it, don't I? It is my job to keep up with musical trends. I am lying restlessly on the pink corduroy beanbag pretending to read the newspaper but finding it hard to concentrate on anything deeper than my horoscope and the Garfield cartoon strip. We have stretched the telephone wire from the hallway to the lounge just to make sure I don't miss a call. I must talk to Connor, to sort out in my head – and especially in his – the mess I managed to create before he left this morning.

Connor and I have always been able to talk about things but simply by his absence the rules seem to have changed. I mean, what will happen if I tell him over the phone that I didn't actually mean to accept his proposal and that I am unsure about marriage? Add to that, what if I tell him just as he lands in California for six months with a bevy of lusty Essex beauties? It is not too hard to imagine a man whose confidence in a relationship has taken a severe long distance battering seeking solace in the heaving bosom of one such lusty beauty, now is it? Not that Connor has ever done anything like that before but then I've never made a gaff like this before. So, I'm not necessarily saying that I am going to come clean but then I don't really want to be living a lie for the next six months. I will have to play the conversation by ear and employ tact and cunning.

Meg turns a page of the magazine and shrieks at the double-page spread on one of France's biggest stars whose legend is quickly spreading across Europe.

'Didier Lafitte,' she drools. 'Didier bloody Lafitte. Jeez-oh, he is the kipper's knickers.'

She holds up the magazine and strokes the picture of the sultry pop star who is sprawled on an empty beach wearing nothing but a small towel.

'Now don't go telling me he's not way horny, pal,' she pouts, 'or I will begin to fret about your hormone levels. You may be in love and gettin' married and everything but you have to appreciate beauty like that.'

I chew my bottom lip and cough nervously at the mention of marriage. 'Er, no, he's pretty fit, I have to say. Nice eyes.'

'Och aye, his eyes are nice but I would rather have a nibble of his baguette.' Meg cackles loudly, her mouth wide open, and bounces up and down on the sofa. I laugh too, relieved to have something to think about other than the mess I have caused with Connor. In fact, I have almost forgotten that I am supposed to be waiting for him to call until I hear an insistent ringing.

I blush when, after diving for the phone like David Seaman for a last-minute penalty, I realise the sound is coming from my front doorbell.

'Don't worry, he'll call,' Meg says sympathetically, reaching up to touch my arm as I walk past.

And what the hell am I going to say when he does? I think.

Forcing a smile, I trudge to the door, open it and step aside for Ceri's entrance.

'I can't make it tonight,' Ceri shouts, barging through the front door with her ankle-length suede coat flapping in her wake. She hugs me as if she doesn't want to crease herself and blows Meg a kiss across the back of the sofa.

'What do you mean you canny make it? You're here, aren't you?' Meg laughs, scratching her ribs underneath her left boob. 'Honestly, Ceri, your head's full of wee motors sometimes. Right, I for one could eat a scabby horse so let's order pizza before I die of hunger.'

'Not likely, Meg,' Ceri smirks, raising her eyebrows suggestively at Meg's velvet-clad figure, 'but you'll have to go ahead without me, my hunnies. I have got a hot date.'

'Who with?' I ask.

Ceri's love life is colourful to say the least. She eats men for breakfast and then uses their bones for toothpicks at dinner. I don't know if Ceri has ever been in love; it would take a lot for her to admit it if she ever had. Right now she seems content to work her way through the eligible men of Glasgow until she finds one who can hold her interest for more than a week. Believe me, he will be a very special man to fill that role.

'Boy Three,' says Ceri, striding to the window on her long, lean pins and peering out into the darkness from behind the blind. 'He's waiting for me in his car.'

'It's a fucken' ginormous Mercedes!' Meg shrieks from the other side of the blind.

Ceri shrugs nonchalantly. 'It's all right, but it smells of sickly aftershave. Can you believe he buys his scent in Boots? You'd never believe he was a millionaire. No taste.'

Meg almost collapses at the word 'millionaire'. I smile and say nothing.

'And he wears cheap jewellery. He assures me the ring he's wearing is solid gold from Goa but I know he's bullshitting.'

'Ooh, ooh, speaking of *rings*.' Meg stretches the last word out as if it's connected to her vocal chords by a long piece of elastic and winks at me. 'Go on, Angel, tell her,' Meg grins, clapping her hands excitedly.

Ceri flicks a lock of perfect hair over her shoulder and eyes me suspiciously. 'Tell me what?' she pouts. 'What's the big secret?'

'It's no secret,' I cough, suddenly finding the nails on my left hand rather fascinating. 'I left a message on your phones about it last night.'

'Oh, that. Yes, you were so obviously pissed and mouthy I couldn't be bothered to listen to you waffling on about Connor going to the bloody toilet.'

'Well, you should have,' Meg says quickly, stepping towards me and linking her right arm through my left. Meg is obviously desperate to break the news to Ceri. What with Ceri being the glossy mag gossip queen of Glasgow, we rarely get the chance to tell her something she doesn't already know. 'Angel,' Meg announces proudly, 'is gonna be a wife.'

'What?'

I'm sure I can see the colour visibly draining from Ceri's face. As I expected, she is not a fan of long-term commitment.

'A wife,' Meg continues happily. 'She's gettin' fucken' married!'

'Who to?' Ceri replies, steadying herself on the edge of the windowsill.

'To Connor, of course. Who else would she be marrying, ya big eejit? They've been together for like a hundred years.'

'Thirteen,' Ceri corrects her sharply.

I nod, searching Ceri's face for clues as to what she is thinking. I have to admit, the vital signs are not looking good.

'Well,' Ceri replies, 'this is big news, isn't it. When did all this happen?'

'Last night,' Meg jumps in before I can reply. 'Took her to the friggin' Ice Palace, but. Och, it sounded so romantic. Beautiful meal and he'd bought the ring and then he—'

'And you said yes, I take it?'

I chew on the end of one of my nails. 'Er, yes.'

'Hmm. So,' Ceri says through pursed pink lips, 'he wasn't going to dump you then?'

'Apparently not,' I reply, sticking my chin in the air. 'Not unless he got very confused about how to dump someone.'

'Hmm, well, his last girlfriend did dump him, of course,' Ceri shrugs, meaning herself. 'Unless,' she continues, 'he's only proposed to keep you on hold while he's away; you know, to stop you finding someone else. Hedging his bets, so to speak.'

'Yes, thank you, Ceri,' I scowl. 'I had considered that possibility.'

'Really?' she smirks. 'Did he give you any indication of anything like that?'

I bite my lip. 'Well, he did say something like now I would be here waiting for him when he got back, but that doesn't mean anything.'

'Loaded words, my dear,' Ceri replies, sucking air through her teeth. 'Men always use loaded words.'

'Och, don't be daft,' Meg interrupts, beaming at us both. 'You and Connor are perfect, Angel, and this is just pure dead brilliant. I think we should celebrate.'

Ceri nods. 'Well, it certainly looks like we've got a lot to talk about. I'd better give my date the cold shoulder.'

'No, you don't have to . . .'

Ceri, however, has already slid the bottom part of the window up and is calling out to her date on the street below.

'Hey, Boy Three' – I still can't believe she gives them numbers. More to the point, I can't believe they actually *answer* to those numbers – 'we'll have to give it a miss tonight, lover, something's come up. Give me a call tomorrow.'

No recriminations, no angry scene. Boy Three simply smiles, starts his Mercedes like an obedient schoolboy (er, a rich schoolboy with a Mercedes) and drives off into the night. Amazing.

'All right, lady,' says Ceri, throwing her coat over the back of the sofa and sitting down. 'Talk!'

CHAPTER SEVEN

Hanging On The Telephone

'You're not sure, are you?' asks Ceri, delicately picking the juicy, buttery part out of the centre of a slice of garlic bread.

I try to hide my reddening face behind a droopy slice of vegetarian with extra pepperoni (I find you get more toppings that way).

'Well, erm, I don't know really.'

'Angel!' Meg shrieks, very close to my right ear, 'how can you no' be sure about gettin' married? And to Connor of all people?'

I shrug helplessly and search for an adequate response. 'I know, I don't know. I'm just confused.'

'As far as I'm concerned,' says Ceri, crossing one long leg over the other on the sofa, 'marriage is for couples who either have nothing left to say to each other or for people who need stuff for their house and can't be bothered to fork out for it themselves. I mean' – she reaches forward to place another lump of soggy bread on the pizza box and screws up her nose – 'wedding presents are great and everything but it's no reason to commit yourself to one person for the rest of your time on earth, is it?'

'That had not even come near to crossing my mind,' I frown, 'and Connor doesn't need *stuff*. We've both got flats full of stuff.'

'You more than most,' Ceri snorts, glancing at my collection of empty Pringle cans on the mantelpiece.

We have now assumed our usual Saturday night pizza ritual positions – Ceri on the sofa, Meg half on the floor with her head on the pouffe and myself on the beanbag – except it's still Friday and this is an emergency gathering. I am finally facing my fears and sharing my feelings with Meg and Ceri about Connor's proposal. They know us as a couple and they also know the mess my parents' marriage ended up in. I desperately need someone's advice. Of course we often discuss men and sometimes marriage (usually instigated by the ever-hopeful Meg) on our girls' nights in but the big 'M' has never been such a burning issue before, just speculation and gossip. This time it is scarily real.

Ceri picks a single herb off her slice of garlic bread and places it gently on her tongue.

'It's strange; we all know Connor so well but I just can't picture him proposing. I mean, I've known Connor McLean since he was ten and he has never been a hopeless romantic. Hopeless, perhaps, but romantic – I think not.'

Ceri's tinkly laugh grates on my nerves, which are already frayed waiting for the blasted phone to ring. She has a habit of doing that. Of constantly reminding me that she knew Connor (and snogged him on the bus) before I was even on the scene. There's nothing I can do about it but it makes me feel excluded from that part of Connor's life. I want to be the only one to know everything about my boyfriend but Ceri knows a lot too and even, I imagine, some parts that I don't.

'Connor is very romantic, actually,' I huff, pulling a cushion close to my chest, 'and his proposal was beautiful. He chose the ring and everything.'

'So where is it?' Ceri asks.

I stand up and trundle to the bedroom, nervously chewing my cheek as I reach for the silver box sitting precariously on top of a pile of books on my bedside table, most of which haven't been touched for months but have not managed to find their own way back to my bookshelf. I squeeze the closed box in my palm and return to the lounge where I shakily hand it to Ceri. She flips open the lid, herself and Meg peer inside and their mouths drop open in perfectly choreographed synchronicity. I allow myself a moment of pride.

'Jeez-oh,' Meg gasps, 'it's fucken' massive!'

'Too right it is,' Ceri snorts, not taking her eyes off the ring for a second, 'what did he do, mug a transvestite?'

A very brief moment of pride.

I snatch the box back and snap it shut, narrowing my eyes at Ceri's mocking expression.

'Thank you, Ceri, that's my engagement ring you're talking about.'

'I know,' she smirks, 'no wonder you had doubts about saying yes if that eyesore is part of the bargain.'

'Och, Ceri, don't be so nasty,' Meg tuts, reaching forward and patting my hand. 'I think it's lovely.'

Ceri slowly moves her eyes over Meg's orange outfit. 'That's not saying much for the poor monstrosity, is it?'

Meg huffily crosses her arms and looks away, the hurt visible in her eyes. I clutch the ring box and refuse to speak while Ceri – who obviously considers it her mission in life to save us women with no taste from ourselves – smiles victoriously. During the awkward silence my eyes flick to the phone, sitting quietly on the coffee table in front of me. Why hasn't Connor called already? I was nervous about him phoning but now I'm starting to wonder why he hasn't called sooner. It's nine o'clock and he flew early this morning. That's more than twelve hours ago. I'm starting to feel a bit pissed off, to be honest.

'So why did you say yes if you had doubts?' Ceri asks directly.

'I, erm, well, I . . .'

'You didn't want to hurt his feelings?'

'Not exactly.'

'You didn't have the doubt until after you had said yes?'

'No.'

Ceri slowly sips her glass of wine and licks her top lip. 'Then why? You and Connor know each other well, Angel. You should have been able to be truthful with him.'

'Well,' I say, my voice wavering slightly, 'it was quite funny when I think about it now.' *Who am I trying to kid?* 'It was actually' – I look up at my two friends – 'it was kind of a mistake.'

Meg's bottom lip almost lands on her shoes. Ceri frowns darkly.

'A mistake?' she repeats. 'How can it have been a mistake? You either say yes or no. That is quite hard to get wrong, Angel.'

'Granted,' I shrug, 'but I managed it. It was early and I was knackered and he was ready to go and he was over-excited and I was about to say "I will think about it". The problem was I only got as far as "I will". He kind of jumped the gun.'

'Oh shit,' Ceri gasps, 'that's a nightmare.'

'Oops,' says Meg, 'poor Connor.'

'Poor me, more like,' I tut. 'I'm the one who fucked it up.'

Ceri flicks her hair behind her shoulders and clears her throat.

'You have to tell him, Angel. You can't let him go on thinking he's engaged when he's not. You have to tell him you didn't mean it and you don't want to marry him.'

'But I don't know that I don't want to marry him,' I whine. 'I'm just confused. Maybe I do want to marry him and it'll just take time to get used to the idea.'

'Well, yous have got time,' Meg nods, 'he's no' back for a while.'

'See,' I smile, 'so I don't have to tell him yet. Anyway, maybe we *should* get married. What do you think?'

'It's up to you, darling,' says Ceri. 'You and Connor have been together a long time but I can completely understand your fears about changing something when it seems to be going all right just as it is.'

I bite my lip and nod.

'If you're having doubts, maybe you're just not the marrying kind.'

'But if you say no, he'll be gutted,' Meg interrupts fretfully. 'You said he was so happy this morning, you canny disappoint him already. It hasn'y even been twenty-four hours yet.'

I nervously grind my teeth and listen to their confab.

'Ah, he'll get over it,' Ceri tisks, flapping her hand dismissively.

'Yous two are perfect together but,' Meg replies firmly. 'And he'd make a great husband and you'd be a pure gorgeous bride.'

'It's not just the wedding you have to consider though, Angel – it's the rest of your life we're talking about here.'

'Aye, and she doesn'y want to mess it up by throwing away a good man.'

I look from one to the other feeling like a spectator at an agony aunt tennis tournament.

'Talk to him,' says Ceri, 'tell him your fears.'

'But what if he dumps her?' Meg adds, shaking her head. 'Proposals don't happen every day, you know.'

'I've had three in the last month,' Ceri smiles, 'and I didn't say yes to any of them. In fact, I didn't answer two of them.'

'Aye, but that's probably 'cos you didn'y know their names and phone numbers,' Meg scowls, the green-eyed monster showing in her eyes. 'This is different.'

'Oh God, I just don't know,' I wail, clasping my cheeks with my hands. 'I love Connor so much but this marriage thing took me by surprise and now he's far away I feel even more confused. I'm desperate to talk to him on the one hand but on the other I just don't know what to say!'

'Say NOTHING,' Meg shrieks.

'Say YOU GOT IT WRONG,' Ceri shouts back.

RING, RING!

We let out a collective gasp and stare at the phone. Ceri motions quickly to Meg and jumps from the sofa with her suede coat in one hand and Meg's right arm in the other (Meg's left arm is trying desperately to reach the scraps of food left in her pizza box before Ceri drags her out of the door).

'Where are you going?' I complain, realising that I am about to be left alone with the hideous task of admitting to my boyfriend that I became a fiancée by mistake and would quite like to undo that mistake, thank you very much.

'This is a matter between boyfriend and girlfriend, it is not for our ears,' says Ceri, nodding insistently at the ringing telephone before they disappear out of the room quicker than kids out of school on the last day of term.

'When the going gets tough, the tough bugger off,' I groan and reach for the receiver. 'He . . . hello,' I say shakily.

I hold my breath during the silence at the other end of the phone. If this is a pervy caller he's going to get a lot more than he bargained for, believe me.

'Hello,' I say again, a little more forcefully.

I hear a click at the other end and finally a voice.

'*Allô, allô, oui, Angelique, c'est maman à l'appareil. Ça va?*'

Damn, it's my mother.

'*Oui, Ça va, Maman.*'

Yes, thanks to my mum who hates the English language only slightly less than she dislikes the country itself, I speak French. More slang than classic Poirot, which often got me a good telling off in my French Higher classes. To be honest, I have hardly used my language skills since leaving school other than to talk to my mother. There isn't really much call for fluent French on a radio station that thinks Wales is 'abroad'. It comes in handy if I want to sound professional ordering a pain au chocolat in the bakery on Byres Road but that's about the stretch of it.

'So you're not out tonight, Mum?' I ask, checking my

watch to make sure we don't keep the phone engaged for too long.

'*En français, Angelique, s'il te plaît.*'

'No, I don't want to speak French, Mum. I'm tired and I'm in Scotland; we speak English here.'

Well, that's not a bad record – we've only been on the phone about twenty seconds and already I have devolved into the cheeky rebellious teenager only my parents and especially my mother can turn me into at the age of twenty-nine.

'Huh,' Mum snorts, 'you should be proud of your French 'eritage, *chérie*.'

Her accent sounds like the Resistance woman from *Allô, Allô,* except that it is real.

'I am,' I grumble. 'I had a croissant last Saturday.'

God, even I am tempted to give myself a clip round the ear. How do I become this person whenever my mother calls?

'So, er, what can I do for you, Mum?' I ask, trying to sound a little more enthusiastic.

'Oh, *charmant*, I cannot call my daughter on an evening to see how she is doing now, uh? And may I remind you that you have called me first, yesterday evening.'

'Oh yes, I was just checking how you were. And you're OK, so that's great. Anyway, it's good to hear from you, *Maman*, but it's just I'm . . . well, I'm expecting a call actually.'

'Oh now, let me guess who it is that this is from.'

The French language uses far too many words and unfortunately Mum tends to import this into her English.

'It's from Connor, Mum.'

'Eugh, I know this. He is keeping you hanging, is he not?'

'No,' I sigh, 'he is not keeping me hanging. He is over in the States and said he'd call me about now so I should really keep the phone free. International calls can be tricky long distance.'

'And what am I? Am I not international, *chérie*? France is not part of your country, you know. You is not even in Europe because of your xenophobic *gouvernement* and all this rubbish about your pound and the Queen. It would do you good to learn some culture.'

Oh here we go. A call from my mother is never simple. She always finds something to jump on her soapbox about and it usually involves British politics or the cultural superiority of France. I choose not to argue and instead make agreeable noises, despite the references to 'my' pound and 'my' government as if I'm directly responsible for the Royal Mint and the Scottish Parliament, which always gets on my wick. After all, I am half French – admittedly I only choose to point this out when they are winning the World Cup or at other such glorious moments, but that's fair enough I think.

'And your Connor – what is it that he is doing in America?'

'He's doing some filming; remember, he's a cameraman.'

'Huh, cameraman.'

Delphine manages to say this word in the same tone that someone might use for 'male prostitute' or 'smelly tramp'. She has never approved of Connor's job, despite her love for the cinema which, as I have often tried to argue (to no avail), would not be quite such an enjoyable pastime without the work of cameramen. Unlike her disregard for my job, however, her disregard for Connor's stems from the simple fact that she disapproves of Connor himself. He could be Prime Minister of France and she would still rate him as a no-good lazy Scotsman with a lack of ambition.

The problem stems from the fact that Connor is neither French nor rich nor a David Ginola lookalike, which he can do very little about. I have tried to discuss the Gary Lineker comparison, but even our most wholesome boy-next-door footballer fails to match Delphine's expectations. Mum is especially wary of British men, having suffered such a useless marriage to my father. What Mum doesn't seem to realise is that I am considerably more British in my outlook than Bordeaux-ish. I don't smoke, I don't have the confidence to carry myself in French society and I like being able to whisper sweet nothings in my Scottish boyfriend's ear without worrying whether they are grammatically correct or whether he's going to get the completely wrong end of the stick. Connor has tried hard to forge a relationship with Delphine, especially during the eleven years that Mum lived in Scotland, but they eventually settled for a mutual dislike combined with a frostily polite way of communicating. It bugs Connor, it annoys the hell out of me but, as they say, c'est la sodding vie.

'And, uh, how long is it that he does cameraman in America?' she asks with such feigned interest that it is hardly worth the effort.

'Six months,' I cough quietly.

'*Six mois!* He has left you?'

The joy in my mother's voice is unmistakable. I draw my lips into a tight scowl and take a deep breath.

'No, he has not left me,' I growl. 'In fact . . . in fact, Mum, he, *Connor*, has asked me to marry him. And . . . and' – my voice wavers mid-tantrum – 'I've said yes. I am getting married. So there.'

A particularly grown-up finish, I must say.

Now I know most French expletives but some of these are lost even on me. I manage to make out the French for ba*#ard, useless son of a b!*ch and not on your f*~#ing life before there is a crashing sound in my ear and the phone goes dead.

'Oh dear, we appear to have lost the votes from the French jury,' I grimace to myself, gingerly replacing the receiver.

I look pensively at the telephone, stick my tongue out between my teeth and drum my fingers on my knee. My stomach churns nervously at the thought of what just happened. I have told someone for the first time in definite terms that I am getting married. Fair enough, Meg and Ceri *assumed* I was getting married but I didn't actually have to say so. Already I am suffering side-effects – hot flushes, shaky hands, stomach pains. Jesus, the strain of the day must have aged me so much I've become menopausal. Luckily the phone rings again before I have a chance to pursue this line of paranoia.

'Yep,' I sigh, knowing exactly who it will be.

Again there is the silent pause and the click before Mum speaks. God knows what she's doing on the other end of the line but it is a particularly annoying habit of hers intended, I think, to give her greeting greater impact.

'It is not etiquette for one to answer the telephone with these word.'

'It's *this* word, Mum, and it is etiquette where I come from.'

Amazing. I can be polite to almost everyone else in the world when the situation requires it, even if I really don't like them very much, but there is no pretending with parents. They know me too well and Mum especially knows how to rub me up the wrong way. At least Dad's too pissed most of the time to be cunning. Mum is like a sly French fox when it comes to manipulating conversations.

'Angelique,' she continues, putting on her sweeter than sugar please-do-as-I-say voice, 'please think carefully before you go and marry yourself with this man.'

'His name is Connor, Mum; you've known him long enough to be on first name terms.'

'*D'accord, d'accord*; *Connor*.'

The pursing of her lips is almost audible as she enunciates his name.

'I am saying please to think carefully before you take such a big step with this Connor. Marriage is a serious thing, *petite*, you must not go into it lightly.'

'I am twenty-nine years old, Mother; I have been with "this man" for thirteen years. I would hardly call it an impulsive, immature decision.'

'Very well, very well, but, Angelique, you know you could—'

'Don't say it, Mum.'

I can feel my blood beginning to boil.

'You could do so much better than him. You could find a nice French boy—'

'I don't believe you!' I seethe into the receiver, the mouthpiece becoming hot and sticky with my breath. 'When are you going to let me make my own choices? Connor is a lovely person; he's good to me, he works hard—'

'Puh. He – what is it – he points a camera and he press play. This is not hard.'

'He works hard,' I continue, 'and he loves me.'

'English men do not know love, Angelique.'

'He is Scottish,' I huff, 'and just because Dad didn't fulfil your dreams you can't tar every British man with the same brush.'

'I have nothing to say about your father. All I *can* say is you should try a French man. I have a friend who has a son—'

'Oh Mum, leave it, would you?'

'A singer, he is famous here and he comes to Scotland soon. He looks like the beautiful Monsieur David Ginola.'

'I don't want to hear it, Mum,' I reply firmly. 'I am with Connor and you'll just have to . . . you'll just have to bloody well lump it!'

Oh my God, I hung up. I hung up. On my mother. I have never put the phone down on my mother.

It crosses my mind that I am now in deep shit, until I tell myself that I am twenty-nine and almost married, which is far too mature to be in deep shit with my mother. Bollocks, I know – once a child always a child as far as parents are concerned – but I have to make myself feel better somehow.

No matter how much I try to deny it, though, I am upset. Upset partly because I acted like a spoiled brat and probably hurt my mother, which is not good behaviour for anyone in their high twenties no matter how far out of joint their mother can put their nose. But I am also upset because – and this is frightening to admit – Delphine in her own inimitable style may well be right about this whole marriage thing. After all, she does have experience of this particular topic and it is largely that 'experience' that is putting me off in the first place.

With my nerves on edge and my mind in complete disarray, I trudge to the kitchen to make myself the proverbial cup of tea. Unfortunately, all my mugs are piled in the sink awaiting the arrival of the washing up fairy, who only seems to appear when Connor is in my flat. You see, his absence is already manifesting itself in very visual ways. Instead I grab a can of Coke from the fridge – caffeine and sugar, always a good choice when your nerves are teetering on the brink of breakdown – and begin to pace quickly up and down my lounge, glancing frequently at the silent telephone. Stopping to flick through one of my CD racks, I select a mellow, soothing Richard Ashcroft album and put it on the stereo, hastily skipping 'A Song For The Lovers' which is the last thing I need right now. I then unhook the small mosaic mirror from the lounge wall and plonk myself on the sofa, holding the mirror out in front of me to see my reflection.

Do I look like a bride? Can I see myself in the white dress and veil, saying 'I do' while I gaze dreamily into the adoring eyes of my beloved? Don't brides have long hair that they can pay ridiculous amounts of money to have curled and tweaked and piled on their heads with cascading tendrils or whatever you call them? Or, if they've got short hair like mine, don't they have to wear bejewelled tiaras which cost more than a small car and will never be worn again?

Never mind being the tiara type or the tendril type, maybe I'm just not the marrying type at all. Maybe I'm not supposed to be a bride, which is why I feel so nervous about the whole thing. Just because Connor and I have been together for thirteen years doesn't mean we have to go down that road, does it? I've heard about people who date happily for years and then get married only to split up a few months into the lifetime commitment. I don't want that to happen to us. I don't want a perfectly good relationship to be derailed just because Marriage Central is supposedly the next stop on the line and we feel obliged to get off there.

I say perfectly good relationship, but considering the length of time Connor and I have been a couple, why can I not just say yes to his proposal without all these fears invading my thoughts? Does it signify a problem I haven't yet identified? Or am I just terrified at the thought of being someone's wife and labelled as a possession. Connor and I have been together for so long that I could not imagine being with another man and I don't think I would like to be, but the thought that I would never have the option again is scary. Especially when, and this is a little secret of mine that only Ceri knows, I have only ever slept with one man in my life – Connor McLean. Would I be silly to commit myself to him when I don't know what I'm missing out on, or are people who sleep around only really looking for what I was lucky enough to find first time?

'Fuck!' I shout into the mirror, flopping my head back against the sofa with sheer exhaustion. 'This is so bloody complicated. Why did he ask me to marry him?'

Good question. Why did he ask me to marry him? Is he the type of man who would do something like that just to 'hedge his bets' as Ceri so neatly observed. I am trying to think positive, to let a little of Meg's optimism into the equation, but somehow the fractions of doubt presented by Ceri are a lot easier to focus on when considering something as huge as this. I can't think clearly on my own. I need advice.

In fact, I am so desperate for advice that I am even willing my mother to call me for a third time so that we can talk this whole thing through.

I visibly jump when the phone rings again. Pausing momentarily, I inhale deeply like a meditating yogi and then dive for the receiver. Again there is the silence and the click at the other end of the line.

'Look, Mum,' I say with feigned calmness, 'I didn't mean to put the phone down on you but you just wound me up with all that Connor business. He's a lovely guy and I just wish in my heart of hearts that you would learn to accept him.'

I pause but decide to carry on when the heavy silence persists.

'Despite that, *Maman*, I was rude and I apologise. I am not myself after the proposal and if you must know I am rather unsure about it all. Connor did ask me to marry him but . . . but it didn't exactly go according to plan, OK? I didn't really mean to say yes but it got out of hand and I don't know what to do. Maybe I should marry him or maybe I shouldn't but I can't think clearly because he's not here. And you and Dad have got me so messed up about marriage with all your antics that I don't bloody well know what to think. So that's about the size of it. I'm being honest and I'm confused and I need help. I need your advice.'

I bite my lip, waiting for the advice floodgate to open. I have never been this honest or humble with my mother before and I am almost intrigued to see how she will react. I wait for a few seconds but nothing happens.

'*Maman*?' I say again. 'Did you hear what I said? Are you going to talk to me or not?'

There is the faint sound of someone catching their breath at the other end of the line. I push the receiver closer to my ear to be able to hear and my stomach almost hits the floor when I hear a man cough. A very familiar man. Somewhere in my head a bell tolls – the sound of impending doom.

'I heard what you said,' says Connor, his voice cold and hurt, 'but I think it's you who should be talking to me, Angel. Don't you?'

As I said earlier, tact and cunning. You can always rely on me.

CHAPTER EIGHT

Whiskey In The Jar

I am officially sad. Not sad as in unhappy, although I am hardly basking in an overwhelming sense of inner peace and joy, but rather sad in the unfortunate sense of someone with an unhealthy obsession for something, like trainspotters and thimble collectors and people who join competition-entering clubs. My new obsession is telephones and other modern methods of communication, as well as some antiquated ones like letters – how square am I?

I have also developed a bad case of e-mail-related neurosis in the last fortnight. I have logged on five times this morning in the space of forty minutes. Logged on – to find thirty-two junk mails of the 'XXX . . . girls, hamsters and penis extensions' and 'End all debt for ever by taking out this giant shark-infested loan' variety – logged off. Logged on, logged off, logged on. And so forth. Just in case Connor had happened to send an e-mail at the very point I decided to log off, like when you're making a call and the phone's ringing but you don't know when to put it down at your end just in case the person you're trying to call picks it up at their end just as you put it down. I worry about things like that. I have been known to slowly lower the receiver to its resting position with my ear still attached until the last possible second. So there I was on the e-mail, on and off five times in quick succession until my computer threw a wobbler and refused to access the Internet any more for someone as 'sad' as me. Probably just as well as I could feel myself being sucked into a never-ending logging circle, which would finally end with me forging friendships via Internet chat-rooms with other nerdy computer people and lonely old perverts.

Of course I am now beginning to fret that I have damaged the telephone line by going into overdrive on the electronic highway. I call the BT Operator who assures me (twice) that all seems well but I simply have to confirm this conclusion by calling both Meg and Ceri and asking them to call me back just to make sure. I then go through the same procedure with my mobile phone, even carefully extracting the battery and giving it a thorough dusting to prevent any impairment of the connection. On the third call, Meg assures me everything is fine before rushing to catch the subway to work.

Ceri, on the other hand, responds with a curt, 'Piss off and stop being such a sad man-obsessed loser at this God-forsaken hour' while Boy Four makes rather off-putting slurping noises in the background.

Bloody charming, what exactly is wrong with calling your friends for a minor bit of assistance at – I glance at my watch – eight o'clock on a Saturday? Morning? OK, point taken.

I know I should stop this ludicrous, pre-pubescent behaviour but I am on a roll. Despite the fact that it is now only quarter past eight, I have already exhausted every method of passing time while waiting for a phone call. I have called my friends, I have made four cups of coffee (probably a very good reason for my angst with all the caffeine coursing through my veins) and I have listened to every song I own for an anxious time such as this. So, in an attempt to be less of a loser I telephone his hotel. Again.

'I'm sorry, *maaam*, but there is *still* no answer in his room. Do you want to leave *another* message?'

She is mocking me; I can hear it in her condescending Californian chocolate-tanned-and-big-boobed voice. What right has she got to question me? Just because I've called a few times this morning. I might have a piece of immensely important news to deliver to the man in room 224B. I might be working for MI5 and be waiting to communicate a matter of national security to one of our spies. OK, it's not very likely I would do that via a hotel receptionist but she doesn't know that, does she? And more to the point, she doesn't know *me*.

He does want to speak to me, you know, you . . . you receptionist, I want to protest. *In fact, he has called me twenty times in between my calls without you realising. That man in room 224B is positively bombarding me with incredibly romantic telephone messages and I am actually calling to tell him to give it a rest.*

But I don't. I simply whisper, 'No, thank you, I'll call later.'

Am I becoming unnecessarily paranoid? Granted he has not been bombarding me with incredibly romantic telephone messages over the last fortnight but he has called me whenever he's had the chance. And that is despite our truly horrendous start that Friday night. God, I still cringe when I think about that conversation and rightly so. After all, what do you say to a man who has just heard you freely admit that you have doubts about him even after thirteen years and that you accepted his marriage proposal when you didn't really mean to? Exactly, even Jeremy Paxman would have trouble talking himself out of that one.

I suppose you would like to know how it went. It may be over two weeks ago but I still remember every word, it being possibly the worst thing I have done to Connor in our time together. To begin with, I started digging in the hope that I had either the natural wit and cunning to find my own way out of the very deep hole I had created. But faced with a wall of silence at the other end of the line and feeling as if I were in a church confessional, I eventually had to resign myself to the fact that Connor was unlikely ever to speak to me again until I attacked his latest essay title: 'You said you were going to marry me and I haven't been gone twenty-four hours and you've already changed your mind, you fickle cow. Discuss.'

So I talked, nervously, Connor listened and all the while I silently prayed that the 'honesty is the best policy' thing was not just a load of self-righteous bullshit made up by the Girl Guides.

'I'm sorry, Connor,' I said sheepishly, sucking in enough air to fill two sets of elephant lungs, 'I can't lie to you about this.'

'About what?' he replied, his voice distant either because of the miles between us or because he was terrified of what was to follow – I couldn't quite tell.

'About this whole marriage proposal and what it means and whether I'm doing the right thing.'

His silence was my cue to elaborate.

'You know I love you, Connor; I have since the first day we met and I do even more thirteen years on. And when you asked me to . . . when you proposed I was surprised and flattered and you did it so beautifully . . .'

'I didn'y, though; I messed it up, having to run off to the toilet and everything.'

'That was fine, Con, it made it more special,' I laughed weakly. 'The thing is, the more I think about marriage and what it means, the more I realise how big your question was. It's something you have to be so sure about or the consequences would be disastrous, for both of us.'

'I see,' he sighed, the pain he was feeling evident even at such a distance.

'I can't really see,' I carried on, gaining impetus. 'I'm so confused, Connor, and I'm really sorry. I think Mum and Dad's break-up affected me more than I realised and I just want to make sure that I don't get this wrong.'

'Of course,' Connor said sadly after a short time delay. 'I want you to be sure too, baby. But can I ask you something?'

'Sure, anything.'

'Why did you say yes if you weren't sure?'

'I didn't actually say yes, Con,' I coughed. 'I, er, said "I will".'

'Aye, so, that's the same thing, isn't it?'

'Not exactly. You see, I was going to end the sentence with "think about it" but it was all so rushed that you kind of jumped in after the "I will". I guess it was a bad choice of words but I wasn't really thinking straight, being up with the lark and everything.'

'Oh.'

We sat in silence, both waiting for the other one to speak.

He hates me now, I thought sadly, *he's going to dump me right this minute and I'll be a lonely old spinster who always harks back to the time a lovely man asked her to marry him and she was too stupid to accept.*

'Right, so,' Connor said just before the pause reached its full gestation period. 'It seems like our wires got a wee bit crossed, doesn't it, Angel?'

'Hmm, just a bit. But I do love you, Connor, it's just . . . well, it's not you, it's me.'

That old chestnut. I could have done better than that.

'And if I asked you again now, now that you've been thinkin' about it for the day, what would you say?'

I looked up at the ceiling and prayed that the sky would not fall through it on top of me when I uttered the words: 'I would say "I will think about it".'

The ceiling stayed put and, thankfully, so did my boyfriend at the other end of the line.

'Well, it's not a no, is it?' Connor replied, clearly making an effort to keep his voice light. 'And that's good enough for me right now. I don't want to push you into something and make you unhappy, baby; I want you to be ready. If it's time you need then take some. I mean, you've got six months to mull it over.'

'Thanks, Connor, I'm so glad you understand. I didn't . . . I don't want to hurt you.'

'I'm glad you can be honest with me, baby; that's all that matters. Take some time and just let me know when you've made up your mind. I've got to go now. I love you, my Angel. Bye.'

And that was that. I had told the truth, spoken about my innermost feelings, even over a distance of thousands of miles when I couldn't see his face to judge his reaction. And therein lay a problem – had Connor really accepted my doubts with such grace or had he been more hurt than he'd let on? Even more than the time he tried to teach me to play tennis and I let go of the racket and whacked him around the head and knocked him out. (I've never been very good with bats and balls.) Or the time I tried to learn to drive and reversed over his boots which unfortunately had his feet in them at the time. Was he going to put the phone down and immediately run for tea and a sympathetic blowjob from one of the glamour girls? I had worried about that before the call but the need to tell the truth had won through in the end. So while I had been truthful and therefore gained some time to think about the proposal, had I also pushed my man into the arms of another woman?

I am ashamed to admit it but that thought has played on my mind ever since, despite my previous preaching about the importance of trust. Which is largely why the fact that Connor has not called me today is becoming an issue. Especially when he promised that he would call me on Wednesday and it is now Saturday. And I have so many things to tell him, all noted down succinctly on my post-it notes by the telephone. Yes, that may sound rather . . . pathetic, making notes before speaking to the man who is supposed to be my boyfriend, but I have discovered that long distance calls involve an immense amount of pressure. Pressure to sound fun and charming and bubbly – like Bonnie Langford only less annoying and not quite as squeaky. Pressure not to talk over the end of the other person's sentences because the time delay makes the whole escapade completely nonsensical. Pressure afterwards when you put the phone down and analyse everything he said or didn't say. You see, all that pressure makes clear thinking and effortless conversation difficult and I kept finding myself either running out of things to say or forgetting to tell Connor all the important things I had wanted to tell him. So I make notes. Notes which are this week becoming very long because I haven't had a chance to tell him ANY BLOODY THING!

Staring dejectedly at the telephone, my eyes filling with tears and my ears ringing to the sound of silence, I come to the decision that enough is enough. So what if he promised to call me on Wednesday? So what if he never seems to be in his hotel room no matter what time of the day or night I call? So what if he is becoming friendly with the Essex glamour models whom he now insists on calling by their first names and has described as fun, intelligent girls? By first names please note that I am referring to Ferrari, Honey, Truly, Pirelli and Kelly. I mean, please; does that sound like a Mensa gathering to you? So what about all of that. I am not going to sit by the phone, or the e-mail, or the mobile phone, and wait for Connor to get in touch. I am going to give him the benefit of the doubt and I am going to be strong and independent and get off my butt and enjoy myself. Fill my day off with fun, exciting pursuits other than hanging around Meg's music shop all day or trailing after Ceri and her doe-eyed admirers. I am going to get on a train and be sociable and visit my dad. Wow, I really know how to party!

Dad lives in Paisley, a town to the west of Glasgow reached by a fifteen-minute train ride from Glasgow Central Station.

I buy a copy of *Star* magazine to read during the journey and spend the next quarter of an hour catching up on all the celebrity gossip without which Ceri's life would be an empty shell. Well, who would have thought it; so-and-so is supposedly doing it with Whatserface after dumping the It girl. Meanwhile, Mr TooRichForHisOwnGood has been spotted in a lap-dancing club with Mr FootballBoots, and Miss HoityToity and her friend Dipsy Double-Barrelled are pictured shopping in the High Street dressed in, God forbid, non-designer label trackie bottoms. I giggle at Ceri's tittle-tattle column, read the make-up tips and retail therapy column and try the free cheapy lip-gloss on my bare lips before almost missing my stop, jumping off at Gilmour Street Station and walking the brisk five minutes to Dad's house.

I say house but it is really part of a house – the bottom floor of a grey pebbledashed ex-Council house to be precise. I always feel a lump of sadness swelling in my throat whenever I visit my dad at his home. In Norwich we lived in a big semi-detached cottage-style house, before moving to the outskirts of Glasgow where we bought an even bigger semi-detached modern house on a peaceful estate in Motherwell, very close to my school. After the divorce, the financial details of which I won't bore you with, Dad could not really afford a big home, nor did he want one as it would only serve to emphasise the fact that he was alone, rattling around inside with only his record collection and drinks cabinet for company.

'Hiya Dad, it's me, Angel,' I say to the thin face peering around the edge of the door.

Why I always say that is beyond me, seeing as I am my

dad's only child and thus the only person who would say 'Hiya Dad' after knocking on the front door. I guess it is just something to say to start the ball rolling. And it's better than 'Hiya Dad, are you sober for once or pissed as a fart?'

Dad lets me in to his dark little house and we hug stiffly. I smell his familiar musky aftershave which seems to have been on the market for at least twenty-nine years. It mixes with a stale whiff of alcohol, like the smell of pub carpets in the cold light of day, and the manly aroma of Brylcreem – the hair product that spans generations thanks to the advertising dream that is David Beckham. In fact, I'm surprised Harmony hairspray and the hairnet makers haven't tried to get that modern thing going with the help of lovely Posh, although I doubt the effect would be quite the same.

'Good to see you, Angel. I was just thinking about you yesterday.' Dad smiles sadly and I know he means it.

He shuffles down the narrow corridor towards the equally dark lounge and I watch him with a heavy heart. When I was little, my dad was the best man on the planet. He was the tallest and the strongest and the cleverest and he could do anything I needed him to do. And he was adored by my beautiful mother who thanked her lucky stars that such a wonderful man had blessed her life. Then I grew up and realised that either I had been living with two different people during my early years or they had changed dramatically for the worse. My dad is not a super-hero or even a super-hero's sidekick. He is an ageing man with a clapped-in face, as Meg would say. His round belly, the product of too much alcohol, hangs off his bones, pulling his shoulders down into a stoop. Dad used to have my nose, small and snub like a cheeky piglet, but the end of his is now red and crusty, again the result of too many toxins racing around his alcohol stream. I wish I could do something for my dad to bring some vibrancy back into his lifeless world and believe me I have tried. But Steve Knights doesn't want help. He refuses to discuss his problems just as he refused to do when he was with Mum, so all I can do is subject myself to these painful visits and hope that I am doing some good simply by being here.

I follow Dad down the corridor, past the minuscule bathroom on the left with the plastic concertinaed door because a normal one on hinges would take up the whole room. Past the kitchen just beyond that, which is emitting an aroma of burnt toast and stewed tea. Past the closed door of the musty spare room and the half-length mirror on the wall, the only decoration in the hallway. I stop briefly and glance at my reflection. There is definitely a family resemblance between my dad and I. He is five inches taller at five feet ten but of similar proportions – long legs, long arms and a long neck. My face is slim the way his always was and I also have slight dark shadows under my eyes, which appear to be a genetic trait and take a trowel-load of highlighter to cover up every morning. I correct the collar of my green striped rugby shirt and pull up my jeans to cover the inch of bare flesh squeezing its way between the two. Licking my fingers, I twist a couple of the short browny blonde spikes on the top of my head, take a deep breath and walk smartly into the lounge.

'Not bad weather today, is it, Angel?' he says, jerking his head towards the net curtain hanging limply in the single window which runs along the far wall.

'Bit of sunshine between the clouds and rain,' I smile, shifting a pile of newspapers from the brown sofa that was once velvet but now resembles the wiry coat of a mucky Jack Russell.

Dad nods and reaches for the television remote control, muting *Football Focus* at the touch of a button. We sit in our respective chairs and stare at the silent pictures on the small screen.

'Did you see Norwich City won the other night, Angel?' he says after a few moments listening to the clock ticking from the top of the television.

'Yes, that's great, Dad. One-nil, was it?'

'That's right, one-nil. Good goal, too; flying header after a great run down the left wing from the half-way line.'

'Brilliant,' I reply enthusiastically.

'Yes, brilliant.'

I clear my throat. 'I see Motherwell lost though,' I say, popping my lips and raising my eyes to the low ceiling.

'Yes, afraid so. And they were doing so well for the first hour.'

'Shame.'

'Yes, real shame.' Dad shrugs. 'Oh well, better luck next time.'

When we first moved to Scotland Dad knew very little about its football teams other than the infamous Celtic and Rangers and the funny-named ones like Partick Thistle and Queen of The South. He was a Norwich City fan and vowed to remain true to the Canaries. Three weeks into his new job, however, Dad discovered that the second cousin once removed of his new colleague and lunchtime drinking partner was a professional football player for Motherwell, a Glaswegian side with a certain amount of success and a lot of hope and fighting spirit but who seemed to have a habit of losing their games in the dying seconds of the match. This new partnership was perfect for my father, giving him the feeling he belonged in the country as a true football fan but supporting a team that would rarely take him to true glory. Dad likes that, I have come to realise – a glint of hope but the inevitable disappointment at the end of the day, much like his own life.

'I'm still thinking of getting a season ticket,' he adds happily.

'You should, Dad, that's a great idea. It would get you out at the weekends. How much are they?'

He rubs his hands together. 'No more than two hundred pounds I believe.' Man United eat your heart out, I smile to myself, this being about the amount most Man U fans spend on kit and memorabilia in a single season, never mind the cost of tickets.

Having exhausted our weather and football conversations, Dad and I move on to local news, national news (anything unless it involves France or French people which is definitely a no-go zone), the young ten-year-old upstairs who has just discovered joy-riding, and the price of bacon at Dad's local supermarket. Then Dad shuffles away to the kitchen for mugs of coffee and biscuits while I take the opportunity to look through his record collection, which is stacked in no discernible order on both sides of the disused fireplace, across the mantelpiece, along the piano and up against the wall next to his bedroom, which leads off from the lounge.

Our love of music is where my father and I are very much alike – both buying it and listening to it. In fact it was Dad's extensive record collection that first gave me the idea of becoming a DJ, much to Mum's disgust. When I landed the job at hospital radio Mum used to tell the neighbours that I was training to be a nurse. My uniform of scruffy jeans and trainers, a bag full of records and my dislike of medical emergencies might have given the game away a bit. Dad, however, was very proud and used to come with me to trawl the record shops in Glasgow for the latest vinyl releases. It is largely thanks to him that I have a similarly impressive music collection that always makes people gasp when they enter my flat for the first time. Of course I have progressed through the waves of technology from vinyl and picture discs to tapes, CDs and mini discs to now downloading songs from the Internet. Dad, meanwhile, has stayed in the realm of records and has more vinyl in his lounge than Jordan has in her wardrobe. His collection ranges from Abba to ZZ Top, taking in The Carpenters, John Denver, Pink Floyd, Jimi Hendrix and Paul Weller along the way. Dad does not just collect 'cool' music but music for every taste and mood. He has his favourites but he is not a musical snob, which was one important lesson he taught me. Dad always says if you like a song, buy it. If you think it will emerge as a classic of its time (for good or bad reasons), buy it. If you just like the album cover, buy it. That way you end up with a collection that will be fit for any occasion and you won't go in search of a song to suit a chirpy mood only to find you've actually only got four hundred rap CDs shouting about drugs and shooting people in various colourful curses or a hundred Morrissey-esque songs for those studenty depressed moments. I, like my dad, may have the trendy stuff but I am not ashamed to admit that my collection also includes Five Star, Steps, The Brotherhood of Man and Keith Harris and Orville. OK, I might be a teensy bit ashamed of the last one but I was young and easily impressed that a three-foot-high bright green duck with a hand up its nether regions could sing with such feeling.

'Have you got the new Travis album, Dad?' I ask when he returns from the kitchen shakily bearing a tray loaded with two mugs and a plate of Tunnocks caramel wafers.

Dad points to a box underneath the piano stool. 'In there. It's great, actually. Borrow it if you like.'

'Thanks.'

I crouch down and rummage carefully through the box, past Runrig, Texas and Deacon Blue until I find what I'm looking for.

'Scottish rock and pop,' Dad says before I can comment on his filing system, 'I've decided to try and stock them by country and then by era and type within each country.' He looks down at his slippers and shuffles one foot. 'That's whenever I get a moment to myself of course.'

I blush and bury my head in the box, knowing that a moment *not* to himself would be more of a novelty.

'That's a great idea, Dad,' I chirp. 'Maybe I should do theme days like that on my radio show, like a whole day of Scottish pop and people could phone in their requests. We might even discover some fresh talent that way.'

'That would be great, Angel, your show definitely needs some improvement.'

Jesus Christ, first Meg has a dig about the music on my show and now my own father. And here I was thinking they were proud of my (extremely) minor celebrity status.

I replace the box and sit back on the sofa, putting the Travis album on the seat beside me. Dad and I both reach for a biscuit at the same time and sit quietly unwrapping the chocolate wafer from its shiny foil wrapper.

'So how is work going?' he asks after a bite of biscuit and a sip of coffee.

'Good, great.'

At least I thought I was getting away with it until you lot got your claws out.

'We still listen to the radio at work. Like I always said, you've got a good voice for broadcasting.'

'Thanks.'

We stare at the muted television and sip our drinks.

'And how is everything with you, Dad?' I ask, having plucked up enough courage to do so.

'Oh, you know, fine. Thanks.'

'What about work, how's that going, Dad?'

'Fine, yes, absolutely fine.'

And that is as deep as my father will let anyone tread when it comes to matters relating to work, money or love. 'Fine' – that empty word that could mean anything, like 'nice' only even more vague. It used to drive me mad when I would ask Connor how I looked and he would reply: 'Fine'. In fact, this created so many heated moments in our first few months together (purely on my part) that Connor soon learned his lesson and banned the word almost entirely from his own vocabulary. Dad, however, has never learned and it drove my mum mad until as far as she was concerned everything was far from fucking fine.

I stay for lunch, knowing that Dad is enjoying my company despite the conversation flowing as easily as a river of setting cement. I like to be with him too – I mean, he is my dad and he has a heart of gold – but I do find his solitary life depressing. At least he's sober now.

Dad makes us Scotch pies that were always my favourite

for Saturday lunch when we first moved to Glasgow. Mum would make her weekly trip to the hairdresser and beautician on a Saturday, leaving Dad and I to fend for ourselves. With the health-conscious skinny one out of the way we would sneak the meat pies into the house and promptly devour them with slices of white plain bread layered with real butter and dollops of brown sauce. The crust of a Scotch pie stands upright like Eric Cantona's collar and the middle is pressed down with a tiny hole in the centre, which releases hot steam and an oozing of the meaty filling. They are still delicious and I feel comforted as I load my bread to make a pie and brown sauce butty. Of course this time I only eat half the filling and three quarters of the pastry, having realised that Mum was indeed right – tasty meat pies with white bread and butter *are* bad for you. *Quel disappointment*. Finally feeling relaxed and comfort-fed, I decide to test my dad's therapy skills. After all, he is a parent and I am his daughter – perhaps Mum and I just never gave him the chance to get personal and offer real advice. I decide to take the bull by the horns and broach the subject of my quickly changing relationship with Connor.

'Connor's gone to work in America,' I begin gingerly. 'He's been away for two weeks and I really miss him already.'

'Oh, let me clear these dirty plates away,' says Dad, jumping to his feet as if the armchair is on fire.

'He, er, he asked me to marry him before he left and I kind of said yes.'

'I'll just get these in some soapy water before the brown sauce goes hard.'

'I didn't really mean to say yes, but I did and then I had

to tell him the truth. Now I'm worried he'll run off with someone else, but I can't just say yes because he wants me to, can I? To be honest, my mind is in a bit of a tiz, Dad.'

'Do you want another coffee, Angel? I can make another one if you want, it's no bother.'

'So I was just wondering: how do you know if you should get married?'

Dad's slippered feet disappear out of the lounge so fast there is smoke rising from the rubber soles.

'Thanks,' I snort, directing my comment at Fran Healy on the front of the Travis album, 'that was very helpful.'

'We've just produced these little things at work,' says Dad, reappearing cautiously after a lengthy delay and with a whiff of Dutch courage on his breath. My heart sinks even further towards the threadbare sofa cushions.

'It's a small bottle of whisky designed to be sold in pubs with this little bottle of mixer so that people can refill their own glass and not have to go back to the bar all the time. Apparently they do that sort of thing with small bottles of rum in places like Barbados.'

I stare at the bottle of dark liquid and smile uneasily. 'That's, um, lovely, Dad. Did you make coffee?'

Dad sways unsteadily across the floor. 'No, no, I didn't. I thought maybe we could try this' – he raises the whisky bottle triumphantly as he tumbles into the chair – 'as a bit of research for my work.'

I glance at the dusty carriage clock on top of the television and frown. 'Bit early for that, isn't it, Dad? It's not even half past two yet.'

Dad shrugs nonchalantly, trying to hide the fact that he is

dying to escape from sober-dom as quickly as possible before we have to talk about anything else meaningful.

'Just a lunchtime taster, Angel, that's all. Nothing wrong with that.'

'Sorry, Dad,' I sigh, 'but I've got stuff to do this afternoon. As a matter of fact, I should really get going.'

Get going to anywhere except here as soon as the fumes of secretly imbibed alcohol appear. I jump up nervously and tuck the Travis album under my arm

We hug at the door – me still stiffly and Dad slightly more at ease than when I first arrived thanks to the bottles of spirits he likes to stash in the biscuit cupboard in the kitchen, usually behind the tin of garibaldis where he thinks no one will find them. I promise to call again soon and to keep him up to date on the developments at Energy FM, then I walk briskly down the path, tripping over a discarded rusty tricycle and a mud-covered toddler on the way. I know I should stay and try to keep my father on the straight and narrow. I know it is my duty to talk to him and to try to get him to the end of Saturday afternoon still sober, but I am selfishly tired of trying and today I don't have the enthusiasm for such a difficult mission. I am so desperate to get away that I even jog to the railway station, which I soon regret when I collapse into my seat only to be overpowered by a wave of Scotch pie burps. The woman beside me reading *Woman and Home* through small, round glasses is, needless to say, unimpressed. I hold my breath for most of the journey, finally tumbling out at Glasgow Central rather light-headed and completely exhausted.

CHAPTER NINE

Imagine

I get off the subway at Hillhead and turn right up Byres Road towards my flat. When I reach the block, however, I keep walking, my head bowed to the chilly October wind blowing straight down the street. I need a place to think and I know where that place is – the Botanic Gardens, a haven of tranquillity situated at the end of my road.

The gardens are quiet and empty as I walk through the double iron gates and up the pathway, past the red brick gatehouses and on towards The Kibble Palace. A solitary grey squirrel stops as I come close, tilting his head to one side and listening to the clip-clop of my denim boots on the tarmac.

'Just you and me today, Squirrel Nutkin?' I say softly, aware of how loud my footsteps sound in comparison to the rustling of the trees and the distant rumble of traffic behind me. 'Can I bend your ear about my life if I buy you a cup of coffee and a cake?'

My furry companion looks up at me and bares his front

teeth before scampering away across the immaculately cut lawn.

'I'll take that as a no, then,' I sigh, kicking myself for feeling self-pity because a rodent with an oversized tail won't keep me company. I really must get a life.

The Kibble Palace is a giant greenhouse that sprawls across the lawn to my right. It is topped by an impressive dome, rather like the Taj Mahal only much smaller, not as Indian and not quite as popular with the world's tourists. It may be rusty and have the odd broken pane of glass but in my eyes this gives the Palace character. When you open the front door and step inside no one can fail to be impressed by the beauty of the fern displays which fill its domes. I have always loved coming here. I adore the smell of the plants and the sound of water running somewhere within its parameters. I revel in the peace, which exists even when the Gardens are full of summer visitors. There are no 'Quiet Please' signs or stern-looking attendants asking for order but the setting begs for a kind of reserved behaviour, even from someone like me who always has the urge to shout out rude words in the library or to sing loudly on a quiet bus. There are other glasshouses, full of tropical plants and rare orchids, but I always begin with The Kibble Palace, largely because it has seats to sit on and sells things to eat but also because it has a wishing pond next to the entrance, which I am definitely in need of today.

'I'll have a cup of hot chocolate,' I say to the young girl behind the counter of the coffee shop as I root around in my rucksack for my wallet. 'In fact, make that a *mug* of hot chocolate. With cream on top. And do you have chocolate sprinkles or a Flake or something?'

The girl nods and smiles, which makes her bright blue lip stud glint in the light. Oh to be young and cool and able to have a lip stud without feeling like mutton dressed as lamb or like Lulu dressed as Kylie. I bet she doesn't have to worry about things like marriage and the future and boyfriends/fiancés running off with tarty girls with big bazongas. Actually, who am I trying to kid? When girls are that age all they *ever* worry about is the future and boyfriends and girls with big bazongas. I give her a sympathetic smile in as cool a manner as I can muster, as if to say 'I'm with you, sister, men are nothing but trouble,' but I thankfully draw the line at adding the word 'man' to the end of every sentence.

'And I'll have a slice of that chocolate fudge cake,' I say, peering at the glass counter. 'Quite a big slice. Or maybe I should just have two normal-sized slices. Ooh, and one of those cookies.'

'The giant choc chip ones?' she asks, raising a very thin pencilled eyebrow.

'Er, yes, the big choc chip one. I wouldn't really call it *giant* as such.'

I self-consciously chew my bottom lip with my top teeth and hand over the cash.

'Bad hair day?' the girl asks suddenly.

I flick my head up to look at her and run my hand through my short spikes. 'Why? Does it look like it?'

Sarky little shit.

'No, your hair's cool, man, so it is.'

I smile proudly, lapping up the compliment from a sixteen-year-old coffee shop assistant as if it is Vidal Sassoon himself congratulating me on my choice of hair-do.

'Thanks.'

'Nae bother. I were meanin' just generally. Are ya havin' a bad day?'

I shrug and begin to dig my fork into one of the slabs of chocolate cake with the urgency of a dog searching for its favourite bone.

'Bad family and boyfriend day,' I mumble with a mouthful of gooey chocolate icing. 'Much worse than a bad hair day.'

'I can tell,' she laughs and I briefly see a tongue stud towards the back of her mouth. 'There's enough chocolate there fer a bleedin' chocolate convention.'

I look at my tray of chocolate delights and cringe. She's right. If Rosemary Conley could see me now she would take me outside and whip me with a bunch of celery sticks. I can already feel my hips expanding and I've only had two mouthfuls.

'Nightmare eh?' I tut. 'Here, you have this one.' I hold out the chocolate chip cookie.

'Nah; oh, well, maybes I will. OK, thanks.'

'No problem, er . . .?'

'Winona.'

Of course it is. No name like Kate or Sharon for this chick.

'No problem, Winona, I don't think I'll starve.'

We lean on our respective sides of the counter and munch our chocolate treats silently, soaking up the sounds and moist aromas of the glasshouse. It must be at least five minutes before we speak again.

'So, what's up with yer man? Is he doin' yer box in or something?'

'No.' I smile weakly.

'Did he dump ya then?'

'No.'

God, I really can't get into the proposal/marriage thing again, especially not with a complete stranger. I'm starting to even bore myself. Before I know it I'll be hanging around at bus stops making small talk with anyone who will listen until they ask me what the problem is. What did I used to talk about prior to that moment when he popped the question?

'So what was it? Did he bone someone else?'

Charming, Winona, do you treat all your customers with such decorum?

'Er, no, he didn't actually.' *Or at least I hope he hasn't.* Visions of Connor's smiling face being enveloped by a silicone breast valley flash across my mind. 'It's just he's in America and he hasn't called for a few days.'

'How many days?'

That's what I love about teenagers; they're so direct.

I clasp my chin as if I have to think about the question for a minute, like you used to do at school when someone asked how long you had been with your boyfriend and you had to stop yourself from shrieking 'Four weeks, three days, eight hours and forty-five minutes!' and instead answer with a nonchalant: 'Bout a month.'

'Hmm, about five days.'

Winona sucks air through her teeth and I hear the metallic clunk of tongue stud against teeth. How do you carry out human functions with one of those things in – like eating and talking and kissing – without knocking all your teeth out or getting someone else caught on it in the process? I once got my brace entwined with the oral train tracks of Daniel Jennings, Norwich High School's answer to Joe

Ninety (I had a thing for the specky intelligent look at the time). It took two teachers most of second break to prise us apart without the use of pliers and wire-cutters and a lot longer for us to explain why our teeth had been touching in the first place. Our excuse – that we were carrying out a science experiment about the magnetic properties of dental appliances – was inventive for a pair of twelve-year-olds but not very convincing.

'The last time a fella I was seein' didn'y phone us for that long,' says Winona seriously, bringing me back to reality, 'he'd been off shaggin' Mary Gordon in my class. Got her up the duff and everythin', so he did.'

'Shit, that's bad news. How old was she?'

Winona shrugs as if this sort of thing happens all the time. 'Och, same as me at the time. Fourteen.'

Fourteen! Jesus, I hardly knew what proper sex was when I was fourteen. Or if I did I hadn't quite got past the giggly stage of pointing at pictures of boys' bits in biology books. Fourteen. I have to admit to feeling shocked. Damn, when did I become a square old fogey without realising?

I take a gulp of hot chocolate to steady my nerves and lick the cream moustache from my top lip. Winona is certainly taking my mind off things with her tales of how life is for a sixteen-year-old but I'm not sure she's doing a good job of cheering me up.

'Och, anyhow, I didn'y mind. It wasn'y like I was gonna marry him or anything. He was a bit of a tosser really and that lassie was a right wee slapper. I don't wanna get married but, I think it's shite. All my pals do too. We wanna be able to have lots of men just in case the one gets boring.'

And they say the institution of marriage is dead and

buried, oh ye of little faith. 'So, ehm, how long have yous two been shaggin'?' Winona blinks innocently.

She is nothing if not blunt.

'How long have we . . .?' I scratch the side of my nose and try to act cool. 'Er, we've been *shagging* for just about thirteen years.'

'Fucken' hell, man!' Winona hollers, her mouth gaping open, studs and all. 'Thirteen years! That's like my whole life nearabouts.'

I blush and shove a generous forkful of chocolate cake into my mouth as Winona continues to laugh like a hyena on E.

'Thirteen years, ha ha, I didn'y think you looked *that* old. That means yous two got together when I was three. Ha, that's amazin'. Isn't that amazin'?'

'Amazing,' I repeat moodily, feeling a sudden urge to poke her eye out with the leg of my zimmer frame. Now not only am I pissed off that Connor hasn't called and pissed off that I am pissed off about it, as well as being pissed off that my only relative to speak of – who won't talk about anything deeper than the Motherwell first eleven – makes me thoroughly depressed, but I am also pissed off that a sixteen-year-old Saturday girl has the ability to make me feel like one of the blue rinse/travel sweet brigade. Who gave her a job here anyway? This is *my* place.

'I really should go,' I grumble, pushing the suddenly uninviting remains of my chocolate treats towards her. 'I've got stuff to do.'

'Aye, all right,' Winona smiles, 'I'm closing up soon anyhow and I've gotta get ready to go clubbin' tonight.'

Please, no more. You've had your fun, now leave me alone to go and enjoy my wordsearch magazine.

I smile weakly and, throwing my bag over my slumped shoulder, turn to leave.

'But you know, pal,' Winona calls out to me before I can escape through the door, 'you shouldn'y hang around waitin' for him to phone. That's not cool, man.'

'I'm not I . . .' A neon sign saying 'Loser' flashes above my head with a giant arrow pointing directly at me.

'You should do something else, pal, to take yer mind off of him. Focus on something that takes up yer time. Then you willn'y care so much. I bet he's havin' fun in America so there's no reason why you canny have fun here.'

I stare open-mouthed at my teenage counsellor who is playing with her lip stud as she looks at me, probably completely unaware that she has just spoken far wiser words than have come out of my own or any of my friends' mouths in a long time. I am surprised to feel suddenly immature in comparison when only five minutes ago she had me down as an old hag.

'Thanks, Winona,' I nod sincerely, 'that is really good advice.'

She waves her hand at me and smiles. 'Och, nae bother. Anyhow, you take it easy . . .'

'Angel.' I finish her sentence for her.

'Wow, cool name, man. See ya, Angel.'

I leave the coffee shop feeling inspired as well as slightly shaky from the amount of chocolate I have just consumed in a very short space of time. I wander towards the wishing pool, delve once more into my bag for a couple of coins and lean against the waist-high metal fence. Winona is right, of course, I do need a focus. She may be too-cool-for-school with more studs than Man United's boot room but she is spot on when it comes to being an independent woman living life to the max. I need something to occupy my mind other than worrying about what Connor is up to every time he doesn't answer the phone or doesn't call. After all, that is completely out of my control. I need something other than thinking about the blasted proposal and trying to fathom what I am going to tell him in about five months' time. And I can't rely on anyone else to give me that focus either. I am a grown up, it is my responsibility. Besides, my dad has enough problems of his own just trying to get through each day without having me to sort out as well, and Meg and Ceri are there to be my best friends not my crutches. I lift my chin and try to think of something that will occupy my time and give me self-fulfilment. For at the risk of sounding like Raj bleedin' Persaud, I have heard that you can't truly make another person happy until you are whole and happy in yourself, so I would in fact be doing myself and Connor a favour.

A fish splashes the surface of the water and I look down to see silver and copper coins glinting in the light. How many coins have I thrown in there in my life, I wonder? There was the time I wished for a puppy for my birthday because I was desperate for a pet to complete my flat. That was two years ago this December. Connor bought me a goldfish instead because he thought I should have a go with something a little less demanding than a dog to begin with. So, the wish came true to a certain extent, although I couldn't really take James Pond for walks or teach him to sit down and beg. Mind you, he did learn one trick which consisted of leaping out of the bowl and flapping violently on my lounge rug until I found him and returned him to the water (he hadn't quite perfected the getting back in part). The day I took one step too many to peer into the bowl was the day our pet and owner bond came to a slippery end. Yuck, I can still remember the feeling of wet scales against the sole of my bare foot. I vow not to wish for a pet as my new focus.

I clasp one of the ten pence pieces between the thumb and forefinger of my left hand and hold it above the water. The really big wish that came true from this wishing pool was the time I came here before my interview with Energy FM. In an attempt to listen to every single one of my CDs to gen up on my music knowledge I got Paul Weller stuck in the CD tray, causing a power surge that blew the speaker and short-circuited everything electrical in my flat. I almost blew a fuse myself until Connor (after making a very poor joke about it being apt that Paul Weller got stuck because he was the lead singer of The Jam) armed himself with a screw-driver and ushered me out of the door with a handful of wishing coins and instructions not to leave the Botanics until I had calmed down. Three hours later I returned, having told every plant in the glasshouses my worries and safe in the knowledge that I had the wishing pool on my side. It worked; I got the job and I have had real faith in this place ever since.

'Of course!' I yelp excitedly at my own watery reflection. 'My job. Jeez, if anything needs help it's that.'

I clap my hands, taking care not to drop either of my coins before I am ready. I smile at my own ingenuity. That's it! While Connor is away I will throw myself into my work and that will definitely take my mind off things. Ceri has done that recently – admittedly she hasn't thrown herself *too* far because Ceri is the sort of girl who could challenge most cowboy builders when it comes to hours of hard slog – but she has been put in charge of developing the gossip column and I have really seen a change in her. It is as if she has a purpose – other than bedding every above-average bloke in a fifty-mile radius, that is.

This is a simply perfect idea. For the next five months or so I will completely focus on my career. God knows the show needs improvement anyway and I am the woman to do it. After all, you only need to play so many Shakin' Stevens and Alvin Stardust records to realise that your career is on the snake route rather than the ladder. Dan is also desperate to take *Angel on Air* to greater heights so we can do it together. We can take on the station controller, select our own playlists, even get special guests on. With a lot of effort and even more enthusiasm we could achieve great things. Much better than putting my life on hold until my boyfriend comes back just because I'm a bit lonely and feeling sorry for myself.

Bursting with new-found resolve, I close my eyes, squeeze one coin tightly and drop it into the pool (after first checking for fish in the vicinity as I would hate to be responsible for two fishy deaths).

'I wish,' I whisper quietly, 'for the motivation to be able to focus on my show while Connor is away and the imagination to make it a real success. Thanks.'

I open my eyes just as a ray of October sun bursts through a missing pane of glass in the dome. I instantly feel brighter and more positive; so much so that I am desperate to embark on my plan. It is Saturday and I am not at work until Monday but I can at least jot down some ideas and get the rusty brain cells working. I am so happy – I have a mission.

Realising that I still have the other coin in my hand, I click my tongue against the roof of my mouth while I think of what to wish for. I whisper under my breath as I drop it into the pool. I then pick up my bag and skip towards the exit with the determination of a bra-burning feminist. Except they would probably not be seen dead skipping and I doubt they would be big on three-inch-heeled denim boots but you know what I mean.

'Thanks, Winona,' I call through the doorway of the coffee shop as she is preparing to close up, 'you really cheered me up.' *Eventually.*

Winona, who has changed from her regulation green apron and sensible black pumps into a fitted Blink 182 T-shirt and glaringly trendy red and black skate-style trainers, looks up and winks.

'Any time, Angel, see you again.'

I nod and then jump suddenly as my mobile phone bursts into song. My Macy Gray 'Why Didn't You Call Me?' ring-tone breaks the silence of The Kibble Palace. I answer it, crossing my fingers that it's not my dad in a developed state of rotten drunk.

'CONNOR!' I whoop loudly, stopping short of punching the sky with my fist. Well, the second wish worked and pretty damn quickly too.

Winona looks out of the corner of her eye and smiles knowingly.

'Hi baby,' Connor replies, his voice distant because of a poor signal, yet warm.

My heart scrambles for its glittery cheerleader pom-poms and does a victory dance around my chest. Give us a C, give us an O, give us an N . . . So much for the feminism vibe.

'How are you?' I chirp at the same time as Connor says, 'It'll have to be a quick call.'

'I'm fine,' he replies, just as I ask, 'Why? Where are you?'

The time delay makes a sensibly flowing conversation practically impossible. I pause to let our words catch up with each other and to wait for Connor to speak. Unfortunately he decides to do the same so we remain in complete silence bar the crackling on the line.

'So, how . . .?' Connor and I say simultaneously.

'Sorry, you first.'

'Oops, go ahead.'

Jesus, this is a nightmare. I feel like a presenter on GMTV trying to interview a guest by long distance video link and making a complete hash of it. I clear my throat.

'Sorry I haven't called you for a couple of days, baby,' Connor jumps in before I can speak.

'No problem,' I reply with a forced air of nonchalance, 'it's just great to hear your voice.'

'And yours, my Angel, it makes my day.'

Hearing my voice makes his day. I am about to melt on to the glasshouse floor when my new independent streak gives me a swift clip round the ear.

'Thanks,' I reply coolly. 'I was really busy anyway. I've got a lot of important stuff on.'

At least I have from about five minutes ago.

'It was difficult to find a phone,' he says apologetically. 'We were on location in the middle of nowhere.'

'On location? Gosh, that sounds glamorous. Is the filming going well?'

'Aye, great. The girls are settling into it well, finding their feet, you know.'

Oh really? And here was I thinking they spent most of their time on their backs.

'Brilliant,' I beam, 'and all's well here. I've decided to really throw myself into my show, make it the best it can possibly be. Dan and I are going to give Energy a real kick up the bum. A complete *Angel on Air* overhaul.'

Well, we are going to, in the very near future. It's only a little white lie.

'Fantastic, I'm proud of you, baby. I'm sure it'll be great. Anyway, look, I'd better run, this is Ferrari's phone I'm using. But I just wanted to let you know that I'm OK and I miss you and I love you, Angel.'

His words reach the part of my heart that is still soft and squishy. I bite my lip to stop it trembling and feel a bubble of emotion rising in my throat. I clasp the phone closer to my ear. I want to shout 'Please come back, it's lonely here without you. I want to feel you lying in bed beside me, I want to see your smile and smell you and taste you and kiss you', but I muster all the willpower I can find to keep it inside. If I give into it now then my wish meant nothing and I may as well not even begin my new mission.

I take a deep breath of fern-smelling air and simply answer, 'I miss you too, Connor,' keeping the sound of a smile in my voice the way I have to do on the radio.

'Right then, well, you keep working on that radio show and time will fly, I promise.'

I nod, then flinch when I hear a woman's voice in the background. I press my ear even closer to the phone until I can almost feel the microwaves frying the outer layer of my brain.

'We're on the move again, baby,' Connor says before I can

ask whose voluptuous body the squeak belongs to. 'Speak to you again soon. Bye.'

I can sense the green-eyed monster rising up inside me as if, any minute, my clothes will tear open and I will evolve into the Incredible Jealous Hulk, which would not be a pretty sight – especially the clothes tearing open part. Jealousy has never really been part of my make-up and I'm damned if I'm going to let myself turn into one of those distrusting psycho chicks now. I swallow the feelings and drag my new inner strength from the dark corner it has retreated to. I force the smile on to my lips again.

'Bye,' I chirp, 'have fun, Connor.'

And tell that Ferrari from me that if she gives you more than the use of her phone I'll pop her fake boobs with a knitting needle.

CHAPTER TEN

Rock DJ

True to my word, I throw myself into my work, beginning by booking a slot in the elusive diary of the station controller Mr G.G. MacDougal – a feat equivalent to the Scotland squad booking a place in the World Cup final – to discuss ideas for *Angel on Air*. No one really knows what the G.G. stands for, although Gone Golfing is currently the hot favourite. Dan prefers Gay Gordon but our G.G. is definitely heterosexual, hiring mainly voluptuous brunettes and the odd blonde as his secretarial staff and being renowned for helping himself to handfuls of women's bums at office parties. With my bum defensively clenched and Dan quivering at my side I knock on the outer door to G.G.'s lair and wait to be summoned by Marjory, his stern, terrifyingly efficient secretary – the exception to the voluptuously beautiful rule – who also appears to be as mad as a box of frogs.

'Daniel, Angie, do come in,' G.G. smarms when Marjory eventually agrees to let us within sniffing distance of her master the Thursday after my wish. He flings open his office door with nothing short of gusto.

'Er, it's Angel actually,' I say apologetically, shuffling past and taking a seat in front of his enormous oak desk.

'Of course it is; anyone for coffee?'

G.G. barks an order for three filter coffees before Dan and I have even had a chance to respond to his question. Dan looks across at me and smirks, both of us suddenly feeling like naughty children called to the headmaster's office.

Dan is younger than me by six months but joined the radio station exactly a month before I did so has no trouble in thinking of himself as my boss. Not that that's a problem, I could have a much worse boss, believe me. He is very laid-back, extremely sociable and would have us both drinking pints before every show to loosen us up if I hadn't explained my fears regarding the alcoholic tendencies floating around the paternal end of my gene pool. Thankfully Dan understood so instead we compete to see who can down the most espresso-choc coffees from the vending machine in quick succession and who can eat the most free bars of chocolate that are often sent into the studio by our sponsors – a perk of the job – by which time we are certainly sparky enough to talk for three hours. Usually shutting me up and bringing me down from the caffeine/cocoa high is the problem. Dan is very tall, lankier than semi-cooked spaghetti, with a freckled, boyish face. I'm not quite sure of his sexual orientation, and I'm pretty certain neither is he, which makes for some great gossip on the odd occasion that we do go for a drink after work. All I know is he is not my type but he has a fantastic personality and has become a good friend. Since I explained my new mission he has also become my partner in crime, just as determined to turn our show into something good. Maybe not to rock the foundations of the broadcasting world but at least to create a minor tremor at some point in the near future.

'So, my bright young stars,' G.G. enthuses, 'what can I do for you this fine day?'

His eyes drift to one of the huge windows covering two of the four walls in his office and I know he is most probably contemplating the weather conditions for a quick round of golf.

'Well,' Dan begins, clearing his throat nervously.

He pauses and we both stare as G.G. reaches into a polished wooden box on one side of the desk and produces a comb in a leather case. Removing it from its sheath, he smooths the tortoiseshell teeth over his dyed chestnut hair. Just like The Fonz, only not quite as cool and with a brown suit and tie where the leather and denim should have been. I am aware that my jaw is dropping but I reel it in when Marjory knocks sharply on the door and appears with cups of coffee, two custard creams and a two-finger KitKat. Dan instinctively reaches for the chocolate but is immediately deterred by a glare from Marjory that could melt eyeballs. Sheepishly, we both select a limp biscuit with a quick 'Thank you, Marjory' and snigger into our cups, well aware that the biscuit signifies our importance in the scheme of things as far as the boss is concerned. You see, G.G. and Marjory have a system around here. Cakes such as fondant fancies or Tunnocks snowballs and posh cookies with real chocolate chips are reserved for the real execs, the people G.G. is trying to keep in favour. Then one moves down the scale to the acceptable but not so suave, like Hob Nobs and chocolate digestives, used for well-positioned members of staff or new DJs on their very first day at Energy. The scale continues to descend through Jaffa Cakes and pink wafer things until we hit bourbons, custard creams and Jammie Dodgers, not at the bottom but a sure indication that G.G. is more interested in keeping his biscuit budget down than in impressing his guest. Thankfully, Dan and I have never slipped below custard creams and we maintain a hope that one day we will be offered at least a plain digestive to dunk in our stewed cup of instant, but such dizzy heights are rare in this company. All I know is the day I enter G.G.'s office and don't get a biscuit at all I am really in trouble.

'Well,' Dan begins again, 'Mr MacDougal, we—'

'Oh, call me G.G., my dear boy; you are a member of my staff after all, aren't you?'

I can't help but notice that this last part is framed as a real question while trying to appear rhetorical. I blush and nod.

'Yes, we do *Angel on Air*, the lunchtime show, Mr, er, G.G. I'm the DJ and Dan's the producer.'

'Of course you do. I know that. I know everything that goes on within these four walls.'

By that I think he means the entire building, although the four walls of his plush office would be more accurate.

'So, Angie—'

'Angel.'

'So, Angel, and you most certainly are if I may say so . . .'

I shoot out my left leg and kick Dan on the shin as he snorts under his breath.

'. . . what did you want to see me about?'

'I' – I sit up straight and try to appear confident and efficient. Act as if, remember, act as if – 'well, Dan and I,' I continue, 'would like to talk to you about plans for the lunchtime show.'

G.G. makes agreeable noises while slithering out of his chair and walking towards an umbrella stand next to one of the windows.

'Carry on,' he orders while rifling around for a golf club.

Dan dunks his biscuit and nods at me to continue.

'Er, OK, we were thinking that the show could do with a bit of a revamp. You know, to bring in more listeners, perhaps more of the younger audience who listen to some of the more, er, trendy stations during the day while they're in their cars or at work or even in cafés and such like.'

I make a face at Dan, wondering whether to carry on as G.G. is clearly far more interested in perfecting his putting skills than in anything a twenty-nine-year-old female DJ has to say. Dan mouths 'Keep going' while chewing on his soggy biscuit.

'Of course we want to keep the essence of the show the same,' I say a little louder, 'but we feel that perhaps the three hours is getting a little staid. I've got a good network of callers and I want to keep them but even my older listeners would prefer something a little different, I'm sure.'

G.G. changes clubs, nodding like a plastic dog in the back of a Ford Cortina, and takes a few practice swings.

'So, what Dan and I were thinking was . . .'

I nudge Dan, trying to encourage him to speak, but he simply opens his mouth to show me his chewed-up Custard Cream and smiles mischievously. I grimace, feeling like a religious preacher standing alone on a wooden box in the middle of the city while people walk hastily past.

'What we were thinking was,' I persevere, 'maybe we could introduce a guest slot on the show and invite someone in the news or a pop star' – fat chance of getting anyone anywhere close to the Top Four Hundred but I live in hope – 'and perhaps begin to have a bit of input in the playlists to make them a bit more . . .'

I glance quickly around the office, taking in the framed pictures of Cliff Richard and The Shadows, Dolly Parton, Des O'Connor and the like on the wall behind me. This man is a musical dinosaur, for God's sake. In fact, I'm surprised God hasn't got an album cover on display too – Jesus and The Apostles, Now 25 A.D.

'A bit more . . . modern,' I cough, diving for my cup of coffee.

G.G. turns towards me, lines up for a bully-off or whatever they call it and swings the club. Dan and I stare, polite smiles fixed on our faces, as our boss watches the invisible ball fly down the invisible fairway and on to the invisible green.

'Great shot,' Dan remarks quietly.

I chew my cheek and wait for G.G. to speak.

'It is a fabulous game, golf,' he says eventually, striding back towards the desk with the club resting on his shoulder, 'so unappreciated by the young people of today.'

'Apart from Tiger Woods, of course,' I beam, thankful that there is at least one famous young golfer whose name I can bandy about whenever necessary.

'A genius,' G.G. nods seriously, 'you're absolutely right, Angie.'

I decide not to correct him when my efforts have so far been futile. I wait to be asked to leave the office with my tail between my legs. G.G. stops and brushes imaginary dust from Des O'Connor's Colgate smile before returning to his huge leather chair with a sigh.

'As you can see,' G.G. begins after an uncomfortable pause, 'I am a man of taste and tradition.'

We say nothing.

'I like the good things in life – a good game of golf, a good piece of music. I don't like noise and the infernal racket some young people call music these days but I am aware that not everyone shares my class and impeccable upbringing. My people brought troops like you two into this company to move us forward and that, Daniel and Angie, is business. So' – he smooths down the lapel of his suit jacket and looks me in the eye – 'we are open to your suggestions as long as you can prove that you are benefiting the station by bringing in your changes. I do not want your playlists full of junk, you understand, we must maintain some level of acceptability for our listeners with better appreciation of a real melody, but I hear what you are saying. I believe I can find something in the budget for you to bring in the music you think will work. Nothing too Top Ten, mind; money doesn't grow on bushes these days. As for guests, we want big names, something that will catapult the station into the headlines. Having given you this freedom, I don't expect to be disappointed. I will keep my eye on your progress and if the changes don't appear to be working we will have to return to the original format' –he pauses – 'or something completely different.'

By that I suppose he means the format of a P45 but I do my best to overlook this veiled threat.

Dan sticks both thumbs up beneath the desk and out of G.G.'s view. I do the same.

'Now,' he booms, rising up from his chair, 'I have a very important meeting to get to.'

Eighteen holes or just the nine? I am tempted to say.

'You prove your worth and it will be good for all concerned. I am sure you won't let us down.'

He finishes with a wink in my direction, which makes me blush although for all the wrong reasons. Dan and I shake hands with our boss and scramble out of the room, gasping for fresh air as we almost run down the corridor.

'You were great, Angel Fish,' Dan grins, jogging along next to me.

'Thanks, Dan; you were shit.'

'Hey, I just didn't want to steal your thunder,' he protests, 'and anyway, I knew he would fancy you.'

'Yuck,' I laugh, 'imagine that.'

'Making out to Des O'Connor,' Dan howls as we jump into the glass lift at the end of the corridor.

'I'd rather make out *with* Des O'Connor,' I giggle, flapping my hands under my armpits which are feeling decidedly sweaty with liquid nerves.

'Your wish is my command, lady.' Dan pretends to wave a magic wand over my head. 'Our first guest on the new improved *Angel on Air* will be Des himself.'

'Yeah right, Dan, you'd be lucky.'

'Watch me,' Dan pouts. 'I'm gonna make some calls right this minute. Our show's gonna be brilliant from this moment on.' He clicks his fingers and winks mischievously. 'We're gonna make you famous, Angel.'

With my new focus at the forefront of my mind, the weeks pass quickly and I begin to realise that Connor's absence is becoming less and less of a black hole in my own little universe. His third week, one month, fifth and sixth week anniversaries of leaving for California go by with little more than a few teary telephone calls to Meg and Ceri and several emergency curry nights. Of course I miss him and I still tick off the weeks gone by on my Didier Lafitte calendar (a present from Meg after our giggly girlie moment over his photo in *Smash Hits*) but I have noticed that I am slowly metamorphosing into Destiny's Child's 'Independent Woman'. It is quite a revelation to someone like me who has been part of a couple for over a decade. It is official, I *can* be alone. In fact, in a lot of ways I can achieve more on my own with no distractions, *and* I can enjoy my own company. Don't get me wrong, I don't want to sound too surprised that I am not finding myself as dull as ditchwater, but the last six weeks have, at the risk of sounding like a self-help book, been a real lesson in the importance of 'me-time'. My flat has definitely benefited as a result. I do things like, would you believe it, tidy up and clear out junk? I play records that haven't been out of their dust jackets for years. I even do some of those girlie things that Ceri has taught me, although bikini waxing is something I simply cannot inflict on myself. Mind you, it also scares me how quickly I can settle in to a whole new way of life when the person I am supposed to be loving for ever is no longer around. What if I can't adapt when he gets back? What if he is experiencing the same sense of independence? Nah, if I were him I'd be missing me like crazy!

Since our meeting with G.G. Dan and I have been extremely busy improving our playlists and having concentrated brainstorming sessions about which star guests to invite on the new-look show. I say brainstorming, but our meetings in the staff canteen usually seem to degenerate into reminiscences about pop stars we used to fancy and lyric-remembering competitions. The truth of the matter is that regardless of how many calls we make to agents of stars (or in some cases PAs to the agents of the agents of the stars) we always get the same answer – 'Mr FarTooFamousForTheLikesOfYou would *lurve* to come on your show, *dahlings*, but he is just so *awfully* busy at the mo.' In other words – 'Please try in twenty years or so when he's washed up and so desperate for public adoration that he would even stoop so low as to appear on a piddly little local radio show like yours, you sad unknown girl DJ.' I am not disheartened, however. All right, I am a teensy bit disheartened, but I am still determined that before the year is out we will have landed a guest that will send a whirlwind of excitement around the whole of Energy FM. Actually make that around the whole of Glasgow, given that someone being offered a cherry bakewell by G.G. is enough to blow the roof off our office. I'm aiming a little higher than that.

In contrast, the playlist thing is improving at a great rate. The idea I had when I was at Dad's to have themed days on the show has been very well received by my listeners and has even pulled in a few more first-time callers, which is always a good sign. We had a Scotland day, an American music day, a Caribbean day and an Irish day before I came to the conclusion halfway through the latter that an overdose of Ronan Keating, a superfluity of Daniel O'Donnell, a plethora of The Corrs and a total saturation of Westlife wasn't good for anyone's health, especially my own. We then moved on to years, for example the best of 1998. Not a new idea, I know, but it is a good way of introducing some modern songs without too many complaints, and the older listeners stay with us in the knowledge that they will get their chance on another day when we concentrate on the best of the 1950s/60s/70s. That said, this week we are stuck in the eighties, celebrating ten years of tragic fashion and big hair (I sneakily dedicated a song to Beth, the woman responsible for my ginormous engagement ring). I have to say it is making me feel rather nostalgic for the delights of the Stock, Aitken and Waterman era. I can almost feel my hands twitching for the scratchy sensation of a lacy fingerless glove.

'That was ZZ Top with "Gimme All Your Lovin",' I laugh as Dan comes to the dramatic end of his air guitar solo, 'which I played especially for Harvey in Bellshill, a long-term member of the ZZ Top International Fan Club, from his wife Cheryl who wants to give Harvey all her lovin' when his lorry gets back to town tonight. Lovely. And keep your calls coming in for the person you would like to hear as our first special guest on a soon-to-be-broadcast show. We are very choosy about our guest list' – *not through choice but because no fucker wants to come*, I am tempted to add – 'so think hard and call me with your suggestions. I aim to please so we'll see if we can make your dreams come true.'

I glance at Dan, who is pretending to pray, and then reach forward to press a flashing red button indicating a caller on hold.

'Angel here, who's on line one?'

'HEY ANGEL!' booms a voice in my ear. 'THE SHOW'S PURE MINTED TODAY, HEN. US LADS AT THE GARAGE ARE HAVIN' A RIGHT WEE HOOLEY TO OURSELVES, JUMPIN' ABOOT AN' THAT.'

'It's our mate Boomer, if I'm not very much mistaken,' I reply, gripping my ear to stop my eardrum exploding out of the other side of my head. 'Glad you're enjoying the music. So what can we do for you today?'

Boomer, another of my regular callers, is needless to say very loud. I have considered suggesting that he bins the telephone completely and just shouts at me from his garage five miles down the road but I wouldn't like to hurt his feelings. Not any more than he hurts my eardrums anyway.

'SEE THIS SPECIAL GUEST, ANGEL, DOES IT HAVE TO BE SOMEONE ALIVE, LIKE?'

Dan falls off his chair with the force of his laughter.

'Er,' I reply, clamping my top teeth on to my bottom lip, 'that would kind of be necessary, Boomer, yes.'

'HOW?'

'Well, it might be a little bit tricky to interview them in the studio if they're, um, dead. That's our plan, you see; to get them in and have a chat and maybe get a listener in to meet them too.'

'AYE, RIGHT, I GET YA. SO I CANNY ASK FER ELVIS THEN?'

Poor Boomer, he's got a heart of gold but he hasn't really got a Scooby Doo what's going on most of the time, bless him. There's a fair bit of storm damage up there if you know what I mean.

'Is there anyone else you'd like to hear from other than Elvis?' I suggest, keeping the headphones a safe distance from my lobes.

'NUH, NO' REALLY. ELVIS IS THE KING, HEN. YA CANNY GET ANY BETTER THAN THAT.'

'OK, thanks for your suggestion, Boomer, and just give us

a call if you think of anyone else *alive* whom we could invite on the show.'

'AYE, SMASHIN'. CHEERIO NOW.'

'Bye, Boomer,' I grin, always cheered up by his 'special' ways. 'Here's a song just for Boomer and the guys at the garage. This is Van Halen with "Jump".'

The guest suggestions throughout the afternoon oscillate between the bizarre, the out of reach famous and the far too boring even for our show. Some of the more unusual include Val Doonican, The Jackson Five, The Frog Chorus, The Tweenies and the woman who sang the Shake 'N' Vac advert jingle, leading me to conclude that many of my listeners are either very young, very old or have more than one screw loose. Clear favourites soon emerge as we draw nearer to three o'clock and the final counting of the votes. The boys/men call in for Kylie (or Kylie's bum, to be more precise, despite this being a radio interview). The girls want Will Young, Gareth Gates and Robbie Williams. Cliff Richard is also a hugely popular choice among the more mature ladies, largely thanks to Gladys who has obviously forced every one of her friends and family to call in and request the Peter Pan of Pop himself. Not that their dedication will help much, Cliff Richard being way beyond my expectations for the calibre of guest that we will be able to attract. If he is A or B list then we are floundering around the range of F-minus.

There is, however, one name that seems to span the sexual divide and the generation gap. Gladys has him down as her second choice behind Sir Cliff – praise indeed. Malcolm from Hamilton – he of the blinkered opinions –

even rates his music although he can't resist adding, 'Mind you, he may be able to sing but he's still a ponce-faced Froggy b—' before Dan can get rid of him. Darling Malcolm, so reliable. Fifty or so girls from my old school, all fighting for control of a single telephone during their lunch break, emotionally scream his name as if they will all drop dead if they don't get to meet him sometime soon; there are even tears. Who is the man stirring up all this sexual chemistry? His name is Didier Lafitte, the smouldering French pop idol who has recently started to cause a commotion in the undergarments of female fans this side of the Channel. His picture is everywhere on posters around the city and in magazines – the one with him semi-naked on a French beach that almost caused Meg to spontaneously combust, the one from his video with him wearing black leather and a billowing white shirt, the boy-next-door one on the cover of the latest *Smash Hits*, not to mention the calendar on my fridge. As a woman it is my duty to admit that he is very good looking and his music is extremely sexual. In fact, such is his wide appeal that most people with an ounce of oestrogen and many with a healthy serving of testosterone fancy him. Didier Lafitte would undoubtedly be a fantastic guest but he has never given an interview in the UK, is notoriously distant and is way, way, *waaaaay* out of our league. We can but dream.

'That was Blondie with "The Tide Is High" and I hope you were singing along as much as Dan and I were.'

This eighties music is starting to possess me. I now have a real urge to go to a roller disco.

'Our last caller on the show today,' I continue, still tapping my feet happily, 'is our friend Tyrone. How are things with you, Tyrone?'

I ask this question gingerly as 'things' are rarely good with Tyrone. He is fourteen, a regular caller to the show and a total sweetheart, yet Tyrone doesn't seem to have a friend in the world.

'Not bad, Angel,' Tyrone replies quietly, his voice so timid and nervous I can practically hear his face blush. 'I, ehm, I . . .'

Frankly I am amazed that Tyrone takes part in the phone-ins at all considering his disposition, but I think he finds solace in the fact that no matter how lonely his real life, every weekday between twelve and three he has a network of friends at the other end of the phoneline. I don't doubt for a second that were it necessary for him to show his face or cast aside his relative anonymity Tyrone wouldn't touch my show with a bargepole. But we never use his second name, I don't reveal where he lives and let's face it, his school bullies who seem to consider themselves the coolest and hardest fourteen-year-olds this side of the Bronx are highly unlikely to tune in to my show. In this instance, thank heavens for that.

'No school today, Ty?' I ask, trying not to make this a loaded question. 'Or did you finish early?'

'Nuh, well, aye, there is school but I couldn'y go.'

'Why's that?'

'Ehm, they took my shoes yesterday and they took my trainers too. I haven'y got anything to wear.'

I look at Dan through the glass and shake my head. 'That's bad, Ty, and did you tell anyone? Your mum or a teacher?'

'Nuh, they willn'y do anything and Mum's not here. It's just my brother and he's always out.'

'And do you know where they put your shoes, these lads?'

'Aye, they chucked them on the school roof. Everyone laughed.'

My heart lurches at the thought of Tyrone, this boy I talk to every week but have never met, standing in the school playground while the kids around him jeer, mock and bully him for their own entertainment. School sounds so tough these days, like army endurance training or a five-year stint on *Survivor*. We had a girl at my school in Norwich who went through a phase of pricking smaller girls in the arm with the end of her compass. Tyrone once had a flick-knife pushed against his neck to make him hand over his mobile phone, making a compass seem rather insignificant in comparison. His tales make me realise that the world never stops changing and, despite having promised myself that it would never happen, I *will* end up sucking air through my teeth and tutting, 'Well, that never used to happen in *my* day.'

'Does your brother have any shoes you can borrow?' I continue navigating my way carefully through his teenage minefield.

'Maybe. But he willn'y let me wear them.'

'Not even if you explain to him what happened?'

'I dunno,' he replies with an audible shrug, 'maybe.'

'He might be someone you can talk to if you give him the chance, Ty.'

'Aye, I dunno. I like talking to you but,' he replies cheerfully.

I allow myself a smile. 'And I love talking to you too, Tyrone.'

'And I'd like it if you could get that Didier on the show. My brother got his album and I sneaked into his room and recorded it. It's pure brilliant. I like the one called "Confidence".'

How apt.

'Well, I'll certainly see what I can do, Ty, but I won't promise anything just in case, OK?'

'Aye, that's fine. Just so long as I know it's not impossible. I can look forward to it anyhow.'

I clasp my hands together and raise them to my lips.

Bless him, Dan mouths silently.

'Right you are, Ty, I'll try my best.'

And a pig might just glide through the studio with Didier Lafitte on its back.

'I guess you're too young to remember the eighties like us old fogies but I'm sure we could make an exception for a special caller like you and play you any song that you'd like.'

Dan nods his approval.

'I do know songs from the eighties, I've got an old compilation,' Tyrone answers proudly, his confidence growing as the call continues. He is happy in this radio world. It seems he can be the someone on my show that he has never been given the chance to be in the playground.

'Wow, all right then dude, impress me,' I chuckle.

'I would like Haircut 100 and "Fantastic Day".'

'Great choice, Tyrone, as ever, and I hope your day gets better as it goes along.'

'I doubt it, Angel, especially after your show ends. All right then, see yous.'

He hangs up the phone, I swallow the lump in my throat, cue the record and bring the show to a close.

'I wish there was something I could do for that kid,' I sigh over a can of Diet Coke in the staff canteen.

'You already do something by listening to him and

making him feel important,' says Dan, scratching his neck. 'He thinks of you as his mate.'

'Yeah, but it's not enough. He needs someone to go into his school and sort it all out. Bullying like that shouldn't be allowed to carry on, it'll ruin his life and he's too scared or embarrassed to bring it to anyone's attention. Not that many people would listen if he did, most probably.'

Dan shrugs and stretches out his long legs in front of him, resting his feet on the seat of a metal chair.

'You're not the person to intervene, Angel fish, you're nothing to do with him.'

'I know but—'

'But nothing. You can't get involved and you can't save the world.'

I sullenly sip my drink, knowing he is probably right.

'Let's face it,' Dan smirks, wrinkling his freckled nose, 'if you can't even get the S Club Juniors to come on your show the chances of you saving the world and all its bullied teenagers are pretty slim.'

'Oh God, that's tragic. Who else has turned us down?'

'Erm, let me see now. Everyone.'

'Everyone?'

'That's right, everyone. Ooh,' he waves his hand excitedly, 'apart from the woman from Bucks Fizz—'

'Who, Cheryl Baker? Oh, I love her, that's gr—'

'No, not her, the other one.'

'The curly haired one?'

'Yeah. What's her name again?'

'No idea.'

'Oh well, never mind, there's her and the school choir that sang "There's No One Quite Like Grandma" about twenty-five years ago. They're getting together for a reunion.'

'St Winifred's? What did you call them for?'

'Dunno really.' Dan winks. 'I just wanted to know our limitations. They did get to Number One, you know.'

'So did Mr Blobby but I won't be rushing to get him into the studio. Bloody hell, Dan, so much for us being famous and turning our show into something that will electrify the radio waves. I think I've just come over all suicidal.'

'Now, now, darling, don't be disheartened. You never know who's just round the corner.'

'Yes, I do,' I grimace, ducking behind my can of drink as a familiar figure appears at the far end of the canteen. 'G.G. MacDougal has just appeared around the corner and he will be looking for a progress report if he spots us.'

'That's if he remembers who we are, *Angie*,' Dan snorts.

'I'm not taking that chance. Not until we've got something positive to report to our boss, and believe me, St Winifred's School Choir is really not going to cut the mustard with the executives around here. Four weeks and no guest – that's not a roaring success. Our P45s are probably already on order. Right, I've got to go and meet Ceri for a coffee so quick, Dan, roll in those never-ending legs of yours and sprint for it.'

CHAPTER ELEVEN

I Heard It Through The Grapevine

I look out of the Sauchiehall Street entrance to Starbucks to see Ceri, immaculate as ever in a pristine white trouser suit, waving her hand dismissively in the face of a beautiful young man with shoulder-length blond hair and more than his fair share of muscles. As Ceri turns to walk away, his face crumples and I realise I am about to see a grown man cry. How does she do it?

'Eugh, what a complete and utter sap,' Ceri tuts, striding across the café and pulling up a chair, which she brushes down before sitting.

Bloody hell, if I were wearing a white trouser suit I'd have to carry around my own white chair, white cushion and a bottle of Vanish all day to prevent stains. I glance down at my slate grey baggy trousers, purchased after I saw Kylie Minogue wearing a pair in Ceri's mag. Of course, Kylie still managed to look petite and doll-like in hers whereas I look like a hippy (by that I mean bodily parts, not tie-dye and joss sticks) girl trying to cover my thighs by wearing two parachutes on my legs.

'Boy Two?' I smirk, nodding towards the window as Ceri folds her long slim frame into the seat.

'What? Oh no, Boy Five. Big mistake.'

Ceri lifts a bony head and signals to our waiter to bring her a drink and some more tea and cake for her less attractive friend. Of course she doesn't actually say that but I think it, as does the waiter who winks adoringly at her before scurrying off to fulfil her every need.

'And what did Boy Five do to deserve such public humiliation?' I ask, always intrigued by Ceri's tales of men won and dumped.

'Oh, nothing really,' she shrugs. 'I've been seeing him since Tuesday. He's a perfume rep for some company or other. He's bought me so many bloody fragrances my bathroom is starting to look like a sodding ferry duty-free shop. He was just starting to get on my tits. He eats with his mouth open for a start and he's way too needy. He wants to see me more than I see myself.' She smooths down her hair with both hands. 'It was all getting a bit too intense, you know?'

'But you've only been seeing him for two days. How can it get too intense in forty-eight hours?'

'I don't know, Angel; I just attract the ones who fall madly in love very quickly, I suppose.'

Ceri turns towards the waiter and flashes her white smile as he bends down to place his loaded tray on the table between us. His eyes take in every inch of Ceri's body. In fact, I am almost of a mind to ask him to please stop salivating in my green tea but he probably wouldn't take any notice. Ceri Divine is too distracting for anyone with erection equipment.

'Right then,' I cough loudly, before Starbucks metamorphoses into a scene from a porno movie, 'what is this big news you've got to tell me, Ceri? This big piece of PRIVATE NEWS.'

The waiter rubs the ear I shouted in and scowls at me before striding away, trying for all he is worth to get Ceri's eyes to follow his clenched bottom. Ceri raises one eyebrow at me and reaches for her giant mug of tea with her tiny hand. The proportions are all wrong; she looks like a Borrower trying to lift a pint of Guinness.

'Well, Angel,' she pouts, 'have I got some gossip for you!'

'I expect so. You are paid to pry, after all.'

I break off a morsel of carrot cake and wait for Ceri's latest release from the gossip-ometer. It had better be good; I compromised a team meeting with Dan to be here.

'Big star,' Ceri begins, raising the palms of her hands to emphasise the statement, 'huge star in many places and going to be even huger here.'

'I don't think huger is a word.'

'I work in glossies, Angel, anything you can make up a spelling for is a word. Now do you want to hear this news or not?'

I nod and chew on the end of my tongue which is still numb from my first sip of too-hot tea.

'Right, I got wind on the grapevine this morning that a rather exciting megastar is coming to Glasgow in one week's time.'

'Don't make me guess who it is, I'm too exhausted for games,' I grumble, tired of the admiring looks Ceri is getting from every man in the café except for the toddler in the corner who is trying to fit his entire head into a packet of crisps.

'Games?' Ceri pouts. 'I don't play games with this sort of thing, Angel honey, especially when this man's arrival on Scottish soil could be the big break *both* of us are looking for.'

Damn, she's got me interested now. I lean closer and smile.

'In seven days' time,' Ceri carries on, clasping her hands together, 'none other than French pop star and delicious eye candy Didier Lafitte is coming to Meg's shop to do an album signing.'

My mouth drops open.

'Meg's shop?' I repeat. '*Our* Meg's shop?'

'Of course our Meg's shop. And close your mouth; regurgitated carrot cake is not a pretty sight.'

I clamp my mouth shut and shift forward on the chair. I am literally on the edge of my seat. Didier Lafitte. *The* Didier Lafitte in our friend's shop. If I could just grab him and ask him to appear on my show . . . Wow, this is perfect timing.

'Didier Lafitte, Ceri, is just the sort of person I am looking for to come on the show. Everyone wants to meet him.'

'I know, darling, that's why I'm telling you. Obviously he would make a fantastic subject for my column and I will be attached to him like an It girl to royalty, but I want to see you make a success of *Angel on Air* and if anyone can push you into the public eye it's this man of the moment.'

'Gosh, thanks Ceri,' I smile, ashamedly amazed at such sincerity and thoughtfulness from the girl I have known inside out for thirteen years. Don't get me wrong, Ceri Divine has her moments of compassion but they are few and far between and, I have noticed, becoming even more scarce as we near thirty.

I beam and clasp Ceri's hand conspiratorially. 'Imagine if we each landed an interview with Didier Lafitte. He's never done one over here; that would be such a scoop.'

'Plus,' says Ceri, running her tongue along her top lip, 'the man is an absolute peach. Clearly mad about music and French too. Sounds like someone else I know. You two might be perfect for each other.'

'Ceri,' I laugh, 'I'm not interested in him for that reason. I'm with Connor, remember?'

'I know that, but you're currently with him in a very distant sense of the word. This could be your only chance to try something new and interesting. To see if someone else rocks your boat before you book the life-long cruise as it were. Might be worth a try.'

It astounds me how Ceri can talk about 'trying' someone new, otherwise known as being completely unfaithful to the man who has asked me to marry him, as if she's talking about testing a new shampoo.

'Say Connor comes back in March and you say yes to his proposal,' Ceri persists, 'how do you know that you're not accepting second best if you haven't had a good look around? I mean, you don't plump for the first lipstick you can find; you test a few, see what suits and then choose the best one. Why settle for a manky last season Rimmel when you can have a hot new Revlon?'

'What? What are you talking about Ceri? Connor's not a manky lipstick.'

'But how do you know that unless you've had a good look around the make-up department?'

I scratch my nose with confusion. How did we get on to this subject anyway? I thought we were being focused career girls.

'I don't need a good look around the make-up department, thank you. I'm happy with Connor, he suits me fine.'

Ceri runs a shapely nail along one of her eyebrows. 'Yes, Angel, he may suit you fine but you haven't exactly had much experience in that area, have you? Or rather no experience other than Connor.'

I shift uncomfortably on my chair and while I think my eyes stray towards the toddler who has now turned his hair into a wig of salt and vinegar crisps. Of course this very question did occupy a space in my confused mind shortly before I told Connor that I needed time to think about getting married. Not that I want to go shagging every bloke with a pulse but I suppose Ceri does have a point. I don't have any complaints about Connor's performance in bed, even if he does need a little guidance sometimes like I'm sure ninety-nine per cent of the male population does, but I can't pretend to know any different. He is, after all, the only man to explore that previously uncharted territory. Bloody hell, Ceri has a real knack of creating doubts in my head, pouring in the ingredients and stirring them round and round like a candyfloss maker until my brain is equally as fluffy. I ruffle my hair and take a deep breath while Ceri grins at her achievement.

'You see, Angel, you do have doubts.'

'Stop it, Ceri, I do not have doubts. Anyway, this is all purely hypothetical. We are talking about a gorgeous European megastar who never speaks to the Press and is as untouchable as the Crown Jewels. I am an average-looking DJ on a Scottish radio station that is stuck in the Jurassic era, who can't even get Cheryl Baker to appear on her show. I hardly think he'll be begging to come on and then go ripping my knickers off with his teeth.'

'Oh, that's completely over-rated if you ask me.'

I can tell she is speaking from very recent experience; Ceri would never have the problem of surplus hormones just waiting for a chance to be released. No sooner has her sex drive recovered from the last session than she's off again giving it a jolly good workout. She's like an endurance athlete only she doesn't need trainers. Unlike yours truly who hasn't seen any action, obviously, since the day before Connor left. I shake myself when I realise I am staring into space, trying to remember what a real live orgasm feels like, with a man. I'm starting to resemble a pre-pubescent teenager all over again, except I haven't resorted to chatting up a poster on my bedroom wall or snogging my pillow. Although I have slept with Connor's James T-shirt on a number of occasions, breathing in his familiar smell that lingers on it to comfort me to sleep.

'OK, it is extremely hypothetical,' says Ceri, her words breaking into my hormonal reverie, 'but forgetting that we're all grown up and you're nearly a married woman and all that garbage, just pretend that Didier Lafitte wants to get you into bed for one night of passion and no one else in the world is ever going to find out.' Her eyes twinkle naughtily. 'Do you think you would do it?'

I laugh and think about her question for a moment.

'Ha!' she shrieks, pointing a spindly finger at me. 'Your delay is very telling, my friend.'

'Don't be daft,' I giggle, 'I'm only messing with you. Of course I wouldn't. I couldn't be unfaithful to Connor, it wouldn't be right.'

'Oh right shmight, who says what's right and wrong anyway? You thought you wouldn't be able to be on your own for six months without a boyfriend and from the looks of you, Angel, you're getting along just fine.'

'I have to get on with it. I can't just sit around and wait for him for half a year, can I?'

'Exactly. And don't pretend that you're not enjoying your new independence a teensy bit.'

I shrug.

'And it's doing you the world of good at work, putting all your efforts into the show, isn't it? You're much more focused than when Connor's here to distract you.'

I finish my tea and plonk the mug down heavily on the table. 'Can we get back to the point of this conversation and stop discussing me and Connor?' I snap.

'If you like,' Ceri pouts, checking out the nails on her right hand. 'I'm just trying to be there for you, Angel, to be a friend you can talk to.'

I sigh and feel guilty for getting annoyed with her when she is doing me a big favour including me in her gossip.

'Yes, I know, and thanks. But let's just get back to our visiting pop star and what we're going to do about him, in a *professional* way. So the great Didier Lafitte is doing an album signing at Meg's shop in one week's time, you say.'

Ceri nods her long blonde mane.

'But Meg hasn't mentioned it and she's the assistant manager. Does she know?'

'I doubt it. Meg's shop and all its contents could be whisked away to another planet with Meg in it and she wouldn't notice. Well, not until she came to go home and couldn't find the subway.'

'Don't be mean,' I frown.

'I don't know if she knows anyhow; it's all pretty hush-hush.'

Not any more, I think, now that the foghorn of Glasgow has got hold of the information. Didier Lafitte may as well send a press release to the BBC detailing his every move when he arrives in Scotland as most people will know by the time he gets here anyway.

'Now, as you know, he is not big on interviews.'

'Not big on them,' I snort, 'he's non-existent on them.'

'Precisely, which could mean either that he's an arrogant prick or that his management are just very tight on who they give access to. I'm sure that between us we have the skills to pin him down to a couple of little chats.'

'Skills?'

'Well, with my looks and charm and your ability to *parlez français* we are bound to get our feet in the door.'

'Er, thanks.' I think that's what you would call a back-handed compliment.

'So all we need to do is get our Megan, once she's genned up on all the movements of our star, to get us a couple of VIP passes to that album signing, lifting us above the masses, so to speak, then we can grab him and *voici*—'

'*Voilà*,' I correct her.

'And *voilà*, the sky's the limit and we'll both be famous. Easy.'

'Easy,' I repeat, although I very much doubt it. Nonetheless I have to admit it is the best chance I've got to land a guest above the level of an ageing school choir.

One week. Seven days to plan our attack and I am determined to make this work. This could be just the opportunity Dan and I need to change the face of Energy FM. One month into my mission and at last I have a target.

CHAPTER TWELVE

Say Hello, Wave Goodbye

In my new capacity as a high-flying, er, make that low-flying, workaholic, I waste no time in planning my 'attack' on Didier Lafitte. Ceri decides to wait until the day of the album signing to secure her interview by relying on the influence of her dazzling hair, even more dazzling smile and pert everything. I guess if I had her assets I would probably sit back, relax and spend the week gazing at myself in a mirror. I, on the other hand, get to work. I may not be able to compete with my friend on a level of technical gorgeousness, but as Ceri herself so delicately pointed out I do speak French.

First I do my research by buying all of Didier's albums, including his latest release 'Enigmatique'. I study the songs – also known as learning all the words and prancing around my lounge singing into a roll-on deodorant like a scene from *Fame* only without the dancing ability – to get into my subject's psyche. I tell Dan the plan, who whoops excitedly, runs around the studio waving his arms in the air and decides he will be gay on the day Didier shmoozes into our offices. You see, now I am talking as if it is a definite arrangement, another integral part of my mental preparation. However, Monsieur Lafitte is proving very difficult to pin down. In true megastar style he has so many 'people' he could be his own country. Finally, having tried to contact the popstar through his agent in the UK to no avail, I find out the name and address of his record company in France. I make a call every day but it seems that people in music are too cool to do such mundane things as answer the main switchboard. It must be direct lines or nothing. I leave what is amounting to an audio tape recording of *War And Peace* on their answering machine but of course a big fat no-one calls me back.

Suddenly I realise that the *Countdown* clock is almost at its last dooby do do dooo and tomorrow is the album signing. Doesn't time fly when you're walking on the spot making absolutely no progress? I can't be defeated, however. So I say a prayer to the Patron Saint of DJs, Saint Dave Lee Travis, down three espressos for energy, eat two chocolatines for luck and switch into French mode to make my final call.

'*Monsieur Lafitte ne donnera aucun interview en anglais*,' the receptionist informs me with what I can only describe as a blatant yawn.

OK, Monsieur Lafitte won't give any interviews in English, but do you really have to *yawn*, for crying out loud? Don't you know that this man you are so happily denying me any form of access to could mean the difference between me continuing as an unknown DJ on a crappy little station and me becoming the next big thing, desired by every radio station and photographed for every glossy as I do my shopping in Safeways? And I was only trying to use her popstar for my own selfish purposes; there's nothing wrong with that, is there? Not forgetting to bring joy and happiness to my listeners, of course.

After a very pronounced sigh from the other end of the line, indicating that our 'negotiation' is coming to a conclusion, I move to the very last resort tactic for getting close to Didier Lafitte. Feeling like a twelve-year-old caller to his fan club, I ask for a signed photograph. I've got to start somewhere.

'*Non*,' she huffs disinterestedly, '*je n'en ai plus*,' and puts down the phone.

'What do you mean you haven't got any left?' I snap. 'He's your only big popstar; the whole bloody office must be wallpapered with photographs of him. Thank you very much for your fantastic unhelpfulness, you useless bint, and I will make sure you get fired when I'm a very famous DJ and you're not.'

Of course I say this for effect because, as I said, she has already put the phone down. Nonetheless, it feels good. I don't really have the capacity to be rude to people on the phone – other than to my mother if she pushes me far enough – but I like to pretend. I slam down the receiver and trudge over to the freezer for a consolatory tub of ice cream. I guess I should have dinner before pudding but I can't be bothered to cook for one tonight (which is probably just as well as those espressos are really playing havoc with my ability to concentrate and I would probably end up burning down my flat or something). Besides, ice cream is a very good source of calcium . . . and chocolate fudge chips and chocolate sauce and pecan nuts.

'I didn't even want a stupid signed photograph,' I grumble

to myself, pushing the freezer door shut with my shoulder and coming face to face with the November page of my Official Didier Lafitte Calendar.

'And you can wipe that pout off your face too,' I scowl, poking his head with the end of my spoon, 'this is all your fault. If I can't get a few words from you then I've let everyone down – Dan, my listeners, G.G., myself – because I don't have many options left other than calling Aled Jones to see if he's free for a guest appearance.'

I swallow far too large a mouthful of ice cream and screw up my eyes as I experience the painful sensation of an ice cream headache.

'Oh why won't you give one frigging interview, you pillocky little popstar?' I growl at his flawless face. 'Can't you string a sentence together or are you just too damn arrogant to bother with the likes of me?'

He gazes back at me with his sultry, almost black eyes and sends a shiver down my spine.

'Well, we'll find out tomorrow, won't we?' I say, recovering my composure. 'Because tomorrow, Monsieur Lafitte, you and I are going to meet. So look out buster, I'm coming for you.'

I have never before seen so many skimpy outfits at five o'clock on a Thursday afternoon in Glasgow. It is freezing cold, the rain is lashing the streets and the sky is a heavy shade of grey and miserable. It must be about five degrees or less with the lovely addition of a northerly wind blowing the essence of the Arctic straight towards us. Yet here in Meg's shop you would think we were in the midst of a heady midwinter heatwave. The girls and boys have turned out in their hundreds, each one of the girls (and some of the boys) wearing so little that indecent exposure would be an understatement. There are even several pairs of teeny hotpants and, believe me, their owners are definitely not Kylie. It is an unbelievable sight and it is all because of Didier Lafitte – due to arrive in ten minutes and already causing hormonal surges that would blow the National Grid.

I have opted for a more casual/smart look – my favourite jeans with glittery stars around the bottom of the legs, a crisp white shirt and a pair of high rainbow wedge-heeled shoes which I like to think of as my lucky wedges (largely because I have never fallen off them and twisted my ankle). I am shifting my bottom nervously on the cash desk, which it turns out is the extent of the VIP area, much to Ceri's disgust. Thanks to Meg, the VIPs are myself and Ceri, who is dressed in a black leather dress slashed to the armpit, and the manager's eleven-year-old daughter. Wow, I have really made it. I have decided that my best bet for getting close to the megastar himself is to glue myself to Meg when he arrives because she carries a certain amount of official status as assistant manager – emphasised by her red and yellow uniform and her assistant manager badge – so she may be able to boss people around and get me to the front of the queue. I will also keep Ceri close at hand because any man who fails to notice her divine body, silken locks and BJ lips is either in need of an emergency appointment at Vision Express or is dead. I am, therefore, hoping for attention by association and the chance to slip in my request in my best French. I have to admit to feeling the onset of adrenalin even at these early stages. Super-dry Sure better not let me down.

'He's coming!' Meg shrieks, rushing towards us and

waving her staff walkie-talkie in the air like a commemorative flag.

A wave of excitement courses through the room and I'm sure I see every pair of boobs grow at least two sizes by being thrust up and out by their owners.

'Why, thank you for your discretion, Megan,' Ceri sneers. 'I am so glad we have the honour of knowing that news before the rest of the population of Glasgow. Perhaps you could shout a little louder next time and his granny in France will be able to hear that he's arrived safely.'

'Och, sorry, I'm just so excited. I'm gonna wet myself, so I am. Didier fucken' Lafitte in *my* shop. Isn't it pure dead brilliant?'

Ceri pulls a tiny silver compact from her bag and checks her lipstick. 'Hmm, well, I just hope this French boy is all he's cracked up to be. I'm missing a one-to-one with Texas to be here.'

'The country or the band?' Meg giggles.

'Texas isn't a country, you moron, it's a state,' Ceri scoffs, looking down her nose at Meg's uniform polo shirt. 'A bit like you really.'

But nothing can dampen Meg's good humour as another message crackles through on her walkie-talkie, which is in itself exciting enough for our Meg even without the imminent arrival of a gorgeous-looking and much adored popstar.

'Big Ten Four Rubber Ducky,' she whoops into the speaker before turning to us and beaming, 'Girls, hold on to your fannies, the lurve machine is in the building.'

He is stunning. Tall, dark, handsome, lean, toned, seductive, mysterious and every adjective synonymous with stunning.

Even more stunning than Ceri and that is saying something. In fact, to have two such stunning people in one building must have about the same probability as winning the Lotto or being hit by lightning ten times. I for one feel as though I've been hit by lightning. The chemistry this man brings to the room is electrifying.

'Pull yourself together, girl,' I scold myself, hopping from one foot to the other in my place in the queue.

The VIP section apparently doesn't carry any benefit other than Meg being able to direct us to halfway down the long snake of people waiting to have their 'Enigmatique' album signed by Didier's own fair hand. The manager's daughter is of course escorted to the front of the queue, at which point I have to forcibly restrain Ceri from pulling the little girl's hair with jealousy. Anyway, after an hour of patient waiting I am now just a few people from the front. Ceri is right behind me, her disgruntled groans and sighs audible above the screams of Didier's fans.

'I wish he would bloody well hurry up,' Ceri hisses, poking her head around the side of the line to see what is happening, 'All he has to do is write his own name. I bet he can't even spell.'

'Not long now,' I say happily. 'Look, we're almost there.'

I grin at a young girl who has just had her album signed and is almost floating towards the front door.

'Not before time,' Ceri tuts, 'I don't do queues. This is way below me.'

'All in the name of business, darling,' I smile, turning round to look at her. 'Just think how good it will be for your gossip column when he agrees to hang out with you and give you the red-hot scoop.'

Ceri shrugs. 'Oh, I can do without him. He's not that special. He's just a lanky karaoke singer.'

'Yeah right, Miss Divine, which is why when he walked in you stood on that cash desk and shouted, "Didier, *dahling*, over here!" Or were you simply looking for a chance to let him know that he's a wanky, lanky, talentless, French karaoke wannabe?'

Ceri raises an eyebrow and moves a lock of hair behind her ear. 'Don't be facetious, Angel. I was just trying to attract his attention for you.'

'Thanks,' I smirk, 'and it really worked.'

Ceri is in a mood because our megastar has so far ignored her usually overpowering presence. I am intrigued to see what will happen when we finally reach the silver table and the man behind it. I haven't met a popstar up close before. This is a whole new experience. We move one step nearer to the table and I giggle with anticipation.

'Do you think he's going to say yes, Ceri? D'you reckon he'll come on my show if I'm really, really nice?'

'I have no idea, Angel, but if we have been standing here all this time for sweet f.a. I am going to give him a piece of my mind.'

'Ooh, I bet Didier's never had a piece of someone's mind before.'

'Maybe he should think about borrowing a piece of mind,' Ceri tuts. 'It might make him a bit bloody quicker at signing those sodding albums.'

I step to the side and peer around the group of girls in front of us to check our progress. Four more lots of fans and then us. Brilliant. I run a hand through the front of my hair to check that my fringe is still erratically spiky – you know, the non-styled look that takes a lot of styling – and I am about to step back into line when Didier Lafitte stops writing on the CD cover and looks up. I stand frozen to the spot for a second as our eyes lock together. He is looking straight at me. Didier Lafitte is looking at me. With those smoky eyes and that jawline and that tanned complexion. Before I can stop them my lips mouth 'hello'. At that moment a thick strand of Didier's shoulder-length black hair slides across his face and falls over his left eye. He blinks and our connection is broken. Realising that my mouth is wide open and that I have forgotten to breathe, I quickly hop back into the line next to Ceri and gasp for air. Ceri stares at me as if I've just sprouted horns.

'What is up with you, asthma girl? You're not pretending to faint so that you get rushed to the front of the queue are you?'

'Er no,' I stammer, struggling to calm the hormones that are whizzing around my body and bending down to collect the contents of my bag that I have succeeded in emptying on to the floor. I shove everything back in, stand up and clasp Ceri's arm, which is rather like holding on to a breadstick only it is covered in black leather.

'He looked at me,' I say in a loud whisper, 'he's gorgeous.'

'My, my,' Ceri smirks, turning to look at my reddening face, 'our little virgin has finally found someone else on the planet attractive other than Connor McLean. I never thought I would see the day.'

'Oh behave,' I scowl, 'this is different. He's not a real person, he's a popstar.'

'A popstar who is very real and very alive at the end of this line, honey, and after this lot of teenagers we're next.'

I gulp as the group of girls ahead of us step up to the table. Luckily they take up enough room to completely conceal our target until I have had a minute to compose myself and remember what I am going to say. I must be calm. I must concentrate. Although I would be able to concentrate a lot better if that plonker would answer their bloody mobile phone. That ringtone is so irritating. I turn to Ceri with a frown when she taps me on the shoulder.

'Answer your phone would you, Angel? And get a new ringtone while you're at it, that one's really irritating.'

I manage to blush on top of my blushes and forage in my bag for my mobile. Did I forget to put my brain in this morning? My head feels like one giant jellyfish. I continue to rummage until the ringing stops, when I take a deep breath and try to relax. Before I have time to exhale, however, the ringing starts again. I put my head down and search for the phone while it rings incessantly. It is then that I see two pairs of enormous feet approaching at speed.

'Got it!' I shriek, pulling the phone out of my bag and thrusting it in the faces of the hulks who must be two of Didier's 'people'. Only these are people with big heads and big muscles and even bigger frowns. The frowns grow more pronounced as my phone – which appears to be trying to ring at the top of its voice – blasts in their angry faces.

'No mobiles,' grunts one.

'Turn it off,' grunts the other.

I fumble with the buttons but my fingers suddenly seem to have turned into long sausages of Dairylea and are completely uncontrollable.

'Jesus Christ,' Ceri spits, 'turn the bloody thing off, Angel, you're causing a scene.'

'I'm trying,' I hiss back, struggling with the phone, my bag and Didier's CD. Too late: the bouncers grab me by the elbows and drag me away from the line towards the exit.

'No mobiles,' snorts giant number one again.

'I know that,' I whine, breathing a sigh of relief as they deposit me at the door and the blasted phone immediately stops ringing. 'Phew,' I laugh, 'sorry about that, guys.'

I delicately extract my arms from their steak-like hands and smile inanely.

'No mobiles,' snarls number one.

I am beginning to think that this is the extent of his vocabulary, although I suppose that's not bad for a brick shithouse.

'Security,' says number two.

'Yes, I gathered that,' I smile, 'but it is only a phone, after all. Just a few microwaves so no harm done, ha ha, unless Mr Lafitte's an android and the microwaves will interfere with his circuits, ha ha.'

They stare at me with hard faces. I bite my lip, wobble on my wedges and look around for Meg or Ceri but they are far too interested in someone else not too far away to be concerned about my welfare.

'Righty ho then,' I whistle, patting both men on their huge arms, 'I'll just get back in line, shall I? Panic over.'

'Turn the phone off,' orders number two.

'Oh, sure. Sorry.'

Using very deliberate movements so as not to distress them, I hold up the phone, point my index finger towards the off button and am just about to press it when the phone rings for the third time.

'Shit,' I exclaim.

I look at the screen and note that the persistent caller is my dad. This can mean one of two things – either he is in the middle of a medical emergency or he is pissed. Whichever it is, I have to take the call. And so, with a sinking heart, I nod to my two new 'pals' and slip out of the glass doors on to the street.

'Hi Dad, how are you? Only I'm a bit b—'

'Went for a fish supper, Angel,' he says, only it sounds more like, 'Wen fer flishuper, Ange.'

I recognise the slurred words and the audible furriness of his tongue. My father is clearly very drunk but I will do my best to translate.

'You shouldn't have so many fish suppers, Dad, they're bad for you.'

'I know,' he slurs as I lean against a wall for support, 'it hurts.'

I clasp my chest in panic. 'What hurts, Dad? Your heart? Does your chest hurt?'

Oh my God, my dad's having a heart attack.

'No,' he says, 'punch hurts.'

'Punch? What punch? Who punched you, Dad?'

'Man in chippy. Big man. Big punch. Hurts.'

I stand up straight and push the phone closer to my ear to make sure I am hearing him right.

'Are you telling me that you got in a fight? Dad, you don't get in fights, you're not the fighting type.'

'I know. I didn't fight.'

'Oh.'

'Didn't punch him back.'

'Oh dear.'

'Hit me three times. It hurts.'

I close my eyes and marvel at my world. At how only five minutes ago I was inches away from meeting a pop megastar who would perhaps have catapulted my career into the stars, or at least somewhere above the smothering atmosphere, and now here I am back down to earth with a bump before I even got a good view of the moon.

'Are you all right then, Dad?' I ask, softening my voice as he is clearly distressed.

'No. Two years.'

'Oh shit, please tell me you're not going to prison. You're not calling me from the police station?'

'No. Two years since she left.'

Suddenly it hits me. Now I know what all this is about. There is usually a reason behind it and eleven times out of ten it begins with Delphine. It is two years since my mother left and I didn't even remember. I blush at my own selfishness and feel a twinge of pain for my sad, lonely father who must have been so distraught all day that he went home, got himself drunk and then went out to annoy the wrong man in a chip shop queue.

'Don't worry, Dad,' I say gently, 'you'll be OK. I'm coming over. Give me half an hour.'

I press the off button, finding it instantly this time, and briefly turn to look at the scene through the sparkling shop window. Ceri is now hogging the silver table, thrusting her body towards a startled-looking Didier Lafitte and oozing the sex appeal of an entire warren of Playboy bunnies. I smile weakly as all my hopes of making my show a real success (and meeting a gorgeous singer in the process) fade away like the pipedreams they were.

'Good luck, Ceri,' I whisper, pressing my hand gently against the window. I turn sadly away and head for the station and the next train to Paisley.

CHAPTER THIRTEEN

Ironic

My journey to work the next day is like slow torture and I'm not just talking about the tiny orange train that rocks and rumbles its way from Hillhead to Buchanan Street, although if it were much noisier the passengers would have to wear industrial earplugs. I am tired after a very late night consoling my dad and trying to make him drink pints of water rather than whisky, and it seems that posters of Didier Lafitte in various states of undress have spread throughout the rail network overnight like an extremely virulent computer virus. He is everywhere and, despite his oiled six-pack and aesthetically pleasing face, he is really starting to piss me off. Especially as this noisy Clockwork Orange is currently propelling me towards a meeting with G.G. MacDougal to discuss the progress Dan and I have made with *Angel on Air* over the last few weeks. As it stands, I am praying to every God I can think of that either Dan has realised overnight that he is directly related to a megastar like Britney Spears or that G.G. got eighteen holes-in-one on the golf course this morning. Fat chance and fat chance.

'Oooh, how was it, how was it, how was it?' Dan screeches, racing across the marbled reception area and practically diving headfirst into the lift. 'Did you get his autograph for me? Did he kiss you when he gave you the album? Did he say yes to coming on the show? Is he as gorgeous in real life as he is in those posters that are every-bleedinwhere this morning?'

I hold up my hand to encourage him to stop and take a breath.

'Er, no, no, no and more,' I reply without smiling.

Dan's boyish face loses its sparkle and he slumps his shoulders.

'So you didn't get an autograph?'

I shake my head.

'And he's not coming on the show?'

I keep shaking my head.

'Bummer. Did you actually go to the signing thing? I knew I should have taken the afternoon off and made sure you got there.'

'Of course I went to the signing but there were lots of people there and some things happened, my dad happened for one, so I didn't get the chance to ask him.'

'Oh.'

Dan reaches out and sympathetically touches my arm. An alien voice in the lift informs us that we have reached the sixth floor. We step out and begin to trudge towards G.G.'s office with all the enthusiasm of a pair of mice walking into a cattery.

'Is that it then, do you think?' Dan asks, clearly trying not to sound too depressed at the prospect. 'Has he gone?'

'No. Meg told me that he's doing something at BBC Scotland tonight, and then apparently he's staying in the country for a bit of a holiday but I don't know where. She found that out by sneaking some freebies to one of his more pliable people.'

'Well, we could always take a trip to the BBC and have a go. That's up near you, isn't it?'

'Yeah, at the end of my road, but I don't know, Dan, they have pretty tight security around him.' I cringe at the thought. 'And he seems to be a real hard nut to crack. Ceri asked him for an interview for *Star* and even thrust her cleavage in his face and Meg says he didn't flinch. Not a hint of drooling or anything. Amazing. Ceri thinks he must be gay but I think he just hates the Press and all that publicity stuff.'

'Bollocks,' Dan groans as we come to a halt at the outer door of G.G.'s castle.

'Yep, and speaking of which I would hold on to them, mate, because I've got the feeling Mr MacDougal is about to kick us both right where it hurts.'

We both hold our breath when, as we wait for G.G. to join us in his office, Marjory enters the room with two cups of coffee and a tea plate on a tray. I peer at the plate and relax a little when I see the two custard creams, which she plonks down in front of us on the desk. Phew, the same biscuits as in our first meeting five weeks ago. It is only when we gingerly take a bite that Dan and I realise our rating has slipped. These are hideously stale custard creams. I swallow my mouthful and feel a sense of impending doom.

'You're not related to Britney Spears are you, Dan?' I whisper.

He shakes his head and frowns.

I cling to the biscuit and pray for that hole-in-one.

'Daniel, Angie,' G.G. booms, bursting loudly into the office.

I whip my head round to greet him but immediately whip it back when I catch a glimpse of his outfit. Tartan plus-fours, a checked Pringle tank top over a crisp lime green shirt and a tartan flat cap. His dyed chestnut hair is slicked behind his ears, I suspect with Grecian 2000, and an unlit cigar hangs from the corner of his mouth. I feel as if I've stumbled across a Jimmy Tarbuck charity golf day. Either that or an inappropriate use of plaids and checks conference. No wonder this radio station can't attract a half decent guest from the music world; the only 'garage' our controller has heard of is the one he keeps his golf buggy in.

'I am rather busy, Daniel and Angie,' G.G. says sharply to us – or at least to *me* and the top of Dan's head, as my producer suddenly seems to be finding a spot of dust on the floor rather hypnotising – 'so I will keep this brief.'

He perches on the edge of his desk and picks up a glossy white golf ball from his desk tidy, rolling it between his palms as he speaks.

'It is duly noted that your playlists have improved, at least in the opinion of some of the younger and less well-educated members of my executive staff, since we last spoke.'

'Thank you we—'

'The ratings are up by a certain amount,' G.G. interrupts without even acknowledging my attempt to speak, 'but that could be due to a number of reasons which I won't go into now – advertising and so forth.'

Advertising? I think to myself, *What advertising? A free ad in the back of* Golfers Monthly?

'Now our last discussion,' he continues, rubbing the golf ball vigorously and staring longingly out of the window, 'was some six weeks ago.'

'Five,' I correct him quietly.

'Five, six, still an ample amount of time for you to have found this star guest you promised us.'

I shift on the leather chair that is becoming increasingly hot and uncomfortable. Dan keeps his eyes focused on the floor.

'Well,' I begin when I realise that Dan has left his voice-box outside the door again.

'You see, your playlist improvements and the ideas you put forward,' G.G. butts in again, 'have made us realise the potential for a show like *Angel on Air*.'

I lift my chin and smile at our boss.

'Indeed, we believe *Angel on Air* could be our flagship show . . .'

My smile almost touches both ears.

'. . . a show for the lunchtime and afternoon audience that spans the generations, dealing with important issues during the phone-ins while bringing great music and a little sparkle into the lives of our listeners by using the magic touch of a special guest.'

Er, sounds great, G.G., but wasn't that our idea?

'This show could be big, really big. We have had talks and we truly believe that this could catapult Energy FM into the next century.'

How about trying for this century first?

'That's fantastic, G.G.,' I beam, 'and we both really feel that potential too.'

I nudge Dan who raises his eyes and nods nervously.

'Jolly good, so we are on the same wavelength. Or should I say the same radio wave.'

He finishes with a wink in my direction and I indulge his weak joke with a forced smile.

'So, you understand my dilemma?' says G.G., closing his mouth into a tight asterisk.

My shoulders, which had begun to relax in the last few minutes, tense up again and I frown. Dilemma? What dilemma? My show is going to be great, I'm going to be famous, Dan will be a legendary producer, blah de blah, everyone goes home rich, famous and happy. I can't see any dilemma there.

Dan and I both look at our boss in confusion, which I suppose is why he then proceeds to don a sympathetic expression and a tone of voice that suggests he is addressing a class of remedial teenagers.

'My dilemma is that you brought the potential of the show to our attention, and you went some way to reaching that potential, but since then, Daniel and Angie, you appear to have reached a plateau. We see the special guest as rather essential to the show's future yet you don't seem to have done anything to fulfil this part of the bargain.'

If only you knew, G.G., if only you knew.

'In fact, you have not even presented us with any potential ideas for a guest. Now would there be a reason for this?'

I consider explaining that we have lots of lovely ideas, thank you, it's just that no one *wants* to come on our show, but my common sense tells me to keep a lid on all that. After all, we don't want to seem as if we lack either the professional negotiating capacity or the celebrity pull to attract any guests worth attracting. The fact is we lack this in spades but I can't go telling G.G. that, can I?

Instead, Dan mumbles, 'We have been making some progress but . . .', his words trailing off as he hits the brick wall at the end of his conversational cul-de-sac.

'The thing is,' G.G. sighs, now throwing the golf ball from one hand to the other and clearly desperate to run out of the room (as am I but for very different reasons), 'running this station requires a lot of time and energy on my part.'

I stifle the snort that is threatening to erupt from my nostrils.

'Which is why I need staff I can rely on to do their bit and make a mountain of effort for the good of the station. Do you understand?'

We nod.

'Now, if either or both of you are unable or unwilling to make the effort to attract a star guest, or at least to come to me with ideas, then either or both of you may not be completely indispensable.'

He stands away from the desk and it is obvious that our meeting is over. Dan and I wobble to our feet and slink towards the door. I suspect Marjory has had a glass pressed to the other side and is enjoying every minute of this discussion.

'Now,' G.G. smiles as we reach the door, 'show me some real progress within one week and everything will be just fine.'

One week. Bloody hell, I may as well pack up my headphones now . . .

'No problem, G.G.,' Dan pipes up, seemingly discovering his vocal chords at the office door. 'In fact, Angel here has a very promising lead in that area. There is a rather famous French popstar in town this very night and, believe it or not, Angel has a meeting with him.'

My mouth drops open and I stare at Dan, willing him either to shut up or to disappear into a very large hole in the office floor.

'We were going to keep it quiet until everything was near enough finalised, a surprise if you like, but you need to know and I am sure we will have something exciting for you by the end of next week.'

'Marvellous,' G.G. gushes while ushering us out of the door. 'I knew you wouldn't let me down.'

'Marvellous,' Dan repeats as we stride quickly past Marjory.

'Wanker,' I mutter, grinding my teeth.

'God, isn't he just?' Dan giggles under his breath.

'Not him, Dan, *you*. You're the wanker and thanks to you I am up shit creek without a boat, never mind a friggin' paddle.'

What am I doing? Ten minutes ago I was standing in my kitchen having a career discussion with my Didier Lafitte calendar and now here I am running, yes running, up Byres Road towards the BBC Scotland building. If Meg's information is correct, Didier Lafitte is there this evening to record a performance of his latest release, 'Confidence', for a BBC show, and I am damned if I am going to let him escape from me this time without at least a modicum of effort on my part. Especially since Dan has practically promised G.G. that I will have a French popstar in his in-tray in some shape or form by next Friday afternoon. I can't let this career slip away from me without a fight, not least because I am about four pedal revolutions from thirty on my bike-ride up the hill of life. Not that I'm worried about that or anything, in fact I've hardly given it a second thought. But you must agree that thirty is a milestone and losing the job that I love – despite the fact that it is still a fair climb from the pinnacle of radio – a week before my birthday would be nothing short of a complete bummer.

I reach the end of Byres Road, dash across the busy lanes of traffic shooting along Great Western Road and jog (I'm pacing myself) up Queen Margaret's Drive towards my destination. I come to a breathless stop close to the rear of The Kibble Palace and bend forwards with my hands on my knees to rest my aching body. Twenty-nine and already incapable of running five hundred metres without a cardiac arrest. I make a mental note to do something about this when I get a spare moment, starting with buying a jazzy new pair of trainers. Essential sports equipment, naturally.

'Wish me luck, wishing pool,' I say under my breath to the glass dome visible above the hedge before marching across the road and into the building.

I instantly regret not having worn high heels or at least a power suit when I approach the female receptionist and don my best polite smile only to be greeted with a stare that would make Rambo tremble.

'Can I help you, er, madam?' the woman asks, scanning me up and down with distrust.

'Yes,' I chirp, while discreetly trying to wipe a liquid

moustache of sweat from my top lip, 'I have come to see Didier Lafitte.'

I shuffle my feet in my comfy Kicker loafers and self-consciously pick an imaginary piece of fluff from my skinny rib jumper.

'And you are?' she replies after an unhealthy pause.

Knackered, perspiring and desperate.

'Er, Angel, Angel Knights.'

'Angel? Is that your real name, madam?'

Cheeky cow.

'Y . . . yes, it is. Why, do you not let heavenly bodies into the building? Ha ha.'

She looks at me as if I have just thrown up all over her desk. I bite my lip and repeat my name.

'And is Mr Lafitte expecting you, Ms Knights?'

'Well, no, not really, but I'm sure it'll be fine. So he is here then?' I squeak excitedly.

This is it. I am going to pull this off.

'I am not permitted to give out that information, madam, and unless you have an appointment I can not let you past this desk.'

Oh pleeease, I want to wail, *pleeease let me in, I have to see him. You don't know how much I have to see him.*

'I'm sure you can if you want to,' I smile mischievously, 'and I'll make it worth your while.'

'I am not open to bribes, thank you, Ms Knights. Now if you don't have an appointment I suggest you leave the way you came in.'

I consider stamping my feet and throwing a tantrum but restrain myself and simply stand steadfast in front of the desk. The receptionist does her best to ignore me but finds this difficult with only a switchboard, a pen, a notepad and a packet of mini rice-cakes to keep her distracted.

Eventually she taps her pen on the desk, sighs dramatically and groans, 'Are you a fan?'

'No!' I retort, increasing the volume of my voice above a commotion erupting behind me in the reception area. 'Well, yes, I mean, I *like* Didier Lafitte but not in that way. I just need to meet him. It's very important – very, very, *very* important.'

'*Excusez-moi*!' shouts a voice that is deep and silky with an almost musical French lilt. I immediately know it is him.

'Mr Lafitte,' gushes the receptionist as he strides confidently towards the desk, 'I was just trying to stop this woman from bothering you.' Raising her eyes to the ceiling she adds, 'She's a *fan*.'

'I am NOT a FAN!' I growl before my brain can tell my mouth to button it. 'I mean, I am a . . . oh.'

He is suddenly beside me, staring into my blushing face with his smouldering dark eyes. I whistle quietly and try to stop my legs trembling.

'She is not a fan,' he says firmly and I feel his hot breath rush past my cheek. Blimey. If I could bottle that stuff I'd make an absolute fortune. I smile nervously when I realise that he is still peering curiously at me as if I am a piece of modern art.

'I didn't mean to be rude,' I whisper, 'it's just I am here for another reason, not as a fan. That's all I meant.'

God, if I were any more vague I would be a faded pencil sketch of myself.

'Shall I get rid . . .?' the receptionist begins, but clamps her mouth shut when Didier Lafitte raises a slim hand and snaps, 'Quiet! Please.'

Hmm, masterful. I never quite realised how attractive that could be. I watch, mesmerised, as he tilts his head, causing his thick hair to spread in a fan shape across his left shoulder, black and shiny against his crisp white shirt. It is the same colour as Connor's hair, I note, only more dramatic. I quickly look down at my feet but I am unable to stop my eyes moving slowly down the long legs of his jeans, from his muscular thighs to the shiny boots on his perfectly proportioned feet. Shit, this is not what I came here for; I am not supposed to be finding this man attractive. The fact that I have not had *real* sex (no need to elaborate, you know what I mean) for almost two months may have something to do with my hormone-charged reaction to the presence of a megastar. I metaphorically kick myself. This is *business*, Angel, purely business . . . But fuck, he's sexy.

'Right, well, the thing is,' I say loudly, forcing myself to look into his tanned face, 'I wanted to have a chat with you, er, Didier, because—'

'I know you,' he interrupts, placing a hand on my shoulder.

'Do you?' I ask, almost swallowing my tongue with shock.

'Do you?' repeats the receptionist who appears to be turning a vivid shade of green.

'*Oui, oui, je vous connais*. I know you.'

I wrinkle my nose in a frown while my shoulders freeze under his grip.

'You were at my album signing yesterday,' he nods. 'You wore rainbow shoes.'

When eventually I roll my tongue back into my mouth I manage a squeaky 'Yes' in response.

He noticed my shoes. Didier Lafitte noticed me and my shoes. I knew he had clocked me but I had no idea he had noticed me in that much detail which, for a bloke, you must agree is bloody good. They are my lucky wedges after all. I make a mental note to retrieve them from the dark corner I moodily kicked them into after the signing. I then make an additional mental note to buy seven pairs and wear them every day of the week from now on.

'I wanted to speak to you actually but before you arrived at the front of the queue you ran away,' he adds with a touch more softness.

'Oh yes, sorry about that. I had to . . . I had some business to attend to.'

'No problem,' he replies abruptly.

In fact he is clearly too well practised at that abruptness thing. It must come from being famous and having a whole posse of people pandering to your every whim. A whole posse of people who are at this moment crowding around us like an army of nameless stormtroopers.

'It is *vraiment* no problem,' he repeats as I hop nervously from one foot to the other, 'but I wanted to see you.'

I catch my breath and stare at the ground. This is weird. This is very weird. Here I am standing face to face with *the* Didier Lafitte and unless I am very much mistaken he is flirting with me. Now this may be part and parcel of everyday life for someone like Ceri but I'm so used to being with Connor I've forgotten what it feels like to be flirted with. Especially by a man like this.

'I wanted to see you too,' I reply, cringing at my own lack of inspired conversation.

The receptionist emits a snort.

'And here we are,' he smiles, the lights above us reflecting off his perfectly white teeth, 'seeing each other.'

He reaches out a hand and I extend my own in preparation for a handshake, but I almost wet myself when he holds my fingers, pulls me towards him and kisses me on the cheek. Oh God, kisses me on *both* cheeks. Bloody hell.

'*Enchanté*,' he breathes into my ear, which sends a shiver down my neck and all the way through my body to the soles of my feet. '*Enchanté*, Angel Knights.'

At the sound of my own name, my head immediately expands to the size of a prize watermelon. He knows my name. I'm famous. I am fucking famous! And here I was thinking that I didn't even have a following to speak of in Glasgow when all the while I had an unknown fan base on mainland France. I didn't even know our station signal travelled that far.

'I have your phone number,' he says before I can offer him my official DJ autograph.

The penny drops. He has my phone number. He has my phone number because I made several hundred calls to his people last week and one of the messages must have got through to him. I smile at my own delusions of grandeur.

'Oh, you got my messages.'

He shakes his head and frowns.

'No, I did not get any messages. Did you call me?'

Only until my dialling finger was reduced to a stump.

'Er, yeah, a couple of times but it doesn't matter.'

OK, this is getting far too confusing now. How does this man know my name and claim to have my phone number if it wasn't as a result of my calls? Popstars *have* stalkers, they don't *become* stalkers. Do they?

'I recognised you immediately, from the photo,' he says to

add to my confusion, 'the photograph that your darling mother has shown me back in France.'

My *darling* mother? Surely he has got me confused with someone else? My mother is many things but she's not what I would call a darling. However, Didier seems so certain and he did know my name. I am surprised that Delphine has a picture of me at all, not to mention the fact that she is proud enough of it to show it off to someone else. Delphine is proud of me. I smile self-indulgently.

'Plus,' he adds, 'you are truly much prettier in real life than your mother said you were. I *like* your curves.'

The image of Delphine as a proud mother showing countless pictures of her beautiful daughter to strangers in the street vanishes into thin air.

'I'm sorry,' I say with an apologetic dip of my head, 'but I am a bit confused. How did you see a photo of me that my mother had?'

'Oh, pardon me. I was there in Bordeaux visiting my mother before I left for this trip. Your mother has shown me your photograph so that I would recognise you when we met,' he chirps, as if it is the most natural thing in the world that he's been hanging out at my mother's house.

Oh shit, please tell me you're not her boyfriend. I would definitely have to puke.

The receptionist is straining her pointy witch ears to earwig our conversation. The stormtroopers are hopping around him like jumping beans out of their box.

'I am sorry, my English is bad, I must be confusing you,' he smiles, I guess in response to the deep frown forming on my brow.

He takes my hand again. His palm is soft and a lot cooler

than mine as my sweat glands appear to have gone into overdrive.

'N . . . no, your English is great,' I stammer, 'but I am still a bit confused. Sorry, you must think I'm a right dimwit.'

'Dimwit,' he laughs. He looks good when he laughs, much warmer and more approachable. 'Dimwit. I like this word. I can see that you are going to teach me some very good English.'

'Am I?'

'*Oui*. That is why your mother has given me your telephone number. In Bordeaux, Delphine and my mother, they are best friends. And when I was there Delphine has told me to come and find you in Glasgow in order that you can help me with my English. I was going to call you but I have been very busy.'

He nods his head towards the stormtroopers. I smile and raise my eyes to the ceiling as if in agreement that it can be a right drag being an incredibly famous sex symbol. Without saying a word, Didier clicks his fingers and as if by magic a small card is immediately thrust into his palm. Pif, pof, poof, just like the Great Soprendo. I look from his smiling face to the glossy card in my hand and back again. Didier Lafitte's phone number. Didier Lafitte's personal mobile phone number. My mother. His mother. Best friends. Maybe I'll just collapse right here on the spot and then when I come round everything will be back to normal.

'*Didier, allons-y*,' commands a voice behind him.

He nods his head gravely without turning towards the voice. 'I am told I must go now,' he says softly.

'*Oui, j'ai compris*.'

'Well, of course you understand, Angelique, I forget that you are French too.'

'Half French,' I cough.

'But twice as beautiful.'

I manage not to wet myself when Didier leans forward again and kisses me gently on both cheeks. My skin burns with the heat of his touch. I look away bashfully, briefly catching the murderous look in the eyes of my friend the receptionist. If I had a set of fireworks to hand I would let them off right here in this reception. My mother knows Didier Lafitte. And more to the point, my mother has come good at last and made the path as smooth as velvet for me to know Didier Lafitte. He knows me, he knows I am a DJ and part of the industry and it clearly doesn't bother him at all. I can't believe it; my job is saved and my show is going to be legendary. That interview is as good as mine. Super-stardom here I come. After phoning my *darling* mother to thank her first, of course.

'At last I meet Angel Knights,' he says, 'the beautiful nurse.'

'Beautiful?' I grin, 'I wouldn't exactly—' Hold on a petite minute there, monsieur – 'nurse?' My grin fades instantly, like a shaken Etch-a-Sketch picture.

'A very honourable job,' he nods, waving his hand, 'not like all this music business.'

'Oh,' I grimace, 'yeah, but you see, the thing is—'

'And so, Angelique,' he says, placing his hands in the front pockets of his jeans, 'I must leave but I call you tomorrow, yes?'

'Yes,' I reply instantly.

'And then we can, how you say, hang out? And you can tell me all about being a nurse.'

'About being a nurse,' I mouth, my voice barely audible.

Darling Delphine, you lying old hag. Proud of me, huh. She may have one sodding photo to bandy around her friends but she still can't bring herself to tell them what her only child does for a living. He thinks I'm a nurse. He bloody well thinks I'm a frigging nurse. My chances of landing that interview have just diminished by about ninety-nine per cent, unless I keep the questions restricted to nurses' uniforms and the National Health Service. While I contemplate the choice words I will use on the phone to my mother, Didier gives a small wave, turns and glides from the building into a waiting limo. The stormtroopers march out behind him and dart into a convoy of vehicles with blacked-out windows before disappearing into the night.

'That was Didier Lafitte,' I grin to the receptionist, who is currently making a voodoo doll in my likeness behind the desk. There may have been a slight blip in the proceedings but I have to make the most of the moment, don't I?

'Yes, I know,' she replies, faking a pleasant smile. 'Um, if you like I could help with those English lessons.'

'Sure,' I smirk as I strut towards the door like a peacock with new feathers, 'thanks for the offer. If he wants to know the definition of a rude, unhelpful and snobby cow I'll know exactly where to send him.'

I think mixing with fame has already started to go to my head. I turn on my heels, flap my new feathers and float all the way home.

I am halfway through the door of my flat when the phone starts to ring. Blimey, he doesn't waste any time, does he? We only said *adieu* less than fifteen minutes ago. I race down the hallway and throw myself towards the phone, panting like Anneka Rice on *Treasure Hunt*.

'H . . . hello,' I splutter, sniffing and coughing all at once.

There is a brief pause and I hold my breath, largely to stop myself coughing a lung into the receiver but also with the anticipation of hearing his voice at the other end.

'Angel? Angel, baby, are you all right?'

Jesus Christ, it's Connor. My boyfriend Connor, whom I had as good as forgotten as soon as I found myself face to face with a popstar. My whole body blushes with guilt. Talk about spectacular timing, and I thought only women had that female intuition thing; unless they've just brought out a male version in America and Connor bought himself the package.

'CONNOR,' I shout far too enthusiastically, '*brill*iant to hear your voice.'

'Angel, are you OK?' Connor asks with genuine concern. 'You sound all weird.'

'Me? Noooo,' I wheeze. 'I'm fine, everything's fine. Fine and dandy.'

There is a delay as my sentence filters its way across the Atlantic.

'Right, OK, it must be the line then. But have you got a cold? You're all breathless.'

'No,' I reply sharply, 'I'm fine. One hundred and twenty per cent fine.'

'*Fine*. That's all right then, I guess. So, what are you up to, my Angel?'

'Up to? What's that supposed to mean? I'm not "up to" anything.'

Me? Guilty? Never!

'Ehm, I just mean what are you doing? Anything exciting happening?'

'Exciting? No, not really. All the same here, Con; nothing ever happens as Del Amitri would say, ha ha.'

Apart from the fact that the biggest pop idol in Europe has just kissed me a total of four times – twice on each cheek – which I happened to enjoy rather too much for a non-single girl, and that the said pop idol has my phone number and I have his and he is going to call me tomorrow. Apart from that, nothing exciting is happening at all.

'Oh well, as long as you're OK. You said you'd call earlier and you didn't so I was a wee bit worried.'

His concern forces me to recover my composure – slightly – and I try my best to concentrate on what my boyfriend is saying long distance from California rather than on the daydreams currently playing in my head.

'No, I'm great. It's just I've had a busy day at work and I had a few things to do and so I thought I'd wait a bit. Save the best for last, you know.'

'Glad I'm still the best,' he laughs.

'Course you are, Connor,' I squeak, desperately searching for some conversation. 'Um, so how is everything with you all the way over there?'

'Great. The show's going good. The girls are very compliant.'

Oh, you don't say. That's the word for it now, is it? Compliant?

'You know, they let me set up shots and they don't get impatient and they're pretty natural.'

Apart from all their fake body parts you mean.

'We've got good footage so all we need now is a bit of

voiceover, a big event for the storyline and great music, for which I might need to enlist the help of my own personal DJ.'

'Huh?'

'You. My DJ.'

'Oh yes.'

Whoops; for a minute there I thought I was a nurse.

'DJ, yes, I'm a DJ. Fab.'

'Ehm' – he coughs nervously, which is hardly surprising considering his girlfriend is acting like a complete fruit-loop – 'Anyway, it should all come together.'

'Brill. Brillio. Fab.'

There is a pause, probably while Connor considers sending the men in white coats around to Byres Road, then he sighs and speaks again.

'I've got stuff to do now, but you take care of that cold or whatever it is.'

'I will, honey,' I say, biting my lip as I realise we are about to end the conversation – 'and, er, I miss you.'

'I miss you too, Angel,' he replies, 'be good.'

'OF COURSE I'LL BE GOOD,' I reply, surprising myself at the loudness of my over-enthusiastic reply, 'I'm always good.'

'I know,' says Connor, sounding relieved, 'that's why I'm so comfortable with our situation. Bye then, baby, speak to you soon.'

I replace the receiver, the word comfortable tapping repeatedly on my eardrum. *Comfortable?* What does he mean, comfortable? That makes me sound like a worn-in Scholl sandal or a pair of baggy old jeans, not like a funky twenty-something (just) DJ who wears her hair spiky and hangs around with popstars. Comfortable indeed; what a bloody cheek. I bet he doesn't go calling Ferrari and Pirelli and Sunny, Money and Bunny or whatever their poncey names are, *comfortable.* Well, not unless he was resting his head on their enormous airbags at the time. I stick two fingers up at the phone, put on my The Bees CD at top volume and stomp into the kitchen to make myself a pre-bedtime hot chocolate with marshmallows and Hob Nob dippers. Comfortable? Me? Never.

CHAPTER FOURTEEN

Black-Eyed Boy

I wake up feeling as if I have just completed a two-hour Step class in my sleep – not that I would really know how that feels but I can well imagine the pain. I then remember that in my dream I was the star of a rather energetic pop video, bumping and grinding in a crotch-length nurse's uniform while I mimed to the female part of a French duet along with Didier Lafitte. I must have been jigging my legs around in bed and, by the unusual angles of my hair, I must have done a bit of breakdancing on my head too.

I trip out of bed, yawn my way to the bathroom and splash some water on my face. I peer in the mirror, the one that Connor bought me that is designed like an LP. Eugh, I look tired. I have more bags under my eyes than a Louis Vuitton luggage shop and my skin is definitely in need of something to make it sparkle. I had a restless night's sleep – making a dance video isn't easy, you know – but I haven't been sleeping too well ever since Connor left for America. My bed feels huge all of a sudden, despite the fact that when he's sleeping with me I sometimes have the urge to boot him on to the floor because he's taking up all the room and stealing the duvet. But this week I especially miss having a man's company, *Connor's* company in my bed. I've heard about the seven-year itch; well, this must be the eight-week itch; I'm itching for him to come back and give me someone to hug. Not to mention some satisfaction, if I may be so blunt.

I wander through to the lounge and lift up a photo frame containing a picture of Connor and I taken on holiday in Ireland using the automatic timer. We are wrapped snugly in scarves, hats and snowboard jackets, which makes it all the more bizarre that we are eating 99 Flake ice creams. The Donegal wind has reddened our cheeks, making us look healthy and very much in love. I wonder what Connor is doing now? Is he lying in his hotel room gazing at a picture of me in one of those Hollywood telepathic love scenarios? After all, he is in Hollywood so it is possible. But, then again, he is in Hollywood, where every woman looks like Pamela Anderson or Cameron Diaz, only prettier, so why on earth would he be lying in a darkened room in the middle of the night gazing at a blurry photo of yours truly? Yours *comfortable* truly. The woman he can happily leave unguarded and single at home while he swans around LA without the slightest fear that another man will even look in my direction – but asks me to marry him just to be on the safe side. Is that what Connor meant when he said he was comfortable with our situation? Am I so much of a done deal that he feels he doesn't have to even try?

The fact that we don't talk so much at the moment only adds to my confusion. Snatched telephone calls, impersonal e-mails when I can be bothered to log on (my sad computer-nerdy behaviour has evaporated recently) and one postcard which told me where he was (which I already knew) are the extent of our communication thus far into our LDR. I stuck the postcard on the fridge with Blu Tack with the expectation of making it the centrepiece of my new postcard collage but I haven't had another one since. I know he's busy, I understand he's at work and not on holiday, but how big is a postcard? It doesn't take a genius to fill the few square inches on the back and whack on a stamp. And as for Interflora . . . have they ceased to exist or something?

God, I'm in a bad mood today. I can see I'm not going to enjoy my own company this weekend. Perhaps Didier Lafitte will call like he promised and I can get on with being focused on my show. Except, of course, he thinks I'm a nurse. Which reminds me, maybe I'll call my mother and ask her what the hell she thought she was doing telling porkie pies to Didier. We haven't spoken since I called to explain that I hadn't actually accepted Connor's proposal – which for Delphine was a reason to celebrate.

'*Allô. Allô, oui*?'

'*Maman, c'est Angel à l'appareil.*'

'Angelique, *chérie*, how is your life?'

'Not bad, Mum. A bit lonely, actually. I'm missing Connor.'

'Why?'

'Because he's in America, Mum, remember?'

'*Oui*, but why is it that you miss him?'

I knew this was a bad idea.

'Because he's my boyfriend,' I reply wearily. 'God, you've

got a heart like a paving stone. Anyway, *Maman*, I wanted to ask you why you told Didier Lafitte that I'm a nurse.'

'Didier Lafitte!' Delphine shrieks, almost losing her inherent cool. 'You have met him, yes?'

'Yes, last night as a matter of fact. It was quite a funny story, actually. I—'

'And he is gorgeous and beautiful and very masculine, no?' Delphine interrupts without waiting to hear my 'funny' story. 'His eyes are like onyx – beautiful.'

'Er, yeah, he's OK I suppose—'

'He does so much resemble David Ginola, do you not think, Angelique?'

'Ginola?' I reach over to my CD collection and pull out Didier's album, which just happens to be close at hand. 'Now you come to mention it, he does a little bit.'

But even better looking, my mind adds before I can stop it.

'It is me that you must thank for this, Angelique. I give him your telephone number of the flat and I tell him that when he gets to Glasgow he must call you. He has told me that he needs a beautiful English girl to help him with his vocabulary.'

I blush.

'I say to him that you are more plain than beautiful but that you speak well.'

I frown.

'You never told me that you were friendly with popstars, Mum. How come I didn't know?'

'Aah,' she breathes smugly, 'there is much you do not know about your mother, *ma fille*. You do not, for instance, know my new lover, Frédéric, and how he brings pleasure to my life.'

'Yeah, and I'd rather continue *not* knowing that if you don't mind, Mother.'

'But now that you know this about Didier Lafitte, Angelique, I hope you will be using this moment to your benefit.'

'I would be using it very much to my benefit,' I huff, 'if I could convince him to come on my radio show, but the fact that he thinks I wear an upside-down watch and a little hat and empty bedpans all day somewhat scuppers my great plan, don't you think?'

'*Comment?*'

Oh here she goes again, pretending that she doesn't understand English when it suits her so that she won't have to apologise for lying about my occupation. Mind you, the part about the upside-down watches and bedpans might have been a little bit confusing.

'Anyway, he said he would call me at some point, so I guess I'll just wait for that.'

'*Non*! You must call him, Angelique. Be like your mother and go out to get things. Do not sit around and achieve nothing like your father. Tell me please that you have his telephone number.'

I glance at the shiny little card propped up against my stereo and bite my lip.

'Um, yeah, I've got it somewhere, I think.'

'Then you must use it. This poor boy, he is in Scotland all alone and you are his only friend and I promised Marie-Pierre that you would look after her son. This is very important to me, *chérie*.'

Something in my head suspects that my mother has a greater scheme in mind than Didier Lafitte's tour of Glasgow and the English language but her motherly guilt trip goes a long way to doing the trick.

'All right, *Maman*, I'll show him around. After all, if it's that important to you I simply must repay all the huge favours you've done for me recently.'

I'm sorry, I just couldn't help myself.

'I gave birth to you, Angelique,' my mother retorts with an audible pout, 'and this is a very big favour from any woman who was born to be a size one with the little hips.'

Thankfully Delphine is speaking in French sizes, so I am not eleven sizes larger than my own mother. Nevertheless, the thought of being a size one in any language makes me feel slightly dizzy.

'OK, Mum, I will call Marie-Pierre's son when I get a free moment.'

Her snort is enough for me to know that she realises my social diary is not exactly bursting its binding.

'I must go,' says Delphine in her this-is-the-end-of-our-little-chat-now-that-I've-got-what-I-want voice, 'Frédéric is arriving and we are going to—'

'OK then, bye, Mum,' I interrupt hurriedly before she can go into any more gruesome details, 'and Dad's fine, by the way. Still broken-hearted and lonely and killing himself with alcohol, but now with a chipped jaw bone to mark the anniversary of your leaving.'

Harsh, perhaps, but fair.

Delphine's heartstrings remain resolutely untugged.

'You know, *chérie*, you and your father should go out of the house more and live your life. You are becoming like stagnant water.'

Oh really? Then you must be the irritating little mosquito buzzing around the stagnant water, I scowl to myself.

Jesus, even my mother thinks I'm boring. I end the

conversation, jump in the shower to calm down and then stomp into my bedroom to get changed. I knew from the word go that calling her was a silly idea. Now I'm even more pissed off because my mother has a better social life, not to mention a more active sex life. I pull on a casually uninspired outfit while continuing to mutter under my breath. Stagnant? Comfortable? Boring? Does anyone else want to add an unflattering adjective while I'm here in my flat alone with my career hanging in the balance and no one to make me feel good?

I swear as I stub my toe on a shoebox lying next to the bedroom door. I am about to kick it across the floor when I realise the box contains my new pair of skate-style trainers. Ah, did I forget to mention that particular shopping trip? It was inspired by Winona after she told me to have a focus, and I felt that if I was going to try to become a trendy DJ the least I could do was start to dress like one, starting with the footwear. I smile in the way only a new-smelling pair of shoes can make me smile and pull on the red and white Globe trainers.

'Just call me skateboard chick,' I ooze to the mirror, feeling suddenly empowered. 'I am going to phone Didier Chuffing Lafitte and I am going to tell him that I'm not a bloody nurse. I am going to make him come on my effing show whether he likes it or not. This is too important an opportunity to miss.'

I march into the lounge and pick up the embossed business card.

'But first I am going to pay a visit to Winona and the wishing pool just to make sure that everything goes according to plan, and maybe I will drink eight espressos to give me the edge that I need.'

Pleased at my own motivation, I throw what I need into my rucksack while singing 'Get Happy' at the top of my voice. I delve into the tin of change I keep in the kitchen for a handful of offerings for the wishing pool.

I am just hollering (the only apt description of my attempt at singing) the chorus when the phone rings.

Eleven o'clock. It'll be Meg, on her first lunch break of the day. I dance towards the phone while trying to support a handful of coins and the tin and quickly shove the receiver between my right ear and shoulder.

'Yep.'

'Uh, *excusez-moi*, I am looking for Angelique, *s'il v* . . . please.'

I immediately drop the coins and the tin and almost the contents of my bladder on to the floor with an almighty clatter. Very cool, Angel, positively ice-like.

'Oh, um, yes,' I stutter, my tongue having turned to cotton wool, 'this is Angel.'

'Ah,' he breathes, 'I am so glad. This is Didier. Didier Lafitte.'

You don't say.

'I meet you last evening, you remember?'

No, it had totally slipped my mind. Didier who?

'Of course I remember,' I reply with a smile, 'how are you today, Didier?'

'*Très bien.*'

I bet you are.

'I was wondering, Angel, if you would do me the honour of spending some time with me today.'

Do me the honour? Mmm, let's hope this man never learns to speak English like a native. I much prefer the

Shakespearean touch. I clear my throat. And clear my throat. And clear my throat again. Didier takes my nervous pause as a bad sign.

'Uh, I am sorry, Angel,' he interjects apologetically, 'you have plans already?'

'Plans? Oh um . . .'

Don't say 'no', you'll sound like a loser.

'. . . well, yes, I was just about to . . .'

And don't say 'go and hang out at a wishing pool by myself' – you'll sound like even more of a loser.

Blimey, this chatting with a popstar is not easy, is it?

'. . . I was just about to, um, go to my . . . Tai Chi class with ten of my closest friends.' (A little excessive perhaps but I'm improvising here.)

'*D'accord*, Angel, that is not a problem. I would like to join you . . .'

Shite.

'. . . but I have already spent this morning in the gym for a great two-hour workout. I think my body is in need of a rest.'

I grimace. Do people really do stuff like that for fun? 'Great' and 'workout' are not exactly two words I would closely associate with each other unless the sentence went something like: '*Great*, thank Christ that crappy *workout* is finished, let's go and eat some Mars Bars.'

'So, uh, I suppose you would not like to spend this afternoon on a boat with myself and a few acquaintances? We are having a small gathering, you see, and I think it will be very enjoyable. There will be music, champagne, aperitifs . . .'

Boat, music, champagne, BOAT, MUSIC, CHAMPAGNE, repeats my brain, hopping excitedly in my skull.

'But if you prefer to attend your Tai Chi class, please do not let me stop you.'

'Er, well, I think I could give Tai Chi a miss today 'cos I've been like eight times already this week. I think my body might need a rest too. A boat party sounds lovely. What time and where?'

Oh my giddy aunt, I've just made a date with a popstar.

CHAPTER FIFTEEN

Wonderland

Did he not say 'myself and a few acquaintances'? Was the afternoon not billed as a 'small gathering'? Yes, that's what I thought, but it seems that Didier Lafitte's idea of a small gathering amounts to about the same number of people that I have met in my entire life. I am on perhaps the swankiest private boat ever to have sailed into Glaswegian waters. It is a floating wonderland and everyone onboard is either a music type, a model type, a fashion type or a television type. You name it, they are here. I'm aware that my mouth is hanging open but I can't help it. I am not terribly accustomed to spending my Saturday afternoons on a boat worth more than my street, nibbling sushi and drinking bottles of champagne that cost more than my monthly mortgage payment. It certainly beats my usual Saturday shoe-shopping trips (just).

As Didier guides me confidently along the upper deck – my elbow apparently glued to his hand – the crowd parts like the excited mob of fans at the top of the mountains in the Tour de France. They stare, they smile, they come very close to us but they never touch, moving away just as the star and his unknown lady friend (*moi*) reach them. I glance nervously up at Didier, who appears completely unfazed by the attention. It is as if he hardly sees the gawping admirers all around him. As for me – the sort of girl who could stand naked at a bar waving a fifty-pound note for an hour and still not get my order taken – this is something very new. Yet despite feeling as out of my depth as a toddler in a diving pool, I take my mother's advice and 'act as if'. I hold my head high, walk with self-assurance and pray that I don't fall flat on my arse.

Today at this 'small gathering' I am going to save my career. I simply have to; it's all I've ever wanted to do and now I am here I can't just let it slip away. In fact, I am not just going to save it, I am going to push it as high as it can go (within the boundaries of Energy FM of course). Once Didier has agreed to appear as my special guest, my career will not exactly be orbiting the moon but I will have a pretty good bird's eye view of Glasgow. However, before that can happen I have to quell the rumours about my nursing ability, get to know my new friend beyond the 'our mothers are chums' stage and pluck up the courage to ask the question. In my opinion much of that will also involve getting Didier on his own which, considering there are packed sardines with more room than us, is not going to be easy.

'Are all these people your friends?' I ask when we finally come to a stop at the stern of the boat.

He shrugs and motions for me to take a seat beside him. He has that kind of authoritative manner that makes one do as he says. I perch carefully on the highly varnished wooden bench for fear of sliding off and landing in a heap at the feet of the beautiful people.

'Uh, they are not really my friends,' he shrugs, pensively sipping his drink as he surveys the babbling crowd with his dark eyes. 'They are more, as I said, acquaintances. Actually, some I have never met but, you know' – another shrug – 'they want to get to know me.'

That's confidence for you, I think with a bemused smile. Yes, I get people banging on my door every hour of the day just begging to get to know me. Only someone famous could say something like that and get away with it. He is right, though, people do want to get to know him. I realise this as I sit quietly next to Didier, discreetly watching him watching them. I see people trying desperately to attract his attention either by following him with their eyes or by throwing their head back and laughing uproariously, trying to be the visible life and soul of the party. It is a strange phenomenon to observe – the human mating/networking game where every player vies for the attention of the same man. The man who just happens to be sitting comfortably by my side. I straighten my back and adopt my best smug git impression as I then notice that when the eyes aren't looking at him they are watching me. I can almost read their thoughts: *Who is she? Why is she sitting with him? Who does she think she is? She's not even a size six and I'm sure that outfit is from the High Street* . . . If the daggers they are piercing me with were real I would look like a human porcupine by now. I have to admit that I am enjoying myself. This is perhaps what it would be like were I not a DJ on Crappity FM but on a big station with even bigger guests. I look over at Didier and grin. He returns the vibe, his mouth turning up at the corners in a slightly crooked smile as one eye narrows into a discreet wink. For the first time in weeks I feel distinctly positive. It seems my mother might for once have done something good for her only daughter.

'*Excusez-moi*, Angel, I must talk briefly with my manager,' says Didier after a while, standing up and thrusting a hand deep into the pocket of his jeans.

I avert my eyes from the pocket/groin area and nod.

'I will return,' he says with a slight bow, 'please stay.'

'I'm not going anywhere,' I reply to his retreating broad back as he leaves me sitting alone.

A waitress appears by my side holding a tray piled high with enough tapas to feed the entire Spanish royal household.

'Just leave the tray,' I smirk, motioning to the bench beside me.

She obliges, asks whether 'madam would like anything else', curtsies (yes, *curtsies*) and wiggles her minuscule backside back to the galley. A wave of happiness rolls down my spine. Now I have always prided myself on being a down-to-earth kind of girl but, bloody hell, if this is how the other half live then I want to defect to their side of the equation. This is great!

An hour passes and still no sign of the man of the moment. I have scoffed enough Spanish omelette to keep a battery farm in business for a month, until I notice that no one else around me appears to be eating anything at all, apart from an enormous man who looks and sounds like an opera singer but even I give him a run for his money in the eat-all-you-can stakes. The rest of the beautifuls act as though they are eating but in fact all they do is move food from one tray to another. Lift up a sandwich, sniff the sandwich, place the sandwich on a passing tray. Lift the cake, sniff the cake, place the cake on a passing tray. The damn stuff never actually touches their mouths. It is like being on a boat full of Ceri Divines, which really makes me wonder about the world. When did eating go out of fashion? If food wasn't meant to be eaten we would never have been given stomachs and no one would have invented chocolate. In an effort to ingratiate myself with the other partygoers, however, I exercise my willpower and put my plate to one side. Admittedly it is now empty apart from the odd scrap as I have gorged everything else in sight but I do not dive in for another helping. Instead, I refill my glass. Now I do tend to have real willpower when it comes to alcohol consumption thanks to my dad's bad example, so I switch from straight champagne to Bucks Fizz, quietly humming 'Making Your Mind Up' to myself as I pour the first glass. Of course this only reminds me of the alternative guest for *Angel on Air* if Didier doesn't help me out (you know, the curly haired one . . .). Gripped by a sudden career-down-the-tubes panic, I face my fears and enter the realm of the beautiful people. I need to ask Didier to come on my show. Here goes nothing.

How many floors can one boat have before it becomes a passenger ferry? And whatever happened to salt-encrusted portholes and smelly fishermen with beards and yellow wellies? This boat is all varnished wood and bright white walls adorned with real art and spotlights and gold fittings. There are spiral staircases and 'banquettes' surrounding widescreen televisions that many a small-town cinema would be proud of. On each floor concealed speakers create the musical ambience. Some tracks I recognise as Didier's from his latest album but other French singers and rappers get a look-in. I nod and smile to everyone I see but I emerge at the very front of the boat having covered what must be the whole interior (unless there are secret passages behind the walls, which wouldn't surprise me) and I still haven't found the only person I happen to know at this party. He's probably buggered off, leaving me to stand here alone like a dork. Just pass me a watering can and call me a wallflower.

I lean on the shiny railing that runs around the bow of the boat and gaze out at the River Clyde. The river I see every day as I walk to work. The river I will probably be booted into if I don't come up with the goods for G.G. by Friday. Great. I peer down into the water, think about my job and try to look insignificant. Unfortunately, a group of beautifuls take my lonesome silence as a self-important detachment and convince themselves I am a 'somebody'.

'Do join us,' gushes the first woman to pull me into the group.

I am sure she introduces herself as Chlamydia but I don't dare ask her to repeat it. If her parents want to name her after a sexually transmitted infection then far be it from me to question their decision. She is taller than me – in fact she is taller than most of the LA Lakers, with legs so long I am almost eye-level with her crotch. Her hair is cropped short and spiky like mine, although I can tell hers was cut with solid gold scissors, and it is dyed a vibrant red. She is dressed entirely in black, as are, I notice, the rest of the group – two older men who favour the giant Rolex, open-necked shirt and slicked-back hair look and a pair of twenty-nothing twins who would make Elle MacPherson check into the ugly clinic.

'Darling little party, wouldn't you agree?' Chlamydia asks in an Edinburgh accent more refined than oil.

'Yes,' I nod with a friendly smile, 'although I wouldn't really call it little. It's all rather grand in my opinion.'

The twins titter as if I have just finished a ten-minute rib-cracking stand-up sketch.

'Really? Wouldn't you?' they giggle in unison.

'You have clearly never been to one of Flash's bashes then,' says Chlamydia, pouting towards the larger of the two older men whose Rolex is about the size of a helicopter landing pad. He's obviously got a small penis.

'Flash's bashes? No, I don't believe I have.'

And if I dropped dead right this minute I don't think I would regret not having been bashed by Flash either.

'So what are you?' asks Flash in such a deep, rumbling voice that I look round to see if there is a train coming.

What am I? I glance at my body and self-consciously pull the hem of my white Diesel top down to meet the waistband of my navy blue bootleg trousers (thankfully I had the presence of mind to change my outfit again once my plans for Saturday dramatically shifted). The last time I looked I was boringly human, although that definition may need some clarification for these people, judging by my first impressions.

'What am I?' I repeat slowly.

'Yah,' reply the twins through mouths far too wide for their fat-free faces, 'are you fashion, music, television, photography, literary or journo? We're in fashion. We're models.'

You don't say, I think, my eyes coming to rest on their pointy hipbones, visible through their clingy dresses like train buffers. And here was I thinking that the modelling profession was only open to your average girl who is a genuine example of the modern woman with curves and internal organs. I must have been mistaken.

'Flash is in music, Julian is in television and I am a little bit of everything,' Chlamydia announces loudly and proudly. 'I do television presenting, I have a CD, I write for' – she sighs – 'oh, I would say every publication worth getting one's laptop out for and I model whenever I have a spare moment.'

'Gosh,' I laugh, 'you could open your own one-woman temping agency with a CV like that.'

'I don't think so,' Chlamydia retorts, as if I have just suggested she become a Bangkok transsexual prostitute. 'Do I look like the sort of woman who would be seen dead in one of those grotty temping agencies? Good Lord, temping is for poor people.'

'Oh, I don't know, I've done some temping in my time.'

Chlamydia's heavily mascarad eyes look me up and down before focusing on the Miss Selfridge logo on the front pocket of my trousers.

'That doesn't surprise me, darling,' she concludes sourly.

'So what are you?' Flash repeats before I can smack the red-head with my champagne flute.

'Well' – I shift my feet – 'I guess I'm in music too, just like you, Flash.'

Sadly that is where our similarities end, my friend.

Flash squashes his orange-tanned chins into the place where his neck should surely be and frowns. 'You are in music, are you, love? Would I know your name? I'm big in the music biz.'

I don't doubt it. Everything about this man is big. Everything visible at least.

'Maybe,' I smile, 'I am Angel Knights.'

He grunts and shakes his gold chains. 'Nope, doesn't ring a bell. Julian?'

Julian also frowns and then growls, 'Never heard of her. Does she sing?'

'Do you sing?' Flash repeats.

I look from one to the other. Funny, I could have sworn that Julian spoke in perfectly understandable English just then but he obviously feels the need to communicate through a translator.

'Do I sing? Only when I'm alone and I don't sing very well. I prefer to play other people's music.'

'She's a musician then,' says Julian to Flash.

'You're a musician then,' Flash expertly translates.

'No.'

They all sigh.

'I'm a DJ.'

This is much better. I see five pairs of ears prick up with interest.

'A DJ, how cool,' chirp the twins.

'Ooh, you could play my CD on air,' Chlamydia twitters, the idea eventually reaching her brain despite it being at such high altitude.

'Club or radio DJ?' Flash queries.

'Radio.'

'Which station is she on?' Julian snarls.

'Which station are—'

'A local one,' I interrupt, beginning to tire of their double act. 'Energy FM.'

This is not so good. The twins let out a disappointed '*Uuhh*', Flash's head disappears even further into his missing neck like a retreating turtle and Julian laughs. No need to translate that one, he just laughs at me. Out loud.

As for Chlamydia, she looks down on me in both senses

of the word and snaps, 'Energy FM? God, you're not worth knowing at all.'

Not good for the confidence. This is definitely not good for the confidence. I knew I hated mingling and now I remember why.

'So how come you're even here?' Chlamydia tuts, I suspect shortly before they completely close ranks on the party loser.

Bloody hell, don't beat around the bush, just come right out and say it.

'Why am I here? I'm here because . . .'

God, I don't know, why am I here? To be publicly humiliated because my clothes don't come on diamond-encrusted hangers? Until now the party had been glamorous and indulgent and eye-opening and fun but I suddenly realise that there are still some places in our fucked-up world where being a pleasant, hard-working, ambitious and caring human being just isn't enough.

Beaten by the school bully and her posse of bully trainees, I mutter something by way of an apology for my selfish use of the planet's oxygen supplies and turn to leave, staring morosely at my moccasin boots. I knew I should have worn my lucky rainbow wedges. I try to avoid their sniggers and purposefully loud comments, all of which seem to contain the words 'Energy FM', 'DJ' and 'crap', while I slip my mini-rucksack on to my back. Time to leave. It is then that I feel a strong arm around my shoulders.

'I am so sorry to have left you for so long, *chérie*,' Didier smiles, his face close to my ear, 'these people, they are like leeches. I could not get away.'

'S'alright,' I shrug, still staring at my feet.

He spins me around by the shoulder to face my intimidators. Even Chlamydia has taken her head out of her arse long enough to look downright cheesed off.

'People, have you met my beautiful friend?' Didier asks.

I think he meant to say, '*Beautiful* people, have you met my *friend*?' but, hey, who am I to argue?

'This is Angel, the daughter of my mother's best friend, *my* friend, my English teacher, a nurse and the party VIP.'

'Gosh,' Chlamydia comments through gritted teeth, 'you could open your own one-woman temping agency with a CV like that.'

'Touché, darling,' I wink, swanning past them all on Didier's arm, 'now enjoy my *little* party, won't you?'

Damn that felt great.

Didier is charming and funny and attentive and real. I know all people are real, even famous people, but the odd one, you must admit, is debatable (naming no members of the Jackson family) and it can be quite hard to see through the media persona to find the real man or woman underneath. I spend the next two hours working my way through the maze to find that genuine person in Didier as he sticks by my side on the back deck and takes care of my every need. If I am hungry he gets me food, thirsty he gets me a drink, cold he gets me a jacket. Of course he doesn't actually move from the seat to fetch and carry because clicking those fingers is enough to get things done. As the beautiful people sashay away with disappointed cheek-to-cheek air kisses, the boat grows quiet and previously invisible fairy lights illuminate the deck like our own personal stars. The temperature drops with the sun and two steaming cups of hot chocolate appear, topped with cream and designer marshmallows. We sip them, burning the tips of our tongues, and snuggle on the deck like old friends. Most of the time he talks and I listen – if my job has taught me anything it is how to be a good listener, even when Boomer is shouting in my ear or Malcolm is airing his controversial opinions. I like listening to Didier; his life is so different to my own.

It turns out that Didier grew up in Bordeaux with Marie-Pierre, his father being little more than a sperm donor, although not in the official sense of the word. At the age of eighteen Didier moved alone to Paris and immediately signed with a modelling agency on the Champs-Elysées, where he set about perfecting the sultry look now gracing his album covers. Of course his real passion had always been writing songs and singing, which he continued to do in his spare time with a friend's band. He was spotted one night by a talent scout for a recording company and Bob's your uncle, career number two.

He makes it sound so easy. A model, a popstar and a very rich young man by the age of twenty-five. Some people have all the luck, don't they? Now, at the age of thirty, he has a penthouse flat in Paris and a townhouse near the beach in Biarritz, along with four cars (and I'm not talking Fiat Unos), two fast motorbikes, a growing career in the pop industry and a valuable art collection.

When we get on to the subject of his pop career, I am poised on my tip-toes (not literally) waiting to pounce. Waiting to tell him about my life and my show and about why I was trying to blag my way into the BBC Scotland building. After all, that is, if I am honest, the real reason for my presence here, other than keeping my mother happy of course. So with a deep breath and a nervous bubble of anticipation mingling with the bubbles of champagne in my stomach, I prepare myself to pop the question. Wow, now I can see why Connor was so jittery the night he *popped the question*. Not that this falls in the same category of question at all but a lot rides on Didier's response. Come on, my new French friend, make my day.

'Didier,' I begin, the air rushing uncontrollably out of my lungs, 'can you do me a favour?'

'*Bien sûr*, Angel,' he nods, pushing his long hair back from his face with one of his smooth hands, 'more champagne?'

'No, thanks. No, I—'

'Something to eat?'

'What? No, nothing like that. I—'

'You are cold? We can move inside if you like.'

'No, I just . . .'

Didier laughs and places the same perfect hand on my leg, stopping me in my tracks.

'Ha, this is what I like about you, Angel,' he beams before I can say anything else. 'You are so undemanding.'

'Am I?' I gulp, trying to stop my leg twitching under his long fingers.

'*Oui*, you are very content. I see you looking happy and it pleases me. I hope you have enjoyed this.'

I follow his arm as he motions towards the rest of the boat.

'Of course, it is fabulous.'

'*Merci bien*. And I am glad that you are here.'

I shift on the seat and glance at his hand, which is still resting on my thigh as if it is the most natural thing in the world. I am aware that mainland Europeans are much more demonstrative than we Brits and that this means nothing to Didier, but if Connor could see me right now he would chop that hand off and shove it somewhere rather unpleasant. I just want to ask Didier my one teeny weeny favour and scarper back to my flat to lie in bed and hug Connor's James T-shirt.

'You see, many of the people I must spend time with . . .' Didier sighs, thankfully removing his hand but then resting it on the back of the seat behind my shoulders. Out of the frying pan and into the armpit. I cough and try to concentrate.

'. . . these people do not really love Didier' – he touches the other hand to his chest – 'they do not want to know the real Didier Lafitte. I do not want to complain but, my industry, it can be hard. I know that the people love me when my music is selling good and they do everything for me but this is not real love. They are very, how you say . . .?'

'Fickle?' I suggest.

'Fickle, yes, I like this word,' he grins. 'They are very fickle.'

I watch his hand, which he moves constantly as he speaks. In fact, he could just as effectively stay silent and communicate via sign language.

'And the worst thing is,' he continues, 'people are so demanding. They all want something from me. They want me to give them things and take them places and do things for them all of the time.'

'Oh,' I breathe.

Bollocks.

'They are not my friends,' he sighs,' none of these people today were my friends. Not like you.'

Shit. Now I feel as shallow as a puddle in the Atacama.

'It is not that I do not enjoy giving to people, you understand, but some things I find very difficult. Like the interviews.'

'Interviews,' I croak. The thought never crossed my mind.

'Yes, in Britain I am very nervous to speak the language in public.'

'But you're great at English, Didier.'

His sun-kissed cheeks flush with perfect symmetry. 'With you, perhaps, Angel, because you are French and you are my friend so I feel relaxed.'

Yes, there is still hope.

'But on the television or the radio or in the Press I may be misquoted or say something in the wrong way, you know, so it comes out different from what I mean.'

Hope leaps over the side of the boat and swims quickly away.

'Because of this I do not give interviews in English, but then I have problems with the media. They follow me and try to catch me in bad situations, and they say terrible things about me because I do not like to give interviews. They believe that I am arrogant and rude but I am not. You understand?'

'I do.'

I understand that I feel like a two-faced cow. I am no better than Chlamydia and the rest of the beautiful people. I was only out for what this man could do for me. But damn, it would have been bloody good to further my career a little bit. Heaven knows it needs it.

Mind you, looking into Didier's eyes I begin to suspect that there is something in the old adage that money does not necessarily bring you happiness. He may be famous and successful with more fans than most Premiership football clubs but the real Didier Lafitte is basically lonely. He needs someone to be his friend and, judging by the arseholes I have met today, I think I am leading the Exit Polls. Not a bad job really; getting to see glamour from the inside will be fun for a week or two. I'm lonely, he's lonely – where's the harm in that?

'I am sorry, forgive me, Angel,' says Didier, standing up suddenly and reaching out his hand. 'I have been talking for much too long and bothering you with my worries, using up all of your day of rest, which you deserve because the job of a nurse is very hard.'

'Is it?' I reply. 'I mean *it is*, yes, *really* hard.'

I take his hand and slither off the seat like the lying little toad that I am. Didier smiles and bends forward to kiss my cheeks. A great custom, I think briefly, vastly overlooked this side of the Channel.

'I will get someone to drive you home,' he says, clicking those magic fingers, 'and we must meet again very soon. But first I must ask you a single favour.'

'Sure.'

It wouldn't be anything to do with a mediocre radio show, would it, per chance?

No, of course it wouldn't.

'Uh, it would be better for me if we can keep our meetings and what we discuss just between us, you know. I am certain that you would not tell the world but I have to explain this right at the beginning. The Press and the media, they can be very cunning, and I would just like to keep this as something special. Something unknown to all the *fickle* people, OK?' he asks with an apologetic, pained expression.

'Of course, Didier,' I smile, hugging my bag protectively in front of my body, 'I understand. No fickle people allowed.' I pat him on the arm. 'Don't worry, mate, I won't tell.'

CHAPTER SIXTEEN

Californication

'You went on a date with Didier Lafitte?' gawp Meg and Ceri simultaneously.

Yes, I know I said to Didier that I wouldn't tell but by that I'm sure he meant not to tell anyone *significant* like big-wigs of the music industry and media. Yes, and I also know that Ceri works for a glossip (my new name for a glossy gossip magazine) but she's not exactly the editor of *Hello!* or *Heat* or the *News of the World*. Besides, her friendship to me would come first rather than an entry in her weekly column. You see, my best friends aren't the sort of fickle people that Didier dislikes so much so I'm sure he wouldn't mind that I let on about our budding friendship.

Of course I didn't mean to say anything at all when we first came out tonight but you know how it is when you're relaxing over a couple of beers and a chicken biryani and poppadums in a cosy Indian restaurant – your tongue sometimes just becomes a little looser than usual. Careless whispers, I think George Michael would call it, although bloody-big-gob-after-a-couple-of-bevvies would probably be more appropriate. Meg and Ceri had been talking about their weekends and asking me what I'd done yesterday and I just didn't want to sound like a sad old spinster with a boyfriend on the other side of the world.

'I told you, it wasn't a date,' I shrug, blinking as I snap a poppadum in half. 'It was just a *small gathering* with several hundred of his friends on a luxurious boat with free-flowing champagne and gold-plated nibbles. It was nothing really.'

Not that I am trying to raise the green-eyed monster from its lair but, hey, I've got to get my ten-pence worth, haven't I?

Ceri scowls and huffily discards the chapatti she has been making a meal of for the last forty-five minutes.

'It was just a friendly thing as a favour to my mum.'

'Fucken' hell,' Meg whistles, 'it's nae wonder you've got a big gigantic smile on your wee fizzer tonight, hen, I'd be grinning like a looper from a spinbin if I'd spent the day with Didier Lafitte. Jeez-oh, I always thought your mum was canny trendy but I didn'y know she hung about with popstars.'

'Neither did I.'

'That's mad, Angel, so it is,' Meg continues, managing to speak, eat and gulp her beer all at the same time, much to Ceri's revulsion. 'Mind you, my mum met Lulu in the bogs in Littlewoods once. And she sat behind yon Billy Connolly at the pictures when she went to see that one with Whitney Whatserchops in it. Well, she thinks it was Billy Connolly but it was a wee bit dark, although my mum's got brilliant eyesight for her age but.'

'Gosh, Meg, thanks for that,' Ceri snorts, dipping her fork in and out of her plate of boiled rice. 'You're practically royalty with connections like that. I am so jealous.'

'Och, away and boil yer head,' Meg replies, wrinkling her nose at Ceri. 'Pass us they indescribables, Angel.'

I lift the silver tray of chutneys – our third helping – across the table and hand it to Meg along with a fresh basket of poppadums. We are in my favourite Indian restaurant, just around the corner from my flat. As always, Meg is on her gastronomic tour of India while Ceri nibbles on the few things neither fried nor fattening on the menu, which largely comprises boiled rice, chapatti, lettuce and the menu card itself. Ceri watches as Meg scoops mango chutney and lime pickle on to a huge piece of broken poppadum and opens her mouth wide to fit it all in. A chunk of chutney drops on to the green and gold tablecloth, sending small globules of orange sticky stuff perilously close to the sleeve of Ceri's pale-pink cashmere jumper – the one that plunges to somewhere around her midriff. Meg and I call it her bungee jumper.

'I bet Monsieur Lafitte isn't eating in a grotty place like this tonight. He's probably tucking into ravioli of lobster at the Devonshire by now, washed down with a delicate chardonnay,' Ceri grumbles, watching Meg with a look of disgust.

'Aye, and he'd probably give his right testicle to be here eatin' a hearty cuzza with us.'

'I doubt it' – Ceri picks a long red hair from the sleeve of her jumper – 'and can you kindly stop moulting like a shaggy dog, Megan? It's very unbecoming.'

Meg takes the hair, giggles as she pretends to replace it in her scalp and then dives back into her chutneys. I laugh uneasily. The girls are particularly feisty tonight; they haven't stopped irritating each other since the first pub we went to about three hours ago. They are like two bits of Velcro – both being the prickly side – sitting uncomfortably together. Why do I feel as if I'm missing something here?

'Och shite,' Meg huffs before I can concern myself any more, 'I've dropped friggin' chutney and pickle on my sweatshirt. Now I look like I've been pooed on by a giant green and orange parrot.' She reluctantly pushes her curry to one side and stands up, her thick curly hair rocking the low copper light as she does so.

'I'm off to the bog, girls; d'ya want me to throw up for you when I'm in there, Ceri? Save you the bother?'

Ceri swallows her mini mouthful of rice and scowls. 'Very funny, Megan, now run along and let the adults talk, there's a good piggy.'

I watch them both with bemusement and quietly return to my curry before Ceri speaks again.

'So congratulations are in order then, I suppose, Angel,' she smiles.

'What for?'

'For landing the hugely popular Didier Lafitte as your star guest of course. That *was* your intention, wasn't it?'

'Hmm, yes, well, it *was* my intention but I haven't *landed* him exactly.'

Ceri rests her chin on her hand and leans towards me.

'Oh dear, babe, he didn't say no, did he?'

'No, he didn't say no because I didn't ask him.'

'Pardon? Why ever not?' She peers at me with narrowed eyes. 'You didn't meet him at all, did you? I think I can feel my leg being pulled.'

I shake my head and search in my wallet for his card while chewing a lump of incredibly spicy chicken.

'I did meet him, look.'

Ceri takes the card between two painted pincers and eyes it silently.

'Well, well, I don't suppose I can argue with that. Perhaps we should give you a job on *Star* if you're that good at networking.'

I smile indulgently and replace the card.

'But why didn't you ask him to come on the show?'

'It was difficult,' I reply, 'there was a bit of confusion and then it was complicated and then, I dunno, I just didn't get round to it.'

Ceri changes hands and leans to the other side, pushing out her cleavage against the table.

'You went on a date with a big pop megastar that you desperately want to come on your radio show and you "didn't get round to it".'

I nod. 'Something like that.'

'Or something like,' Ceri smirks, 'you don't want him for that at all. Perhaps you want him all for yourself.'

I choke on my mouthful of hot curry.

'Ah ha, you're blushing,' Ceri giggles.

'I'm not blushing,' I cough, catching my breath, 'I'm choking to death. This curry is bloody hot.'

'Oh really?'

'Yes really,' I snap, gulping down a glass of water.

'So you told Didier that you're engaged then?'

'No, it didn't come up. Anyway, I'm not engaged, I'm *thinking* about becoming engaged. It's different.'

'Of course.'

Ceri's knowing answers are really beginning to annoy me.

'One's taken and the other is still largely a free agent. But I suppose you told him that you've got a boyfriend.'

I fiddle with the edge of my napkin. 'Er, no, that didn't come up either.'

Ceri's 'knowingness' steps up a notch to burning bush proportions. I avoid her eyebrows-raised expression.

'And has he got a girlfriend?'

'Yes. Well, probably. People like that always have girlfriends, don't they?'

'People like what? Like very sexy French singers with tight bums?'

I sigh. 'Look, Ceri, just because you're addicted to sex doesn't mean that the rest of us have to be. I am capable of having a completely platonic relationship with a man who happens to be my mum's friend's son. It doesn't necessarily compute that I'm going to jump into bed with him for a quick bonk.'

Ceri raises her hands defensively. 'Of course, Angel, you're right. And I'm sure Connor saw it like that too.'

I hate blushing. It always makes me look so guilty even when I'm not.

'You have told Connor, haven't you, Angel?' Ceri continues, leaning even closer.

I fold and unfold the napkin. 'Not exactly. I've tried to tell him but, you know, he's never there and then when he is we just have quick chats because he's so busy making that programme . . .'

My voice trails off. I did actually have a fifteen-minute chat with Connor this morning but somehow I just couldn't seem to get Didier Lafitte into the conversation. Connor was on a high. Truly had just landed a big audition for some advert or other – probably one for a bikini-waxing salon or a lobotomy clinic – and if she gets the part it would apparently be a fantastic boost for Connor's documentary. He was full of vitality and I was so proud of his efforts that I didn't want to steal any of his limelight for myself. Plus the squeaky, happy voices in the background were reducing me to a lip-quivering bundle of self-pity. Like a once-shiny helium balloon with all the helium squeezed out of it. I'd wanted either to jump on a plane for LA and get my boyfriend back for real or to check in to a hotel for excluded losers; a room for one with no television just in case Truly's chest was making its debut.

'Oh, I'm sure he would understand,' Ceri nods, 'you have to be proactive to make a success of a career like yours. I'm sure he's being *proactive* out there in Hollywood.'

I tense my shoulders and glance towards Ceri, who is innocently refilling her glass with what must be her eighth gallon of water. I'm surprised she doesn't drown with the amount of H_2O she manages to pour down her throat. Either that or expand to the size of a family lilo. In fact, I wish she would, purely for the satisfaction of us women with normally insulated bodies.

'What's that supposed to mean?' I ask with a scowl.

She looks at me with a wide smile as Meg returns to the table sporting a huge discoloured watermark on her pale yellow sweatshirt.

'I just mean that he's doing well, Angel,' she replies, 'especially since Truly got that Dr Pepper advert audition. These documentaries need highs like that to counterbalance the lows.'

'Dr Pepper ad?' I repeat mid-chew on a mouthful of garlic naan. 'How did you know it was a Dr Pepper ad?'

Ceri lifts her pointy pixie chin that only pointy pixie-type people could ever imagine lifting, flashes one of her I-know-everything-there-is-to-know smiles and pauses. A meaningful pause. Meg, I notice, lowers her eyes and concentrates on dissecting an onion bhaji with the intensity of a brain surgeon at work.

'How do I know?' asks Ceri, holding my stare.

'Yes, how do you know? I didn't say she had a Dr Pepper ad audition. In fact, I didn't even know it was a bloody Dr Pepper ad audition. So how come you're brimming over like the fountain of knowledge all of a sudden?'

It is the lager talking. Myself and beer products do not get on too well on or after the third bottle. I get moody and opinionated and irrational; much like Ceri is when sober. Over and above the influence of a couple of bottles of Tiger Beer, however, this conversation is making me feel decidedly uneasy and that is not just because my G-string has become wedged like a bike tyre in a drain with the amount of shuffling around I have been doing since we started to discuss Didier and Connor.

'E-mail,' Ceri pouts after another pause. Her pauses are so pregnant tonight they'll be giving birth to a baby any minute now. 'Connor sent me an e-mail.'

'Several e-mails,' Meg butts in with an emphatic nod of her head.

I swallow hard and lift my chin this time – not a pointy pixie one I might add but it does the job of keeping my face where it should be.

'E-mail? Since when have you and my fiancé been e-mail buddies? That sounds very cosy.'

I'm jealous. Why am I jealous? After all, it's only a bit of long distance computer interaction. Then again, e-mails are the modern-day version of a letter, aren't they? *And* he's got the nerve to be telling Ceri stuff that I don't even know. If they were writing letters to each other across the Atlantic I would have the right to feel a bit jaundiced about it, wouldn't I, so is an e-mail – *several* e-mails – really any different? Damn these new-fangled modes of communication, they don't half complicate matters.

'It's no big deal, hon,' Ceri tuts, patting me on the hand like an upset child.

I grind my teeth and slide my hand away from Ceri's manicured talons.

'It's only a few e-mails, Angel, don't get all funny about it,' she continues. 'And Connor and I are friends, remember. I've known him even—'

'Longer than I have. Yes, yes, you don't have to keep reminding me.'

'So don't be a silly jealous *girlfriend*. You said yourself that he's not your fiancé and that you're only thinking of becoming engaged, so you can't just keep bandying the term around when it suits you.'

Meg looks from Ceri to me and back again before returning her watery green eyes to the plate of bhajis. I narrow my gaze at the girl who is one of my two best friends but who sometimes has a tongue that could poison an adder.

'I am not jealous,' I reply eventually, ignoring the latter comment, 'it's just a bit odd, that's all. You didn't tell me and he didn't tell me and you don't usually e-mail each other.'

'He's not usually thousands of miles away. Anyway, you haven't told him about Didier so what's the difference?'

I shift on my chair again, sending my G-string so far up my bum I could use it as dental floss.

'No, but—'

'And it's not like he only e-mails me; he sends them to you too, doesn't he?'

I nod. Of course he does but not that often. Besides, I prefer to hear his voice than to check his spelling on a computer screen. But who else is he bloody well e-mailing, I think – Melinda Messenger, Jennifer Lopez and the entire female cast of *Baywatch*? (You see, I told you beer made me irrational.)

'Although I'm sure his ones to me are a bit different than the ones to you,' she adds with a flick of her hair.

I relax. Yes, of course they will be. In Connor's e-mails to me he says he loves me and misses me and wants to see my smile and hold me. That's as far as we go on the computer sex thing. Hardly Pammy and Tommy Lee admittedly but you never know when Big Brother is hacking in to your e-mails, having a good laugh at what I would like to do with a jar of Nutella and my boyfriend's bits. Anyway, Connor's e-mails to me may not be Playboy material but they are sweet and I doubt Ceri's are anything like . . .

'I mean, yours will be the edited version,' Ceri scoffs loudly. 'I doubt he'd write the bits about Ferrari and the girls and how well he *relates* to them, and how much he likes hot tubs and that funny thing about Honey's stars and stripes thong bikini.'

I feel the rage building up in my throat, racing the humiliation to my cheeks.

'What stars and bloody stripes thong bikini?' I hiss. 'And what the hell do you mean by *relates*, Ceri Divine?'

I screw my hands into fists under the table. Meg's eyes seem to have swollen to fill her entire face.

'I don't know what you mean,' Ceri shrugs.

'Yes, you do. You said *relates* with a big emphasis like it was written in italics. You were insinuating, Ceri, inbloody-sinuating, and I would like to know what you mean.'

My voice is rising like a loaf of bread in a hot oven. I can feel sweat on my lip and I have a pain in my chest, like bad indigestion. Except it is not in my stomach, it is in my heart. Heartburn, the real version.

Ceri smiles sympathetically. I don't want sympathy, I want to know exactly what my boyfriend is doing over there that Ceri seems to know so much about. And I want to know if people are feeling sorry for me behind my back while I skip along thinking everything is hunky dory.

'I don't mean anything, hon,' Ceri replies eventually, 'I'm only teasing. I'm sure you know just as much if not more about Connor's trip than the rest of us. After all, you're the one he asked to marry him the day before he left, aren't you, Angel? You're the lucky one.'

Yeah? Right now I'm not so sure. I'm beginning to think the whole marriage thing was a way of keeping his cake at home to make sure he can eat it later if he's still hungry after his American-sized feast (not to mention after a quick floss with Honey's stars and stripes thong bikini). I grind my teeth and find myself backing down. If I show Ceri I'm angry then she'll think I think she knows more about Connor than I do and I'm damned if I'm going to let that happen. I lift my chin (obviously the exercise of the moment) and force a smile on to my lips. Meanwhile I pray to the Patron Saint of Long Distance Relationships – Saint Is-It-Really-Worth-The-Bloody-Hassle? – that my boyfriend is not cheating on me. I would detest that more than anything else in the world.

I would hate to be the last person to know that my darling man of thirteen years has let me down. It would destroy everything we ever had.

'Clamp it, Ceri!' Meg seethes with surprising force when Ceri opens her mouth to speak again, and amazingly Ceri obeys.

We fall silent and I play with the globule of mango chutney on my side plate, my appetite suddenly having shrunk to supermodel proportions. The pain in my chest clings to my heart and I can almost see the flame that has been burning there for my Connor since that first day in the lower sixth flicker and begin to die as the tears inside me rain down upon it. Unlike the heart-rending orchestra music that would start to wail for me now in a movie soundtrack, Indian techno music crashes its way painfully out of the speakers above our heads while Ceri sips her water with a faintly victorious smile. God, she knows how to get my back up. If she carries on like this I'll be moving to Notre Dame to ring a bell and wail 'Esmerelda' for the rest of my sorry life.

I am distracted by my phone vibrating in the pocket of my combat trousers. Finding the right pocket is the first task (I have been told that multiple pockets are fashionable, although if I put something in every one of them I would scarcely be able to lift my legs and would have to be wheeled around on a trolley), hearing the person on the other end over the twanging of an electric sitar is the second.

'Hello?' I screech, even more shrilly than the Indian singer who sounds as if she is being strangled with one of the sitar strings.

'*Allô, Angel, c'est Didier Lafitte à l'appareil.*'

His voice oozes out of the receiver and into my ear like

soothing aloe vera gel. I feel a sudden stirring between my legs, although I put this down to my G-string cutting off the circulation to places of reproductive significance. I allow a smile to move across my previously sullen lips. Just what the doctor ordered; innocent attention from a man whose voice could make flowers grow. My heart wakes up from its depression and takes out its little silver whistle to play along to the techno.

'Didier,' I reply, loud enough to ensure that Ceri hears his name, 'how are you?'

Meg instantly chokes, sending a globule of semi-ingested sag aloo flying across the table. I dodge the spit bomb and grin. The grin almost splits my face when I catch the look in Ceri's eyes – as if she has just been told that her water is in fact one hundred per cent fat and that she will wake up in the morning a size fourteen.

Ooh, anyway, back to Didier, who has been oozing away in my ear while I have been enjoying the moment far too much to listen.

'Blah de blah . . . tomorrow?'

I know it is a question from the tone of his voice but I don't feel sufficiently informed to blag it.

'Er, sorry, Didier, I didn't catch that, the music in this restaurant is a bit loud.'

'Ah, but you are in a restaurant already. I was wanting to bring you to a restaurant tomorrow night but I suppose you will not want to, no?'

'No, I mean yes, I mean . . .'

Shit, what do I mean? This man has the knack of catching me off-guard. A restaurant. That does sound a bit, well, cosy; just Didier, me and a candle burning romantically on a table for two. Yikes, it's a bit different from mingling among his people or sitting in a dark cinema staring at the screen without actually having to converse. I click my tongue nervously against the roof of my mouth. A meal for two. Well, why the hell not? It sounds as if Connor is having a *Moby Dick*-sized whale of a time in the hot tubs of LA so why can't I have an innocent meal with my new friend? No reason at all as far as I can see *and* I get the opportunity to rub the bad news fairy's (aka Ceri's) nose in it, which I have to admit is a very good reason to say yes.

'I mean, a restaurant would be lovely, Didier, thank you,' I reply firmly, even allowing myself a celebratory pout. 'But let me pay this time after the fantastic day we had at your expense' – I'm really working the crowd now – 'It'll be my little treat.'

'Well, Angel, I was thinking of a restaurant I have heard much about since I have been in Glasgow. It is owned by a famous chef and it is called the Devonshire.'

Pants. Big, badly fitting pants with holes in. That's all I'll be able to afford if he makes me pay. What did I have to go getting all feminist/Dutch/even-stevens for?

'The Devonshire,' I whistle, causing Meg to knock over a jug of yellow yoghurt dip. Ceri's nightmare balloons to a size twenty-two.

'*Oui, le Devonshire*, but I must pay, Angel, I absolutely insist. I will not hear of you paying for your meal when I have asked you to come; this would not happen in France.'

Thank fuck, vive la France.

'Well, OK, Didier, that would be great. Lovely,' I reply in my best girly voice, stamping firmly on the dying embers of my burning bra.

'And shall I meet you with a car at the hospital?'

I wrinkle my nose as my face flushes as red as chicken tikka.

'Er, no, don't meet me at the hospital' – I cough over the last word – 'I'll come and meet you at your hotel, if you like.'

'Perfect, Angel; eight o'clock tomorrow night, *alors*.'

'That's fine, see you there.'

'Fine!' Meg screeches when I press the off button. 'She's on the friggin' phone to Didier bloody Lafitte making a date for the Devon-bloody-shire and she says it's *fine*. Jings, I'd love to see what you think's better than fine, hen. And' – she points a stubby finger at me across the table – 'I'd love to see what your Connor thinks of all this.'

I don't really give a shit right now, I think stubbornly. I nonchalantly flick my wrist and try my best to play it as cool as Ceri does when one of her many admirers presents her with a priceless diamond (which does happen, believe me).

'This is entirely a friends thing, Meg, so don't go getting carried away and Connor won't mind at all.' I look at Ceri through narrowed eyes. 'I'll send him an *e-mail* to let him know. That seems to be the best way of communicating with my boyfriend these days.'

Ceri blinks slowly. I am sure I can see jealousy in her eyes. Ceri Divine, jealous. I never thought I would see the day!

'Now, not a word about this to anyone, girls,' I carry on smugly, thoroughly enjoying my moment. 'I'm relying on you both as my best mates to keep Didier's comings and goings a secret, because I promised as a *friend* and I don't want him getting mobbed because of my big mouth.'

'Och aye,' Meg nods, 'nae bother, Angel, but it's pure mental all this. You'll be off at they celeb bashes every Saturday night before we know it.'

'Of course she won't. Angel's hardly a Saturday night party kind of girl, at least not since nightclubs were invented. She's too scared to go that wild and crazy,' Ceri sniffs through pursed lips.

'Och, you're just jealous,' Meg grins, much to my amusement. She rubs her hands together and bounces up and down on the chair. 'You and Didier Lafitte; mates, dates and everything. Jeez-oh, just wait till I tell . . .'

I inhale sharply.

'. . . till I *don't* tell *anyone* at work about all this.'

I turn to Ceri and condescendingly pat her hand.

'You don't mind, do you, Ceri? I know you were the one who told me about Didier coming to Glasgow and that you wanted him for your gossip column but things are just, well, a bit *different* now.'

'Absolutely,' Ceri replies with a smile as tight as if her teeth are stapled to her lips. 'I understand.'

'So you don't mind keeping it under wraps?'

'Nope.'

'And you won't tell?'

Ceri raises a willowy hand and places it on the plunging neckline of her cashmere jumper.

'I won't tell,' she says wearily, 'cross my heart.'

'That's funny, Ceri,' Meg grunts, tilting her glass in Ceri's direction, 'I didn't know you had one.'

CHAPTER SEVENTEEN

Something About The Way You Look Tonight

We went to the Devonshire – *we* meaning Didier, myself and two of his people who sat ominously at the table next to us like the Men In Black. As far as I could tell they spent the night listening to our conversation but they were apparently guarding our bodies, his clearly rating above mine on the 'I will die to save you' scale. Despite our two silent mysterious chums, we spent a very enjoyable evening in the plush surroundings. We sat among the posh people as if we were members of High Society, drinking flutes of champagne and eating food richer than Bill Gates and rather more attractive. Didier was totally at home in the surroundings, adorned as he was in Gucci, Gaultier and Guttingly Expensive. The staff immediately knew who he was; indeed, I was surprised our waitress didn't just serve her ovaries on a plate for him, seeing as she so clearly wanted to have the man's babies. The other diners knew who he was too, which became obvious when I realised that ninety per cent of them were watching us eat rather than looking at the food on their own plates. It was all rather stressful, trying to eat without dropping any sauce on my white fitted shirt while holding in my stomach and constantly scanning my teeth with my tongue for bits of lodged food. It did wonders for my appetite – suppressing it, I mean. No wonder so many famous people have a lower fat content than Skeletor.

It was incredible how once again just being with this man gave me a valid stamped passport to Glamourville. Despite my reservations about being alone with him without the conversational safety net of a crowd, our banter flowed surprisingly easily, it being a comfortable mixture of English and French when the English word eluded him. I did feel strange being at a table for two with someone who wasn't Connor but it was good for my confidence to know that I hadn't lost all ability to converse with a man and keep him interested after spending thirteen years with the same boyfriend. When he laughed at my funny comments or hung on my words as I told a story I felt a flush of self-assurance that I hadn't felt in a long time. After all, Connor knows the majority of my stories now; he's *in* most of them. Conversing with Didier made me feel like a new, interesting, exciting person. Now and again I checked myself when I realised how much I was getting a kick out of an evening alone with a very attractive man, but the fact that I had promised to keep Didier company as a favour to my mum helped to ease my conscience. And Ceri's comments about the e-mails and the stars and stripes you-know-what spurred me on to enjoy myself even more.

Didier told me stories about the music industry when I probed him for information and I – being a nurse on this occasion – nodded with interest without letting on that I knew more than he realised. He told me more stories about his life in France, jetting between his city existence in Paris and his weekend life centred around the Grande Plage in Biarritz, where he would surf, take walks on the beach and watch the sunset from a café on the promenade. He also relayed tales about his mother and Delphine, which instantly brought my mum closer to me, another alien feeling seeing as she is usually as distant as the horizon. I also felt as if I was doing something worthwhile in teaching this man English, while gaining the benefit of a male perspective on things, which has been sadly lacking in my life since Connor went away. Long distance calls just don't give me the time to talk about everything I need or want to discuss with the man in my life and Dan, to be honest, comes a poor second on the male perspective front. He's often more feminine than I am.

I was so at ease in my new friend's company that I agreed to meet him again on Tuesday night, when we did something that 'normal people would do' (his words), namely going to the movies. It was normal in the sense that we held the tickets like excited children and stocked up on giant popcorn and vats of Irn-Bru (you see, I'm introducing him to real Scottish culture) with too much ice. It was abnormal in the sense that Didier wore a disguise – not the false moustache and wig kind but a baseball cap and scarf – that we entered through the back door, that we were given the best tickets without handing over a penny, that we could have emptied the entire food stall into our pockets without anyone uttering a word of complaint and, of course, that the Men In Black sat cosily in the row behind us. I have to admit that being famous by association is pretty cool. And

I figure I may as well make the most of it to help pass the days of my long distance relationship which is proving to be harder than I ever imagined it would be. Conversations with Connor are diminishing, the flowers have still not arrived and I almost can't imagine what it would be like to have him back with me again. I love him dearly, of course, but right now he feels like a stranger. I am sure when he comes home we will slip into our relationship as easily as pulling on a pair of worn-in trackie bottoms but I can't just curl up in a ball and hibernate for the next four months, especially since Connor is out in LA furthering his career and finding himself (at least I hope that's all he's finding). I have to use the time to expand my world too, and making the most of Didier's friendship is as good a way as any. And that is all there is to it. This evening's destination is unknown, although he has promised me glamour with a capital G. Glamour. Good for my social status as an up-and-coming (I can pretend, at least until Friday) DJ, but perhaps not too good for my hips which are starting to feel decidedly J-Lo thanks to all this indulgence (although without the Latino looks to match).

'THERE ISN'Y ANY PROBLEM WITH INFIDELITY,' Boomer hollers into my headphones, 'NOT IF YA DINNY WANT TO HAVE ANY KIDS.'

'I think you're getting confused with in*fertility*, Boomer,' I smile. 'We're actually talking about cheating when you're in a relationship.'

'AYE, RIGHT, I SEE. WELL, THAT ISN'Y ALRIGHT AT ALL. BUT, SO WHERE DO THE KIDS COME IN?'

'Er, I don't know, Boomer, but how's about I play you a song?'

'AYE, ANGEL, ME AND THE LADS AT THE GARAGE WOULD LIKE "BAT OUT OF HELL" OFF MEATLOAF IF THAT'S OKEY-DOKEY.'

'Of course, no problem.'

Try as I might to improve the playlists to an acceptable level, there is no accounting for the taste of my regular listeners.

Infidelity. Gladys's choice of discussion topic for today's (Wednesday's) show – yes, I have still got a show, at least for two more days. Gladys has just discovered that her daughter-in-law, Mandy, cheated on Gladys's son Michael with the man who came to install the widescreen TV. It seems that after fitting the set and handing over the instructions he then gave Mandy a detailed practical demonstration of how the *knob* worked with the accompaniment of surround sound. It then emerged that Mandy had also cheated on Michael with the meter man, the washing machine man, the postman and seemingly every other man who happened to knock on the door, bar the Jehovah's Witness representative (one hopes). Gladys was our first caller and as usual got our discussion off to a flying start.

'Our Michael's been torn-faced ever since he found out, Angel, so he has, the poor wee soul,' said Gladys, who thinks nothing of airing her dirty laundry on the radio washing line. 'And he has been as faithful to that lassie as an auld dog. I said to him – Michael, I said, you are worth more than that. Give her the heave-ho and find a girl who'll not go off havin' her way with every fella who passes her in the street. But he's blinded by the wee tramp, so he is. Blinded.'

Gladys noisily slurped her tea into the receiver while I cued the next track and made a conscious decision not to jog her selective memory by mentioning the fact that 'saint' Michael had been known to wander from the path of the faithful old dog and down to the stray dog pound on occasions himself, which Gladys had admitted on my show. It sounded to me as if this dog had met his match in Mandy the alley cat but I let Gladys wax lyrical about the importance of trust while I wondered to myself about couples like Mandy and Michael. If they were both going to cheat on each other then what was the point of them being together and pretending to be devoted? Or perhaps that was the point. Perhaps people who are destined to cheat find each other and enjoy the security of a relationship while keeping little sub-relationships alive elsewhere. Or perhaps their relationship is the norm these days. After all, Dan and I read only this morning in Ceri's glossip that thirty per cent of all relationships are not monogamous. So if that is the case then who is to say that the whole fidelity thing isn't getting a bit out of date?

Of course, infidelity wouldn't have been my first choice of topic for today's show, or my last for that matter. Although hearing different views may help me gather the thoughts that have been tearing around my head like greyhounds after a hare since our curry night on Sunday. I have turned into a doubting Thomas. When I close my eyes I see hot tubs and thongs and things that only happen in low-budget pornos. Worst of all I see Connor as the lead man and Honey (whom I have never met but who looks distinctly Barbie-like in my dreams, which can't be far wrong) as one of his leading ladies. I hate myself for doubting him but with such a distance between us how can I be sure? The thought of him with another woman makes my skin crawl. Connor McLean is mine. He's been mine for thirteen years. His body is my territory – cared for, massaged, licked, stroked and sucked by me for (I worked this out on a calculator) about forty-four per cent of my life. I've taken such good care of that body, as if it were a flower garden in need of close attention. If someone else has been fondling the flowerbeds then I don't want it any more. The thing is, before Connor went to America I would never have believed he could cheat on me. But Ceri has put doubts in my head.

With all of this in mind, I spoke to Connor this morning before I went to work, still telling myself that I was being ridiculous for having doubts about someone I know (or did know up to nine weeks ago) better than my own parents. Judge for yourself – our conversation went something like this:

'So, have you been trying out anything new over there in America, Con?'

'Like what?'

'Like, you know, American things.'

Hot tubs, you idiot! Like big frothy hot tubs with women in!

'Ehm, aye, I guess so. The food's massive over here, so it is. I might have love handles for you to hold on to when I get back if I'm not careful, babe. Pirelli and Kelly introduced me to their favourite doughnuts and I can't get enough of them.'

Did they now? They didn't happen to be big squidgy ones attached to their chests, did they?

'And, er, has the hotel got any gym facilities, like one of those hot tubs?'

There you go, I said it.

'Och, aye, it's great, Angel, you'd love it. Over here they love havin' parties around the hot tub with everyone in their swimsuits so we've been to a few of them. It's well funny.'

Yeah, Connor, it sounds fucking hilarious, ha ha.

I couldn't bring myself to mention the stars and stripes thong so I hastily changed the subject.

'And have you been in touch with any of your mates recently?'

Or any of my mates?

'A wee bit. I speak to the lads at work just when I have to ring about the show and that but, you know, the calls are well expensive from these hotels. Bit of a nightmare really.'

'Yes, it is. I hear e-mails are cheaper.'

I was beginning to feel like one of those nasty police-women on *The Bill*, grilling him for a confession.

'Aye, well, that's why I've sent you some e-mails rather than call all the time but I know you don't like them that much, my Angel. You're not really up on all that, are you?'

Unlike Ceri bloody Divine it seems.

'I just like to hear your voice, Connor.'

'And I yours, babe; you always brighten my day.'

'Thanks but' – no time for compliments I want answers! – 'you haven't been e-mailing anyone else then?'

'Like who?'

'Ooooh, I don't know, like, er, you know, other people, 'cos those e-mails take ages to write and send and you have to look after your hands being a cameraman and everything. You don't want to get RSI from typing too much, ha ha.'

Pathetic, I know, but I'm not trained in this relationship espionage.

'Ehm, right, well, don't worry about that, babe. I'm not sending e-mails to anyone else apart from you and work so I think I'll cope.'

So there it was. What seemed to me to be a bare-faced lie,

but I suppose it could have been a simple omission to tell me that he had in fact been e-mailing my beautiful best friend and telling her all the gossip about hot tubs and so on. And to mention the hot tub so nonchalantly, as if bikini parties are as natural as a night at the Megabowl – that is not the Connor I know. My suspicions are aroused. What do you think? Am I still being irrational?

Bugger it – why can't he be here where I know what he's doing and who he's doing it with? Double bugger it – how can I even think of marrying Connor when my trust in him is so weak that I want to keep him on a leash (nothing kinky implied) tied to a lamppost outside my flat where I can keep an eye on him? I'm beginning to sound paranoid, which I promise is not like me at all. It's just that everything seems to have changed so fast. It's such unfamiliar territory and I have not felt this vulnerable since the day I walked into St Bridget's Sixth Form without a single friend. Shortly before I fell in love.

Anyway, it was our Gladys who earlier brought up the subject of infidelity and so don't go thinking it's on my mind every minute of the day. It's not. Sometimes I interrupt my worries about infidelity to fret about the impending doom of my career. Oh happy thoughts. I'm sure life used to be easy-peasy once upon a time. At the moment it seems that as soon as I solve one problem there's another just around the corner waiting to pounce into my head and sprout another grey hair. At this rate I'll be joining Gladys and her blue rinse brigade by the time I hit thirty.

Having initiated the discussion, Gladys scurried off to fulfil her duties as a volunteer hospital visitor. Happy to bring this topic to a close, I thankfully turn to my last caller of the day.

'Tyrone,' I chirp as Meatloaf goes like a bat out of hell into the distance (thank God), 'how are you today, my pal?'

I glance at the clock. A quarter to three. There is a chance he went to school and got out early for Wednesday afternoon sports but somehow I doubt it. I decide to give my young friend a break and not mention the 'S' word.

Tyrone sniffs and sighs lightly into the phone. 'My Mum cheated on my dad,' he says sadly. 'That's why he left us.'

I look at Dan who smiles supportively through the glass.

'And how old were you when this happened, Tyrone?' I ask gently.

'Och, really young, like six, but I remember the fights an' all that. And my brother, well, he tell't me what it was all about. She cheated with my dad's brother and they had this massive barney and his brother went to jail, so my old man left and then Mum got drunk and she's been steamin' ever since.'

I inhale quickly and hold my breath.

A drunk parent. What I could tell you about a drunk parent, I think morosely. Not that it would help much as I am twenty-nine and yet still haven't been able to find a cure for my 'old man', who is getting older by the measure. I doubt it would do us much good simply swapping stories about their mood swings, their minor accidents, the mixture of pity and anger you feel as you watch the person you were taught to look up to reducing themselves to a dribbling, pissing, waffling wreck. This young teenager needs answers but unfortunately I haven't got them and, I am ashamed to say, unlike him I don't have the courage to air my personal problems on air. No matter how small my audience. I guiltily hold my tongue as he continues to talk as if to himself.

'Cheatin's pure bad,' he continues with a certain firmness to his voice. 'It hurt my dad and by doin' it my mum hurt herself. I'm not an adult but I know that canny be a good thing, right? If she hadn'y cheated we'd still be a family and I'd have an uncle and it'd all be just minted.'

Somehow I don't think Tyrone's family life would ever have been 'minted' but I make agreeable noises into the microphone to encourage him.

'I'd never cheat on a lassie, never.'

'And have you got a girlfriend, Ty?'

He pauses. I cringe at my own stupidity. Of course he hasn't got a girlfriend. In between hiding from his alcoholic mother, playing truant from school and getting kicked around the playground I doubt the poor lad has had time to confidently ask a girl out and fall madly in love. You plonker, Angel.

'Nuh,' he replies eventually. 'I haven'y got a lassie but . . . but if I did she'd be like you.'

Dan grins and blows me a kiss across the studio.

'She'd sound like you and she'd be dead nice like you and pretty and funny an' I'd treat her like a princess, so I would.'

'And she would be a very lucky girl, Tyrone, I hope you realise that.'

He humphs dismissively into the receiver. I warn myself not to condescend. This lad is probably more mature than Ceri with all the things he's been through in his fourteen years. What he needs from me is support and honesty, not radio DJ bullshit.

'Have you got a boyfriend, Angel?' Tyrone asks suddenly, taking me by surprise.

'Me?' I anxiously nibble my cheek. *Oh well, what harm can it do?* 'Yes, Tyrone,' I answer, 'I have got a boyfriend. We've been together a very long time, actually – thirteen years. But he's working abroad for a while so I'm just getting used to that.'

'Abroad for a while,' he repeats. 'But you're faithful to him, right?'

'Of course I am,' I laugh. 'I wouldn't cheat.'

'Aye, I know that, you're too nice,' he replies happily. 'Not like my mum. She's cheatin' all over again and people'll get hurt. She's got this new boyfriend, see, but she still has loads of other blokes through to the house. She says they're friends but I know she's bonkin' them, although she thinks I don't.'

Dan stuffs his fist into his mouth and I stifle a gasp. 'Well, maybe that's a bit too much information, Ty, but thanks for your input in the debate.'

'Nae bother,' he sniffs. 'Anyhow, when I get older I'm gonna be faithful and I'm gonna make sure I don't hurt anyone. It just isn'y worth it. And I hope your boyfriend doesn'y cheat on you, Angel.'

'So do I, Tyrone,' I reply with a strangled laugh, 'I so do I.'

One hour before I am due to be picked up by one of Didier's cars, I suddenly experience a sartorial crisis. I mean, picked up by one of his cars, that's enough in itself to send any working class girl into a fashion panic. We're not talking being honked from the street by an irate, overweight, chain-smoking taxi driver in a food-stained ancient Mondeo. I've seen the cars Didier and his people use and they are not the sort to be found in the free ads. I can't let Didier down; he has a reputation as a glamorous sex symbol to protect.

Besides, any fashion faux pas is bound to get back to Delphine via Marie-Pierre and my mother doesn't need any more excuses to disown her disappointing daughter. Didier promised me glamour, sorry, *G*lamour, which means I have to give Glamour in return, doesn't it? Fuck.

I stand naked in the bathroom facing the mirror and try to imagine what Ceri would do in a situation like this. Then I admit to myself that Ceri wouldn't have to do anything but spritz on some perfume, slap on a bit of her expensive make-up and choose one of the designer outfits from her wardrobe. Ceri has dates like this every day of the week, sometimes twice a day, and she doesn't exactly have to start with the same raw materials that I have to work with.

I suck in my stomach for the benefit of the mirror and try my best to suck in my hips – my 'problem area' as I guess the body police working for women's magazines would call it – before resigning myself to the fact that hips can not be sucked smaller, at least not from the inside and not without the help of a giant Hoover.

'Give it up, Angel,' I tut, pointing at my strained expression in the mirror, 'you are not Ceri Divine and you never will be. Not unless you spend the next three months on a rack with only celery for comfort.'

My stomach relaxes apologetically. Thankfully my hips don't relax any more than they already have since my early twenties. I may be thirty in ten days' time but that is no excuse for a mid-life crisis. Thirty isn't mid-life any more anyway – the thirties are the new twenties. Tonnes of famous and successful people are thirty-somethings like Kylie and Jennifer Aniston and Nicole Kidman. Granted I am not a sex symbol of their calibre but I should be accepting Angel

Knights for who she is and what she looks like and what her potential is, not fretting about who and what I am never going to be. Damn it, I can be as glamorous as Ceri and Truly and Honey (thong bikini excepted), I just have to be myself. *Be natural* was the advice Dan and I read in *Star* about how to realise your attractiveness. So, when I step into Didier's glamorous world tonight, I will be *natural*.

Three razor cuts, a hot wax incident, several tonnes of make-up and a whole tube of hair gel later I am about as natural as I am going to get. I slip on a kingfisher blue knee-length silk skirt, matching basque top with georgette sleeves and my mermaid blue pointed shoes with heels high enough to make my legs look long but low enough that putting one foot in front of the other isn't too much of a challenge. My hair is not in spikes but sculpted around my face, decidedly pixie-like, I must say, although admittedly my chin still isn't doing it. I glance at my watch, take it off when I realise that a chunky sporty thing doesn't quite go with my glamour look and sit on the edge of my sofa staring inanely at the television, waiting for the horn to honk while practising the art of twiddling one's thumbs.

'Your carriage awaits, *mademoiselle*,' Didier smiles, bowing his head of dark shiny hair and motioning towards a silver stretch limousine.

'Wow,' I twitter, skipping forwards to open the door.

'Uh, we must sit in the back,' he grins. 'Only the chauffeur sits in the front seat.'

'Of course, whoops, I always forget where to sit when I get into limos. Sorry.'

Feeling like a prat, I skulk through the door and almost

fall into the back. This isn't a car; it's an island on wheels. I could fit my flat in this thing, not to mention Connor's Peugeot and a double garage. There are televisions and bottles of champagne and rows of sparkling glasses and canapés. Not to mention the cream leather *sofas* masquerading as car seats, the sheepskin rugs and, Heavens to Bentley, is that a jacuzzi?

'How many friends have you got joining us?' I laugh, picking a sofa and sinking into the folds of soft leather.

'None,' Didier replies, taking a pew opposite me and reaching for the champagne, 'tonight is just for the two of us.'

'What, no bodyguard hulks?'

He laughs and his face instantly softens.

'No bodyguards. Just me, Didier Lafitte, and my beautiful friend and English teacher, Angel Knights. I hope you have a very enjoyable time.'

'Well, it's pretty crap so far,' I giggle and blush all at once as the door clicks shut and the chauffeur seems to magic himself into the front seat. 'You're going to have to try harder if you want to be my friend.'

'Ah, a challenge,' Didier replies, raising his smoky eyes to look at me from beneath his perfectly sculpted eyebrows. 'I love a challenge.'

I squelch further into the sofa under the sudden intensity of his gaze, realising that not only is the car very overwhelming but that the man in the back of the car with me is also overwhelming. We are alone; just me and him and no bodyguards. Fair enough we have a driver, but he is invisible on the other side of the dark screen that closes as we begin to drive. We are alone in a quiet, confined space and all of a sudden I am verging on uncomfortable. I immediately see Connor's face – what would he think of me being in a limousine with a famous male sex symbol? Connor may be indulging in the odd hot tub party but we've got one of our very own in the back of this ridiculously extravagant car. I feel guilt rush through my veins, not only for relishing such luxury that I could never afford but also for not having told Connor about my plans for this evening. I suppose I should let you know the other half of that telephone conversation this morning. Give you all the available information, as it were. It was shorter than my interrogation of him and it seemed harmless at the time:

'It's your birthday soon, my Angel. It's the biggie.' (Him)

'The big three-oh, as they say. Ha, yep, that's me. Ten days' time and counting.'

'What do you think you'll do? Have Meg and Ceri got any plans for you?'

Well, I don't know, Con, why don't you ask them yourself, on E-MAIL perhaps?

'Nah, I don't think so. It'll probably be a quiet one. A bit of champers and a cake and not much else.'

'Och, that sounds a bit rubbish. Your birthdays usually last about a week, babe.'

'Yeah, but you're not here and I haven't got anyone else to go out with so it'll probably pass by unnoticed.'

'Shame. Well, you never know, something might come up.'

Yep, another candle on my cake. It'll be getting pretty crowded on there.

'I doubt it. My diary isn't exactly jammed with offers.'

(This is where the truth began to bend like a spoon under Uri Geller's gaze.)

'Really? You haven't been going out much then?'

'Er, no, not much.'

'No new adventures or new friends or anything exciting?'

Well, there was a music industry get-together, and a dinner at the Devonshire, and a free movie with as much popcorn as I could shove into my mouth, and have I mentioned my blossoming friendship with The Didier Lafitte?

That is what I should have said, but what actually made it past the invisible censor on my voicebox was: 'No new adventures, really, everything's much the same. You know, good old West End.'

And that was it. Why didn't I tell him? I told myself it was because I didn't want to bother him unnecessarily, to give my boyfriend anything to worry about when it was all completely innocent. But sitting in this car with the smouldering Didier Lafitte a pheromone away I am not so sure. Did I not tell Connor because I feel guilty about spending time with an undeniably attractive man? Or did I not tell him because I want to get him back for having fun and frolics with the glamour models? On the one hand I feel confused but on the other I can safely say that I am in a car with a man whom I am suddenly and surprisingly beginning to find very alluring. The simple fact that I am attracted to him scares me. The additional fact that we still have the whole evening ahead of us positively terrifies me.

My eyes dart from Didier's tanned face to the wide collar of his black shirt. The top two buttons of his shirt are open, the neckline seeming to point intentionally towards his smooth chest. I see his breast bone and immediately avert my eyes, but they fall on his slim legs and the black velvet-covered knee that protrudes towards my bare one. *Don't look between his legs*, I order myself, just as my eyes slip to his groin. OH JESUS! I immediately stare at his boots. Big feet, what does that mean again? Stop it, Angel, just behave yourself. I take a deep breath and move my eyes back to his face. His are still focused on me and a smile is touching his soft lips. Damn, I am sure he looked just the same on the other occasions we got together but either I have tumbled to new depths of vulnerability or there is, in the words of Elton John, something about the way he looks tonight that is making me lose my cool quicker than an ice cube in a sauna.

'Champagne, my darling?' he says, holding out a crystal flute filled almost to the brim.

I lean carefully forwards and reach out for the glass, almost dropping it as his hand moves down and touches mine.

'I've got a boyfriend!' I screech and throw the champagne into my mouth like a single shot of tequila.

'Good for you,' Didier replies with a twisted smile, 'but it is not him I am interested in.'

CHAPTER EIGHTEEN

Who's That Girl?

The Ice Palace. Didier Lafitte has brought me to The Ice Palace; the place where only nine weeks ago I was proposed to by my boyfriend. That was undoubtedly the poshest meal we had ever indulged in during our time together and it took thirteen years to get there. Now, here I am with Didier Lafitte, having met him only five days ago. He doesn't hang about, does he? Then again, he is a European pop god, not a cameraman. Not that one is necessarily better than the other, but meals like this are ten-a-penny to a man like Monsieur Lafitte. He's probably not even excited, although he does appear to be enjoying himself, as am I. It would be hard not to really, seeing as this time we are on the best table with an entire waiting staff to ourselves, and people are looking up at me instead of down. How things can change in a short space of time, including the fact that I am lapping up Didier's flirtations in order to make myself feel better about the fact that I am currently as celibate as Mother Teresa and that my boyfriend seems like a distant stranger in a busy hot tub.

Ennio Morricone plays softly in the background as I gaze at the lobster on my plate and wonder who first tackled a creature with a shell that hard and pincers that vicious to discover the tasty meat. It must be one of the best examples of beauty being on the inside.

'What does he look like?' asks Didier over the heartstring-tugging melody of *Chi Mai*.

'What? Oh, a bit like yours really. Pink, crusty, a bit ugly but tastes heavenly. Look.'

'No, not the lobster,' he laughs, holding his stomach (or should I say his six-pack), 'I mean your boyfriend. He is not pink and crusty, is he?'

I laugh too and respond when he lifts his glass to clink it against mine.

'You are very funny, Angel.'

'I wasn't trying to be, but thanks.'

'You should be an entertainer.'

Er, well, now you mention it.

'So?'

'So what?'

'So what does he look like?'

'Oh, right.'

Is that a bad sign? That I can forget that we were talking about Connor in the time it takes to clink two glasses together?

I describe Connor while Didier listens intently. I describe all the things a girl will remember – every feature from his hair to his body and his topaz-coloured eyes. I then move on to his personality, using the words I always use to describe my boyfriend – kind, down-to-earth, faithful, tidy, not overly romantic in a chocolate/flowers (definitely not flowers, as I have recently discovered) kind of way but thoughtful nonetheless. But as I talk I begin to wonder. Is Connor McLean still all those things now that he has spent nine weeks away from me in Hollywood with girls who make me feel like a librarian in comparison? Will he still be down-to-earth and faithful when he returns or will he have discovered the joys of sowing his seed? Will he still enjoy playing Pat in the *EastEnders* omnibus as we cuddle on the sofa on a Sunday afternoon? I don't know any more. While I sit here, patiently waiting for the return of the same man I kissed goodbye on that hazy Friday morning, am I building myself up for a disappointment? And am I missing out on a golden opportunity, as Ceri said, to find out what life has to offer a girl like me before I settle for the one I already know?

Didier refills my champagne flute. I'll rephrase that: Didier motions to the waiter to refill my champagne flute, which is swiftly done. We seem to have a waiter for every minor task. I'm just waiting for one of them to offer to chew my food for me.

'You and Connor,' Didier says once the waiter leaves us alone, 'are you serious in your relationship?'

'Yes, we are. We've been together since we were at school in the sixth form, which is a long time. It's also been a great time. We have fun, we know each other so well; you know, just the general old relationship stuff.'

He nods knowingly while I nervously sip my champagne and hope that if I keep quiet he might just change the subject. It doesn't feel right discussing Connor with another man. Then again, it's not like I've got many other options for airing my thoughts on our relationship. Meg thinks Connor and I are as destined to be together as Scott and Charlene on

Neighbours, my mother would rather poke out her own eyes than see me commit to him for life, my dad shrinks away like a salt-covered slug whenever I mention matters of the heart and Ceri . . . well, Ceri has an electronic personal hot-line to Connor, doesn't she?

'He asked me to marry him,' I say, giving in to my urge to discuss my long distance boyfriend, 'the night before he left for the States.'

'And you said?'

'I said . . . I said maybe,' I reply, studying a lobster claw and trying to imagine what it would be like to be caught in its sharp grip. 'He has given me time to think about it until he comes home. I suppose you could say we are in a kind of pre-engagement situation at the moment. In the queue waiting to buy tickets for the big adventure, as it were.'

'Well, I hope you buy the right ones,' Didier laughs softly.

I am drawn to his whiter-than-snow teeth, framed by the full and soft, even slightly tanned lips that are naturally formed in the sort of pout that only the French do best.

'So does this mean that you are not sure?' he asks, interrupting my very private thoughts about what it would be like to kiss that beautiful mouth. (Come on, give me a break, I haven't had a kiss for so long I'll have forgotten what to do with my tongue. It is no fun for a mouth to be demoted to mere eating and talking duties.)

'Am I sure?' I ask myself.

Of course I am sure. Kissing him would be as delightful as sucking on a giant Magnum ice cream, only possibly less messy. But we weren't talking about that, were we? Concentrate, Angel, for heaven's sake.

'If I am honest, Didier, I don't suppose I am sure,' I smile weakly. 'I mean, I love Connor and I have never wanted to be with anyone else' – I could add that I have in fact *never* been with anyone else, but that might be just too much information and I don't want him to think I'm frigid or anything – 'and he probably is The One but marriage is such a big thing, even these days. I just don't want to get it wrong. Like my mum and dad, they definitely got it wrong.'

Didier shrugs.

'Maybe, maybe not. Their marriage produced you, Angel, and the world is much better for that.'

Wow, he's smooth. I blush the same colour as the lobster on my plate and nervously guzzle more champagne. Actually, I am definitely getting a real taste for bubbly the more time I spend with Didier. Not necessarily a good thing when you've got a bank balance like mine, plus it slips down far too easily and one bendy juice addict in the family is more than enough. I move from guzzling to sipping and look across the table at my new friend. My new friend who is currently reaching across the table and, *fuck me*, placing his hand on top of mine and squeezing it gently. His hand is warmer than I remember it being when we have shaken hands before. My skin sizzles under his touch.

'It's a man,' my nerve-endings giggle to each other, 'remember what one of those feels like?'

'My advice is,' Didier says, looking deep into my eyes, 'marry this man if your body and soul fit properly with his. If you have seen what else is out there and he is the best fit for you. Marry him for sure if living without him is something that you just cannot do, but if marriage scares you be certain before you commit. Otherwise, *chérie*, you will not settle into it and you will not give it the time it needs to grow.' He gently strokes my fingers, putting my nerve endings on red alert. 'We have only one life, Angel, so why live it safely? Stepping out into the unknown can be the best thing in the world and also the most frightening but often it is worth the risk. I went to Paris alone, I took a risk and look at me.'

Do I have to? Looking at you is making me dizzy. If I were standing up my knees would definitely be weak.

'You may think you are happy with what you have,' he concludes, 'but how do you know you cannot be happier?'

All of a sudden Ceri's words of, er, I suppose I can call it wisdom when we first discussed Didier's imminent arrival in Glasgow start ringing in my ears: 'How do you know that you're not accepting second best if you haven't had a good look around?' Now Didier himself is saying practically the same thing. Am I missing out? If I marry Connor, or even if I just stay with Connor as my boyfriend for the rest of my life, will I be making the most of what the male species has to offer? Is sleeping with one man in my whole life just like sticking to the same sandwich filling day after day until my teeth fall out and I can't eat sandwiches any more?

I frown and look down at my hand. Or rather at Didier's strong, masculine hand that is totally covering mine. The heat from his skin warms my fingers and shoots up my arm like a sudden bolt of lightning, electrifying the champagne bubbles in my head. My mind spins with the confusion of it all but my eyes focus firmly on his.

What was the other thing that Ceri said, this time about Didier himself?

'The man is an absolute peach. Clearly mad about music and French too. Sounds like someone else I know. You two might be perfect for each other.'

And she was right. If Ceri knows one thing well it is men. She could probably win *Mastermind* with that as her specialist subject. Didier is a peach and we do have a lot in common, despite living in completely different worlds. And he is right in front of me, stroking my hand and giving me his undivided attention, ignoring the fact that he could probably have any woman in Glasgow he wanted. And Ceri tells me that Connor is off having a whale of a time in good old Tinseltown. Am I missing something so big that I would have to be blind not to see it?

Didier's fingers move from my hand to my wrist. He turns my arm over and massages the pressure point at the base of my palm with his smooth thumb.

'Erm, I'm a little bit confused at the moment, Didier,' I cough. 'It just keeps going round and round in my mind.'

'You should just relax. Let yourself go. Do what you feel like doing at each moment.'

What, getting naked and having full-blown sex right on this table? Probably not a good idea.

'Hmm,' I squeak, trying desperately to focus on thoughts of Connor, 'but how do I know if he is The One?'

He continues to stroke my wrist. I don't tell him to stop.

'I think it is impossible to know that, Angel,' he replies in his sumptuous French accent. 'It is not written in stone. It is simply something that your heart will tell you.'

I watch as he places his other hand on his heart, rather too close to the open collar of his black shirt for comfort. My eyes register the tanned skin of his chest and I squeeze them shut to prevent them sending an unsightly drooling command to my mouth. Thankfully the waiter interrupts Didier's poetic theories to clear away our lobster dishes and replace them with the prettiest steaks I have ever seen, which gives me time to regain some composure.

'One thing I must say,' says Didier when we are alone again, 'is that your boyfriend is a very lucky man, Angel. I hope he realises this and I hope he treats you with the respect you deserve. You are a wonderful woman – you should be living a wonderful life.'

I shiver as he clasps my hand between both of his and then thankfully releases it before I explode as the result of a hormonal surge. I am living a wonderful life, Didier, I want to say aloud, but I keep my thoughts to myself. Limousines, parties, champagne, glamour and good conversation with a very attractive and attentive Frenchman who is the darling of women all over Europe – how can that not be a wonderful life? Only last week I was lonely and drifting along in the get up, go to work, buy some shoes, go home, see Meg and Ceri way of life. Now I am doing new and interesting things and my horizons have instantly broadened. Dare I say it, Didier makes me feel sexy, alive and like a new woman. One question though, can I be a new woman with forty-inch legs and a bum like Kylie's? Just checking.

We eat our pretty steaks, served as they are with pretty sauce and pretty flowers and even prettier vegetables (definitely the sign of a good restaurant if they can make carrots look exciting). We have a lemon sorbet course and a chocolate sorbet course and a cake course and a brandy snap and handmade chocolate course, followed by coffee and an aperitif (or is that the one that comes before the meal? I can never remember). Anyway, we have a drink of something strong after what feels like fifty courses and I finally collapse back in the ivory velvet booth seat like a stuffed foie gras goose. I am completely relaxed thanks to the food, the champagne and the restaurant's easy-on-the-ear chill-out album piped softly through the air. Any more relaxed and I would be completely horizontal (I hope I didn't say that out loud).

'Did you enjoy your meal?' Didier asks, sliding around the seat until we are at adjacent edges of the table.

'Did I? Wow, of course, I'm stuffed.'

He smiles and raises his glass of deep red wine.

'My grandfather was a winemaker,' he says, running a finger slowly around the rim of the glass.

I watch his digit with fascination until I realise that my tongue is making the same motion around my lips. Girls, I really must apologise for the lack of available female hormone right now, it appears I have got it all.

'Did he crush the grapes himself,' I grin, 'with his feet?'

'No, I think he had a machine for that, *chérie*, but he did pick the grapes himself. He grew them and tended them with his own fair hands.'

Well, if his grandfather's hands were anything like Didier's, I'm not surprised they produced a good wine.

'You will not join me, Angel, in having one small glass of *vin rouge*?'

'No thanks, Didier, that champagne was more than enough and I can already feel that shot of whatever it was having an effect on my legs.' Or is that just from being close to you? 'I'm not really a big drinker.'

'You are not a big anything,' he laughs, 'you are very petite.'

Petite? I like it. Short, maybe, but has the guy not noticed my hips?

I look on as Didier raises the drink to his lips (yes, it's those lips again) and takes a long, lazy sip. All the while his eyes are focused on mine through the glass. I bite my lip and picture the red liquid running smoothly down the back of his throat and trickling into his firm stomach. He gulps and I gulp too, pushing the rush of adrenalin back down into my body.

'Beautiful,' he nods. 'I taste plum and berry flavours, with a subtle aroma of oak. Perfectly formed.'

His knee brushes against mine beneath the table, sending an urgent wake-up call to my ovaries. He moves closer along the seat until our shoulders touch and I can smell his fragrance, masculine and modern, so rich and oaky, just like the wine, that I want to fill my lungs with the aroma. As for the body that is dangerously close to mine, talk about perfectly formed. I can feel the chemistry leaping from him and burning its way through my clothes. I should move away, run to the toilet, whistle to the waiter for the bill, anything to stop this, but I can't. I am hypnotised. I am floating up to the sky like an Angel on air.

'You must taste a little of the wine,' he breathes, holding the glass up between us.

'All right,' I smile uneasily, 'I'll have a sip if it's that delicious.'

I reach out for the stem of the glass but my fingers touch nothing as he swiftly moves it away from my grasp and once again lifts it towards his mouth. His moist lips part teasingly and the rim of the glass disappears between them. His top lip glistens under the dim lights as the wine touches the skin. I am mesmerised. He lowers the glass but I continue to watch his mouth as he swallows and then parts his lips in a wonderful smile. When I reach for the glass my hand is shaking as if I've got a vibrator up my sleeve, and when I raise it to my own mouth I am overwhelmed by the thought that this same glass was only seconds ago being caressed by the lips of a gorgeous man. Now that the glass is against my mouth, it feels as if we have kissed. The wine is warm with a strong flavour, but I can't concentrate on the taste as it fills my throat. How can this moment be so intense? And why are my lips now aching to be pressed against his?

I should leave before the ache grows so strong that I cannot resist it. This is wrong. I shouldn't be here. Now the hand that Didier Lafitte is raising towards his mouth looks like mine, and it appears to be attached to my arm, but it simply can't be mine. After all, I wouldn't let another man kiss my fingers without putting up a fight. I wouldn't allow him to run his tongue along them and take them into his mouth gently, one by one, kissing them passionately. And I certainly wouldn't just sit motionless while that man placed his other hand on my leg underneath the table, pushing up my silk skirt and caressing my bare inner thigh with a touch capable of causing an earthquake from here to India. I am Angel Knights – good student, good worker, good girlfriend and all-round good girl. I don't do the sort of things that this girl is doing here at our table in the middle of a crowded restaurant. Didn't I promise Tyrone only today that I wouldn't cheat on my man? Didn't he agree that I was too nice to do such a thing? Didn't I tut to myself at the unfaithful antics of Gladys's daughter-in-law and son? I'm not like them. I'm not that sort of girl.

Who is this woman and why is she giving in to his touch? His hand moves up her thigh and I hear a distant groan. He kisses the palm of her hand, breathing in the aroma of her perfume – the perfume her boyfriend bought for her in the shiny red bottle. He leans across the corner of the table and she does the same, longing to be nearer to him. She closes her eyes as he cups her chin in his hand and runs his finger down her cheek.

'You are truly a beautiful woman,' he breathes, his mouth so close to her ear that his lips touch the lobe. '*T'est vraiment belle.*'

'Thank you,' I hear her reply quietly, her voice also breathless.

Just 'thank you'. Not 'Am I really?' or 'Do I look all right in this outfit?' Tonight she is beautiful, she knows it and she wants more than anything to make the most of the rush she is feeling.

'I want to be with you tonight,' he whispers.

The words make her body spasm with lust.

'I want to be yours. Come home with me tonight.'

Her eyes find his and she is instantly pulled into their deep, dark vortex. His face moves nearer until their lips are almost touching, the electricity shooting between them like a Jean Michel Jarre laser show.

'OK,' she whispers, her voice barely audible, 'I will come home with you.'

As their lips briefly touch she thinks she sees a flash of light illuminating them from one side but she can't move. And as he takes her hand and leads her away from the table towards the exit, her mind spins like a record.

'Don't go,' I warn her, but she has already succumbed.

'I want to make love to you, Angel,' he whispers, placing a strong arm around her body as they reach the waiting limousine.

Angel? Why is he using my name? I'm not that sort of girl. Am I?

CHAPTER NINETEEN

I'm No Angel

What *am* I doing? I'll tell you what I'm doing. I am sitting in a grandiose hotel reception, trying not to look like a call girl while I wait for France's biggest (by that I mean record sales, not . . . yes, anyway) popstar to take me to bed. That is what I am doing. The question I am now beginning to ask myself is why? I am someone's girlfriend. Someone who only a couple of months ago I was buying a thirteenth-year anniversary present for. And I have only ever slept with that someone in all my almost-thirty years. So am I really going to go ahead with this and try a different sandwich filling?

It seemed like a good idea in the restaurant and even to a certain extent in the limo – which, thankfully, Didier had too much style to turn into a shaggin' wagon. It didn't seem real, so caught up was I in the whole seduction thing. But as I sit here now reality is setting in. Should I resist him? Is this wrong? Will this moment change my life for ever? Or should I just stop worrying and go for it to ensure that I don't wake up one day in the future wondering what it would be like to have slept with two men in my life? I don't want to live with regret. Then again, I don't want to live with the reputation of being a two-timing slapper either.

Didier has gone to clear his room, or rather his *suite* of rooms, of the stormtroopers who gather there to protect their megastar from women like me. Meanwhile, I am sitting alone on this plush sofa, struggling with the realisation that maybe I, just like the original stormtroopers in *Star Wars*, am also being drawn to the dark side of the Force. Just give me a black helmet and an asthma problem and call me Darth.

I glance at the lift doors behind me, which remain steadfastly shut, then look around the reception, trying to keep my mind occupied. The staff busy themselves at the desk, hardly giving me a second glance. People wander in and out, all of them looking as at home in these surroundings as I would in a motorway services Travel Inn. A dark-haired man in a James Bond-esque suit and coat eyes me suspiciously from an armchair at the other end of the foyer. From the look on his face he's got me well and truly summed up. I look away and occupy my shaking hands with the task of finding my mobile phone in the depths of my bag. Time for some modern-day text message therapy.

I wait for the buttons to be activated before I can type a message. Mind you, what am I going to write and who am I going to write it to? *Hi Ceri, just off to shag Didier Lafitte, what do you reckon? x Angel.* Yeah right, and find myself in her gossip column in a couple of days' time. And I already know what Ceri would tell me to do. So how about – *Hiya Meg, what you up to? Didier kissed me and set my heart on fire. Is that a bad thing? x Angel.* But that would destroy Meg's vision of Connor and I as the perfect couple – the same thing that Meg has strived for her whole life, without a whole lot of success. I couldn't do it. That leaves my mum, who isn't even up to speed on fax machines let alone text messages, my dad, who doesn't believe in mobile phones, and Connor – er, even if his mobile did work in the States, this is not a very good time to send him a news-filled text of recent goings on, is it? Anyway, he's probably tucked up cosily between Truly's pillows by now.

The phone suddenly emits two shrill beeps, causing me to drop it on the hard floor with a loud crash. The man opposite sneers at me in disgust before returning to his newspaper. I scrabble on the floor for the phone, then curl up and try to become invisible. The screen informs me that I have a voicemail message, probably left earlier when I had the phone switched off during dinner. I take one quick look at the lift doors – still shut – then dial my voicemail number. Anything to pass the time that is slowly turning me into a nervous wreck.

'You have one new message,' the posh electronic woman tells me.

I press the phone to my ear and listen. The voice is wheezy and stilted but I instantly recognise the slurred words of my dad. He hates answering machines. It is very unusual for him to have left a message at all.

'He . . . hello? Hello, Angel, are you there?' He pauses. 'Oh well (cough) . . . I . . . um . . . Angel, I was watching the football. And (cough) Motherwell, they won.'

He sounds so happy that his team have won that it brings a tear to my eye. Simple pleasures, that is all my father has left.

'Two-one in the very last minute. Scored wi . . . with thirty seconds to go. Amazing. So' – I hold the phone away from my ear as he coughs a lung into the receiver – 'I was having a little cele . . . celbation . . . celebration.'

'I bet you were,' I comment cynically.

'Just a couple, you know, just a couple. And it has been fun. I have had a fun night.'

I press my lips together as I listen to the man I once admired more than any other in the whole world telling me that sitting alone watching his favourite Scottish team winning a match with only a bottle of whisky for company is a fun night. I suddenly feel guilty. I should have been with him, not out trying to be glamorous and getting as far away from my roots as I could.

'A fun night,' he repeats with a lingering wheeze. 'Only now, Angel, I . . . I don't feel too good. I was wondering if you could come over. I . . . (cough) . . . I think I'm ill.'

I freeze at the last word. Yes, of course my father is ill. He is a drinker, pure and simple. But Steve Knights is also of the generation of men that sees illness as a weakness. I have never heard my dad admit to feeling ill. The adrenalin I have built up throughout the night surges through my veins in the form of fear. Something is wrong.

'Can you hear me, Angel?' he asks, his voice weakening, 'I'm sorry.'

'Dad,' I say aloud, forgetting where I am. Forgetting the man staring at me across the quiet reception.

My fear turns to panic as my eardrum is enveloped by a pitiful cry before the phone goes dead.

'Dad,' I say again, my whole body starting to quiver.

No, this can't be happening. Not tonight. Tonight was all

so perfect and magical and . . . I stare at the phone in my unsteady hand.

'You have no more messages,' the electronic woman says dully.

'No!' I wail, leaping up from the sofa and clattering across the floor towards the lift doors.

I hammer the button and pray for them to open. Tears stream down the cheeks of my reflection in the mirrored doors but I don't feel them. I am numb. A bell sounds, the lift doors slide open and I fall into the arms of the man inside.

'Help me, Didier,' I cry, pointing towards the exit, 'it's my dad. I think he's dying.'

Now I can imagine the pain of being caught in the grip of that lobster's pincer – a sharp, crushing pain that goes right to the bone. The pain I am feeling as we drive westwards out of the city towards Paisley and my dad's house won't go away. Didier's driver senses the urgency and pushes the car to its limits, like the Delorian car in *Back To The Future*. Maybe we will burst into flames and emerge unscathed in a different time zone just like Michael J. Fox. One where things like this don't happen. One where life is generally less complicated. It doesn't feel right racing to his aid in a top-of-the-range luxury limousine and it feels all wrong pulling up alongside my dad's grey pebbledash house in this street where limousines are of another world entirely. I could stop to think of the significance of this – my world against Didier's world – but I don't. I throw open the door before the car has come to a standstill, stumble on to the pavement and race up the path.

'Dad, it's me, Angel,' I shout, banging my fist against the door. 'Dad, are you there? Are you OK?'

I press the bell but the battery must be flat. I hammer on the door as hard as I can with my bare fist. I run to the front of the house and peer through the kitchen window but I can't see him. I try the lounge window but my view is blocked by the net curtain that hangs lopsidedly from the wire above the window.

'I can't see him,' I call to Didier, who is banging on the front door and calling my father's name.

'It is OK, we will get in there,' Didier says softly, touching a calming hand to my shaking shoulder. 'Don't worry, Angel, it will be fine.'

'It's NOT fine,' I sob loudly. 'He's in there and he can't hear me. Oh God, what's happened, Didier? DAD!'

I want to smash a window, kick the door down, anything to get inside and help him.

'I should have been here,' I cry. 'He shouldn't be living here all by himself, he's so lonely. Break the door down,' I yell at Didier's driver, who I notice is about the size of a yeti now that he is out of the car.

'*Non*, wait,' Didier says firmly. 'Would anyone have a key? Uh, a neighbour, a friend?'

'What? No. He doesn't have friends. Stop being so calm. Why are you so fucking calm?'

I wrestle myself from his firm grasp and run towards the back garden. Finding a heavy brick among the rubble that is supposed to be a rockery feature, I raise it above my head and trip towards the front door. Just as I am about to smash the window a neighbour appears, a transparent-looking young woman in a pink velour tracksuit with a cigarette hanging from her bottom lip.

'Bloody hell, hen, you gave us a fright, so ya did,' she

wheezes. 'Put that bloody rock doon the noo before ya hurt yersel or some'dy else.'

The brick remains frozen above my head. 'My dad,' I splutter, staggering around in front of her, 'I need to get in to my dad.'

She looks at the adjacent door and shrugs. 'Och, Mr Whatsit doon the stairs, is it now? I'm sorry, he's already gone, hen.'

I drop the brick, narrowly missing my foot, and stumble backwards. Didier catches me before I can fall.

'Gone? No, he can't be gone,' I sob. 'Don't tell me he's dead.'

She stubs the cigarette out with the sole of her slipper.

'Nuh, no' dead, love, he's just went to the hospital. Din'y look too good, but, when he shouted on us to help him. Put the shiters up my wee-uns, so he did. But the ambulance came and he went. Yous should get there and see the poor wee soul. I think he went to the Royal Alexandra Hospital.'

She continues to talk but I am already in the limo and away.

At the hospital we wait, we pace up and down, we wait some more. A doctor arrives and, speaking at a hundred words a minute, delivers a stream of jargon that my aching head struggles to comprehend.

'Miss Knights, your father has had an attack of Angina Pectoris . . .'

I am with him so far. Just.

'This is a sudden chest pain, which is caused by a lack of adequate blood supply to the heart as a result of low haemoglobin . . .'

Words are getting a bit long and complicated now. I wrinkle my brow and concentrate, feeling like I am back in my GCSE biology class.

'Now this can be caused by a number of things, but in your father's case I suspect that it's largely due to his drinking habits – he is a drinker, yes?'

I stare blankly for a second, then nod when I realise I have been asked a question.

'Well, I believe your father has developed oesophagitis, an inflammation and eventual erosion of the oesophagus over a period of time. He may have had symptoms such as heartburn and indigestion?'

I nod again as his voice rises at the end of the sentence, but my brain is tired and I am having trouble keeping up.

'Anaemia . . . ECG . . . blood count . . . blood transfusion . . . endoscopy . . . diagnosis . . . drugs . . . keep him in . . .' the doctor continues.

I nod and frown and beg my brain to discover its genius IQ sometime in the next five minutes until I realise he has stopped talking. He looks at me. I blink. He smiles, somehow without turning up the corners of his mouth, and mutters: 'OK, I am glad you understand. I'll get back to him then.' He then scurries away like the frantic white rabbit in *Alice In Wonderland*, probably to work another seventy hours before he can stop for a cup of tea.

I turn towards Didier with my mouth open. I let him pull me back down on to the hard plastic chair.

'So, erm, is he OK or not?' I ask shakily.

'Oh, uh, I think he said that your father is all right but that he must stay here and have many tests just to be sure. I do not remember the name of his illness but you will know better than me, being a nurse.'

'What?'

He pats my arm. 'Your father is still having treatment so

we cannot see him for a while yet. Can I get you anything, Angel? A cup of tea?'

I smile weakly.

'Huh, you're becoming very British, offering cups of tea in times of need. You'd better get back to France quick before you start standing in queues, moaning about standing in queues and talking about the weather.'

'*Pourquoi*?'

'Great British traditions,' I explain.

We laugh and I feel a second of release before I realise where I am and why. The clinical white walls close in swiftly around me and my laughter fades.

'I will find us something to drink,' Didier nods, lifting his tall frame out of the seat and striding off down the corridor.

I hear giggles and whispered comments as he passes a nursing station but I am too worn out to be amused at the stir my hospital companion is causing. I had better keep him in one place, though. The doctors are rushed off their feet enough already without having crowds of over-excited fainting women to deal with.

'Can I interest you in a drink of Irn-Bru, *mademoiselle*?'

Didier hands me one of two cold cans and sits down again.

'Perfect,' I reply, suddenly realising that my shocked body is craving an injection of sugar, 'and it's about time you drank something normal, Didier. Champagne followed by more champagne is not a varied diet.' I take a long, slow gulp of the fizzy liquid, hiccupping as I try to swallow too much at once.

'Oh là là, what colour is it?' he shrieks, peering into the can. 'I did not notice how bright it is when we drank this in the darkness of the cinema.'

'Bright orange and not a colouring in sight,' I wink. 'I love the stuff and my friend Meg absolutely swears by it. She says that's why her hair is so red because she was brought up on this and red lemonade.'

'Not really,' I smirk when Didier touches a hand to his charcoal locks, 'but it is great stuff, especially for hangovers. My dad has some every morning and he's—'

I stop mid-sentence, choking back tears and a mouthful of pop. Didier drapes his arm around my shoulders and pulls me towards him. I sob quietly into his chest, my tears spreading across the black silk of his shirt like a shadow.

'I'm sorry,' I sniff when I eventually pull away, 'I shouldn't be crying on your shoulder. This isn't your responsibility. You're a popstar – you should be off doing popstarry things.'

'Like what?'

'I don't know, like getting Number Ones and signing women's breasts and stuff. Like having the sort of evening we were having before all this happened and I dragged you into my reality with a bump.'

'It may surprise you, Angel,' he smiles down at me, 'but I would much rather be here with you.'

'Why? You don't have to stay, you know. I'll be fine on my own.'

'I will not leave, *mon amie*. This is not the sort of place for you to be by yourself.'

He tilts his head and his hair fans out across his broad shoulders. I stare at him numbly, secretly very glad of his company in this hospital corridor.

'Thanks,' I croak, accepting a hug. 'I appreciate it.'

'And anything else I can do, please just ask.'

'Make my dad get better? Stop him slowly killing himself by having wine and whisky for breakfast, lunch and dinner?'

Didier looks down at the floor and says nothing.

'Sorry. I just feel so . . . so angry about all this. Angry at my dad for drinking. Angry at my mum for not being there for him. Angry at Connor for not being there for me. Angry at myself for not being there for my dad. Fuck, it's just one big circle of anger.'

I leap out of the chair, my body jittery with pent-up emotion.

'What's taking them so long? Why don't they come back and tell me what's happening? When can I see him?'

'They will be back when they have made him comfortable, Angel. He is in the best place right now, with the professional doctors and nurses just like yourself.'

'Huh?'

'Now, while we wait can I do something? Perhaps I shall call Delphine?'

'Delphine? Why the hell would I want you to call her?'

'Well, she is your mother,' he replies seriously, 'and she was married to this man for many years.'

'So?'

'So I think perhaps she might like to know what is happening to him.'

'Why?' I huff, setting my lip in the surly expression of a stubborn toddler. 'So that she can thank her lucky stars that she got rid of him when she did and saved herself all this bother?'

I feel the anger building inside me like floodwaters behind a dam, just waiting to burst.

'It's *her* fault he's in here in the first place,' I hiss. 'If she hadn't left him he would never have got this bad. He wouldn't be so lonely and sad, and then console himself with alcohol. I mean, there's only so much I can do and she's just left me with it while she swans off to François or whatever his bloody name is.'

'Frédéric,' Didier interrupts quietly.

'Fred, Frank, whatever. Yeah, well, if it wasn't for her and the way she behaves he wouldn't have had this angina attack thing. She *broke* his heart. She ruined him.'

Didier looks at my tear-stained face and presses his lips tightly together. 'But perhaps,' he says quietly, 'Delphine had to leave for herself, so that she did not ruin her own life.'

'Yeah, that'd be right. Self, self, self, that's all she's ever been. She just looks after number one and to hell with the rest of us.'

'I don't agree. I think Delphine cared very much for your father but their love just did not work. Sometimes this happens.'

I grind my back teeth and fight the anger inside me. How dare he stick up for her? Just because he's famous and rich and successful he thinks he knows everything. Well, he doesn't. He may think he knows my mother but he doesn't. I need someone to blame and right now she fits the bill perfectly.

'Why couldn't she just love him as much as he loves her? Then he wouldn't be here and everything would be fine.'

It suddenly hits me that I've heard that theory somewhere before. It was Tyrone, talking about his mum and dad, and I thought it sounded too simple then. I plonk myself down on the chair and let out a deep breath.

'This is what comes of marrying the wrong person, Didier. This is where it leads.'

He crushes the empty Irn-Bru can with one hand. 'Maybe, or maybe your father would have ended up here anyway. Maybe that was why Delphine decided to leave. Perhaps she made the hardest decision anyone ever has to make.'

'Well, she's definitely got you on side,' I say snidely. 'You appear to think she's great.'

'And she thinks that you are great too, Angel.'

'Oh yeah? Are you sure you haven't got me mixed up with someone else? I'm her only daughter – the size twelve daughter with a boyfriend she detests and a job she despises.'

'*Non*, she loves your job, Angel. Being a nurse is a wonderful thing.'

I laugh and shake my head as the Defence's case breaks down in front of me.

'Oh Didier,' I sigh. 'I'm not a nurse. If I were a nurse I'd probably have been more use to my poor dad.' I squeeze my eyes shut and rest my head in my hands. 'I'm a DJ, *mon ami*. A crappy DJ on a crappy station with a small group of listeners who haven't got anything better to do than call my show on an afternoon in the hope that I'll solve all their problems. Well, I can't. And I definitely won't be able to after this Friday.'

'Why?'

'Because I'll be getting the sack,' I snap, the self-pity setting in like squatters in an empty flat. 'I only came to meet you at the BBC to convince you to come on my show and do one poxy interview, and I can't even get that right. There you have it. Now you know everything there is to know about Angel Knights and her dysfunctional family. Bet you're glad you didn't sleep with me now, aren't you?'

CHAPTER TWENTY

Anything Is Possible

I didn't see Didier again after we left the hospital. That was on Wednesday, right? And today is Friday, isn't it? I think that's correct, although since I was forced to recognise the fragility of my dad's existence my mind has been in such a spin that I hardly know what day it is. Mind you, the fact that today is Friday has hit me like a rounders bat in the face because today is the day that Dan and I must face G.G. to admit that even Pinky and Perky are too famous to agree to appear on our show. You know one of those days when you are feeling so sorry for yourself that you think all the bad vibes in the world are being transmitted directly at you to give you a month's worth of bad days all rolled into one? I am having one of those days.

Now I am not the sort of girl to wallow in the depths of despair but I think this week I am entitled to feel distinctly pissed off.

Firstly, my dad is in hospital having slow blood transfusions and drugs and tests, and although they have assured me he will recover I don't know how to fix his life to stop this happening again. Secondly, though I would like to forget this fact, I kissed a man who could in no way, shape or singing voice be mistaken for my very long-term boyfriend. Not forgetting the fact that I was about to succumb to his charms between the sheets had my dad not had a very timely health crisis. I then succeeded in alienating my new friend/kissing partner by admitting in the heat of my built-up anger that I had been using him all along for my own DJ devices, thereby putting the final nail in my career's coffin by scuppering any chance I might have had of actually using Didier Lafitte to further my career. That my own mother had had the audacity to encourage the aforementioned Didier Lafitte to seduce her own daughter is staggering (more about that later). So it turns out that he was using me just as much as I was using him. Wanker. Lastly, I am thirty in exactly eight days' time. I had not exactly aimed to be a thirty-year-old unemployed love cheat. Aim high, achieve low, or so it seems.

OK, there are several solid reasons for why I am feeling Prozac-worthy. I think that will do for now.

Yesterday passed by in more of a blur than Damon Albarn. I got back from the hospital in the early hours of Thursday morning, having sent Didier packing in his limo well before I managed to see my dad and hold his hand and tell him everything would be OK. I snatched a couple of hours of sleep and then awoke to a jolly postcard from Connor. Although a nice thought, it arrived with spectacularly bad timing. The picture on the front was of Mickey Mouse holding a surfboard, sandwiched between two gorgeous beach beauties. His message conveyed the same happy-go-lucky theme.

Dear Angel,

Hope all is cool with you. Having an all-American fun time. The series is great, the storylines are BIG, the sandwiches are BIGGER. Everything in California is HUGE and extravagant but great to see. I think this show is going to be the making of me. Wish you were here to share it all, my baby. The girls say hi. Hope you're having fun.

Love always,
Connor xx

'Great, fun, *cool*, super-dooper, tell the girls to fuck off,' I sighed as I dropped the card in the bin.

It was strange for me to realise how out of touch my boyfriend is with my reality. I promised myself I would call him later once I had summoned the strength.

I then called my mother.

'Dad's in hospital,' I said calmly, 'with angina. The doctors say he'll get better but that he'll need to change his lifestyle if he doesn't want it to happen again.'

Delphine was moved, but not to the extent that she would race to Bordeaux airport and jump on the first plane to be with us.

'Poor Stéphane,' she sighed, 'but he knows what it is that he is doing to himself. He must not continue like this. I hope you are coping, Angelique. Had you to deal with this all by yourself?'

'No, I was with Didier. He stayed with me at the hospital.'

How one woman's mood can change so quickly is a scientific phenomenon.

'Didier! Aaah, *chérie*, I knew that my plan would work.

Mais oui, you are made for each other. You may think that it is interference, my daughter, but I was doing this for your own good. He is a wonderful man, *vraiment beau*, and I hope that he has shown you what it is that a man can be for a woman.'

'Mum,' I breathed wearily, 'I have absolutely no idea what you're talking about. Can we stick to English please? I only got back from the hospital a few hours ago so I'm a bit knackered to be bilingual in English and Delphine-ish.'

'*Alors*, I did not want you to tie yourself to one man without having first tried the beauty of a Frenchman. And this was too good an opportunity to miss.'

'What was?'

'Asking Didier to seduce you, Angelique, as a favour to me. This was a perfect opportunity, *non*? And you see, *chérie*, he was there for you when your boyfriend was nowhere to be seen, so I think I did good, yes?'

I don't think I need to tell you the exact words that followed. My own mother had asked her friend's son to try and get me into bed because she doesn't like my own choice of boyfriend. Does this woman have no morals at all? And to make matters worse, I had almost fallen for it. Here was I thinking that an international sex symbol found me irresistibly attractive and all the while he was just doing Delphine a favour. So now I have another woe to add to my list – the fact that I feel like such a prat for putting my relationship in jeopardy for that. Thankfully we only kissed and it was very brief – just lips, no tongues and the minimal exchange of saliva. I was lonely, my body needed some physical affection, that was it. Admittedly he did turn me on but deep down I wanted him to be Connor. Oh God, Connor, what am I going to tell him? Or rather, am I going to tell him anything at all? I mean, what would it really achieve other than hurting his feelings and destroying our trust? Suddenly my honesty-is-the-best-policy way of looking at life doesn't seem quite so workable.

I mentioned the subject briefly on the show yesterday. Of course I referred to this person who had kissed another man as 'a friend of a friend' as I would never discuss something so personal in public. Gladys said my friend should 'come clean', Boomer told my friend to 'KEEP QUIET ABOUT IT', Ty expressed his surprise that someone as nice as me even had friends like that (oh, the guilt) and Malcolm asked for her phone number because he fancied a bit of 'slapper action'. Opinions were mixed among the rest of my callers but the subject came to an abrupt halt when another listener raised the topic of late-return charges at Renfrew library and we were instantly off on a sharp tangent. And to think I'll miss these random discussions. I must be sadder than I thought.

One positive thing did emerge from yesterday's three-hour airtime, though. While Gladys was on the line she reminded me for what must be the thousandth time that she is a volunteer hospital visitor. The idea leapt out of my head in the shape of a light bulb. I had been concerned about leaving my dad alone in the hospital while I went to work but there was no way I could leave Energy FM in the lurch, especially not with the current state of my career. Now was the time to call in a favour from one of my listeners. After all, I'd been there for them over the past twenty-one months so one little favour wasn't much to ask. I talked to our Gladys off-air while I played 'Have A Nice Day' (not likely) by the Stereophonics and asked whether she or any of her volunteer visitor friends could possibly find a slot in their diaries to visit a lonely man called Steve Knights. Gladys was only too happy to oblige and raced off to catch the next bus to Paisley, on a mission to bring cheer to my poor old dad. I hope he'll thank me. Either that or he'll charge me for the reconstructive surgery on his ears after Gladys has given them a good old bashing with her incessant stream of gossip and chit-chat.

Meg and Ceri, it must be said, did their level best to help when I informed them of Dad's heart condition. Meg joined me at the hospital for half an hour after work, bringing with her a box of chocolates and a bottle of Lucozade. She then proceeded to polish off the lot, having discovered that Dad was supposed to be nil-by-mouth. Ceri made her apologies – she was out with the photographer again, much to my surprise as one week is surely some kind of record (he must buy *very* expensive presents) – but she did send along a gift for Dad with Meg. Dad looked bemused at the moisturiser for modern men and mistook the exfoliator for a DIY product but it was a kind thought all the same. The copy of this week's *Star* magazine that Ceri also gave Meg to deliver should certainly keep Dad occupied until I get back to visit him later this afternoon. The pole dancer exposé will definitely be an eye-opener although probably not the best thing to leave lying around a male heart patient's ward.

'Penny for the Guy?' says a voice beside me as I lean on a white-painted railing and stare down into the dark green waters of the River Clyde.

'Bonfire Night has already gone,' I smile at Dan, who leans on the railing beside me.

'I know, but I need to start saving for next year if I'm going to be out of work in less than an hour.'

I wrinkle my nose and sniff. 'No last-minute career-saving ideas then, Mr Producer?'

'Nope. Other than getting my mum and her mates to write a sackload of gushy fan mail.'

'Could work,' I nod.

'Och, and I did manage to wangle a phone number for the agent of a bloke who won *Stars In Their Eyes* a few years ago but he was too busy doing panto in the Outer Hebrides.'

'Who, the winner?'

'No, the agent. Seems business is bad so he needed some extra cash.'

'Tell me about it,' I snort. 'I guess I could be a tramp,' I add with a sigh, nodding my head towards a hairy, wizened old man trudging along the path and carrying his worldly possessions in several carrier bags.

'Nah, you'd never fit all your shoes in those bags,' Dan smiles, 'and the soup kitchen would never be able to keep up with your appetite.'

I nudge him playfully in the ribs. 'I'm going to miss working with you, Daniel.'

He nudges me back, a pitiful look on his boyish face. 'Thank you for the compliment, Angel Fish, but you never know, it might not come to that.'

'Maybe not, but I wouldn't be too quick to put my faith in G.G. We're young, trendy non-golfers, we mess with the playlists and we don't deliver top-class guests by' – I glance at my watch – 'five minutes' time.'

'Maybe only one of us will get the shove,' says Dan, 'and you're better-looking than me so he'll keep you on. Or maybe we'll just get demoted to a twilight slot.'

I turn my back on the Clyde and squint at the tall silver

building looming majestically on the other side of the road, the headquarters of Energy FM.

'Whatever the outcome, Dan, I think it's time for us to go and face the music.'

Rather apt for a DJ perhaps, but I suspect that this music will not be the sort I will rush to add to my extensive collection. This music is going to be anything but easy listening.

'Can I get you a coffee?' Marjory grunts in a tone of voice more befitting the question: 'Can you just piss off out of my face and stop being so demanding?' That's our Marjory, professional to the last but always begrudgingly so.

'Yes, please,' we whisper meekly as she stomps to the door of G.G.'s office.

I glance quickly around the room for G.G., half expecting to see him propped up in a corner like one of his golf clubs.

'Mr MacDougal is a very busy man,' says Marjory, reading my mind. 'He will be with you in due course.'

'After he's seen everyone more important than us,' I whisper, jumping in my chair when the door slams shut.

We sit and wait for our boss to arrive – me anxiously chewing my cheek and tapping my fingers on my knee, Dan singing as many Carpenters' songs as he can think of under his breath to pass the time.

'Do you think he's coming?' Dan asks mid-way through his third rendition of 'Please Mr Postman'.

'Dunno, I guess so. It is his office after all.'

We wait. I tidy my hair by peering at my reflection in a framed photo of G.G. with his arm around a grimacing Jane McDonald. Dan moves on to 'Calling Occupants of

Interplanetary Craft'. We wait some more, the realisation sinking in that we have seemingly slipped out of the Top Ten, make that the Top Forty, of G.G.'s list of Friday morning priorities.

'I want to run away,' I groan as the tension mounts.

'I want a wee wee,' Dan sniggers just as Marjory shuffles into the room.

'Toilets on this floor are for executives only,' Marjory comments with a look of disgust.

She places two coffees on the desk in front of us.

'I'm fine, thanks,' Dan mumbles, grabbing the cup, taking a slurp and letting out a yelp when he burns his tongue.

'Thank you, Marjory,' I beam, but she has already turned to leave.

I half-stand, reach out for the coffee and stare fretfully at the doily-covered metal tray.

'Either she's coming back, Dan, or we are really in the shit,' I say grimly.

'Why?'

'No biscuits, Dan,' I gulp, nodding at the tray. Not even a stale custard cream.

'Sorry, sorry, sorry,' announces G.G. from the doorway, 'emergency, ah, meeting of the Board at the, ah . . .'

He attempts to deposit an enormous red leather golf bag complete with wheelie trolley discreetly by the door and marches around his desk to face us.

'Anyway, I'm here now, but only briefly, so' – he moves Jane McDonald two inches to the left with a puzzled frown – 'where were we?'

Dan once again becomes a deaf mute in the presence of

our boss so I take a deep breath and answer meekly: 'Um, we're here to give you a progress report.'

'Progress report?'

'Good one,' Dan mutters.

'Yes, on our show, *Angel on Air*.'

'That's right, well done,' G.G. nods, as if I am simply affirming what he is already up to speed on. 'Jolly good, Angel.'

Bloody hell, the man knows my name. I raise my eyebrows in surprise. How ironic that he finally gets to grips with it today. He will probably be calling my replacement Angel for the next two years, man or woman.

G.G. slams the palms of his hands down on to the desk, making Dan and I jump in our seats. He leans forward and smiles a thin-lipped smile.

'Progress, progress. Where are we on the progress front?'

I open my mouth, close it again and kick Dan's ankle with my foot. I'm beginning to think my producer is not really in the room but has sent a hologram of himself instead. What am I supposed to say? *Progress is great, thank you, G.G.* – and hope that he is too busy to have the inclination to pry, thus buying us time? Or, *Well, we didn't quite manage to secure the services of the big European pop-star but the reunited St Winifred's School Choir have their bus passes at the ready and can be on the next coach to Buchanan Street faster than you can say There's No One Quite Like Grandma* – in the hope that this is one of his favourite hits of all time (which actually wouldn't surprise me but I doubt the rest of the executives would be so easily swayed).

'Progress,' I whistle, shuffling on my chair. 'Now progress

is a funny thing these days. Sometimes it is quick and, erm, sometimes it's rather slower.'

'You are so right, Angel,' G.G. jumps in, fortunately covering up the suicidal groan erupting from Dan's throat. 'Because everything seems to take so long these days, don't you think?'

I nod very slowly.

'I find it almost impossible to get anything done in this day and age in the working environment.'

Try staying in the office for longer than half an hour each day, I think snidely, that might help.

'It is always *mañana mañana* with people these days' – he shakes his head at Jane McDonald but I believe he is talking to us – 'especially, I am afraid to say, with the young people. So quick to shirk their responsibilities to perform well at work. Do you know what I mean?'

I continue to nod like a jammed robot. Dan has by now lost all will to live.

'Now to be honest with you both . . .'

If you really must.

'. . . I half expected you to let me down. To turn up here today with some bodged-together project and think that you would be able to get away with it the way young people do these days.'

Us? Never!

'I expected you to turn up here and say, "We have a guest for you, G.G., but due to blah and blah and blah it is not quite the guest we promised you".'

'Really? Ha ha ha,' I laugh mechanically, desperately looking around for the nearest emergency exit.

'But no.'

He dramatically thrusts his arms open and beams at Dan and I.

'No?' My voice is shaking.

'No. You have not let me or yourselves or Energy FM down, nor the dedicated listeners out there who tune in every day expecting us to bring a little joy to their lives.'

'Haven't we?'

Somebody draw me a flowchart of this conversation because I am now utterly baffled.

'Well, of course you haven't, my bright young stars, and I am so pleased to have you both as part of this team.'

The colour starts to return to Dan's face.

'I mean, gosh, Didier Lafitte,' he continues merrily. 'Even I have heard of Didier Lafitte. He will be an absolutely perfect guest on your show. I couldn't have expected this much but now, my friends, you have set the standard.'

Dan turns as white as a chameleon in an igloo.

'Ah, about Didier . . .' I squeak, my vocal chords contracting so tight with fear I make Minnie Mouse sound husky.

G.G. raises both hands to stop me. 'We can go into the details later, Angel and Daniel, as I' – he glances at his golf bag – 'have another meeting very soon, but I must just say how proud I am of you both for giving your all to this company.'

He leans across the table towards us and I swear I see a tear in his eye.

'This is a very big thing for us and I hope you both realise that this is a very big thing for the two of you.'

'But—'

'This could be the making of you both, my bright young things,' he continues tearfully, 'and I will be proud to know that I encouraged you to rise to such high standards.'

Dan snorts beside me. I bite my lip and try to concentrate.

'When Didier Lafitte called me yesterday I knew . . .'

Wait a God-damn minute, did he just say . . .?

'. . . I knew that this was the moment we had all been waiting for at Energy FM. And the fact that he chose to call me directly rather than through his manager shows just how much he respects both me as the station controller and also the people who approached him to do this interview in the first place.' He beams at us. 'He speaks very highly of you, Angel. You must have done a very good job with him.'

'You must,' Dan pipes up, raising an eyebrow and looking at me questioningly.

I shuffle uncomfortably under their weighty stares.

'Well,' I cough, 'you know, I . . . er . . . Dan was a great help too, G.G., I couldn't have done it without his professionalism backing me up.'

G.G. claps his hands together and gushes, 'Marvellous, this is truly marvellous.'

He presses a buzzer on his desk and almost immediately Marjory shuffles into the room. I always suspected she was remote controlled.

'The interview will take place next Friday,' G.G. continues while my head struggles to take it all in. 'One week today, so we must rush straight into the preparations. But I am sure your hands are very capable.'

My hands are very clammy right now, actually, but give me a minute.

'Marjory, refill the coffee cups of Energy FM's brightest

stars and bring us a tin of the finest chocolate-dipped Scottish shortbread. This calls for a celebration.'

Chocolate-dipped Scottish shortbread? Dan, my friend, I think we've made it!

CHAPTER TWENTY-ONE

Star People

The week that follows oscillates between the glamorous task of arranging Didier Lafitte's debut interview in Britain on none other than *my* radio show, and visiting my dad on a grim ward full of ill men. The difference in these two commitments could not be more marked but each one brings its own rewards. The interview is taking shape with the assistance of Dan as well as Didier's stormtroopers, who seem to want to know anything and everything about the show, from details about the regular callers Didier is likely to encounter to details about what biscuit we favour to dip in our Maxpax coffee. I don't talk to or meet with Didier himself all week – largely because he has decided to see more of Scotland than just Glasgow and so is off each day with his driver doing the tourist trail in style. But also because I do not yet have the courage to face him, look into those dark eyes and admit that not only were we using each other for what we could get from our friendship but that, once the friendship blossomed of its own accord, I was only a condom-machine away from jumping into his four-poster bed. I know it and I am sure he knows it too. Thankfully, Connor doesn't.

Connor and I speak to each other more times over the next six days than we have in the last month. Connor is supportive and loving and concerned. I could not have lasted through the week without his support.

'Just checking how you are, my baby,' he says each morning when he calls and again every evening before I go to bed, regardless of the time difference. 'Are you eating properly? Do you need me to do anything? Do you want me to come home?'

I tell him to stay and work on his programme, that Dad and I can cope, at least while he is in hospital. I tell him that having my show to concentrate on is a great distraction and that I would be too busy to be with him were he to come home anyway.

I tell him all that but really what I want to say is – 'Come back and hold me, Con. I need you. I don't want you to be over there and me over here. I nearly ruined everything and now I've realised that you're my rock. Come home.'

But I don't. Nor do I tell him that the star guest who has the potential to shoot *Angel on Air* at least into division one if not the premier league of radio shows is a personal friend of mine. A rather *too* personal friend. I think that can wait for now. So I tell him the basics – 'Dan really helped to set it all up', 'It came out of the blue really', 'I think the interview is going to be the best moment of my career', 'How good is it that it's happening the day before my thirtieth birthday? I'm not going to be a failure after all!' Connor is proud, I can hear it in his voice, and I, by taking the time to talk to him, suddenly feel near to him again despite the geographical distance between us.

You see, the postcard that arrived the day after Dad's health scare frightened me. I realised how out of touch Connor and I were from each other's lives, and how easy it had been to let the perfect communication we had developed over thirteen years together waste away to empty telephone calls, the odd e-mail and a dog-eared square of hastily scribbled-on cardboard. I also realised that I had to take half the responsibility for what was happening to us. I had been so caught up in the problems of our LDR – not being able to see my boyfriend every day, not knowing what he was up to and not being the centre of his universe – that I hadn't looked at the good points. Connor's temporary absence had allowed me to concentrate on myself, on my career, on making friends and finding a bit of independence. I had been able to discover that I could survive in the world on my own, but also – and this is the most important part – that although I could do all that I would rather do it with Connor. I had got caught up in Ceri's circle of doubt and I had come very close to giving in to my loneliness with a sex god called Didier. The point is, coming that close woke me up to the fact that although Didier is gorgeous and fun and has a kiss that could send most girls' lips into spasm, he is not *my* man. Nor do I want him to be *my* man. And I'm sure he doesn't see me as the prime candidate to be *his* girl. I mean, he's probably just as lonely as me when you consider the fickle, arse-licking butt-heads he has to hang around with most of the time, so it's not surprising Didier took my mum up on her offer (eugh, how cheap do I feel?). We simply mistook our friendship for something else, even if there was a bit of lust lingering on the fringes and trying to complicate matters.

But my Connor is more than lust on legs. He is the man who makes my soul, not just my fanny, sing with delight whenever he is around (apart from the days when he's pissing me off but then that's just real life). I hope Connor's time away from me has made him realise the same thing. He may have been tempted but I can't chastise him for that because I was also tempted. I never expected to be but I was. I just hope that even if he was tempted, he has not come to the conclusion that what he has been looking for his whole life comes in the shape of a tanned hourglass in a spangly thong. Please don't let him want that. I want him to want me.

Anyway, the truth is I am far too busy to fret about whether Connor still loves me or not. I have been starting the publicity train chugging along its tracks. To be honest, though, I didn't have to do much to stir up interest because once people got wind that Didier Lafitte was planning to give an interview for the first time in English, the rumour spread like an oil slick on the ocean. Is it true? It can't be true. Why would someone like *him* do an interview at a radio station like *that*? Energy FM my arse, ha ha ha! All week long there has been a city-wide game of Chinese whispers, all beginning and ending at Energy FM's door, with, I suspect, Ceri Divine playing an important role somewhere along the chain.

'You're joking, right?' Ceri pouted when I met her in a café on Byres Road to tell her about Didier.

No, of course I didn't tell her *that* about Didier. I kept things on a very professional level and simply said: 'Didier has agreed to give an interview on my show on Friday. Do you want to come along and write something for your column?'

'Why would Didier possibly want to make his debut on Energy FM?' she scoffed. 'He's way above that level. Anyway, I thought he thought you were a nurse.'

She still hasn't got to grips with that tact thing.

'We sorted out the nurse business, it was all just a bit of a misunderstanding.'

'Which date did you sort that out on then? The boat one, the Devonshire one or another one?' she smirked suggestively.

'Not on any *date*,' I answered firmly. 'Now do you want to be a special guest or not?'

'I never thought I would be relying on you to invite me to a ticket-only star-studded event, Angel, but I suppose I will have to graciously accept. As long as my column takes precedence over every other magazine in the city.'

'Of course, madam. And we'll get a gold plastic chair for your designer bum to sit on too.'

So Ceri was coming, which of course meant that Meg would have to be a special guest on the big day too. I wrote her name on Dan's guest list as an important player on the front line of the music business. Meg was so excited she wrote me a thank-you card every day for five days until I told her that any more pretty-enveloped cards written in girl's handwriting and my postman would start to think I was in the throes of a lesbian affair. I don't need any more complications in that department right now.

The studio is very small, so many more guests and we wouldn't have had any room for Didier and his inevitable entourage of people. Dan was quite happy not to bring a friend as he decided it would make him more nervous on the day, and I knew my dad would not be up to the strain, so in big-time radio station fashion we ran a competition. Our listeners were asked a question about Didier Lafitte every day for the first half of the week. They then had to phone in their answers to get their names 'entered into our computer'. Not that we had a huge computer database, it was more of a tattered list on Dan's desk, but it sounded impressive that way. Thursday was the day of the final, when two of our listeners would go head-to-head on air for the chance to come into the studio and meet the man himself. By that I mean Didier, of course, although meeting 'Dan the Producer' would, I assured our Dan, be a definite bonus prize. Now at this point I have to admit another of my little white lies of late. You see, I knew who the winner of our competition would be before I even set the first questions. Not that I was fixing it exactly. I was just going to *help* it along a little bit. You know, *steer* it towards the right result. In my opinion (and Dan agreed wholeheartedly), my youngest caller Tyrone needed this good thing in his life more than most. Despite his problems and the ups and downs in his life he had given so much to our show from the very beginning. Why not slightly manipulate one measly little contest in order to bring a bit of happiness to the poor lad's week when it was in our power to do so?

I had originally thought it was going to be easy. After all, we don't have that many listeners, fewer still who can actually be bothered to pick up the phone and call the show. At least, we *didn't* have. Not until we announced the fact that Didier Lafitte was coming to our office. All of a sudden our audience began to grow, our phones began to ring and we had more entrants for our competition than for all the other competitions ever run at Energy FM put together. (Which sounds unbelievable, but when you consider that previous prizes have included a Dolly Parton tea towel and napkin set and an Energy FM-engraved shoehorn the record wasn't too far out of our sights.) The listeners, both new and old, entered in good faith and on Thursday morning I battled with my morals over whether fixing a high profile (relatively speaking, we are still not Radio 1) competition was a good idea. However, my desire to help Tyrone in the only way I could won through in the end. Thus it was no coincidence that the other caller on the head-to-head final could only answer one out of the five questions. And it was definitely not surprising that the caller sounded strangely like Dan's chronic impression of Sean Connery. We got away with it and I am glad. Tyrone's sheer delight at having won the competition was worth all the cheating.

'We will send a car for you tomorrow, Ty,' I told him off air, 'and you can spend all afternoon with myself and Dan and Didier Lafitte in the *Angel on Air* studio. Congratulations.'

I could hear him biting his lip even down the phone line. 'Thank you so much,' he croaked quietly. 'I'm just . . . I can't believe . . . thank you, Angel. This is pure brilliant. This is the best moment of my life.'

'Good,' I beamed, 'but just wait, Tyrone, tomorrow will be even better. Tomorrow is going to be great.'

'Dan, why are you cowering under a railway bridge?' I frown, bumping into him on my way to work.

'I'm not, I'm—'

'Cowering under a railway bridge,' I finish for him. 'Who are you hiding from, the Minging Yellow Trainer Police?'

Dan looks down at his shoes, glowing like two radioactive bananas on the end of his legs.

'These aren't minging, they're very fashionable, actually.'

'According to whom, the National Association for Colourblind People?' I giggle, pulling his sleeve and dragging him towards the Energy FM building.

'Very bloody funny, Angel,' he pants as he tries to keep up with my urgent pace, 'but you might just be laughing on the other side of your high-heeled cowboy boots when you have to run away from *that* little lot.'

I follow the direction of his outstretched hand and gasp.

'Oh SHIT! What's happened?'

'Hmm, let me see. Maybe there's a hostage situation inside and everyone is waiting to see the shoot-out. Or perhaps G.G. has finally lost it and is threatening to throw himself from the top of the atrium unless he is given a lifetime supply of fondant fancies.'

'Wow, do you really think so?'

'No, Angel Fish, I don't,' he snorts. 'I think that there is a small event happening in the Energy FM building today that just happens to involve you, me and the man that every woman and gay man in that crowd over there would like to eat alive given half the chance.'

'What? No way.' I gawp at the crowd of people surging towards the entrance to the building. 'You mean this is all for Didier? For our interview?'

I can hardly believe it. The last time there was a crowd this big outside Energy FM's building was when . . . What am I saying? There has never been a crowd this big outside

Energy FM's building. In fact, nobody knew where it was and nobody cared. Until today.

I link my arm through Dan's and we creep along the road towards the people. It is a scene of organised chaos. There are crowd-control barriers and policemen and photographers and television cameras and . . . Damn, television cameras?

'Does my hair look all right?' I ask fretfully. 'Shit, I knew I should have worn something different. I'm a radio DJ, we don't *do* cameras. Everyone will see how I look.'

'You look great,' Dan smiles, placing a calming hand on my arm. 'Your jeans are tight enough to be foxy but not so tight as to make you look like a denim duvet. Your jumper is trendy and red really suits you, and your cowboy boots are . . . weren't they pink before?'

'Oh yeah,' I grin, 'I had to buy a red pair. It was an emergency.'

Dan raises his eyes to the sky and then fiddles with the spikes on top of my head, his tongue between his teeth.

'There, perfect, Little Miss Spiky Locks. You are fab and cool and everything a DJ should be.' He opens his arm towards the crowd. 'Now come on, hon, it is time to face your public.'

'That lassie must be the DJ,' says a voice as we scurry past the metal barriers towards the front door of the building.

'Her name's Angel,' says another. 'Angel Knights.'

'Och, I love her boots,' says the first voice again, 'and her hair is mega cool.'

'Angel, hey Angel!'

I turn stiffly and wave robotically, like the Queen. A dazed smile fixes itself to my gobsmacked lips. I suddenly feel like a Hollywood actress at a film premiere, being watched and admired by the world's press and my loyal fans as I sway my petite hips down the red carpet, tottering on the heels of my three hundred thousand dollar diamond-encrusted Manolo Blahniks. Not that stomping my red cowboy boots through the entrance of a Glasgow office block in front of the cameras of the Glasgow *Herald* bears any resemblance to that at all but I am so overwhelmed my imagination has gone into overdrive. People know my name. People are calling my name. Dare I say it – I think I might have found some fans. Fickle they may be but right now fickle is good. I tell you, if I forgot to wake up this morning and this is all one of those vivid dreams I am going to be in a very bad mood.

'Mind your head, Angel Fish,' Dan comments, waking me from my ooh-I-love-being-famous reverie, 'something that big is never going to fit in the lift!'

Inside the building the fifth floor has become a circus. I swear, what was once a run of the mill verging on dowdy radio station has metamorphosed into an all-singing all-dancing theatre of manic hyperactivity. The usually sombre women at the reception desk have traded their sensible clothes and their sour faces for bright florals and so much make-up that their heads all look too big for their bodies. There are Energy FM logos slapped on every spare surface in the form of posters, stickers and, bloody hell, there is even *bunting*. Didier Lafitte's husky singing voice drifts from previously redundant speakers and even G.G. can be seen breaking into a fast crawl along the corridors with not a golf club in sight. He barks orders at everything that moves and even some things that don't. We finally catch up with him deep in conversation with the water dispenser.

'Ah, right, we have a DJ, jolly good. That is one thing going right this morning. At least we have a DJ.'

'And a producer,' Dan adds apologetically.

'Marvellous. Now do us proud team' – he gives my arm a firm tap, almost knocking me sideways into the wall – 'it's time to get to work. Your other guests are in the studio already. Enjoy the show but, please, don't mess this up.'

'Blimey, no pressure,' Dan mutters as G.G. hurries off shrieking, 'Marjory, have those sausage rolls turned up yet? I don't want a fainting popstar on my hands!'

'Look, Angel, you're in a fucken' magazine,' Meg hollers, bounding up to Dan and I before we are fully through the door of the studio. She waves the glossy pages of the latest edition of *Star* in my face.

'Just out on the shelves today. You're famous, hen! And guess what? Ewan McGregor's name is on the same bloody page. Imagine that.'

'She doesn't have to imagine it, Megan,' Ceri yawns, kissing me on the cheek, 'it's all there in glorious gloss.'

I take the magazine and perch myself on the edge of the desk, my stomach flipping merrily like a pancake on Shrove Tuesday.

'Didier Lafitte, the most edible man in pop, is to give an exclusive interview this week,' Dan reads aloud over my shoulder, 'at the city's Energy FM radio station, to one of Glasgow's top female DJs, Angel Knights.'

'I didn't write that last bit,' Ceri interrupts, sitting herself beside me, 'my editor must have added it in.'

I grin and pat one leg of her deep pink leather trousers.

'Will Angel get the longed-for gossip on the man we all desire? Will Monsieur Lafitte send this Angel to Heaven?' Dan continues. 'Find out what the pair get up to in next week's Divine Gossip.'

'Wicked,' says Meg, clapping her hands.

'Sounds a bit juicy,' Dan smiles with a squeeze of my shoulder.

'It does,' I nod, but any discomfort at the implication of what we 'got up to' is surpassed by the thrill of seeing my name in print. And not just any old print – glossy print in a popular weekly magazine no less. Wow, this morning I am getting so many kicks I could be a football.

'Thanks, Ceri,' I smile, giving her a friendly nudge.

'No problem.' Ceri flicks her hair over her shoulder. 'Good luck, Angel. I hope this all works out as you want it to.'

Dan gets to the end of the page and looks up, sticking out his lip. 'Don't I get a mention then?'

Ceri does the hair-flicking thing again and treats Dan to a knee-melting wink.

'Maybe next week, darling, depending on whether you are a good boy or not.'

I knew inviting her was a mistake. Dan will never be able to concentrate on the technicalities of running a radio show with Ceri's pheromones wafting around the building. As for Didier, she will probably swallow the poor man whole (no crudeness intended). As long as she lets me do my interview first, I don't mind. Honestly, I don't.

While Ceri does her best to look like a VIP and Meg single-handedly devours G.G.'s prize buffet (do popstars eat tuna mayonnaise-filled vol au vents?), I prepare myself for the show, occasionally prodding my producer to ask him to put his energies into helping rather than just being flirted with by Ceri and nattering with Meg. I re-read my questions and edit them as appropriate. I prepare the music for the show and double-check that no one has pilfered our copy of Didier's album as no doubt he will be expecting at least a certain amount of ego-tripping. A wave of excitement reaching giant proportions rumbles through the studio when we are given the nod that our male guest has arrived. Ceri's boobs instantly spring into pert position, Meg wipes chocolate cake crumbs from her mouth with the sleeve of her jumper and Dan starts to race about in all directions like a deflating balloon. Calm is somewhat restored when the male guest is revealed to be Tyrone, but no one is disappointed. The small boy who peaks his strawberry blond head around the door and blinks at us even turns Ceri's heart to putty. OK, maybe not putty, but at least a softer stone than usual.

'Ehm, I'm lookin' for Angel,' he whispers, clearing his throat between each word. 'I'm, I'm, ehm . . .'

'Tyrone,' I beam, 'and I am very pleased to meet you.'

He takes my hand and shakes it with surprising firmness, smiling up at me with his big blue eyes. He has a freckled nose like Dan but must be a third of Dan's lanky height. He is adorable and polite and so awestruck by every button and light in the studio that he wanders quietly for half an hour just gazing and gasping but never touching. After a while in our company he relaxes a little and perches gingerly on my chair with a wagon wheel in one hand (supplied by Meg) and a plastic cup of pop in the other.

'I never thought I'd be here,' he smiles, wrinkling his nose just, I note, like I do. 'It's amazing. I must be the luckiest kid in the world.'

I very much doubt it but I am glad he can have at least this moment of believing he leads a charmed life. I smile at Tyrone and clink my plastic cup against his. He laughs happily. Despite the laughter on his lips, though, his eyes still hold a sadness that may never go away. Why, I wonder, is he the one who has to have the dysfunctional family and get picked on at school? So what if he does not have the designer clothes and his scuffed trainers do not have fresh Nike ticks on them? So what if his hair has ginger tints – how that particular hair colour ever became the butt of the nation's jokes I have no idea. He may be small and delicate but he is wonderful and appreciative and heart-warming. Let's face it, if he can bring a smile to stony old Ceri's lips then he must have something special going for him. I realise that exciting though the crowd of fans outside the door and my mention in the *Star* column may be, this is definitely the best part of the day so far. Tyrone is the magnet keeping my feet firmly on the ground.

While Meg entertains Tyrone and Dan with her banter and Ceri wafts around looking at herself in any reflective surface, I steal a moment for myself and slip out of the studio to call my dad. I wait while the nurse takes the phone to his bedside.

'Dad, hi, it's me, Angel. How are you feeling?'

'Not bad,' he chirps – obviously an accepted variant of 'fine' when one is in a hospital bed wired up to more machines than a nuclear reactor – 'the doctor has been round and he says he is pleased with my progress and I am back on my food now.' He pauses to slowly inhale. 'We had lovely chicken for dinner last night after you left, with these unusual little potato things called, um, what were they called, Gladys? Gnocchi, that's it, gnocchi. They're Italian and very soft and tasty, like pasta except they are made of potato, and quite healthy as long as I don't eat too many.'

Woah there, Dad, back up the bus a minute. Enough of the potato talk, didn't I just hear you mention—

'And Gladys is reading to me from the *Reader's Digest*.'

I *did* hear him mention . . .

'Gladys tried to read a couple of articles from Ceri's magazine but it wasn't really our kind of thing, was it, Gladys?'

'No, Steve, no' really.' I hear her laugh very close to the phone and hence to my father's bedside.

'So I take it Gladys is there again, Dad?'

'Oh yes. She was doing her voluntary rounds and she decided to keep me company while your big show is on because, of course, she knows when you go on air. We are going to listen to it on the radio, Gladys and I. She brought one with her and the nurses have given us permission to tune in because you are my daughter. That's great, isn't it? We are so excited, Angel, I can't wait. Are you all set?'

I pause to consider whether that is possibly one of the longest string of sentences I have heard my dad utter in a long while. He is in hospital with a heart condition, he almost died and yet my father appears to have suddenly discovered 'chat'.

'I am nearly organised,' I reply, relieved that my father is not alone. 'I've just got to welcome our guest and then firmly cross my fingers, so wish me luck.'

'Good luck,' he responds proudly, 'and double good luck from Gladys. She apologises for not being able to participate in the phone-in during the show but you should be able to manage without her, shouldn't you?'

Without Gladys from Motherwell's take on the French pop industry? I doubt it.

'I hope so, Dad. All right, I have to go, but I'll come by later, OK? Don't get too over-excited.'

'Sure,' he breezes, 'and, Angel, I just have to say I am so proud of you. This is a great thing you are doing today and I hope you enjoy it.'

'Thanks, Dad,' I croak, emotion pushing big fat tears into my eyes.

What did he have to go getting all sincere and affectionate for? He's not even drunk and this mascara isn't waterproof.

I turn off my phone and move towards the studio and my big moment of truth.

'I hope you are not crying because I am here,' says a deep French voice beside me just as I reach the studio door.

I bite my lip and turn to face him. He kisses me gently on both cheeks, his soft hair brushing against mine as he leans towards me.

'Didier,' I greet him while trying not to inhale his sensual aftershave, 'thank you so much for offering to do this.'

He shrugs. I pull my eyes away from his lips as he smiles. Those lips (and the body attached to them) got me into trouble last time and I am not going to make the same mistake again. But just between you and me, they do look incredibly chewable.

'It was the least I could do, Angel. You have been so good

to me since I came to Scotland. You have provided me with real friendship.'

'Even though . . .' I begin.

'Even though you did not tell me about all this.' He gesticulates towards the studio with his arm. 'You should have told me, Angel. I can tell that you are not one of these fickle people. You are too lovely to be fickle.'

I blush and look at the floor. 'Thanks. I know I should have told you but you didn't seem too keen on the music biz crowd and Delphine had already told you a few little white lies about me. The subject just didn't seem to come up.'

He pulls his hair back from his face, accentuating his angular jawline.

'Uh, probably because I was talking about myself too much. Troubling you with my concerns when you have many worries yourself with your father and everything. *Je m'excuse*, sometimes I can be very wrapped up in myself.'

Understandable really, I think, glancing at his beautiful face. If I looked like that I wouldn't mind being totally wrapped up in myself either.

'I want to do this for you, Angelique,' he breathes while reaching out and touching my arm. 'I did not like to see you upset and I think you deserve some good luck.'

If I wasn't wearing a jumper my skin would be tingling by now. I can't help it, he is just one of those born-to-be-sexy types. Even if I don't want to sleep with the man, I would be dead if I didn't find him attractive. Although, wait a second, Miss Knights, may I remind you that he is a hired seducer? A disciple of Delphine despatched on a mission to temptation. So let's just stick to business, shall we?

I discreetly pull my arm away and shove my hands in the back pockets of my jeans.

'All right then, *mon ami*, how's about we get this show on the road?'

'The road?' he frowns.

'Let's go, *allons-y*, time to do your first interview in our beautiful language.'

'OK, but if I have trouble you will help me, yes? In French?'

'Sure, but don't worry about it, you'll be great. Don't try to be too British because that accent of yours will knock them dead.'

I fling open the door and gently push him into the studio. As if to prove my point, Meg, Ceri, Dan and Tyrone stand in dumbstruck silence, gazing at the handsome man in front of me.

Silence, that is, until Meg drops to her knees, clasps her hands together and gasps: 'Jeez-oh, thank you God. Now I understand the point of men.'

Surprisingly, the cool, outwardly arrogant figure of Didier Lafitte is even more nervous than me by the time he places the headphones on his immaculate hair and sits to my left in front of the second bulbous microphone. Ceri, Meg and Tyrone have all retired to Dan's room, leaving Didier and I alone in the small studio, although it is hard to ignore their faces (and in Ceri's case her perfect boobs) pressed up against the adjoining window. I cue the first song, give Didier's hand a reassuring squeeze and pause to contemplate the fact that the next three-hour show could change my career for ever. Between us, Dan, Didier and myself are about to put Energy FM on the map. Please let it be a good map – a treasure map with a big X marking the spot where our rewards are buried.

'Ten seconds,' says Dan into my headphones.

He gives me a thumbs-up through the glass. I close my eyes, open them, inhale deeply and wait for the red light to indicate that we are on air.

'It's Friday, it's twelve o'clock, you're listening to Energy FM and now it's time for *Angel on Air* with our one and only heavenly host, Miss Angel Knights.'

Blimey, couldn't they have at least splashed out on a new jingle?

'Here we go,' I grin at Didier as the music plays us in.

'*fantastique*, Angel,' he smiles back. 'I am all yours.'

CHAPTER TWENTY-TWO

Livin' La Vida Loca

Amazing, wonderful, fantastic and brilliant! If one more person pays me a compliment my head is going to explode like a detonated watermelon. I must admit, though, the show was amazing and wonderful and the rest. We had more callers than our phone-lines could deal with and I loved every minute of it. It all ran smoothly and there were no real slip-ups. Well, apart from when Malcolm from Hamilton questioned our guest's sexuality over his decision to wear leather trousers in his video. However, Didier dealt with it like a true professional, accepting Malcolm's question as a compliment and not confirming on which side of the sexual fence he tended to fall.

'Why Malcolm?' he quipped, winking across at me. 'Did you find me attractive?'

Malcolm hung up before you could say 'homophobe'.

On the whole, though, the interview was a dream. Our conversation flowed, we were clearly comfortable together and his English was strong, just peppered with the odd

French word – like a light dusting of icing sugar to add a sweet touch to his voice. In fact, any time Didier did make a mistake in English I would simply smile encouragingly and imagine at least half my listeners sighing, 'Aah, I love it when he does that.'

We talked about Didier's life, his accelerated rise through the ranks of the music business, the highs and the lows, and his likes and dislikes. We discussed love and his take on Scottish women: 'I love the red hair that glows like the sunshine and the natural beauty of freckles that you could kiss one by one. For me they are some of the most beautiful women in the world.'

Now if that doesn't get him a Number One I don't know what will. We talked about Didier's childhood growing up in a one-parent family in Bordeaux. The one parent part alone made Tyrone's dinky little ears prick up. The next part made his mouth gape open as if his jaw were wired with elastic.

'You may not think it to look at me now,' Didier began, 'but I was bullied as a child at school.' He shrugged, the sad memory reflected in his deep eyes.

'Maybe we were not rich enough, or we were different because I did not even know who my father was. The other kids, they did not like me no matter how hard I tried. And, you see, I was not good-looking at school.'

It was then the turn of my jaw to bounce on elastic.

'I was too tall and my features were not in proportion. Uh, and the teacher would say my eyes had no colour. Just black. The black-eyed boy.'

I stared silently into the eyes which, though black, were responsible for setting many fans' hearts on fire.

'They would tease me and steal things from me and, you

know, call me names. It was awful. *Vraiment* awful. But' – his tight-lipped expression softened as he continued – 'I think I have shown them all. I was lonely and so I lost myself in my music. I tried so hard to be good. I learned to be comfortable within myself *et voilà* – here I am. I look at them and many of the beautiful ones from school, now they are not so beautiful. Now they may not have achieved as much. You are in control of your life. Don't let them break you and be kind to people you meet because you never know who or what they will become.'

When he finished, he inhaled deeply and smiled before turning his head to look at Tyrone across the studio. While I played the track 'Confidence' from Didier's album they smiled knowingly at each other. Didier may have only met Tyrone briefly but he knew. Somehow we all recognised that this day was going to make a difference to Tyrone. The gorgeous, confident, successful, sensuous Didier Lafitte was a bullied ugly duckling. Well that's a fuck-off big poke in the eye to the bullies, isn't it?

Notwithstanding this headline-making moment, the mood of the show was far from sombre. Didier laughed and joked with the callers; he gave advice and he took it – even that of Shanice from Rutherglen who advised him to get his long hair trimmed every six weeks to avoid split ends and to use a good leave-in conditioner.

'*Merci bien*,' Didier smirked, blowing a kiss down the phone. I suspected she wouldn't be giving that handset a clean for a while.

Didier spoke of his travels in Scotland, his penchant for the Glaswegian accent and of his wish to return to our shores again soon. When our Gladys did eventually call in from the hospital in Paisley – I knew she wouldn't be able to resist getting her ten-pence worth – he sang to her live without accompaniment (other than Dan who warbled along in the next room but thankfully out of the public earshot).

The people adored him – Didier, I mean, not Dan, although I do see a fan base building from the reactions to Dan's sporadic on-air comments – which was obvious from the moment the red light went on. And as I said goodbye to the listeners, as that red light went off, as we gave each other a congratulatory hug and as we emerged into the real world, the adoration was right in front of us and all around us, just waiting to sweep us off our feet and on to an awaiting cloud. Tyrone ran into the studio and gathered us both into a group hug. Dan high-fived me and patted Didier on the back with an accompanying – 'Thanks, mate, that was fab' – before gazing happily at the palm that touched the megastar's shoulder. Meg bounded up like a hyperactive puppy but thankfully stopped short of licking our faces (although I am sure it crossed her mind when Didier's cheek was only a coat of lip-gloss away). Even Ceri expressed her approval, but in her own 'special' way of course. 'Pretty good, darling, you are wasted at this lame radio station. I would say that went rather well and it is always good to throw in a bit of childhood trauma. Great for the after-show publicity.'

If Ceri Divine were a counsellor, Britain would not have a problem with overcrowding, that's for sure.

And now, as we stumble euphorically into the corridor, G.G. rushes into our midst.

'Wonderful job, Angel, great show,' he hollers, shaking my hand and almost pulling my arm out of its socket. 'And here's to more of the same. We have already had offers galore for more interviews so marvellous job, well done.'

Dan whimpers when his offer of a handshake is passed over for a hearty slap on Didier's back.

'Didier, my lad, you are welcome here any time. Any time at all. Thank you so much for giving us your time and we hope to welcome you back to the Energy FM family in the very near future. Tell me' – and at this point I am cringing for him as he does one of those mimed golf swings that only over-keen golfers do – 'do you play?'

We escape golf chat thanks to some spectacular conversational manoeuvring by Didier, who is clearly well practised in the art of getting away from people, and strut through to the reception area with Tyrone, Dan, Ceri and Meg in tow. The rapturous applause hits me with the shock of unexpected bird droppings, only much more pleasant. The room is full of the blushing, gushing, swooning and generally hormonal women of Energy FM. They are gushing over Didier of course (although I am positive a small lady in a box-pleated pinafore was giving me the eye). I am surprised to see Marjory clapping along with the others. Funny, I never knew robot clones had feelings.

We are cheered en masse out of the reception, along to the lifts and enjoy a moment of relative peace before the doors open again and the noise hits us once more. Didier's army, milling around the atrium, springs into action and swoops on the lift like a US Task Force given the all-clear to attack. Our star is immediately surrounded and guided smoothly to the glass front doors.

'Bring my friends,' he orders them and we are instantly enveloped by our own street of brick shithouses.

'Wow,' Tyrone laughs, clinging to Didier's right sleeve, 'I wanna be real famous, just like you.'

Didier beams down at him and pats his hand. 'You already are, man,' he smiles and steps through the doors.

Lights, flashes, shouts, screams, sobs, more flashes, questions, requests for photographs and autographs and kisses and waves come at us from all sides. Can this be the same entrance I trudge through anonymously every day of my working life without anyone so much as stopping me to ask directions? Today I can barely walk the few steps to the pavement because of the crowd of people surging forwards. And they are here to see us. Well, Didier mainly, but some of them are here to see me. They want *my* autograph and *my* photo (I knew I should have had a shifty look in the mirror before we left). They want to ask *me* questions. A couple of them are even holding banners with *my* name on. And do you know what? It may be shallow, and I may have succumbed to our generation's obsession with fame, but as I stand here in front of these people and sign posters I feel as if I have made it. These fans are telling me that my work was good today. This is what I have wanted ever since I got my first DJ gig. Admittedly I did gain a certain amount of notoriety on hospital radio, but to be honest, being asked to sign Biddy's 'hope you get over your bunion operation' card did not evoke quite the same thrill.

I chat, I laugh and I soak up the compliments like a double-quilted super-absorbent kitchen towel. I am overwhelmed and slightly scared by the attention but at the same time I am loving this moment. Then the shiny black cars arrive with their darkened windows and burly, peak-capped drivers and we are shepherded past the barriers and the screaming fans.

'It is all arranged,' Didier grins at our startled expressions, 'you are coming with me. Work is done, now for some fun. *Oui*?'

'*OUI*!' Meg and Dan shriek in perfect unison, sprinting towards one of the open car doors as if their shoes are on fire.

'Wow,' gasps Tyrone again, so awe-inspired that his vocabulary has been reduced to a single word.

With a final wave to the crowd we are whisked into the cars and through the streets while cocktails (a non-alcoholic one for Ty) are whisked and shaken into our hands. I take a sip of my creamy, coconutty drink and wriggle down into the sofa seat between Didier and Tyrone. I then realise that I have been holding my breath for about the last ten minutes and I inhale sharply.

'Are you all right, my Angel?' Didier whispers quietly.

'All right would definitely be an understatement right now,' I smile back. 'I am having the time of my life. Thank you.'

'No, thank you,' he nods in response. 'I have just done my first interview in English.'

'No, thank *you*,' I reply.

'No, thank *you*.'

'Thank you both!' Tyrone giggles happily.

And so it continues until the three cars come to a halt outside a red brick building and our doors are magically opened from the outside.

'My school,' Tyrone gasps, retracting his head back into the car like a frightened tortoise. 'What are we doin' here but?'

'You are going to help me with, how do you say, a little PR exercise.'

Didier reaches his hand into the car and helps me out, then does the same for Tyrone. Tyrone steps nervously on to the pavement; his head droops and his body suddenly appears to shrink ten inches.

'I asked my people to find out more about the person I was to meet today,' Didier continues. He bends his knees until he is eye-level with Tyrone. 'We spoke to Dan here and he told us that you call the show often. *Alors*, then we called your brother and he told us that you have problems at school.'

Tyrone lowers his eyes. His shiny red hair glistens in the daylight. He shrugs a skinny shoulder and says nothing.

'So here we are at your school.' Didier sweeps his arm towards the building just as the tatty brown doors open and children of all shapes and sizes emerge from its corridors. 'Let us see if we can make things better. Hold your head high,' Didier instructs Tyrone. 'Never apologise for being who you are.'

Tyrone slowly nods his head and thrusts his chin into the air. I wipe away a tear as I watch him and then slip quietly back into the car. As Dan pointed out, I couldn't save the world but I have at least helped to make it better for one bullied teenager. I am suddenly so glad I met Didier Lafitte; just for this moment it has all been worthwhile.

'Do you think I will have earned some good karma from all this?' I whisper to Ceri.

She flaps her hand dismissively. 'I don't believe in all that hippy crap, Angel. In my opinion, no matter what you do life will throw whatever shit it wants to your way and there is nothing you can do about it.'

'Er, thanks, Ceri, that's a very cheerful thought.'

'No problem,' she sniffs, 'and don't ever say I didn't warn you.'

CHAPTER TWENTY-THREE

It's My Party

Warm sunshine in Glasgow during December may be as rare as an Eskimo in a tanning salon but today the golden sky seems appropriate. Our tour of the city feels like a fun-packed holiday squashed into one afternoon. We stop for gargantuan ice creams in a swanky café (Ceri just nibbles the edge of a fan wafer); we eat doughnuts dipped in hot chocolate at another when Tyrone mentions that the jam ones are his favourite type of cake (Ceri orders a black coffee, no sugar). We race into a sports shop in Sauchiehall Street with Didier's PA while our star hides in the car and emerge twenty minutes later with a newly suited and booted (well, *trainered* actually, but that doesn't rhyme) Tyrone grinning from ear to ear. We deposit Tyrone at home with a promise from Didier to keep in touch – and he will – along with lots of tearful goodbyes, mainly from Dan and myself who have grown very attached to our now number one caller. We then pull up outside a fruit shop and one of the stormtroopers is ordered to purchase the best seedless grapes and tropical fruit basket money can buy.

'What are they for?' I ask.

Didier taps his nose. 'You will see, Angelique, just one more stop on our tour.'

All becomes clear when the magic car door opens again and to my surprise we are at the front entrance of the Royal Alexandra Hospital.

I say to my surprise, but when our colourful troop marches on to the ward and Didier shakes Dad firmly by the hand, it's fortunate Dad is already taking angina drugs because if he wasn't he'd need them now.

'Stone me,' he gasps, his vocabulary indicating his age even if the heart monitor and old-fashioned pyjamas didn't.

Meanwhile, a woman with soft white hair in tight curls and a face lined with years of smiles, whom I assume to be Gladys, falls off her chair and displays definite signs of high blood pressure when Didier Lafitte helps her up and kisses her on both cheeks.

'Dad,' I smile, gently hugging his bony body, 'how are you feeling?'

'Fine, I'm feeling fine. No, in fact, Angel, I am feeling *great*.'

Blimey, that's a first.

Dad lifts a transparent anaemic hand and places it on top of Gladys's plump one. She looks at him with even more feeling than when she gazed at Didier. Hmm, I can sense something is going on around here. I blush like a giggly schoolgirl who has just seen her parents snogging. Dan nudges me in the ribs.

'We, Gladys and I, heard your show and it was one of the best moments of my life, Angel. You showed us all that you could do it, thanks to Didier here.'

Didier bows his head politely.

'And you made me so very proud to be your dad.'

Gladys nods her cotton-wool-haired head encouragingly at my father.

'Now,' he coughs, 'I have got some good news for you. The doctor has said I can go home tomorrow.'

'Oh Dad, that's brilliant.'

Oh God, it is all downhill from here. Once he is let out of the safety of hospital who knows what—

'I know what you will be thinking, Angel,' he continues. 'That I can't do this on my own. But I've got you, and Gladys is also going to help me. And I promise in front of your friends here' – he blinks at his rather impressive audience – 'that I am going to make my daughter proud. I can do it. I can pick myself up, dust myself off and start all over again.'

I smile at my dad's use of lyrics, at the spirited man who encouraged my love of music. I am sure I see some of that old spirit returning.

He lifts up the bag of bulbous deep red fruit.

'I think I will stick to grapes in this form from now on,' he says, his eyes twinkling as he laughs. 'After all, as Gladys pointed out, if I managed not to drink for the first sixteen years of my life, then there is no reason why I can't do it now, is there?'

Simple, I think, but it might just work.

'What a mad, crazy day,' I yawn, as I lean against the front door of my block of flats and squeeze my eyes shut. My dad said today was one of the best moments of his life. Has this been the best day of my life? It's up there with the day I met Connor, the day I discovered glittery shoes and the day I bought my first record with my carefully saved pocket money.

No doubt about it. In fact, if Connor were here to share it all with me I think it would be vying for the Number One slot. So perhaps I should just end the day here and curl up under the duvet with a mug of something hot, Connor's James T-shirt and a good book before slipping into a happy, dreamy sleep. Then I can wake up tomorrow to headlines (good ones, I hope) and birthday cards (lots of them – with money inside, I hope).

'You know, I might just . . .'

'Don't say it, Little Miss Squarey McSquare,' squeals Meg, stamping her flowery DM boot on the pavement. 'Do not say that you willn'y come to Didier Lafitte's party when he only dropped us off with the promise that we'd come back once we'd made ourselves beautiful.'

'We haven't got that long, Megan,' says Ceri, looking down her nose at Meg's orange velvet outfit (her current favourite). 'The party is tonight you know.'

'Aye, I know,' Meg frowns, missing the point of Ceri's disparaging comment, 'and our Angel here is the special guest so she cannot just bomb the whole thing out. Och, come on, Angel, please. I want to be your VIP friend.'

I slump my shoulders and sigh. 'But I'm tired, Meg, and all that flitting about this afternoon was enough for me. I think I'm on a bit of an adrenalin drop.'

'I for one am not surprised,' says Ceri. 'It is Friday night, after all; the night when young people go out on the town and discover the joys of letting it all hang out.'

'And?' I look questioningly at Ceri.

'You don't *do* Friday nights, do you, darling? You're too

comfortable, remember. Besides, it's the big three-oh tomorrow, isn't it?'

Meg jumps up and down with all the grace of Darcey Bussell in iron boots.

'Yippee de do dah! I love birthdays. Just wait till you see what I got you – it's mental. Anyways, come on, hen, this can be your pre-birthday celebration party. We can have a few lemon tops, get a wee bit guttered, dance our bloody legs off and watch Ceri going off to podger one of Didier's pals.'

'Podger? What the hell is that?' Ceri scowls.

'Pull, shag, ride, have sex with, your usual Friday night performance.'

'Look, I'm just a bit tired,' I interrupt before the scene turns violent, 'and, to be honest, it's not the same without Connor here to share this with. I'll be at the party wishing he were with me and everyone will be in couples and "podgering" all over the place and it will just make me miss him even more.'

'Och, away ye go . . .' Meg begins at the same time as Ceri mutters something that sounds distinctly like – 'It hasn't stopped you so far' – but Meg is off.

'. . . come on, Angel, your Connor wouldn'y want to see you sitting at home by yourself on your big day, would he?'

I shrug.

'He'd love you to be out having fun, wouldn't he? And it's no' like I'll be off snogging a popstar so I can be your dancing pal all night.'

I smile at Meg's self-deprecation.

'Look, Angel, don't be wet,' Ceri says with more force. 'This party is for you and the Frenchman so just get upstairs and get dressed and meet us here in half an hour.'

'OK, but I might call Connor first and ask him.'

'Suit yourself,' Ceri huffs.

'But isn't he . . .?' Meg starts to say.

'And while you're at it, remind him that it's your birthday tomorrow to give the poor sod time to pretend he remembered.'

I grit my teeth against the icy wind that has started to blow down the street. I think it is emanating from Ceri Divine's cold heart.

'I don't need to remind him, thank you. Connor never forgets things like that.'

'Oh yeah' – Ceri raises a thin eyebrow – 'and did he remember about today?'

'Yes, of course—'

'Did he call to wish you good luck or send you a telegram or a good luck bunch of flowers?'

I drop my eyes and rustle in my bag for my keys.

'But I thought he—' Meg begins again.

'No, he didn't,' I reply with a sharp inhalation of breath, 'but Connor's never been that big on flowers. And anyway, he's probably busy or saving it all for tomorrow or something.'

'Sure,' Ceri replies with a thin smile. 'You don't need to make excuses for him, honey. I am simply trying to point out that while you are standing here missing him and not wanting to go to the party of a lifetime because he's not here to share it with, he might not exactly be giving you the same amount of consideration.'

'But, Ceri, I thought you said—' Meg stutters.

'I will meet you here in half an hour,' I interrupt, 'unless I call to tell you otherwise.'

I shove my way through the front door and stomp up the stairs to my flat. Sometimes I really wonder why I am still friends with Ceri Divine; she is so . . . harsh. Then again, everything she just said was the truth, wasn't it? He hasn't called me today. He hasn't sent me any flowers (not that I should expect any after the dry season my vases have been experiencing in the two and a half months since he left). The thing is, Connor has been so supportive and loving over the past week since Dad went into hospital that I am surprised and disappointed. Right – I fling open my wardrobe doors and squint at the jumble of clothes inside – enough of this reading into things that aren't even important and feeling sorry for myself when this day has been as close to perfect as Brad Pitt. I am going to that party and I am going to enjoy it. After all I deserve a celebration.

I choose a pair of bright pink velvet trousers, a little pink Roxy shirt with just a tiny scrap of material between my cleavage and my belly button (blink and you'll miss it!) and team it all with shiny white boots that I bought in last winter's sale. I style my hair in smooth, thick spikes, take care with my eye make-up and finish off with lip-liner and a diamond-effect pink lipstick, which makes my lips look like they've been sucked into the nozzle of a vacuum cleaner. Who needs collagen when a good bit of colouring-in will do? I stand in front of the hall mirror and blow myself a kiss.

'Pretty damn good, even if I say so myself,' I say to my reflection. 'Angel Knights, you scrub up all right. In fact, I would say' – I wander through to the lounge – 'you look like the very image of a top Glasgow radio DJ. What do you think, Connor McLean?'

I pick up a photo of Connor and I at Glastonbury, welly-deep in mud and looking every inch the scabby hippies. I run my finger down his grinning, dirt-covered face.

'What do you think of your girlfriend being a successful DJ, hey?' I sigh, and look quickly around to check no one is watching me (although it would be a little worrying if they were as I would probably be about to feature in a real life version of *Scream*). Then I kiss the picture.

'I miss you, Connor McLean. I want you here doing all the silly things we used to do and asking me to marry you all over again. I think right now I would probably say yes.'

The realisation suddenly hits me and a tear runs down my cheek. Damn, I really am going to have to invest in some waterproof mascara; my eyes seem to be leaking more than usual at the moment. This has been such a good day, a perfect day, except for the fact that one person is not here with me. It just shows me how special that one person is. He is bigger than all the fame and the glory and the gallivanting. I want him even more than I want all that.

'Sod it,' I sniff loudly. 'Ceri may think I'm a sap and I might make us late but I have to speak to you. It's not every day a girl gets asked for her autograph and then decides that maybe she might want to get married after all.'

I put down the photo, scamper excitedly (this moment requires scampering) to the phone and dial the number while my heart pounds in my chest like King Kong, only from the inside.

'Come on, come on, answer the friggin' ph— Oh, hello? Yes, hello. Could you put me through to Mr McLean in room 224B please?'

'Actually, *maam*, I am not sure—'

'Room 224B,' I repeat in my best tea-with-the-Queen voice. 'This is Mr McLean's girl . . . his *fiancée.*'

'I understand that, *maam*, but Mr McLean—'

'And I actually have some very, very important news for him, so if you could just put me through that would be lovely.'

I tap my foot impatiently.

'I could do that, *maam*, but as I tried to explain Mr McLean is actually—'

That's it, yankee doodle, I've had enough.

'Look, lady, I am calling from Scotland. That is in Europe, and as much as you might be craving a bit of small talk this call is expensive. So if you could just put me through to room 224B, that would stop me having to come over there and—'

'If you insist, *maam*, but there's no need to be rude.'

'Cow,' I grumble, before taking a few deep breaths to rid my body of the receptionist-induced angst. I need to be calm for this. I need to find my inner peace.

'Be in,' I whisper, hoping that Connor chose today for a lie-in.

The telephone in the room rings a couple of times in that monotone way that lets you know this is a long distance and hence costly call. I bite my lip as he lifts the receiver. Only it is not a he – it is a she.

'Hello,' she breathes, 'who's this?'

My blood turns to ice in my veins and I am about to shatter into a million broken pieces until I realise the mistake. She has put me through to the wrong room of course, the stupid dizzy tart. I laugh uneasily.

'Oh, I'm sorry, I was actually looking for room 224B but—'

'This is room 224B.'

My wide eyes shoot down to the notepad next to the telephone where I have scribbled Connor's room number over and over again among the kaleidoscope of doodles.

'Er, but there must be some mistake' – my knees are shaking – 'I was looking for a Connor McLean.'

My lungs feel like two deflated balloons. I struggle for saliva to keep my mouth operational. There is a pause as the girl yawns down the phone line.

'Yeah, this is Connor McLean's room but he's . . . Oh, wait a bloody minute, who's this? This ain't Angel, is it?'

I stare at the mirror in front of me and drop the telephone as the pronounced Essex accent turns my mind a shade of blood red. No, no, no, no, NO! This can't be happening. He wouldn't do this. This isn't how it was meant to be. My body is stiff but a sudden bolt of energy shoots my arm out to grab the receiver.

'YES, this is ANGEL,' I wail, 'but who the FUCK are you?'

The line is already dead.

Nicole Kidman and Robbie Williams' love duet spills from the speakers of Didier's 'after-show' party. Sack the DJ, that's what I say. Why doesn't he play something about death and destruction and hating people? Especially people in room 224B.

'Men,' I mutter, pointing at one of the speakers. 'Waste of bloody space the lot of them.'

'Well, I don't know about that,' Ceri pouts, rubbing her bare leg suggestively against the crotch of her photographer friend.

He looks vaguely familiar but in my present state I just can't place him. Ceri introduced him as James or Jeff or something equally non-descript and James or Jeff has since uttered a total of one word – 'Hi'. The poor bloke is good-looking enough but more wooden than Pinocchio. As I said, he must buy very expensive presents.

'Why don't you just forget about him for a while?' suggests Meg. 'I'm sure there is a perfectly innocent explanation, isn't there, Ceri?' She hisses the last part like an adder that's just been trodden on by the heel of a stiletto.

Ceri inspects her French-manicured nails and shrugs her chiffon-covered shoulders. That is about all she has covered. She appears to have left most of her dress back home. Revealing is not the word.

'Oh, I don't know, there will be an explanation. Whether it is innocent or not is another matter.'

'But you said . . .' Meg begins, tugging on Ceri's elbow.

Ceri slips deftly out of her grasp and brushes her arm as if to wipe away germs. 'I said nothing, Megan, and neither will you.'

'Eh?' I hiccup, swaying on the high bar stool. 'What are you talking about? And why doesn't all this slushy lovey-dovey music just FUCK OFF?'

I stick my fingers up at the DJ who has just subjected my ears to 'Whole Again' by Atomic Kitten. I have only just stopped crying for God's sake; does he want me to have eyes like a pufferfish?

The party is, as you might say if you were hip and cool – something I am really not feeling right now – 'going off'. We are in a private venue somewhere in the city but I couldn't tell you where. My eyes were too busy crying to notice where the car was taking us after it picked me up from Byres Road. Wherever we are, there is music and lots of people and even some of the stormtroopers have taken off their helmets and let their hair down enough to wiggle a bit on the dancefloor. Yep, I am sure it's a great party and Didier is glowing like a firefly with the pride of pulling off his first interview in English.

The sad thing is, this party is supposed to be partly in my honour, but I am too upset and angry to care. I don't want to be here among all these happy people, all celebrating their happy success. It just emphasises how quickly my day rose like a rocket, spluttered, shed an engine and plummeted to Earth. How could Connor do this to me, today of all days? And now he has made me drink too much, which makes me feel worse. Not to mention the fact that my dad has been in hospital all week because of the demon drink, which makes me feel doubly worse. Racked with guilt, in fact. I just want to go home. Home is where the heart is, supposedly. I think I left mine broken into pieces on the floor beside the telephone. I must remember to pick the pieces up when I wake up tomorrow, newly thirty, alone and cheated-on.

'Tomorrow I will wake up newly thirty, *hic*, alone and cheated-on,' I slur while trying to extricate myself from this impossibly high stool. 'Now isn't that just, *hic*, *très bien*?'

Meg catches me as I fall towards her. 'Och, don't say that, pal. You willn'y be alone and you haven'y been cheated on. I think you've got it all wrong.' She props me up against the bar. 'Remember Beth and the shopping trip for the ring? You got it wrong then, hen, didn't you?'

I stick out my bottom lip. OK she has a point, but only a very faint one, like a pinprick on a hedgehog.

'Maybe, but then Beth wasn't in Connor's bedroom on a lazy Friday morning, was she?'

I finish with a wholly indiscreet burp, just as Didier appears at my side, still looking as fresh-faced as a model in a Clearasil campaign. I rub the skin under my eyes in case I am doing an unwitting impression of a panda. Didier places his arm around my shoulders.

'Is everything OK with my favourite radio DJ? You are not crying, are you?'

'She's over-excited, Didier, which is partially your fault.' Ceri narrows her almond-shaped eyes. 'Perhaps you should take her home.'

'Och, don't be daft, I'll take her home. We'll jump in a taxi. Come on, Angel, we're off-ski,' says Meg, tugging on my arm.

'*Non, non, non*, I would not hear of you taking a taxi – we have cars for you. Megan' – Meg's mouth drops when he uses her name, displaying the extensive range of fillings in her back molars – 'you must stay and enjoy the rest of the party.'

'Yes, Megan, and besides, Dan needs a dancing partner and I think you're the only one who can match his style.'

Ceri flicks her head towards Dan, who is shaking on the dancefloor like an epileptic chicken. Meg's face instantly brightens.

'Aye, well, okey dokey, if you're sure but?'

'*Absolument* certain,' Didier nods, taking me by the arm. 'These parties happen all the time.'

'On your planet maybe,' Meg snorts. 'I haven'y been at one this big since my granny died.' By way of clarification she adds, 'She was very popular with the old men.'

'Hmm,' Didier replies with a confused smile. 'OK, we will go now. My PA tells me there are many fans at my hotel so perhaps I can hide at Angel's apartment for a while.'

'You do that,' Ceri nods. 'Take care of her.'

'But no hanky-panky mind,' Meg laughs loudly.

'Excuse me, I am still here and capable of, *hic*, making my own decisions, you know,' I hiccup before collapsing in a heap on the floor.

The next thing I know I am being deposited on my sofa with a loud grunt. Did he really have to grunt? Could he have not just exhaled lightly to avoid giving me the impression that I would qualify as a rival to Lennox Lewis? I groan and look down at my crumpled pink outfit. Where earlier I felt like a lithe, sexy Penelope Pitstop-type, now I feel a closer resemblance to a pink squidgy flump in a marshmallow suit.

'Oh no, I clash with the sofa,' I mutter, and commando roll myself off the red throw and on to the floor. I stumble towards the bedroom, slump backwards on the bed and stare at the ceiling while trying to uncross my eyes.

'Good thing, bad thing, good thing, bad thing. That is how my life goes. I said, that is how my life goes.'

Didier pokes his head nervously around the door. His hair drapes across one shoulder.

'Good thing – Connor proposes to me. At least *partly* good. It freaked me out but at least it showed he cared enough to ask. Anyway, bad thing – Connor immediately buggers off to LA and messes everything up. Good thing – I meet Didier Lafitte, a very lovely person.'

Didier bows to accept the compliment.

'Bad thing – I kiss him and almost jump into his bed.'

'Oh. But this was not *so* bad.'

'Good thing – I have the best day of my radio career ever. Bad thing – my boyfriend jumps into bed with some Hollywood slapper. Not that he necessarily jumped today. I mean, he could have been jumping in and out for months now and muggins here just hasn't realised. I knew Ceri was trying to warn me with the stars and stripes thong and hot tub thing. He's even been e-mailing *her* in secret. She was right.'

I sit up, sniff and squeeze my eyes shut. They hurt as if they want to cry but they have run out of tears. I suddenly feel heavy-hearted – sobered by the thought of my man in bed with someone else. Didier sits beside me. He brushes a hand over my hair.

'You know, Angel, I would not believe everything your friend Sheri—'

'Ceri,' I interrupt, surprised at him for getting the name wrong. No one ever forgets Ceri. (Except Connor of course, when he started going out with me, but that's different.)

'Ceri, yes, perhaps she is not always right about these things.'

'Why?' I huff. 'She's perfect in every other way so she may as well always be right too.'

'Perfect?' Didier laughs gently and shakes his beautiful head. 'Huh, I would not say your friend is perfect. She may work hard at perfection but, believe me, she has many flaws.'

I wrinkle my nose thoughtfully. If anyone would know about perfection it is him. Never mind the fact that over the past fortnight he has emerged as a really genuine person lost in a world of fickleness, especially with everything he has done for me and for Tyrone and my dad today. But he is almost too perfect for me. Despite his good looks and glamour he just doesn't do it for me – basically because he is not my Connor. My heart wails inside my chest at the thought of him. I want Connor here with me where we are so good together. We should be cuddled up on the sofa right now, toasting my success with pizza for two and a bottle of five-quid something. Why did it go so wrong?

'You are much more perfect than Ceri,' says Didier, interrupting my melancholy moment by stroking my hair again. 'And if Connor is cheating on you he is a very stupid man. But do not charge him with the crime before you are sure, Angel. Do not rely on someone like Ceri. Trust in yourself.'

I sigh. 'Thanks, Didier, I'll think about that.'

'*Très bien.*'

We sit awkwardly on the edge of the bed. One thing I do know, I am glad I didn't sleep with him. It feels rather alien just being in a bedroom together.

'Erm . . . Didier, I, er – you're not waiting for a snog or anything are you?'

He throws back his head and laughs. The sound reverberates around the room.

All right, Mister, snogging me isn't that hilarious a concept you know.

'Oh, I am sorry, Angel,' he smirks, 'but you are so funny.'

Hmm, thanks. I think.

'No, I am not waiting for a, how you say' – he makes quotation marks in the air with his hands – 'a "snog". Of course I enjoyed the brief kiss we shared . . .'

My eyes dart nervously around the room to check no one overheard that admission.

'. . . but I realise now that we are just friends.'

I blush. 'Delphine had a little bit to do with that first kiss anyway, didn't she?' I ask. 'How much was she paying you to seduce me?'

Now it is his turn to blush.

'Ah, I see. *Alors*, she did ask me to *help* with your love life a little, and to check that you are OK, but, believe me, after I met you I did not need encouragement.'

Blimey, this blushing is reaching epidemic proportions. It's like we're having a game of hot flush tennis.

'I had feelings for you because you are so genuine compared to the people I meet.' He presses his hands to his chest. 'I still have feelings for you but I think it is just a deep friendship because I know it is not me that you want. You want Connor and I will tell your *maman* this when I return to Bordeaux. So I am simply staying to make sure you are not unhappy with all that has happened this evening.'

'Thanks.'

'I am positive things will work out with Connor and that you will be very happy together.'

'Thanks again.'

He may not be a relationship expert but I am glad to hear a little reassurance about Connor and I. Didier always seems to know the right thing to say.

I try to stifle a yawn that suddenly pushes its way out of my lungs.

'OK, *mademoiselle*, now you are tired and it is time for bed. Uh, and if you don't mind, I may just stay on your sofa in the other room because my hotel is mobbed and it is late.' He grins shyly. 'It is not often that I have the chance to do something as normal as this.'

I smile, pull off my boots and walk around to the head of the bed.

'Sure,' I nod, pulling back the duvet and slipping into the comforting warmth still fully clothed. (I am hardly going to get naked in front of a man like that, am I? I think I'll wait until he's asleep and then quickly change into a T-shirt.)

Didier strolls towards me, bends down and softly kisses my forehead.

'*Bonne anniversaire*, happy birthday for tomorrow, *chérie*, and I hope it is a very enjoyable one. Goodnight.'

Goodnight? Good *day* I would agree with, good *night* is certainly questionable. Then again, there is an internationally famous French popstar kipping on my sofa so . . . yeah, I guess it's not all bad.

CHAPTER TWENTY-FOUR

Torn

I wake up to the sound of a bell ringing in the near distance. My first thought is – *hangover*. My second thought is – *I don't care because it's my birthday!* My third is – *wow, I'm thirty*. Angel Knights, thirty years old, a newly initiated member of the thirty-something club. I can hardly believe it. In my eyes I'm stuck somewhere around my mid-twenties and I am sure I used to be much more mature than I am now. I mean, God, when I was eighteen I knew near enough *everything*.

What *is* that incessant ringing? Shit! It's the doorbell. Presents! Presents too big to fit through the letterbox so the postman has to ring the doorbell, and there must be lots of them because he is pretty insistent. Yippee! I fall out of bed and clump across the room, stepping on discarded clothes and shoes as I go.

'Happy birthday to me, happy birthday to me,' I sing as I burst into the lounge, 'happy birthday top female radio DJ, happy birthday to me.'

I skip across the rug and past the empty sofa towards the hallway.

'Didier? Hey Didier, where are you? Come here and give me a great big birthday—'

Hug. I was going to say 'hug' but it comes out more of an 'urggh' when I round the corner and see the person standing at my open front door. In fact, the *two* people standing at my front door. The two *men* facing each other in complete gobsmacked silence.

Connor? Is it Connor? I rub the sleepydust out of my eyes. His usually tanned skin is even more golden than before. He has shorter hair and is surprisingly thinner than he was when he left – back to the same lithe figure I first met – but it is definitely Connor. My Connor. Opposite him, with one hand on the open door and the other on the waistband of his fitted black boxer shorts, is Didier. Wait a minute, *boxer shorts*? Boxer shorts and naked torso. I look down at my bare legs poking out from beneath Connor's old James T-shirt. I run a hand through my ruffled bed-head hair. Now stop me if I'm getting the wrong end of the stick here but . . . this looks pretty bad, doesn't it?

'Connor,' I breathe in a distant voice that seems to come out of my ears, 'what are you doing here?'

I know I could have done better but just seeing him is a shock. As for the two-men-at-the-door scenario, this is definitely an added complication. Granted there is a perfectly innocent explanation but I just have one of those guilty faces. Put me in an identity parade and I would be picked out even if they were looking for a six-foot bald man with tattoos, just from the expression on my face. Right now I am totally confirming the suspicious look in Connor's blue eyes.

I eventually find my voice. 'Connor, I can't believe it's you.'

I race towards him, literally whacking Didier out of the way en route. I lunge forwards, wrapping my arms around the familiar body and inhaling his smell – Dune aftershave enriched with his natural manly aroma. Unmistakable. He's real. My boyfriend is here but his body is cold. Cold in the metaphorical sense. I hold his slim hips and step back so that I can look up into his face. He looks tired and a little drawn from the journey but he looks good. Fit and tanned and even better-looking than I remember. His black hair is cropped at the front and back, giving him an American boy-next-door image. He is dressed in khaki jeans and a smart blue sweater, with a denim jacket that broadens his already square shoulders. I glance down to see his faithful (an unfortunate word on this occasion perhaps) scuffed boots. A lump forms in my throat. He seems so . . . so manly, so tall and slim, so *mine*.

'You look wonderful,' I say softly.

I smile up into those piercing blue eyes, letting all my love for him show itself on my face. But he doesn't smile back. I frown and then gasp as his eyes begin to blur and a tear trickles down his cheek.

'Connor, no. What's wrong?'

Call me old fashioned but I don't like to see my man crying. At least not sad tears. It makes me uncomfortable. These definitely look like sad tears.

'Hello, baby,' says the lilting Scottish accent, 'I thought I'd pop over to wish you a happy birthday.'

I grin and hug him to me. Why isn't he hugging me back?

Has he forgotten how to do it in the last ten weeks? Come on – arms out, bodies together and squeeze; easy. I try again but detach myself when I realise Connor is looking at Didier. He clears his throat.

'But it looks like I already missed the party.'

'What? Connor, no, it's not what you think.'

I look from one man to the other and then down into the fiery pit of hell and damnation opening up in the floor below me.

'Ha ha, I know this looks a bit . . . er, *odd*, Con, but honestly, ha ha, it's just—'

'Ceri warned me about this,' he interrupts sternly.

'Ceri? What's she got to do with anything?'

'She warned me you were up to something; she says she's even got proof. I didn't believe her. I thought more of you than that but I suppose this is all the proof I need.'

'Stop, Connor' – I grab his arm – 'this isn't proof of anything. Come in, come inside and let's talk about this. Then we can have a happy birthday day and—'

'Did you kiss him?'

The question stops me dead, like a fly hitting the windscreen of a turbo-injection sports car.

'Did I what?'

'Did you kiss him?'

Connor's voice is monotone. I stare at him, my jaw locked in an icy paralysis. Now what am I supposed to say to that?

Our eyes lock and in that second Connor knows the truth. He has studied my eyes – the so-called window to my soul – since I was sixteen. I can't hide anything.

'Perhaps I should go,' says Didier, his voice suddenly an unwelcome sound to my ears.

'Perhaps you should,' Connor agrees coldly.

'Wait!' I yelp. 'This is silly.'

'I would call it many things but not that.'

Connor steps back to leave just as a man appears in the corridor behind him. He is wearing a hat and a camera masks much of his face. The thought briefly enters my brain that he is familiar but I can't place him. Forgive me; I'm in the middle of a crisis here.

'Hello, what—?' I begin.

'Did you kiss him?' Connor says again.

'I must go,' adds Didier.

'Yes, I kissed him but it was no—'

There is a blinding flash that forces my eyes shut before I can finish my sentence. I clasp my hands to my face. Am I falling? Am I going to hell? Or was it just a camera flash? When I open my eyes again the man is gone. I whip my head around in confusion.

'What's happening?' I whimper.

The end of the world as you know it, my mind tuts impatiently, *keep up girl*.

Connor hands me an envelope, then turns to leave. 'Goodbye, Angel,' he says firmly, 'and happy birthday.'

The tears are dripping from my chin. I can feel them just like I can hear my sobs but I have no control over any of it.

'Connor, honey, wait,' I call after him as he disappears. 'WAIT, PLEASE!'

I stare at the sight of him running away. Of the man who hates arguments trying to get as far away from this confrontation and from me as he possibly can. Oh my God. What just happened?

My heart lurches suddenly as a figure appears at the top of the stairs but the hope evaporates when I realise he is not Connor.

'Flower delivery for Miss Angel Knights,' says the man.

'Yes. Hmm?'

He thrusts a forest-sized bouquet of flowers into my hands. I peer at him in bewilderment through the wall of cellophane and the overwhelming cloud of pollen that fills my nostrils.

'I'm really sorry, madam, eh, these were s'posed to be delivered yesterday but we had a wee mix up. Sorry 'boot that.' He clears his throat and shows me a row of uneven teeth. 'They're from a Mr Connor McLean with love. So, eh, enjoy them. Cheerio now.'

At that moment, with a humungous bunch of flowers in my clenched fists and Didier's hand resting on my shoulder, my whole world falls apart. And it keeps on falling until I hit the bottom of nothingness with a bone-breaking crash.

'Happy birthday, Angel,' I whisper before everything turns black.

If Marilyn Monroe lived her life like a candle in the wind, then over the next day or so I am like a lit match in a bloody hurricane. Everything turns upside down, back to front and inside out as I try to figure out how it all went so wrong. As I told Didier the night before that fateful morning: good thing, bad thing – that is how my life goes. Good thing – Connor flying all the way from LA to surprise little old me on my thirtieth birthday. Bad thing – a French pop legend opening the door to him in his boxer shorts. Good thing number two – I starred in Saturday's newspaper headlines after my interview with Didier and was named as one of Glasgow's top female DJs. There were even a couple of surprisingly flattering photographs depicting my radiant smile on that day. Bad thing, no, *very* bad thing – on Sunday I then starred in a Scottish tabloid's headline about Didier Lafitte bedding one of Glasgow's female radio broadcasters, which also included a rather unflattering photo of Didier, Connor and myself gawping at each other on my front doorstep. If the story wasn't bad enough, the photograph was awful. God knows what lens the guy had on his camera but my bare thighs resembled two of those kebab shop skewered meat things and my eyes had all but disappeared into my puffy face. How can I ever face the world again? It is safe to say that at that moment the proverbial shit hit the fan, but more about that later.

On Saturday I learned that the mere fact that it is your birthday does not necessarily guarantee you a day of fun and frivolity, cakes and balloons and an endless stream of unconditional love. In fact, despite it being my birthday and a significant one at that, I had one of the worst days of my life, competing in the ratings with the day I discovered my dad had a drink problem and the day my mother left him. How strange that only the day before I was recollecting the best days. Yes, my thirtieth birthday was crap. I cried from the moment Connor left until the moment my head hit the pillow that night. In fact, I think I may even have carried on crying in my sleep because when I woke up my pillow was like a wet sponge and my eyes were stuck together with some sort of teary glue.

Meg tried her best to cheer me up throughout the day. She appeared at my door, after Didier had scuttled nervously away, with a bag of croissants, a family-sized jar of Nutella, two presents that I still have not had the strength to open and a pile of cards that she'd found on my doorstep. This was after I had called her and said something like: 'M . . . M . . . Mmeg, I . . . sob . . . I . . . Connnnnor, left me . . . sob . . . Didier . . . waahh, kiss . . . all shit . . . HELP.' She understood.

Good old Meg. She is so optimistic. If a meteor was about to hit earth and we were all going to perish in a ball of fire and ash Meg would still look on the bright side. How she could be so positive when I had made such a giant hash of things I will never know.

'It'll be fine,' she assured me, trying to hide Didier's calendar without me noticing before helping me to open my cards as I cried and wailed and blew my nose. 'He'll see sense, hen. You two were made for each other. Dinny worry, Angel.'

So I tried not to worry but I couldn't help it. The look in Connor's eyes had upset me so much. I knew I had destroyed his faith in me but I couldn't find him to try and heal his wounds. We spent the day calling everyone we could think of. His mobile, his old home number, his friends. His parents both died a few years ago and his only relative is some distant aunt in the Highlands who only talks to cattle so I came to a dead-end there. I tried his TV company but it was the weekend and nobody was there so I even rang his hotel in LA (despite the fact that he could not possibly have returned there already). When the groaning receptionist put the sobbing mess on the other end of the line (me) through to room 224B, a familiar female voice answered the phone.

'Yep, 'ello, who's this?'

'Erm, this is, erm,' I began hesitantly, 'this is Angel Knights here.'

'Oh Angel, fuckin' hell,' she laughed in a husky Essex accent. 'Listen, mate, I am so sorry about the other mornin'. It must 'ave sounded well dodgy when I answered the phone an' that but I didn't know what to say. Connor 'ad left to come and surprise you an' we'd all moved rooms cos, like, he 'ad a nice view from 'is one. And we was all bein' a bit lazy, what wiv the boss gone. Thing is, right, he told us to keep it all shtum so I was a bit, you know, off me guard. Anyway, mate, bet you're 'avin' a lovely time. He's mad about you, that bloke is. Never looks at anyone else, even when we tease 'im and I get me stars and stripes thong out. Hope you don't mind, just a bit of a larf, but he is a one-woman man that one. So what can I do for ya?'

As you may have guessed, that was Honey and her infamous stars and stripes thong. I don't think she knew what hit her when I erupted into howls. She was very sympathetic when I explained what had happened and assured me that she would let me know if Connor came back and would even enrol the other girls' help in trying to talk him round. Never in a million years did I think Honey, Truly, Ferrari *et al* would be helping me correct my love life but I needed all the assistance I could muster. Her kindness almost killed me, so wretched was I feeling. Mind you, I suspect she was secretly thinking – you selfish little tart, fancy treating your Connor like a disposable take-away carton.

After that, just to ensure that my emotional state would be worthy of the title 'depression', I read the card Connor had handed me at the front door.

Darling Angel

I am writing this on the plane and if I could make the pilot fly any faster I would because I can't wait to see you. Happy birthday, baby, and I hope it is the best one ever. And I know I should be giving you presents but maybe you will give me one and agree to be my wife. All my love always, from the bottom of my heart,

your man,

Connor xxx

I shouldn't have read that.

The thing is, I can't believe that it can be over. Not just like that. Connor and I have done too much and shared too much of our lives to just say goodbye. Perhaps that is what happens when relationships end these days. Like my mum and dad, who have only spoken once since she left and only then because Delphine couldn't find her favourite Chanel bolero jacket. But I can't accept that Connor has gone for ever. His stuff is all over my flat for God's sake; his pictures adorn my walls, my memory is full of him. Perhaps I overlooked this fact when he was away because of the distance between us but our lives have become intricately entwined like the knotted ropes of a string hammock. And if you take half those ropes away the whole thing falls apart and the support and comfort is gone. I know now that I allowed myself to lose faith in our relationship simply because it became long distance. I was scared of the marriage thing, I soaked up Ceri's doubts and I succumbed to Didier's charms too easily. If I could change it I would but I can't. If I could explain it I would but I can't because he's not here. All I can hope is that, wherever he is, he doesn't believe everything he has read in the papers because it is simply not true. I guess I should explain a little more about the tabloid story.

'Jeez-oh,' Meg tutted, bursting into the flat and waving a Sunday tabloid like a surrender flag. 'You'd better sit down, hen,' she whistled, ''cos you're no' gonna like this.'

I didn't. Like it I mean. I did sit down. I fell down in a heap when I read the headline.

ANGELIC DJ BEDS LAFITTE AS BIRTHDAY TREAT

That was bad but it got worse when we turned to pages four and five. There were photos. Lots of photos. Didier and I going for dinner at the Devonshire. Didier and I slipping in the back door of the cinema. Didier holding my hand over the table at The Ice Palace. Didier and I *kissing*. Me waiting in the reception at Didier's hotel and – *la pièce de la résistance* – Didier, Connor and I in various states of undress and distress at my front door.

'Wow, that's a funny one,' Meg remarked, pointing at the last picture. 'Didier looks like Ginola, only younger, and Connor looks like Gary Lineker, only better-looking and without the sticky-out ears. If you looked like Des Lynam that could be a football pundit studio line-up.'

I didn't laugh. Famous one day, notorious the next, and I had no idea how it had happened.

'Paparazzi,' Meg kept repeating as if that explained everything.

Although my career in the limelight was only two days old, suddenly I didn't want to be famous any more.

I tried to call Didier, only to be coolly informed by his PA that he had left the country and gone into hiding. I resumed my efforts to find Connor but he had apparently gone into hiding too. Even Ceri had done a disappearing act when I tried to get in touch to ask her why she had taken it upon herself to warn Connor about what I was up to. I am well aware of her status as the gossip queen but how did she know what was going on and why didn't she just talk to me first? I was getting frustrated. There were so many discussions that needed to be had but there was no one to have them with.

Apart from my mother, of course. She had to stick her very special type of oar in at the first possible opportunity.

'Angel, it's your mum,' screamed Meg, who had started fielding my calls as if I were a true celebrity.

'Oh God, that's all I bloody need right now,' I croaked and trudged robotically to the telephone from my hiding place under the duvet.

'Angelique, *Maman*,' she began sharply. 'Now what on bloody earth is it that you have done to upset Marie-Pierre? Thirty years old, my daughter, and *toujours* you give me trouble. *Merde*, I can not rely on you to get a single bloody thing right.'

A kind word as always. After explaining to Delphine that the darling son of Marie-Pierre wasn't entirely free of guilt and thanking her for her assistance in bodging up my love life, I put her straight on the fact that although there may be many more '*poissons*' in the sea, I had lost the special *poisson* that should have been mine for ever. (I don't think it came out quite so poetically at the time but it was something along those lines.)

So here I am in bed on Monday morning. I am in pain. I feel ill with a cold and depressed and sorry for myself but I must go to work. Friday may have been a spectacular high at Energy FM but since then I have managed to drag the station's name through the mud along with my own. I can't call in sick – it's not as if my mum is going to write me a note – so I must show my face, pale and tear-stained as it is, and accept what is coming to me. After all, I can't possibly feel any worse than I already do. First, though, there is someone I must speak to.

CHAPTER TWENTY-FIVE

Walking Away

'Ceri Divine please,' I say to the very tall, very thin woman at the plush reception desk.

She has a facial expression as if she is sucking on a bitter lemon, all pouty lips and pointy cheekbones.

'Do you have an appointment?' she asks without moving her mouth, her eyes quickly scanning my body from the thick woolly scarf wrapped tightly around my neck to the black puffa jacket, baggy jeans and chunky Buffalo boots.

'No' – I shuffle my feet – 'but if you tell her Angel Knights is here she will definitely see me.'

A knowing smile touches the corners of her mouth. She peers closer at me. I pull the scarf up a little.

'Angel Knights, eh? I'll just buzz her for you.'

Ceri appears moments later through an invisible door in the bright white wall to my left. She is dressed as immaculately as ever in a tight black polo neck and even tighter black stretch trousers. She looks like a stick of liquorice, only with a shock of waist-length blonde hair, and she is glowing. In fact, she appears more radiant than ever.

Well she bloody well would, wouldn't she? I think sourly before forcing a smile on to my pale, dry lips and accepting her kiss to the air beside my cheeks.

'Angel, darling, how are you feeling?' she gushes, shepherding me through the door.

'Oh, you know—'

'Yes. Sorry I haven't been in touch but I had plans this weekend. What a dreadful business though, hon. I simply can't imagine how bad you must feel, although from the look of you it must be pretty dreadful.'

Thanks for that, Ceri, I needed a confidence boost.

I follow her to her office. 'We need to talk, Ceri,' I say, plonking myself down on one of her chrome and leather chairs that are embarrassingly narrow for a normal-sized female bottom like mine.

'Sure, yes' – Ceri shuts the door – 'I imagine you need a shoulder to cry on.'

'I've done plenty of that, believe me. Meg got the brunt of it.'

I begin to shed my wintry disguise. Ceri perches on the edge of her far-too-tidy-to-ever-produce-any-work desk.

'You must be devastated,' she sighs, 'losing Connor after all these years. You two have been like hand and glove ever since school. It's hard to believe it's over after such a long time.'

I smart at her comment. It is the first time someone has told me that Connor and I are over. I blink back the stinging tears and lower my head.

'How do you know it's over between us?' I ask, my voice cracking mid-sentence.

She laughs lightly and tosses her glossy mane of hair. 'I think it is pretty obvious from that dreadful newspaper story, darling. I don't think many men would stick around after that. Also, I have to admit to having a little first-hand knowledge here. You see, Connor needed somewhere to stay and . . .'

I whip my head up to stare at her.

'Connor stayed with you!' I yelp. 'Connor stayed with you and you didn't tell me.' I take a breath and try to control the volume of my voice. 'How is he? Is he still there? I need to talk to him, Ceri. I need to explain that some of it is not true. I never slept with Didier.'

'Ah, but you thought about it?'

'Only because you kept telling me I was missing out on something and that Connor was off shagging everything that breathes,' I snap.

'I never said that, Angel,' she replies calmly. 'That is just how you interpreted it. That must be what you wanted to believe.'

I shake my head.

'Plus, you *did* kiss Didier.'

I look at the floor. 'Briefly, and it was a mistake. I was lonely. I love Connor and I need to see him. Where is he?'

She shrugs nonchalantly, as if I have just asked her something as unimportant as what she watched on television last night. Her attitude grates on my already frayed nerves.

'I don't know, Angel, he left this morning.'

I bite my lip hard to divert the pain from my chest.

'He was pretty cut-up though, if that's any consolation. He even cried. I think he is going to miss you.'

She smooths one hand over the other as if she is applying moisturiser.

'It's a shame.'

'A shame?' I repeat in disbelief. 'Is that all you can bloody well call it, a shame? It's not a shame, Ceri, it's a disaster, a nightmare, an apocalypse. I need to explain it to Connor but I can't and if *someone* hadn't gone around warning him that I was up to something then he would probably be more ready to discuss things, wouldn't he?'

Ceri wrinkles her usually line-free brow. I try to contain the rage that has been bubbling inside me since all this happened.

'I did not go around "warning" him about you. It's probably just the way—'

'He "interpreted" it, yeah, yeah.'

Ceri tosses her hair again. 'Sometimes e-mails can be misconstrued, Angel.'

Ooh, I'd almost forgotten that little gem. I perch on the edge of the hard seat.

'Ah yes, the e-mails. That was very cosy too, wasn't it? Actually, Ceri, I'm beginning to wonder whose side you're actually on. You e-mail my boyfriend in secret and you take him in when we've had a fight and don't bother to tell me. Are you my friend or his?'

Am I being unfair? Am I taking all my troubles out on her? Who cares, this is therapeutic. Ceri removes her bum cheek from the desk, stands straight with her hands on her hips (all twenty-six inches of them) and looks down at me.

'I don't like what you're insinuating, Angel. There is nothing sly or calculated about what I've done and, besides, I am Connor's friend as well as your friend. After all, I have known him—'

'Even longer than me,' I interrupt sarcastically.

'Well someone had to look out for him after what you did. The poor boy – if I had known what you were up to I would have told him not to bother surprising you when he e-mailed me to say he was coming.'

'I wasn't *up to* anything. All I did was—'

I stop mid-sentence and press the rewind button on our conversation.

'Hold on a minute, Ceri,' I begin slowly, 'you *knew* he was coming?'

She flicks her hair proudly. 'Of course I—'

Now it is Ceri's turn to stop mid-sentence.

I stand up and face her, crossing my arms in front of my body.

'So that's why he was e-mailing you, was it? It was all about a birthday surprise for me, but you allowed Meg and I to believe that you had a special personal chatline going between you.' At the back of my mind a light flicks on. I frown at my friend as the thoughts begin to take shape in my brain. 'You were trying to put doubts in my mind about my boyfriend, weren't you? That's what the e-mailing thing and the hot tub thing were about.' Ceri clasps a hand to her chest as if my words are mortally wounding but I haven't finished yet.

'And unless I am very much mistaken, *you* were the one who made Didier take me home from the party when all the time you knew Connor was due to arrive the next morning. Plus, you knew that Connor was on his way to see me and so couldn't possibly have been in that hotel room when that girl answered the phone, yet you let me carry on thinking there was something going on. Now why would you do a thing like that, Ceri? Please tell me because I would really like to know.'

Feeling like Miss Marple at the crucial crime-solving moment, I introduce a weighty pause and wait for my suspect to confess all. However, this isn't a detective movie and, pauses or not, Ceri flatly denies any foul play.

'Meg knew he was coming too,' she snaps. 'I told her about it.'

I consider this for a moment. 'But you kept telling her to shut up. As you always do.'

'I didn't tell Didier to stay the night.'

'It was late, I was upset, he is chivalrous and his hotel was mobbed, so you knew there was a chance he might.'

We stand facing each other, our tempers locked like clashing antlers, but Ceri accepts none of the blame I am trying to push on to her. Suddenly the office door flies open and a petite young woman with a very loud voice marches into the room.

'Ceri, a word,' she yells, exuding importance despite her size.

'Actually, Amber, I'm just—'

'Look, we need those photographs of that DJ floozy and the French popstar ASAP for this week's issue, so can you ask your boyfriend to stop arsing around and get them couriered over from the tabloid before the whole story goes arse over tit? There's a good girl, chop-chop.'

She marches out before the final full stop, without so much as a hello or goodbye. I stand rooted to the spot, completely dumbstruck for a second, before I hear a crack inside my head and my internal lights explode into a full floodlit firework display. Oh. My. God. The photographs. Ceri. Her boyfriend. The tabloid. Of course. The man in the hallway with the camera on Saturday was the same man in the reception of Didier's hotel that night. And when we kissed in the restaurant there was a flash like a camera going off . . . How could I have been so stupid? That man was the same guy standing beside Ceri at the party on Friday night, being introduced as James or Jeff or whatever his bloody name was. My arms drop lifelessly to my sides and I flinch as my body reacts to the invisible kick that comes from knowing I have been betrayed. Ceri stares back at me, her mouth slightly open, a dazed expression in her eyes. I want to scream but I feel as if the air has been sucked out of my lungs. A tear drops heavily out of one eye.

'Oh Ceri,' I whisper, my mouth completely dry, 'what have you done? Why?'

She set me up. My friend of thirteen years set this whole thing up. Fair enough, I broke Connor's trust with that kiss, but I would never have done it if it wasn't for all her scheming. So much of it was Ceri's doing.

There is a silence for what feels like an hour while we stand two feet away from each other and just stare. Already I know I am mourning the death of a long friendship. Eventually Ceri speaks. Her voice is hard.

'He was mine,' she says calmly. 'Connor McLean was mine long before you came along, Angel, and he was everything I ever wanted.'

I blink slowly, trying to take all this in.

'OK, so we weren't officially an item, but everybody knew not to touch him,' she hisses.

I see hate in her eyes and I take a step back.

'Then you show up, with your la-di-da ways and your sense of humour, and all you talk about is music and that bloody band, whatever their fucking name is.'

'James,' I croak, shocked at the harshness of her words.

'James,' she spits, shaking her head. 'I hated that band.'

The tears are falling from my eyes with the force of a power shower. My head pulses with pain.

'And suddenly,' she continues, as if hypnotised by the memory, 'it was "Angel this" and bloody "Angel that" and even Meg thought you were so bloody wonderful. And then you and Connor were an item and no matter how perfect I was and how much prettier I was and how much nicer my clothes were he wouldn't look at ME.' Now Ceri is crying too. Her voice rises to a sobbing yell. 'He didn't want me any more. He wasn't interested in what we had. And I had to watch while you became the dream fucking couple and I had to be friends with you because that was the only way I could be near him. Connor and Meg were all I had; everyone else hated me for being pretty.'

I shake my head, waiting for her to tell me this is all a lie, waiting for the punchline that never comes.

'I HATED YOU,' she screams, her beautiful face horribly distorted, 'and I could never find anyone to match him, even though I've tried a few.'

Now that would be an understatement.

'When you said he wanted to marry you I didn't know what to do. I always swore that I would get him back, make him realise that I'm the star prize, so I had to try something.'

'So you did this,' I say with a calmness that surprises me.

It is a strange thing to discover that someone hates you enough to go to that much effort to destroy your life. Especially when the person is one of your two best friends. Connor, Didier and now Ceri; I have lost them all in such quick succession. Only Meg and Dan to go before I am applying for full hermit status.

I use all the energy I have left to raise my chin and focus my eyes on Ceri's.

'Yes, I did this,' she rasps, 'and I got some satisfaction out of it, but it didn't work. He doesn't want me, does he? I tried when he was at my flat and the bastard pushed me away!' She rubs her eyes frantically, smearing mascara across the face that I have never seen to be anything other than flawless. 'Can you believe he doesn't want me?' she sobs. 'Do you know how much that hurts? He laughed, he actually laughed. He must be a fool choosing someone like you over this.'

She thumps her fist against her chest and I hear the sound of bones hitting her hard shell. I smile weakly as I am reminded of that lobster.

'Beauty is only skin deep, Ceri,' I say, as if talking to a child. 'What really counts is what you have inside. And now I have seen what's inside you I know I don't want to be near it any more. You're hard, selfish, shallow and twisted, Ceri, and I do feel sorry for you. Not sorry for the hurt that you are feeling but sorry for the lonely, miserable person you will become.'

The words catch in my throat and I stop to inhale sharply. Suddenly I need air, to be away from this smothering hate. I am probably supposed to yell at her or pull her hair or scratch her eyes out but I don't. I just want to return to a world where good things happen and good people live.

I squeeze my lips tightly together, collect my things from the chair and walk away. We don't even say goodbye.

*

The fact that I *run* all the way from Ceri's office to my studio is enough of an indication that I am in shock. I keep my head down as I battle against the bitter chill of the December morning and the icy feeling in my bones that is threatening to stop me dead. I rush along Renfrew Street towards the hotel where Didier stayed. Turning right at the eighteen-screen cinema where we were pictured sneaking in the back entrance, I race down West Nile Street. I pass Ceri's favourite Starbucks where we met that day for her to tell me over green teas that a famous French popstar was coming to town. Swallowing the lump in my throat in one painful gulp, I charge across the road without waiting for the green man and dodge the crowds of daytime shoppers and tourists milling around the pedestrian precinct. I don't register a single face; I just keep my eyes focused on the red and grey paving stones stretching out in front of me. Turning to run down Buchanan Street, I am plunged into shadow. I pull my scarf further up around my ears and try not to glance at the huge construction to my left that is the Buchanan Galleries – the shopping centre where back in September Connor went out, nervous with excited anticipation, to buy me an engagement ring that has remained in its silver box ever since. He wanted to show me how much he *loved* me. I say 'loved' because it appears our relationship has stumbled into the past tense after all.

Further down Buchanan Street, I stop for breath and turn to look through the glass shop front to my right. I see Meg in her music store uniform, her curls flying at all angles from her head like orange sun rays. She is talking to a customer at a hundred words a minute, demonstrating something with her hands and occasionally throwing back her head and laughing as if she has just heard the funniest joke in the world. I watch for a minute to catch my breath before I run on, happy – relatively speaking – in the knowledge that she is still my friend. Meg may have been put down all through school and ever since for not being as pretty or as sought-after as Ceri but it never seemed to get to her. She may not have a supposedly glamorous job like mine but she is content. Meg is kind and funny and loyal and she is worth ten of Ceri or I. I just hope someone else realises that one day.

I run onwards past Princes Square, where Connor and I would sometimes meet after work to marvel at its golden staircases and designer shops. At the banks of the River Clyde I turn right and trip along the pavement. The cars rumble past in both directions and a train screeches across the bridge above my head. I enter our building at high speed and charge into the (thankfully) waiting lift as if I am on a mission. The doors swoosh shut behind me and I finally exhale.

On the way up to the fifth floor, I unravel my scarf, undo my jacket and rummage in my bag for a mirror. My skin looks pale and jaded. My cheeks are pinched and where my once shiny brown eyes were there are now two grey dots like buttons sewn on the face of a rag doll. I look awful but, then again, it is Monday – the day when only the keen few look their sparkling best. Perhaps if I just paint on some lip-gloss and smile no one will notice.

'Blimey O'Reilly, Angel Fish, you look bloody terrible!' Dan exclaims as I step out of the lift.

He noticed.

Dan puts his arm around me and guides me to the studio.

'I, er, saw the, um . . . you know,' he says, clicking his tongue against the roof of his mouth.

'The newspaper? Yeah, you and everyone else who had fifty pence to spend on gossipy trash yesterday.'

'Bit of a shocker, wasn't it?'

'Uh-huh.'

'I was sorry to hear about Connor too,' he coughs, stopping at the studio door and hopping from one foot to the other.

'Thanks. How do you know about it?'

We go inside. I slump wearily into my chair.

'Meg just called me to let me know.'

'Ah.'

'Sooo,' he whistles nervously, 'er, it wasn't a good birthday I take it?'

'Dan' – I fix my eyes on him – 'shall we forget the small talk, just accept the fact that I have created a nightmare for me and all who know me and get on with the next act of my public humiliation, namely the show?'

He quietly claps his hands with relief. 'Yes, let's. Oh but first, hon, I think G.G. wants to see you.'

CHAPTER TWENTY-SIX

Sit Down – the acoustic duet version

I see him before he sees me – marching down the corridor from his office, dressed entirely in green corduroy and trying to juggle two golf balls with little success. I attempt to side-step into the ladies' executive toilet but he notices my escape and drags me back with a booming: 'ANGEL KNIGHTS!'

This is it. This is where I get totally bollocked for ruining the reputation of Energy FM. Quite an achievement really considering the terrible reputation it had in the first place. I line up the excuses in my brain, right behind the row of 'sorry's, and turn to face my boss.

'Young lady,' he begins pompously, 'I am a very busy man so I will keep this brief.'

You're sacked, is that brief enough?

'Firstly, I want to reiterate how absolutely marvellous Friday's show was. Perfect in every way, it could not have gone any better for us. I was so jubilant I went out and treated myself to some new threads. Do you like?'

I follow his hand gesture towards his suit and nod violently, not trusting myself to come out with the appropriate word if I open my mouth.

'So that was Friday and then there was Saturday, the day of great publicity. Marvellous, superb; I thought it could not have been any better. Terrific' – he kisses his thumb and forefinger like an expressive Italian waiter – 'wonderful.'

I chew my cheek with apprehension.

'Sunday,' he booms, 'was the day of sordid revelations about our top DJ and our interviewee. Local tabloid front page news about the kiss and the night of passion and the boyfriend caught in the love triangle.'

No more details, please.

'I'm sorry, G.G.,' I begin, 'I really am. It just got out of hand and there were some evil forces at work. I am so, so sorry.'

I jump when his hand lands on my shoulder.

'Sorry?' G.G. repeats, his face perilously close to mine. 'What on earth have you got to be sorry about? I thought it could not get any better for us but it did. This was spectacular stuff, scandalous!'

He is so excited that I am half expecting his eyes to spring out of their sockets and whirl madly around.

'Admittedly I was a little concerned at first, but it turns out that this is just what our station needed. We have got guests and their agents coming out of our proverbial ears, my dear. They are ringing the telephones off the hooks to get on your show. Indeed, we have already lined up a boy band, an ex-boy band and that lovely fellow who sings those catchy swing songs. Marvellous voice, cheeky smile, you know the one.'

I nod and shake my head all at once.

'We are famous, Angel, we are newsworthy, we are HOT PROPERTY!'

I step discreetly backwards to dodge the droplets of spittle hurtling themselves out of the corners of his mouth. I think I am about to see a grown man explode.

'Now,' he adds firmly, smoothing back his hair which is getting more mahogany by the day, 'tell me, do you have any other scandal lurking behind that angelic little face of yours? An illegitimate child to an ageing rock star perhaps? A sexuality crisis?'

I stare at him blankly.

'No? Well, be sure to let me know if you come up with anything, young lady,' he chirps, giving me a salute and strutting away. Calling over his shoulder, G.G. adds with a twitter: 'Any little gem will do, Angel. A criminal record for pilfering a pedalo even. Ha ha. Jolly good, *ciao* for now.'

My boss is a lunatic. Thank goodness for that.

'It's Monday, it's twelve o'clock, you're listening to Energy FM and now it's time for *Angel on Air* with our one and only heavenly host, Miss Angel Knights.'

'Hello there,' I try to smile as the music – which sounds more like the product of a Morris dancing convention than a trendy jingle – starts to fade. 'I hope you all had a great weekend' – my voice cracks before I can cover the microphone – 'especially after Friday's show. For those of you who tuned in, wasn't it brilliant? For those of you who didn't, where were you?'

I discreetly clear my throat.

'Thank you for all your positive comments. Our Dan has been working his way through them all morning.'

Dan gives me a thumbs-up.

'As we suspected, Didier Laf—' – I wipe a line of sweat from my top lip – 'Didier Lafitte is very popular with all of you out there.'

God, this is hard. Here I am trying to chat away as if nothing is wrong when my listeners were probably snorting into their Sunday morning cornflakes over the sordid details of my supposed love life. How can I pretend?

I swallow and glance anxiously at Dan. He smiles encouragingly. I stare at the sheets of paper on my desk, searching for some urgent assistance.

'OK, right then, I . . . er, on today's show we' – I blink my weary eyes – 'have some great, er, music and our subject for dis . . . discussion is, um . . .'

I look again at the show outline but the words make about as much sense to me as the menu in a Japanese sushi bar. I try to focus but my eyes refuse to cooperate. My head starts to pound, my tongue metamorphoses into a lump of polystyrene and my gut twists itself into alphabet spaghetti. I gaze helplessly at the microphone inches from my mouth.

'*Come on*,' it huffs impatiently, '*say something then. I'm getting bored here. You're supposed to be a bloody DJ*.'

It is at this point that I realise I cannot carry the weight of the world on my shoulders and simultaneously broadcast entertaining chat to the whole of Glasgow. I've had a weekend more depressing than watching twenty consecutive episodes of *Dawson's Creek* (am I the only person who has realised they are always crying on that programme?). It is all too much. Anyway, I don't mean to complain, and I know I brought a lot of this on myself, so . . . back to my stage fright, which is still in full swing. I must be suffering from panic-induced hallucinations because the giant black microphone has morphed into Ceri's face and she is cackling nastily at my predicament. Now it has become Connor with a distant look in his eyes and a tear on his cheek.

'Come in, Angel Fish,' Dan prompts urgently in my headphones.

I turn my stiff neck to look at him. *I can't*, I mouth silently, my voicebox entirely frozen.

'Erm, right,' Dan immediately cuts in on air, 'we have got some fab stuff for you today on the show so don't go away. Here is the first track and this goes out to John and Elaine on their fifth wedding anniversary. This is "My Endless Love".'

Jesus Christ.

'I can't do it, Dan,' I flap when he appears beside me as if by magic, just like the shopkeeper in *Mr Ben*. 'There are all these new listeners and there's too much pressure and . . . I just can't.'

Dan swivels my chair around, places his hands either side of me on the faux leather arms and peers at me with his endearing hazelnut eyes.

'Yes you can and you will,' he says firmly.

'But I—'

'No buts, Angel.'

I clamp my mouth shut at his surprisingly authoritative tone. So much for tea and sympathy.

'You just had a bit of stage fright; it happens to the best of them.'

'It's never happened to me before.'

'Well, you've never split up with Connor before.'

I bow my head sadly while Lionel and Diana croon about two hearts that beat as one.

'Just like you've never been in the papers for porking a popstar before.'

'Hey! I—'

'I know you didn't, darling, but that's beside the point.' He crouches down on his haunches. 'It has all taken its toll on you and you're knackered, mate.'

'You're making me sound like a shire horse.'

'Sorry. I'm just trying to say you're unhappy and you have every reason to be but it will get better.'

'Will it?'

'Yep, and in the meantime you need this show.' He nods at the microphone, which has thankfully reverted to just being a microphone again. 'Just like your listeners out there need you.'

'You sound like Oprah,' I say, forcing a smile.

'Why thank you. I'm going for earnest and emotional.'

'You got it.'

'Cool. Now, let's get back to the show. This is the good thing in your life, lady, use it like therapy.'

'Therapy? Torture more like. I suppose you're the sort of person who advocates facing your worst fears by climbing into a bath of tarantulas.'

He scratches his head comically. 'Hmm, well, we haven't got any tarantulas but there is a big creepy crawly in G.G.'s office if that will do.'

I laugh lightly, which suddenly releases the pressure in my head like a ring-pull being opened on a shaken can of pop.

'That's better,' Dan winks, turning me to face the microphone again, 'now just have a go.'

I grimace. 'But it's hard keeping that smile plastered on my lips, Dan.'

'Then don't, Angel Fish,' he shrugs, heading for the door. 'Just tell them how you feel. They have all had enough advice from you so why not ask for some back? It's an interesting concept but it might just work.'

I press my lips together, deep in thought.

'Now, can I get you anything?'

'A compilation of depressing songs to match my mood and an eat-all-you-can Prozac buffet?' I suggest with a smirk.

'Two espresso-chocs and a king-sized Mars Bar coming up.'

I slip the headphones back over my ears. 'That was Lionel Richie and Diana Ross for a special couple with an endless love of their own, John and Elaine. Now' – I pause and wait for my confidence to catch up – 'it is time to reveal today's topic of discussion and I really hope all of you out there are going to help me with this one. A while ago I talked about a friend of mine who had kissed someone while she was in a relationship with someone else. Well, that *friend* was actually me and you may have read about it in the paper yesterday. I have made a big mistake and now I need your help because today, listeners, we are going to talk about me.'

Talk about being a glutton for punishment, I am positively gorging on it!

I explain everything as best I can without being slanderous (in other words not shrieking 'Ceri Divine is a scheming bitch' across the airwaves). I then describe my relationship with Connor and how I think I just got cold feet: to use an appropriate shoeaholic metaphor, that I was temporarily distracted by a pair of sparkly stilettos (Didier) but that I soon realised I wanted my old shoes back because nothing would ever fit me as well as they did.

I then stop my soul-bearing before the whole studio turns into a giant lump of cheese and stare at the telephone. I cross my fingers into reef knots in the hope that I have not just made a complete prat of myself and given a few bored listeners the chance to say: 'Ha, she's just made a complete prat of herself.' Thankfully the lines soon begin to glow a welcoming red. I uncross my fingers and press line one.

For once, Gladys does not start the discussion. That dubious honour goes to Boomer.

'DINNY FRET ABOOT ALL THAT TRASH IN THE PAPERS, HEN. NAEBODY TAKES ANY NOTICE OF ALL THE GORY DETAILS. I READ IT ALL OF COURSE BUT ME AN' THE LADS ALL AGREE THAT IT WAS JUST BRILLIANT TO SEE WHAT YOU LOOKED LIKE AFTER LISTENIN' TO YA FOR SO LONG.'

'AYE!' chorus the lads in the background.

'AND I'M NO' BEING SLEAZY, ANGEL, BUT ME AN' THE LADS, WE THINK YOU'RE A WEE BELTER, SO YOU ARE, AND IF YOUR MAN DOESN'Y COME BACK HE NEEDS HIS HEID LOOKED AT. GOOD LUCK HEN. CHEERIO NOW.'

'Bye Boomer,' I say shakily, hoping that he doesn't make a habit of talking in long sentences because my ears simply can't take it.

Malcolm from Hamilton is then put through by Dan (the wanker, I'll get him later) on line two. I hold my breath and wait for the barrage of tactless comments.

'I agree wi' Boomer, so I do; you are a wee belter, Angel hen, and it's nae wonder you've got all they men fightin' over you.'

Hardly. The men-fighting-over-me count is currently at a big fat zero.

'What I just wanted to say was, ehm, thanks to you fer bringin' us a pure braw show and fer gettin' us through the crappy weeks and all that. You're a brilliant DJ so that's somethin' to be proud of, eh? It's nice to know you're human just like the rest of us too. And you've got a great pair of legs, hen.'

And that is it. No swearing, no real sleaze, no need for Dan to hurl himself at the controls to cut him off. Our Malcolm seems to have experienced an epiphany. Whether looking at my bare thighs in the papers had anything to do with it I wouldn't like to speculate but Malcolm from Hamilton has just come up trumps and, at the risk of sounding as if we are running some sort of self-help group here rather than an up-and-coming radio show, I feel almost proud of him.

My third caller admits to being a new listener and I can instantly picture G.G. rubbing his hands together with glee. Even Dan holds up a scribbled note which reads: 'I sense a Pay Rise!'

'I'm Fiona from Cowcaddens,' she informs me quietly, 'and I just wanted to know where you get your hair done. It's wicked.'

Next comes Guy, who's calling from a pirate radio station 'somewhere underground', as he puts it. He tells me I'm great (keep it coming) and offers me a job. He then asks for my chest size so that he can send me a station T-shirt. Pervy but resourceful, I'll give him that, but I think I'll keep my chest measurement a private matter.

After playing as many songs as I can that don't include the

word 'love', which is not an easy task, believe me, I then return to the phones and talk to Sue, a visitor from Guildford. Sue is appalled by my antics and expresses her views (or should I say rants on) about young people today having no self-respect. I only escape when Dan executes his terribly discreet cutting-off trick. Sue from Guildford is quickly added to our list of people to give a berth wide enough to contain the Ark Royal to.

I then hear from Geraldine, an arts student from Kelvinbridge, who just wants to say that she was pleased to see from the T-shirt I was wearing in the paper that I have good taste in music.

'D'ya know James are playing a gig at the SECC tonight?' she informs me proudly.

'Yes,' I reply sadly, adding silently to myself – *I had two tickets, actually, one for me and one for my boyfriend to celebrate our thirteenth anniversary together. I didn't think we would be going but if his surprise had gone to plan this weekend we would have been there tonight. Wouldn't that have been grand?*

Learning a lesson from Sue, I keep my rant inside and simply say, 'If you need a couple of tickets, Geraldine, I know where there are two going spare.'

Tyrone's call is a timely distraction.

'Hiya Angel,' he says in a much stronger voice than I am used to from my fourteen-year-old friend, 'I just got back from school . . .'

Ah-ha, I sense progress!

'. . . so as I could call you. I didn'y see the papers but I heard 'boot it. A boy in my class called you a honey.'

'Did he now?' I smirk. Behave yourself, Angel; you can't go

on an ego trip just from being called a honey by a fourteen-year-old adolescent. That would be rather sad.

'Aye, and I told him that you're my friend and that you're no' just a honey but a really special person. Because I know I said I don't like cheatin' and that but I don't think you meant it. I think you were lonely and, well, I know what that feels like. And if your boyfriend doesn'y come back then' – I can almost hear him puffing out his skinny little chest – 'I'll go out with you.'

I can see Dan laughing through the glass. He makes a motion with his hand as if to lasso me with an invisible rope.

Blimey, I've pulled!

'Thanks, Tyrone, that's really nice of you but—'

'Och, I know you're really old and stuff compared to me but I just wanted you no' to be lonely, so give it a thought, eh?'

Did I say ego trip? More like ego trip-and-fall-flat-on-my-wrinkly-old-face. Good old Tyrone, he knows how to keep my feet firmly on the ground.

Just when I am thinking that we are going to get to the end of a show without the input of Gladys from Motherwell, Dan puts the last call through on line four.

'Angel,' says Gladys in between her audible slurps of tea, 'you've been a naughty wee thing, haven't you?'

I bite my lip and smile over at Dan, who slaps his wrist and points at me.

'Now you ken I'm no' into all this hopping from bed to bed like a bed bug but I'll say no more on that subject.'

Thank the Lord for that.

'It's actually my friend who wants to have a wee word on the radio today, so it is. His name's Steve.'

I frown as I listen to the clunks, clatters, 'mind yourself's and 'watch my tea there's that accompany the receiver being handed over. It is as soon as he says – 'Hello, Angel, it's me' – that my throat constricts like a snake ingesting a mouse. Speaking of Lords, I hope he isn't as drunk as one. After all, it is almost three o'clock and the voice on the end of the line is my dad's.

'Now, Angel, Gladys told me to call you,' he wheezes.

Did she? God help our daily discussion slot if Gladys has become my father's mentor.

'Because I felt I should just say this to you.'

I felt? Where have these feelings come from all of a sudden?

'I wanted to say that just because of what happened to me in my relationship and because I fell apart when it did, please do not let that make you scared of marriage so that you don't allow your own relationships to grow. My marriage didn't work in the end but I would much rather have had those years with Delphine than to never have had her as my wife at all. What is it that they say . . . Gladys?'

I hear her murmur over the click of knitting needles.

'Yes, that's the one. "It is better to have loved and lost than never to have loved at all". You see?'

Yes, I see. I see that epiphanies are going cheap today and I suspect that Gladys has had a lot to do with my dad's sudden emergence as a modern man who expresses his emotions. I admire his courage and I largely agree with what he says. After all, it's good to hear that other people think there is a reason behind my idiotic life-destroying behaviour other than me just being a useless plonker. But although it is nice to re-reverse the roles and have a bit of fatherly guidance at last, it might have come in handier the day I told him that

Connor had proposed rather than now when that proposal has been revoked. Nice try anyway, Daddy.

I bring the show to a close with my own personal tribute to James (just to rub another packet of salt into my gaping wounds).

'This is "Come Home", which I play especially for Connor,' I say softly, 'if you're listening. I just want to say: remember the good old days.'

Finally the red light switches off and I sit back and close my eyes. It is a great thing to realise that you have very few reasons to be lonely even if you've just lost the man who makes you complete as well as one of your two best friends. Sometimes it just takes that extra bit of courage to reach out and ask for help in order to make friends you never really realised you had come running. I am lucky to have my listeners as my extended family, even if half of them are bonkers, as they are a pretty good bunch all in all. The sky in my world may not be a glaring Mediterranean blue at the moment but there are at least some breaks in the cloud. My life hasn't been a complete waste of time. Like Dan said, I have got something good in *Angel on Air*.

Perhaps the sun would have come out in my world if Connor had invested in one of those epiphanies. But he didn't ring at the last minute to announce to the people of Glasgow how much he loves me and how he can't live without me. All right, I accept it was a lot to expect, but it would have been nice, wouldn't it?

I climb the stairs at Hillhead subway station and walk briskly up Byres Road, past the man selling lighters and plastic scissors from his battered suitcase. The December chill wraps his fingers around the tip of my nose. I buy a copy of *The Big Issue* from the girl with the knee-length multi-coloured dreadlocks and stop for a brief chat as I usually do.

'Hey, Angel,' she says, 'I love your show. I never realised it was you before but then I saw the paper on Sunday and now I know. Huh, I've got a famous customer.'

That is a new dimension to our conversation.

'I wouldn't really say I was famous,' I cringe.

'Aye, you are, you're a famous DJ. It's wicked.'

I thank her gracefully and carry on up the street. *I am a famous DJ*, I think to myself. Well, it's what I always wanted, isn't it? I didn't exactly aim to get fame in the way I did but it worked, didn't it? People know who I am. So my wish to the wishing pool achieved something – I became successful in my career. The problem is that fame alone isn't all it's cracked up to be. Not if you haven't got that special someone to share it with. No wonder so many famous people are lonely mixed-up fruitloops.

I reach my flat and look up at the partially closed blinds in my kitchen window. I don't want to go in and be alone with only my photographs and music collection for company. I can't even call Meg because she's got some top-secret date and Ceri . . . Ceri doesn't even figure in the equation any more. Now this is where the problem lies – my listeners may have been great at giving the love back but I'm hardly going to hang out with them, am I? Imagine: me, Boomer, Malcolm and Gladys rocking the dance floor at The Garage nightclub. Somehow I don't think that will ever happen. I put my head down and keep walking towards the end of Byres Road. There is one place where I don't mind being alone.

*

I reach the entrance of The Kibble Palace just after four o'clock and slip through the creaky wooden door. I look around the first glass dome and see that I am alone. It is a different kind of alone from being at home though. This is a peaceful, thought-provoking alone. This is my place. To be sociable, however, I peer into the coffee shop to look for Winona.

'Och, she's left,' a woman with a gingham bandana tied around her head informs me. 'Went off 'roond the world with a new fella. Totally in love, so she was.'

Shit; even Winona the angst-ridden teenager has got a 'fella'. Where's your solidarity, sister?

I wander back out to the wishing pool and lean on the railing where I made that wish back in October.

'Well, it worked,' I sigh, my breath forming clouds of steam in front of my face which float up to the top of the giant glass dome to eventually form droplets of condensation. 'I wished for motivation and success and I got it. We went a little off target at some points but I guess my wish came true in the end so, er, thanks.'

A deep orange fish stops swimming below me, pushes his bubble-blowing mouth to the top of the water and pauses there. It is as if he catches my eye to say 'you're welcome' before flicking his tail and swimming away towards the second dome of the Palace. I rummage in my bag and pull out my purse, taking care not to make too much noise. The only other sounds are the trickle of a hosepipe somewhere in the fern house and the odd clink of cups from the coffee shop as the woman prepares to close.

'The thing is,' I whisper down into the murky water, 'I need another favour and this one is more personal. You see, in getting my success I lost something very important to me. The most important thing in my world.'

My voice begins to shake. I stare at the reflection of the tired, sad person looking back at me from below.

'He was perfect,' I continue softly. 'Perhaps not in that obvious outward appearance way although I think he is gorgeous. Huh, he's hardly changed since school except to get even more good-looking. He is kind and funny and I think he was my soul mate but I hurt him and now I can't find him to let him know that I'm sorry. I didn't trust in us when I should have done and now . . . now he's gone.'

I breathe out another cloud as my mind fills with thoughts and images of Connor. Where is he? Will I ever see him again? Is he out there learning the rules of the dating game or is he thinking of me? How can I survive if I never kiss those lips again or feel his body against mine? What do I do with the memories we made if they are too painful to keep inside? How could I have been so stupid?

Now I know what people mean when they say they need 'closure'. I feel as if everything happened too fast and I didn't have a chance to stop and take stock of the situation. Now it is too late.

'Thirteen years and then it ends just like that,' I say sadly. 'How can it be? I don't know how to live without *us*. Even if I meet someone else, I'll be forty-three by the time we build a bond like the one Connor and I had. Forty-three. Bloody hell.'

I blink and a tear drops into the water below me, making a strangely loud splash in this quiet glass haven. The deep orange fish appears again and once more rises to the surface. Another tear drops into the water beside him.

'I'm sorry,' I sniff, 'I thought I had run out of tears, I've cried so many.'

He wriggles his body and then swims away again towards the other side of the pool. I rub my eyes with one hand and then rub the coin that is cupped in the other.

'Right, I've got a pound,' I say to the wishing pool. 'That should be enough for a pretty good wish, don't you think? I could use this pound to buy some very comforting chocolate fudge cake but I am going to give it to you, so help me out here.' I tightly clench my fist. 'I just need to know where Connor is and that he is happy. Of course I wish for him to come back to me but I think that is too much to ask. I wish for the pain to go away, both mine and his, and I wish that the man who is more important than anything will realise how much I love him. I love him even more than I love music. You see, that is how special he is, because I could be listening to the best song in the world, to a one-to-one live James gig even, but without Connor the music just doesn't sound the same.'

I drop the coin into the water and watch it disappear. Then I squeeze my eyes shut and hope that by some act of magic that we don't yet understand my wish will get through to Connor McLean.

'Are you all right, hen?' says the woman from the coffee shop whose concerned face appears suddenly beside mine.

'What? Oh yes, I'm fine.' (Now I sound like my dad.) 'I'm just a bit tired really.'

'Aye, you look it,' she nods. 'You look terrible.'

Thanks. You know, sometimes honesty just doesn't wash with me.

'Well, I've got stuff to do so I willn'y be closing for about ten minutes. Maybe you should have a wee sit down. There's some benches down there' – she points deeper into the glasshouse – 'that are nice and comfy and you can have a wee relax. It's good for the soul.'

I smile weakly and nod. 'Yeah, perhaps you're right. I've had a tough couple of days. Maybe I should just have a little sit down.'

She strokes my arm sympathetically and then I walk around the pool and along the wide, fern-lined path. I close my eyes as I wander into the second dome and breathe in the calming aroma of the plants. My feet scrunch on fragments of hardened soil and the sound of the water fills my head as if it is cleansing my mind. God knows it needs a damn good cleansing after the capers it has been up to lately.

I continue around the circular path towards the benches that are almost hidden among the foliage. Stopping just before the first seat, I reach out and touch the fronds of a particularly lush fern plant. The leaves are cold and moist and comforting to feel. I close my eyes and take another deep breath. I would try that yoga/didgeridoo-style circular breathing thing but I never could get the hang of it so in and out will have to do. At first I think it is my mind playing tricks on me but I open my eyes with a start when I hear the music. I look sharply around me but see no one. It must be the woman in the coffee shop, although I would have labelled her as more of a classical music buff than . . .

James. Someone is singing James.

The voice is quiet and lacking in confidence but I can just make out the words. The lyrics I know so well float through the moist air and wrap themselves around me. I move shakily towards the trailing end of the last note as if in a dream.

Rounding the edge of the large, soft fern I see him. He is sitting on the white iron bench, his blue eyes looking up at me expectantly. I gasp and the tears return sharply to my eyes. I still remember what Connor was wearing the day we first met and here he is thirteen years on – a little older, more refined perhaps, his clothes much smarter and more expensive, although beneath his jacket I spy his new James T-shirt. His eyes are tired from the pain I have put him through. He is still my Connor, just a more worldly-wise version. Life has taught him some tough lessons since then, just as it has taught me, but he is as beautiful as he ever was, and more.

'Connor,' I breathe, 'how . . . ?'

'I knew you would be here,' his lilting Scottish accent tells me softly.

'How . . .?'

Come on, girl, think of another word, for heaven's sake.

He shrugs those broad shoulders. 'Because I know you too well. I knew you would come here, baby, just as I knew you would wake up this morning sad and tired but would still find time to do your hair and devour a bowl of Coco Pops, checking in the packet for the free toy.'

I stare at him, incapable of a reply.

'Just like I knew you would choose a pair of comfortable but colourful shoes because you needed comfort but also something to brighten your day.'

We both look down at my Buffalo basketball boots. Purple ones with pink and silver swirls. My heart beats fast, hitting my chest wall so hard I fear it will break.

'Just like I knew you would go to work and do your job amazingly well because that is how you are.'

He listened. I lower my eyes under his gaze.

'Those listeners love you and I know why. Because you are funny and kind and loving. Maybe sometimes a little *too* loving.'

I whip my head up. 'Connor, look, I'm sorry about . . .'

He raises a hand. 'I know you're sorry, my Angel.'

The last two words give me a glimmer of hope. I hold my breath. The 'but' doesn't come.

'I know that because I know your life as well as I know my own. Maybe we lost sight of that over the last couple of months and maybe I rushed you with the proposal, didn't think about you being here all alone to deal with it.'

'I think too much,' I interrupt.

'Just like you talk too much,' he replies.

I melt as a smile crosses his lips. It is faint but it is definitely a smile.

'But then that is why you are the *Angel on Air* and that is why I am proud of you.'

'After all I've done?' I croak.

He pauses. The pause feels like a lifetime. More tears spring to my eyes. And then he nods, slowly but surely.

'Yes. I've tried to be in the same city as you but I can't do it and not be with you. I know where you're going and what you're doing just by thinking about you because half my life is your life. Half my life is you.'

I swallow the giant sob that is threatening to burst out of my throat and clasp my hands in front of my face. 'Oh Connor, do you mean . . .?'

'I mean, what is the point in living half a life if I can live a whole one with you? What do you think?'

What do *I* think? Blimey, by now I am completely incapable of thinking. My brain is exhausted, my body is exhausted and my tear ducts are producing more water than all the mineral springs in the Scottish Highlands put together. Every part of me aches and only one thing, one person, one man, one love can take that ache away.

'I think,' I say shakily, 'I think . . .'

My heart seems to burst as he reaches out a slim, familiar hand and touches my fingers. A rush of blood blasts up into my head like a celebratory firework.

'Oh God,' I groan, 'I think I need to sit down.'

He pulls me gently on to the seat beside him. I let my body fold itself into his and feel the warmth emanating from his hug. We fit perfectly, me curled into the side of him, his arm pressed around me. I inhale his aroma and I immediately know I am back in the right place. Back with my shoe that fits.

'Then sit down,' he says, cupping my chin with his left hand and lifting my face up towards his. 'Because I've come home.'

'I'm never losing you again.' I smile at the references to the band that brought us together. 'The music sounds better with you.'

EPILOGUE

We Have All The Time In The World

'Ladies and gentlemen, I present to you the stars of the latest series of *Dollywood Or Bust* – Truly, Honey, Pirelli, Ferrari and Kelly.'

'And their co-stars, bouncy, booby, juggy, bazongas and wabs,' Meg snorts, nudging me in the ribs.

'Shhh,' I giggle as the girls waddle on to the stage chest-first. I clap like a performing seal and breathe a sigh of relief that there is no sign of a stars and stripes thong.

We are at the premiere of Connor's TV show, which has been heralded as the big audience-grabber of this September. In the six months of filming in America the girls all experienced brushes with fame, except Honey and Pirelli who spent more time brushing against the sweaty bodies of sleazy directors, but their relative successes produced some fascinating (and at times unbelievable) footage. Beyond the casting couch, Truly landed the Dr Pepper advertising campaign, Ferrari got a walk-on part in a spin-off of *Baywatch* and Kelly was signed up to appear in the next Tom Hanks movie as a glamour model from England. She has three lines to learn. Give her another six months and she should have them down like a true professional.

To Meg's right sits Dan, my friend and producer. He turns his boyish face and grins at Meg as she throws back her head and attempts to laugh quietly but still reaches the decibel levels of a hyena with a megaphone. Dan's hazel eyes are full of love. He leans to one side and kisses Meg on the cheek.

'You're more gorgeous than all of them put together, Meg,' I hear him whisper.

'Och, away ye go, you big softy,' she snorts, tapping his leg playfully, 'and my waist is about the size of all of them put together too.'

The two of them giggle and I smile along with them. Meg has found her man and I have to admit they make a good team. She is a hearts and flowers and cuddly teddy bears type of girl. He is in touch with his feminine side and so is quite happy to receive them – the hearts and flowers and cuddly teddy bears, I mean. His desk at the radio station is like a branch of Clintons. One more shiny helium balloon and the whole building will take off.

I lean forward and wink at my dad, who is sitting next to Dan on the row of red cinema seats. He can't see me because his eyes are covered by Gladys's hand.

'Och, there's way too much chest there fer a man like you,' she tuts, peering distastefully at the girls on the stage. 'You'll give yourself a heart attack.'

Not much chance of that, I think happily – my dad is now healthier than me thanks to Gladys. He hasn't touched a drop of whisky since the angina scare, although he is allowed a small glass of red wine every time Motherwell win. Not to cast aspersions on his team but I'm just grateful he doesn't support Man United. Incidentally, that was a deciding factor in their blossoming relationship – Dad discovered that Gladys has a season ticket for Motherwell FC How could he refuse?

Connor returned to LA after his trip to Scotland to surprise me, but not before I had requested and booked a holiday from Energy FM and bought my airline ticket. I never thought G.G. would agree to my gallivanting off just as our interview bookings began to intensify but it seems I can do no wrong at the radio station. In fact, Dan and I are up to the Hob Nob (occasionally chocolate-covered) rating right now.

I would like to say that Energy has emerged as the station to rival Radio 1 but that would be the same as likening a fluffy brown slipper to a Jimmy Choo. Nevertheless, we have made progress over the last year. The playlists on the show are now down to just one Shakin' Stevens track a fortnight and the guests are coming thick and fast (many of them being *thick*, their flash cars usually being *fast*). Our audience figures are steadily rising and G.G. has invested some of his corporate golf day budget in publicity. Only this week, Meg and I stumbled out of the Clockwork Orange at Buchanan Street on the way to work to be greeted by a four-foot poster of my face that was locked in a grinning contest with the adjacent poster of Suzy McGuire. 'Angel Knights is the *Angel on Air*' it read in bold gold letters. My teeth looked eyebrow-raisingly enormous but it was definitely an improvement on the T-shirt and thighs photo (but let's not dwell on that, it is all but forgotten).

*

Our regular callers are still regular, although they do find it harder to get through to us these days – the price of popularity, I suppose. Tyrone, however, has my personal mobile number and keeps us up to date on his progress. He doesn't phone every day because of *school* commitments. Tyrone has just started his final year and two weeks ago formed the first anti-bullying support group run by bullied kids for bullied kids. The project is sponsored by a well-known French popstar who was himself bullied at school and it promises to be a huge success. Tyrone has already been asked to give talks in other schools who want to set up a similar scheme. We have booked him in for an interview next Friday before he gets too famous for a station like Energy FM.

Didier Lafitte is more popular than ever and now gives interviews in English without batting a perfect eyelid. He and Connor made peace with each other during a recent trip to Bordeaux to visit my mother, when Connor swallowed his pride and thanked Didier for his help in making my show a success. Didier's latest single 'Angelic' is riding high at Number One.

My mother . . . well, she's just my mother really. As opinionated as ever and living the life of a young French beauty who refuses to accept that she is approaching sixty. No change there then. Mind you, she and Connor did call a truce during our trip when I threatened her with grandchildren if she didn't at least pretend to like my boyfriend after all the trouble she had helped to cause. More importantly, I have secretly forgiven her for leaving me and Dad. Perhaps Didier was right – maybe it has proved better for them both in the long run. Gosh, being a thirty-something has made me come over all mature!

Ceri Divine ballooned to a size twenty-five, developed acne, was dumped by every man she met and ended up living in a skip under a bridge on the Clyde. OK, I made that up, but for those of you who believe in karma this wouldn't be an unbalanced result. If the truth be told the last I heard she had left *Star* magazine to take a job on a big glossip in London . . . as a food critic. The mind boggles.

The lights dim, the audience falls silent and my nerves grow as the credits start to roll. In the darkness, Connor slips on to the seat beside me and tightly clasps my hand.

'Good luck, baby,' I whisper, 'I'm sure they'll love it.'

'Thanks,' he whispers excitedly, 'and Angel?'

'Yes?'

'Happy anniversary.'

'Fourteen years,' I whisper back, 'amazing.'

'You are,' he smiles, his eyes dancing in the reflective light of the screen. 'Oh, and just one thing. Don't let me forget I've got something to ask you tonight.'

'Oh God,' I groan, squeezing his hand playfully, 'not again.'